also by
Laura Thalassa

THE BARGAINER SERIES

A Strange Hymn

LAURA THALASSA

Bloom books

Sourcebooks and the colophon are registered trademarks of
Sourcebooks. Bloom Books is a trademark of Sourcebooks.

Published by Bloom Books, an imprint of Sourcebooks
P.O. Box 4410, Naperville, Illinois 60567-4410
(630) 961-3900
sourcebooks.com

Originally self-published in 2017 by Laura Thalassa.

Cataloging-in-Publication Data is on file with the Library of Congress.

Printed and bound in the United States of America.
LSC 10 9 8 7 6 5 4 3 2

Astrid,
For you, the universe.

Mighty Nyx came,
Mighty Nyx sought
All that he could
Of his dark lot.

In the deep night,
His kingdom rose.
Beware, great king,
Of that which grows.

Easy to conquer,
Easy to crown,
But even the strongest
Can be cut down.

Raised in the shadows,
Reared in the night,
Your child will come
And ascend by might.

And you, the slain,
Shall wait and see
What other things
A soul can be.

A body to curse,
A body to blame,
A body the earth
Will not yet claim.

Beware the mortal
Beneath your sky.
Crush the human
Who'll see you die.

Twice you'll rise,
Twice you'll fall,
Lest you can
Change it all.

Or perish by day,
Perish by dawn.
The world believes
You're already gone.

So darken your heart,
My shadow king,
And let us see
What war will bring.

—THE PROPHECY OF GALLEGHAR NYX

CHAPTER 1

Wings.

I have wings.

The iridescent black feathers glint under the dim lights of Des's royal chambers: now black, now green, now blue.

Wings.

I stand in front of one of Des's gilded mirrors, both horrified and transfixed by the sight. Even folded, the tops of my wings loom well above my head, and the tips brush the back of my bare calves.

Of course, wings aren't the only difference about me. After a particularly nasty skirmish with Karnon, the mad King of Fauna, I now have scaly forearms and claw-tipped fingers too.

And those are just the changes you can see. There's nothing—except maybe the wounded look in my eyes—that I have to show for all those parts of me that were altered in different, more fundamental ways.

I spent the better part of a decade fighting the idea that I was a victim. I'd done a damn fine job of it too—if I do say so myself—before I came to the Otherworld. And then came Karnon. A small shiver courses through me even now as I remember.

All those cleverly crafted layers of armor I wore were shucked away by a week of imprisonment, and I'm not quite sure how to deal with it.

To be honest, I really don't *want* to deal with it.

But, as bad as I have it, the Master of Animals got it worse. Des vaporized the dude so completely that all that's left of him is a bloodstain on the remains of his throne room.

Apparently, one does not fuck with the Night King's mate.

Mate.

That's another thing I've acquired recently—a *soul mate.* I'm bound to Desmond Flynn, the Bargainer: one of the most wanted criminals on earth and one of the most powerful fae here in the Otherworld.

But even that—matehood—is more complicated than it appears.

I still have so many questions about our bond, like the fact I never knew I had a soul mate until a few weeks ago. Other supernaturals find out this kind of thing back when they're teenagers and their magic Awakens.

So why didn't I?

There's also the fact most soul mates can feel the bond that connects them to their mate like it's a physical thing.

I place a hand over my heart.

I've felt no such thing.

All I have is Des's word that we're soul mates—that and the sweet ache in my bones that calls for him and only him.

I drop my hand from my chest.

Behind my reflection, stars glitter just beyond the arched

windows of Des's Otherworld suite. The hanging lanterns dangle unlit, and the sparkling lights captured along the wall sconces have long since dimmed.

I'm stuck here in the Kingdom of Night.

I doubt there are all that many supernaturals who would complain about my situation—mated to a king, forced to live in a palace—but the simple, sobering truth is that a girl like me cannot waltz back onto earth with giant wings protruding from her back.

That sort of thing wouldn't go over well.

So I'm stuck here, far from my friends—okay, *friend*, but, in all fairness, Temper's got the power and attitude of at *least* two people—in a place where my ability to glamour, a.k.a. seduce, others with my voice is essentially useless. Fairies, as I've learned, cannot be glamoured; my magic is too incompatible with theirs.

To be clear, that's not a two-way street. They can still use their powers on me; the bracelet on my wrist is proof enough of that.

My eyes return to my wings, my strange, unearthly wings.

"You know, staring at them isn't going to make them go away."

I jolt at the sound of Des's silky voice.

He leans against the wall in a shadowy corner of his dark bedroom, his expression irreverent as usual. His white-blond hair frames his face, and even now, even when I'm bashful and exposed and oddly ashamed of my own skin, my fingers ache to thread themselves through that soft hair of his and pull him close.

He wears nothing but low-slung pants, his muscular torso and sleeve of tattoos on display. My heart quickens at the sight. The two of us stare at each other for a beat. He doesn't come any closer, though I swear he wants to. I can all but see it in his silver eyes.

"I didn't mean to wake you," I say quietly.

"I don't mind being woken," he says, his eyes glittering. He doesn't move from his spot.

"How long have you been there?" I ask.

He crosses his arms over his bare torso, cutting off my view of his pecs. "Better question: How long have *you* been *there?*"

So typical for Des to answer a question with a question. I turn back to the mirror. "I can't sleep."

I really can't. It's not the bed, and it's definitely not the man who warms it. Every time I try to flip onto my stomach or my back, I inevitably roll over a wing and wake myself up.

There's also the little matter of the sun never rising in this place. The Kingdom of Night is perpetually cast in darkness, as it draws the night across the sky. There will never be a time when the sun glances into this room, so I never know when exactly to wake up.

Des disappears from his spot against the wall. A split second later, he appears at my back.

His lips brush the shell of my ear. "There are better ways to spend long sleepless evenings," Des says softly, one of his hands trailing down my arm.

My siren stirs at his words, my skin taking on the faintest glow.

His lips graze the side of my neck, and even that lightest of touches has my breath hitching.

But then I catch sight of my reflection and see the wings. The glow leaves my skin in an instant.

Des notices the moment my interest wanes, moving away from me like he was never there. And I *hate* that. I feel

4

the distance between us. But I don't want him to give me space—I want him to pull me closer, kiss me deeper, make me extinguish this new insecurity I have.

"These wings…"

Des comes around to my front. "What about them?" he asks, blocking my view of the mirror.

I lift my chin. "They'd get in the way."

He raises an eyebrow. "In the way of what?"

As if he's unaware of exactly what we're dancing around.

"Of playing chess," I say sarcastically. "Of…intimacy."

Des stares at me for several seconds then his mouth slowly curls into a smile. It's a smile full of tricks and mischievous things.

He steps in close, only a hairbreadth between our faces. "Cherub, I *assure* you, your wings will not be an issue." His gaze dips to my lips. "But perhaps your mind would be better eased with a demonstration?"

At his suggestion, light flares beneath my skin, my siren immediately ready to go. Whatever my insecurities are, she doesn't share them.

I look over my shoulder at my wings, and my worries come roaring back. "Aren't they a major turnoff?"

The moment the words leave my lips, I wish I could catch them and shove them back down my throat.

The only thing I hate worse than feeling like a victim is airing my insecurities. Normally I don all my emotional armor to hide them—sometimes so deep, I forget they're there—but after my ordeal with Karnon, that armor is lying scattered somewhere around my feet, and I haven't yet had the time or the will to refashion a new set for myself. I'm horribly raw and painfully vulnerable.

Des raises an eyebrow. At his back, his own wings, which

I haven't noticed until now, expand. The leathery silver skin of them pulls taut as they extend to either side of him, blocking out most of the room.

"You do realize almost all fae have wings?"

I know they do. But *I* never have.

I hold up a forearm. In the dim light, the golden scales that plate my arm from wrist to elbow shimmer like jewelry. On the tips of my fingers, my nails glint black. They're not sharpened at the moment (thanks to meticulously filing them down), but the second my siren gets a little angry, they'll grow back into curving points.

"How about this?" I ask. "Do most fae have this?"

He clasps my hand in his own. "It doesn't matter one way or another. You are mine." Des kisses the palm of my hand, and somehow, he manages to make my insecurities feel small and petty.

He doesn't release my hand, and I stare at the scales.

"Will they ever go away?" I ask.

His grip tightens. "Do you want them to?"

I should know that voice by now. I should hear the warning notes in it, the dangerous lilt. But I don't, too consumed with my own self-pity.

I meet his eyes. "*Yes.*"

I get that I'm being a poor sport. Rather than making lemonade out of lemons, I'm pretty much cutting open those lemons and squeezing them into my eyes.

My heart speeds up as he fingers one of the hundreds of beads that still circle my wrist, each one an IOU for a favor I cashed in long ago.

His eyes flick to mine. "Truth or dare?"

Des's gaze twinkles as he plays with the bead on my wrist, waiting for my answer.

Truth or dare?

This is the little game he loves to make out of my repayment plan. To me, it feels less like the game ten-year-old girls play at slumber parties and a whole lot more like Russian roulette with a fully loaded weapon.

I stare the Bargainer down, his silver eyes both so foreign and so familiar.

I don't answer fast enough.

He gives my wrist the lightest of squeezes. *"Dare,"* he says for me.

The part of me that enjoys sex and violence quakes with excitement, wanting whatever Des offers. The rest of me is starting to think I should be scared shitless. This is the same man known around these parts as the King of Chaos. Just because we're mates doesn't mean he'll go easy on me. He's still the same wicked man I met eight years ago.

Des smiles, the sight almost sinister. A moment later, a pile of leathers fall to the floor next to me. I stare down at them dumbly, not understanding what it is he dared me to.

For all I know, I just got royally fucked over.

Actually, I'm almost positive I got fucked over.

"Suit up," Des says, releasing my wrist. "It's time to start your training."

CHAPTER 2

How hard is it to fight a warrior king without the use of glamour?

Really freaking hard.

The bastard dared me to train with him. And if that sounds vague, that's because he meant it to be.

I don't know what I'm doing, why I'm doing it, or how long I'll be doing it for. All I know is that Des gave me leathers and a sword several hours ago, and ever since then, he's been systematically nicking those training leathers and swiping my sword out of my hand.

Above us, little orbs of light—fairy lights—glitter from the trees arching over the royal courtyard that's doubling as our training ground. They hover over the gurgling fountain and dot the hedges that surround us. Beyond them, the stars shine like diamonds, brighter and denser than any constellations I've seen on earth.

"Lift your elbow," Des says for the millionth time, snapping me back to attention. This is just one of his many instructions...

"The strike must start from your shoulder. The arm is merely the follow-through."

"Keep your center of gravity steady. Nothing but a death blow should make you lose your balance."

"Fleet-footed, Callie. What you don't have in girth, you must make up for in speed."

"Your wings are an asset, not a liability. Don't let them slow you down."

Des comes at me again, and if I weren't already intimidated by his experience, I would be by the predatory glint in his eye. That's only a good look on him when he's about to sully me. Otherwise, it's plain terrifying.

I weakly block one of his strikes then scramble back. The Bargainer follows, a slight grin on his lips—like he's actually enjoying this.

Gah, training sucks balls.

Big ones.

"Why…why are we doing this again?" I gasp.

"You know why." He rolls his wrist, swinging his sword around.

Meanwhile, I'm over here, still panting like a dog. "That's…not an answer."

"Your one weapon—your glamour—doesn't work here in the Otherworld," he says, continuing to advance. "No mate of mine will be defenseless."

Finally, an answer, and damn it, it's a *good* answer. I don't want to be defenseless either. If only training weren't so bruising, both for my body and my ego.

"How long…will this…task last?" I ask, panting as I shuffle away from him. It feels like it's been days since we started.

"You told me you wanted to be someone's nightmare," Des says. "I'll stop training you once you feel you are."

Teach me again how to be someone's nightmare. I remember the words I said only days ago. I hadn't imagined they'd lead to this.

And then the rest of what he's saying registers.

"Wait." I stop backing up. "You mean to tell me this task isn't over when we stop today?"

Des rushes me, and his blade strikes mine with the force of an anvil. For the hundredth time, my sword clatters to the ground.

And once again, I get trounced.

The edge of the Bargainer's blade finds my throat a moment later. The two of us stare at each other from across it.

"No, cherub," he says. "This is just day one of the task."

Damn it all to hell.

"I hate training." The skin of my neck brushes the edge of Des's sword as I speak. I don't know if he's used magic to dull the blade, but regardless, my skin doesn't split beneath it.

"If it were fun, more people would do it," he responds.

I raise my eyebrows. "Celibacy isn't all that fun either, but perhaps it would do *you* some good," I say tartly.

His expression brightens with excitement. Only this crazy fairy would find the threat thrilling. "Is that—?"

Someone behind me clears his throat. "Is now a bad time to introduce myself?"

I jolt at the new voice, and only Des's quick movements prevent me from slicing my neck on his weapon. He drops his sword and reluctantly tears his eyes from mine.

I swivel around, noticing the outline of a man a few feet away from us, his body cast mostly in shadows.

Next to me, the Bargainer slides his sword into its scabbard. "Your timing is apt as ever, Malaki."

The fairy steps out of the shadows.

The first thing I notice is the man's staggering frame. He and Des are nearly the same height, and like Des, he seems to be made entirely of muscle.

Seriously, what do they feed these guys? I thought fairies were supposed to be lithe.

The second thing I notice is the eye patch covering his left eye. That's just not something you see very often on earth. Peeking out from the edges of the eye patch is a thin, deep scar that trails up his forehead and cuts into his cheek. His skin is a deep olive color, made all the more striking against his deep brown hair.

"I thought I might be interrupting something—at least, until the lady mentioned celibacy." The man, Malaki, laughs as he approaches, something that causes Des's mouth to quirk. "How the mighty king is finally being brought to his knees."

Malaki's gaze moves from Des to me, and I see his stride falter as his eyes flick over me.

"No wonder you've been hiding her," he says, stopping in front of us.

I glance between the two men, not sure whether I should be offended. I'm suddenly, painfully aware of my wings. The training leathers I'm sweating through don't help either.

"He hasn't been hiding me," I say.

Self-conscious or not, I haven't come all this way to let someone make me feel bad about myself.

But based on the way Malaki continues to stare at me—not like I'm a freak, but like I'm a fascinating oil painting—I realize maybe I let my insecurities get the better of me. Perhaps a man with an eye patch wouldn't immediately think to degrade another's appearance.

11

Maybe his words were meant to be a compliment. How shocking.

"Callie," the Bargainer says, "this is Malaki, Lord of Dreams, my oldest friend."

Friend? My attention turns to Des, whose expression is guarded. How had I not realized Des had friends? Everybody has friends. I've just never heard about his.

Not for the first time, I feel like the man next to me is a mirage. I was so sure I saw him clearly this whole time, but the closer we get, the less apparent that becomes.

"Malaki," Des continues, his eyes lingering on me for an extra second, like he can hear exactly what I'm thinking, "this is Callypso, my mate."

I get the distinct impression Malaki wants to pull me in for a hug, but instead, he takes my hand. "I've waited centuries to meet you," he says, bowing deep enough to press his forehead to the back of my hand.

His words cut through all my jumbled thoughts.

I give him a quizzical look once he straightens. "*Centuries?*"

He glances at the Bargainer. "You haven't told her—?"

"Malaki," Des cuts in, "what is so pressing that you had to interrupt our training?"

"He hasn't told me what?" I ask Malaki.

Malaki flashes Des a wolfish grin. "Oh, this is going to be fun, I can already tell." The fairy begins to back away. "Desmond, you have urgent business in the throne room."

The King of the Night nods, his attention moving to me.

"I'll be there in five," he says, his eyes locked on mine. "Bring in a chair for Callypso. She'll be joining us."

Joining Des? In his throne room? In front of other fairies?

Oh, *hell* no.

I put my hands up in protest. "Whoa, whoa, whoa—"

Magic settles over me for the second time today, and I know without checking that the Bargainer took another bead.

"The time for hiding is over."

CHAPTER 3

I crack my knuckles nervously as Des leads me down the halls of his palace, his hand on my lower back. The ceilings arch overhead, fitted with painted tiles, and starbursts of light sparkle from the sconces lining the walls.

The simple bronze circlet Des wears as a crown currently adorns his head, and his war bands are now visible on his upper arm, the three cuffs proof of his valor in war. Like me, he wears training leathers, and I try not to stare too hard at just how good he looks in them.

Instead, I glance over my shoulder at Des's wings. He hasn't put them away all day. In fact, ever since he retrieved me from Karnon's throne room, they've almost constantly been present. Over a week ago, Temper told me male fairies like to display their wings around their mates.

He catches me staring at them, and his eyes shine.

Just that look triggers all sorts of inappropriate responses, and I have to remind myself that this guy forced my cowardly heart to face not one but two unpleasant challenges today: training and now this.

Ahead of us, Malaki and a team of royal aides and black-clad guards stand in front of an innocuous door, clearly waiting for us.

"What's the situation?" Des asks when we make it to the group.

"The last of the Fauna leaders sent a messenger," one of the aides says. "He refuses to give his message to anyone but you."

Just hearing a mention of the Fauna fae has my blood running cold. I know it's unfair to judge an entire group of fae based on their twisted leader's actions, but the truth is, I didn't just suffer at the hands of Karnon. Every Fauna fae who dragged me to and from their king, every one of them who walked by my cell and didn't stop to help, every one of them who aided the madman—they are all to blame.

"Very well," the Bargainer says next to me, his voice just as silky as it ever is, "let's meet the messenger."

I begin to retreat because I'm really not ready to face a Fauna fae right now, but Des's firm hand on my back holds me in place.

One of the fairies slips through the door, and he announces Des, and then, much to my growing horror, my name is announced as well.

I'm not sure Des means to, but his wings flare out and curve around me for several seconds before they fold back up.

I feel more than a little ill as the two of us file into the throne room.

If I weren't so distracted by my emotions, I could probably feel awed by the room itself. The ceiling that arches above us is enchanted to look like the night sky. The chamber is lit by two grand bronze chandeliers and several wall sconces, light glowing from each of them. The pale stone walls are intricately carved, and tiny bits of colorful tile cover most of them, making the room look like one grand mosaic.

Des's throne room is currently filled with dozens and dozens of fairies who line the walls or peer down from a balcony on the upper level. As soon as they see us, they begin clapping, the sound setting me further on edge. My wings hike up with my nerves, so I breathe deeply to calm myself.

Des's throne is made of hammered bronze and fitted with cushions of deep blue velvet. Next to it, someone's brought out a smaller seat made of the same materials.

My seat, I realize with a start.

Mechanically, I take it, my wings arching over the back.

This room is a far cry from the Fauna King's throne room, and yet staring down the long expanse of it still brings back unwanted memories. Not to mention that this one is filled with an audience.

Only once Des and I settle does the applause cease. In the silence that follows, one of the fairies in attendance steps in front of the throne, bowing deeply.

The fairy essentially repeats what we already heard. "My king, a Fauna messenger is here to see you."

"Bring them in," Des says, his voice booming.

I slide a glance over to my mate. Back in high school, I used to imagine all the lives he must've lived when he wasn't around me, but I never pictured this. Even after I knew he was a king, it was just too hard to envision the wily Bargainer as some benevolent ruler. But right now, he wears the role like a second skin.

A strange combination of awe and fear washes through me. Awe that for the first time in eight long years, I'm being let into Des's world. He's showing me things about himself that I've *begged* him to share in the past.

16

But then there's the fear that accompanies the wonder. The one truly concrete thing I know about my mate is that he's a man made of secrets. And perhaps for the first time, I'm having a certain amount of trepidation when it comes to exactly what those secrets are.

At the far end of the room, the arched double doors open, dragging my attention away from Des. A man with a lion's tail and mane is escorted into the room.

Just seeing the Fauna fae has me squeezing my armrests. One of my jailers had looked similar, and it's dragging my mind back to that cavernous prison with all its horrors.

A warm hand envelops my own. When I glance at the Bargainer, he's staring down our guest, his face set into uncompromising angles, even as he gives my hand a squeeze. I wouldn't want to be on the receiving end of that look.

I relax just the slightest bit. Whatever happens here, Des won't let that Fauna fae touch me. I feel the fierceness of the Bargainer's devotion even across the space that divides us.

The Fauna fairy strides down the aisle, carrying a large leather bag. He doesn't look intimidated by Des. If anything, the Fauna fairy seems like he's all pent-up aggression, his tail swishing back and forth agitatedly.

"The Fauna Kingdom has a message for the King of Night," he announces. Even his voice is aggressive.

I would've thought this would frighten me. Everything else about this moment has struck fear into my heart. But seeing this Fauna fae walk toward Des—toward *me*—full of anger rather than repentance…

My nails begin to curve back into claws.

I feel my bloodlust rising, the siren whispering all sorts of grim thoughts at the back of my mind.

Remember what his kind did to us. To those women.

He deserves to die.

One quick slice across his throat would be enough…

I push those thoughts far, far away.

The Fauna fae reaches the end of the aisle, several feet away from the dais where Des and I sit. In one smooth motion, he throws his bag on the ground in front of him. It lands with a dull, wet thump, and four bloody severed heads roll out.

I nearly fall off my seat. "Holy *shit!*" My wings flare out, accidently bowling over a soldier standing too close.

Seriously, what the hell is wrong with this world?

Around me, Des's subjects gasp, their eyes riveted to the sight of all those decapitated heads.

And the dead…the dead look as though they're still screaming, their eyes wide and their mouths gaping.

The gasps turn into cries for vengeance, and soldiers reach for their weapons. I'm acutely aware that this room is one hot minute away from taking this Fauna dude *out.*

The only one not reacting is Des, and that should worry me deeply. He looks almost bored as he stares down at the severed heads.

Des holds up his hand, and the room falls silent. He sits back against his throne, his gaze moving to the Fauna fae, who looks on challengingly.

"Who are they?" Des asks, his voice echoing throughout the room.

"The last of the Night Kingdom's diplomats staying in our territory," the lion-tailed messenger responds. "Our people demand justice for the murder of our king, the destruction of our palace, and the death of all the Fauna fae trapped inside the castle when you destroyed it."

The Bargainer smiles at that.

Holy crap, if I were that messenger, I would've just wet myself.

"Refuse us, and the Fauna fae still left will not rest until every last Night fae in our realm has been dealt with," the messenger says.

The crowd hisses its displeasure, and something ripples through the room, something darker and more insidious than the night.

"What sort of justice do you demand?" Des asks, leaning forward and placing his chin on his fist.

"We demand that the Night Kingdom pay for the construction of a new palace and that the current king abdicate his throne."

All right, this guy has some serious cojones walking into this place and requiring the Night King step down from his position—to his face.

Surely this guy knows his demands won't be taken seriously?

Des stands, and you can hear a pin drop, the room is so quiet. He steps down the stairs, his heavy boots echoing throughout the hall.

Had I thought he seemed kingly a moment ago?

I was sorely mistaken.

With his white hair brushed back from his face, his black battle leathers curving around his defined muscles, and his talon-tipped wings neatly tucked at his back, he looks like some dark prince of hell.

His ominous footfalls only stop once he stands right in the middle of the carnage. He toes a bloody head.

For several seconds, as the room waits with bated breath, all we hear is the slick sound of dead flesh as the severed head rolls under the Bargainer's boot.

"You pose a striking offer," Des finally says, still staring down at the remains of his diplomats.

The messenger looks resolute, only now his tail has stopped flicking back and forth. I can't imagine what is going on in his head.

"But I'm going to have to decline."

Des's voice is like a swallow of Johnnie Walker after a long day. So smooth, you barely feel the burn of it.

The Fauna fae squares his jaw. "Then expect—"

"*No.*" Power ripples out of Des. Instantly, it brings the messenger to his knees.

"You come here and lay the severed heads of my diplomats at my feet," Des says. His hair ripples a little with the force of his words. "Then *you* demand justice for a mad king who kidnapped, tortured, and imprisoned soldiers—a man who kidnapped, tortured, and imprisoned *my mate.*"

Suddenly, all eyes are on me. My skin burns at the attention.

"Finally"—Des continues staring down at the fairy—"you threaten to kill my people should I not meet your demands."

The messenger tries to talk, but Des's magic keeps his lips sealed.

The Bargainer begins to circle the Fauna fae. "Do you even *know* my subjects? I rule over monsters from your wildest imaginings, creatures made of fairies' deepest fears. And I have their respect." Des pauses at the man's back, bending down to whisper into his ear, "Do you know how I've gained their respect?"

The messenger glances over his shoulder at the Bargainer, his lips still sealed.

My heart begins to beat faster and faster. Something bad is about to happen.

"I let them feast on my enemies."

The messenger looks rattled, but he's not panicking.

Des straightens. "Bring in the bog."

His order is met with fearful whispers. Fairies in the audience shift nervously.

A minute later a side door opens to the throne room.

At first, nothing happens. Then, from the doorway, a shadow slithers over the wall. The fairies nearest to it scream and scatter. It seems to expand, growing larger and larger, the shape of it hulking and horned.

Heaven help me, from the shape of it alone, it looks like Karnon's mutant cousin.

I'm waiting to see the monster that accompanies it when I realize this *is* it. It's a shadow, nothing more. Only, the longer I stare at it, the more terrible it seems. It might not have any sort of physical presence, but on some deep, primordial level, it terrifies me.

It slides down the wall, losing its shape as it pools against the floor. The audience members nearest to it are practically trampling each other to get away, but it pays them no heed. Instead, it creeps toward the messenger.

The Fauna fae struggles, trying to rise to his feet as the bog comes closer, but whatever magical hold Desmond has over him, it pins him in place.

Now the messenger is showing the first signs of panic. My guess is that whatever this bog is, its reputation precedes it.

Des steps away from the fairy.

"Wait, wait—" the messenger says as the creature nears him. "Don't go."

This makes Des's lips quirk, though his eyes are as hard as ever.

Cruel Des. Dark Des. I'm catching an elusive glimpse of the beast behind the man.

The Fauna fae is still trying to move, but it's like his lower legs are glued to the floor. "I'll make a deal," he says, his eyes pinned to the shadowy creature heading his way.

I'll make a deal.

Des's shoulders stiffen at the temptation, but he ignores the fairy.

The creature is only mere feet away.

"Please, *anything*!"

For a fairy who had enough courage to threaten a fae king in his own court, he sure is quick to fall apart. I don't know what he expected would happen. Des doesn't bend to other people's wills. He's the force that contorts and crushes them. I've seen it happen time and time again with his clients.

The Bargainer heads back for his throne, his face steely. His eyes find mine, and they flicker as they take me in. That might be the closest he comes to regret in this moment. And then the look is gone, and he's made of stone once more.

There's a darkness in this man, and I've yet to plumb its depths.

The shadow closes the last of the distance to the Fauna fairy, moving over his feet. The messenger's ankles begin to disappear, then his calves.

That's when the screaming starts.

Des mounts the steps to his throne and takes a seat next to me, all while the bog continues to swallow the fairy.

I dig my fingernails into my seat as I hear the man's cries. I have every reason to enjoy the justice of this moment, but now that the Fauna fae looks less like a villain and more like a victim, I find I can't.

I don't want to sit here and watch this. It's too inhuman, too fae, too wicked. All at once it becomes too much.

I get up and, among the screams and the stares, I leave the room.

No one stops me.

CHAPTER 4

I stand on the balcony connected to Des's royal suite, the night sky glittering above me. After leaving his throne room, I wandered the palace grounds for a bit before eventually finding my way back here.

Far below me, I can make out fairies coming and going across the palace grounds. Beyond them is the city of Somnia.

I don't know how long I've been leaning over the railing, watching this terribly foreign world pass me by. Long enough for me to question just about every life decision that led me here.

"Tell me, cherub, do I scare you?"

I glance over my shoulder. Des stands at the threshold to the balcony, his predatory eyes glittering. He stares at me like I'm the dangerous one.

I don't answer right away, instead choosing to simply watch him. He steps out onto the balcony, still wearing— like me—his training leathers from earlier.

He appears half-wild, the moonlight carving his face

into sinister shapes. He looks like he wants to devour my soul.

Does he scare me?

"Yes," I say softly.

Despite my words, he comes closer. And I'm glad he does. My fear hasn't stopped me from wanting him. Our relationship was forged on bloodshed and solidified through deception. I am the dark creature that craves sex and destruction, and he is the king of it.

When he gets close enough, he places a hand on the back of my neck and pulls my forehead to his, not kissing me but simply holding me to him.

"Truth," he says. "Does this change things for you?"

I feel his magic delicately wrap itself around my windpipe. His question is vague, which is so unlike him, but nonetheless, I understand what he's asking.

"No," I say, my voice hoarse.

Maybe it should change things for me. It feels like I've just conceded a little bit of my soul. But Des has been collecting pieces of my soul since the night I took my father's life. As far as I'm concerned, he can have it; I know he'll take good care of it.

Des's stance doesn't change, but I swear I feel him relax. He smells like sweat and the sweet night. My terrible king. My mysterious mate.

His thumb strokes my cheek, and for several seconds, neither of us speak.

Cruel Des. Dark Des. *My* Des.

"What was that thing?" I finally ask.

"The bog?"

I nod against him.

He straightens, pulling away without letting me go. "It's

a sentient nightmare. It eats fairies alive, subjecting them to their worst fears as it digests them."

A shudder courses through me at the thought. "That's horrible."

It's his turn to nod, his face somber. "It is."

And yet it hadn't stopped him from unleashing it on one of his enemies. Even now he doesn't look regretful.

He's a fairy. What did you think you were getting yourself into when you decided to be with him?

I run my fingers through my hair, emotionally and physically exhausted. The training leathers I've been wearing all day are sticky and chafing in places they really shouldn't be.

"I want to go home," I say.

I'm tired of my wings and perpetual night. I'm tired of being surrounded by monsters and feeling powerless against them. Most of all, I'm tired of living in a world that doesn't have Netflix.

Des's eyes soften. "I know."

"You haven't offered to take me home." This comes out more accusingly than I intended.

"You haven't asked," he responds as smoothly as ever.

"If I did ask for you to take me home, would you?"

The Bargainer's jaw tightens, and for a second, I see something alien in his eyes. Something predatory and very fae.

And then it vanishes.

He nods. "I would."

We both fall silent, and I know he's waiting for me to ask him exactly that—to take me home. If only wanting could make something true. But I can't leave, not as I am. If Des dutifully took me back to earth, I'd still be a human with wings and scales and claws.

"Where do we go from here?" I ask hopelessly.

26

Des's mouth curves up. "You seem to have forgotten that you still owe me a great deal of favors—"

There is that.

"—and that you happen to be my mate."

There is also that.

He takes my hand and leads me back inside his rooms.

"But, as far as where we go from here, I'd say for starters that we get you a bath."

I crack my first smile of the evening. "Look who's talking." I swear man sweat is at least twice as stinky as woman sweat. I'm pretty sure it's a scientific fact.

Des releases my hand. "Is that an invitation?" he asks, raising an eyebrow.

"You're the Lord of Secrets—I think you can figure that out for yourself," I say.

His eyes brighten with mischief.

While he looks at me like I'm the most delicious macaron he's ever laid eyes on, I reach around my back and paw uselessly at the training leathers I wear. For what feels like forever, I've been trying to unfasten the ties that criss-cross my back and hold the leather bodice in place, but I can't quite reach them—

Des's warm hands brush mine away before turning me around and unlacing the ties. Each graze of fingers feels like a kiss. Suddenly, my heart's thundering all over again, and the humorous moment we were having is replaced by something that smolders like embers.

My bodice loosens then falls to the floor in front of me, the air caressing my exposed torso.

Des rotates me back around and places his hand over my pounding heart, as though he's trying to capture the beat of it for himself.

His gaze moves to mine. "Cherub, we have a lot of catching up to do."

I feel his words all the way in the pit of my stomach. Love, romance—the whole thing feels like a rabbit hole, and I'm Alice, about to plunge into it.

His hand slides to my wrist, and I tense as his fingers roll over my bracelet. What will he ask of me now? More training? Some kinky sex act? Not going to lie, I'm pretty sure I could get behind the latter.

And I do mean *get behind*.

"Tell me something about your past, something I don't know."

Of course, the moment I'm eager to participate in one of Des's dares, he blows my mind by asking me a simple question.

A second later I realize the Bargainer's magic doesn't grip me as it usually does. He didn't take a bead. He just wants to know a bit more about me…as I stand topless in his chambers.

"Ummm, what do you want to know?"

I bring my hands up, hiding my breasts from him. I aspire one day to shamelessly have topless conversations with Des…but that day isn't today.

"How did you and Temper meet?" he asks.

That's what he wants to know? Right now?

He reads me like a book. "You think I'm concerned about losing an opportunity to make love to you?"

Those words go straight to my core.

His eyes dip to where I cover my breasts, and he lowers his voice. "I'm not."

I narrow my eyes at his arrogance.

He steps forward, into my space, and it's all I can do not

to edge backward. Des is still overwhelming, still a force to be reckoned with. "I knew who you were the night I left you, Callie, and I'm learning who you are now, but I want to know about everything that came during those seven years I lost you."

That has my breath catching as I stare up at him. We are lovers and old friends and strangers all at once.

He's absolutely right; there's so much we have to catch up on. Things no amount of physical intimacy will make up for. And those things are what he wants from me.

"I met Temper senior year at Peel Academy," I say, my mind jogging back to the final year at my supernatural boarding school. That was a rough period. I'd lost Des only months beforehand, and I found myself with no friends and no family. The only thing I had in abundance was heartbreak.

"It was the first day back, and I wasn't sitting next to anyone in my morality of magic class when she dropped into the seat next to me. And then she started talking." She talked to me as though we were already friends and I just hadn't gotten the memo yet. "It was the first time since you left that another student tried to befriend me."

It doesn't hurt so bad, admitting to Des I was once a social pariah. That, he already knows about.

As for my friendship with Temper, it was only later that I found out how hard it had been for her to take that seat next to me and put herself out there. She knew I had no friends, something the two of us had in common.

It took me weeks to learn people avoided Temper even more than they did me, largely because of the type of supernatural she was. Of course, considering my own troubled past, Temper's infamy only made me like her more.

"Ever since then," I say, "we've been inseparable."

Talking about Temper only makes me miss her all the more. The past seven years might've been the pits when it came to my love life, but not when it came to everything else, and that was largely thanks to Temper. She must be losing her mind right now, wondering where I am.

I shove my worries away. "How did you meet Malaki?" I ask.

I'm not even sure Des will respond. He never answers these things. He stares down at me, standing so close, I feel the heat of his body.

"Will you unfasten my leathers?" he asks instead of answering.

I deflate at his response. I shouldn't be disappointed. Des has already shown me so much more of himself than I ever thought he would.

Pressing my lips together, I nod.

He turns around, his wicked-looking wings still out.

My hands find the ties that secure the leather armor to his back. One by one, I unfasten them.

"I met Malaki when I was a teenager," he begins haltingly.

My fingers still for a second.

"Back then I had…lost my way," he continues. "I found myself in Barbos, the City of Thieves, without a cent to my name."

I bow my head, letting a small smile slip out before I resume unfastening the bindings.

"That was around the time I joined the Angels of Small Death," he says.

"The gang," I say, remembering the explanation he gave me for his sleeve of tattoos.

"*Brotherhood*," he corrects over his shoulder. He takes a

deep breath. "Malaki was another member. He was several years older than me but still the closest fairy in age."

I can tell dragging out these memories is hard for him. His mind is a steel trap. Things go in, and they don't come out.

"Living on the edge like we were," Des continues, "brought us close together. He's saved my life before, and I've saved his."

I unfasten the last of the ties at Des's back, and the leather slides off him. Just like me, he's bare from the waist up. I guess this is our weird version of show-and-tell—show some skin, tell a secret.

He turns back around to face me, his chest bare. "He's my brother in every way but blood."

I meet his eyes. It's rare that I catch Des laid bare like this. Like me, he's spent years building armor around himself… and now it's coming off. He's no longer the terrifying king or the slippery Bargainer.

Right now, he's just my Des.

"How long have you known him?" I ask.

He pauses.

"Long enough," he finally says.

I know enough about fairies to know *long enough* can just as easily mean centuries as it can decades. And the comment Malaki made earlier…

I've been waiting centuries to meet you.

I tilt my head to the side. "You're really freaking old, aren't you?"

A sly smile creeps along Des's face. "I can answer that, but it will cost you."

I don't need to buy a favor to know the dude must be ancient.

I back away from him, heading toward the bathroom. "Rain check…Grandpa."

I only have time to see his grin widen, and then he's scooping me up, throwing me over his shoulder.

"Naughty thing," he says, smacking my butt.

I shriek then begin to laugh. "No wonder your hair is so white. How many centuries ago did it lose its color?"

I feel Des's rumbly laughter shaking his shoulders.

"I'll have you know it kept its color until the day I met you," he says.

He marches us to the bathroom. As he does so, my boots tug themselves off my feet before clattering to the ground. My pants and underwear go next.

"*Des!*" Now just about every inch of my bare skin is pressed tightly to his.

"*Callie.*" He mimics my tone.

"What are you doing?"

His hand caresses my upper thigh. "Disrobing my queen."

That stops me completely.

Oh God, his *queen*.

"Des, you don't mean that, do you?" Because—nope. Nope, nope, nope.

I'm just getting used to the idea of there even being an *us*. Anything more is beyond what I can handle.

"It was a turn of phrase," he says smoothly. "If you'd rather, I call you a scullery maid—"

I whack his back, which only makes him laugh again. The sound has me relaxing again. Just a turn of phrase.

As he carries me, his own pants slide off his hips and down his ankles. Gracefully, he steps out of them.

And now we're both naked.

Ahead of us, the grand bathtub's spigot turns itself on.

He steps into the giant tub, setting me carefully on my feet. For a moment, I stare at my soul mate, his face just as painfully lovely as the first time I laid eyes on him, his white hair loose. His crown and war cuffs are gone, and the only remaining adornment he wears is the ink that runs down his arm.

Without clothes, Des is all the more appealing, his torso massive, large ropes of muscles cording it.

Just as I drink him in, he drinks me in, his eyes moving to my breasts then downward to my waist and hips.

He steps in close, tilting my chin up. "I want to be good at this, cherub. At us."

I reach out and run a hand down his sleeve of tattoos, my finger lingering over the tears inked onto his skin. "I do too."

For several seconds, the only sound is the spray of water filling the tub we stand in. Then, out of the near silence, Led Zeppelin's "Stairway to Heaven" comes on, the song flooding the room.

As I look around for the phantom speakers that must be playing the music, I catch sight of a polished wood tray resting to the side of the tub. On it sits a steaming mug of coffee, an espresso (in an impossibly small cup), and a plate of macarons. It's our usual order from Douglas Café.

And for whatever reason, that does me in.

I take a shaky breath and laugh, though it comes out more like a sob. "Stop it," I say, my voice soft and rough all at the same time.

But rather than stopping, Des pulls me in close, his pretty, pretty muscles pressed against my soft curves.

He leans in, his lips a hairbreadth from mine. "Never."

CHAPTER 5

Des is a romantic.

Ugh.

That's so not what my heart needed. It's not like there's any turning back at this point, but still. It wounds my ego a little to know how easily I can be done in by a few thoughtful gestures.

Close to an hour after the two of us get in the tub, I step out of it, my stomach full of macarons and coffee as I dry myself. I watch Des—wings and all—as he saunters out of the room, a towel wrapped low around his waist.

Once he gets to the far side of the bed, his towel drops to the ground, and holy virgins and saints, that backside is *everything*.

I wrap my own towel the best I can around myself, accidently plucking a few of my feathers in the process, my eyes fixed on the Bargainer. I am absolutely creeping on this man right now, and I have zero regrets.

He glances over his shoulder at me, his pale hair slicked

back. I should be embarrassed that he caught me blatantly ogling him, but his own expression heats at whatever he sees in mine.

We still haven't done anything together—naked espresso drinking and macaron eating aside—and the need to rectify that situation is growing.

I wring out my hair as I pad into his bedroom, the hanging lanterns above us glowing softly.

I'm about to head to the fancy armoire already stocked with a million fae outfits for me when Des reaches into a dresser drawer near the bed and tosses me a piece of black clothing. I catch it, the material soft beneath my fingertips.

"What's this?" I ask.

"A consolation prize. It's the next best thing to earth I can give you."

I furrow my brows.

He nods to the garment in my hand, and reluctantly I tear my gaze from his to shake the faded material open.

A huge grin spreads across my face when I see the giant lips and tongue printed across the faded T-shirt. It's one of Des's vintage Rolling Stones shirts.

"That's on loan to you," he says.

"On *loan*?" I say, raising my eyebrows.

Des steps into a loose pair of pants. "Just because I love you doesn't mean I'm going to give you one of my most prized possessions."

He just made it official: I now fully intend to keep this shirt.

Taking my cue from Des, I let my towel drop to the ground and drag the shirt over my shoulders. My light mood wipes away the moment the hem of the shirt grazes my wings.

I forgot all about them. Now that I have wings, I can't just pull clothing over my shoulders.

Before I can consider throwing myself a pity party, the T-shirt's soft material, which was bunched above my wing joints, now slips down my back as if there were no obstacle in the way, the hem of the shirt falling to midthigh.

My head snaps up to Des, who's smirking a little. "How did you—?"

"Magic, love."

I reach around myself, feeling for where my wings connect to my back. The shirt is split around my wing bones.

I'm so focused on the logistics of Des's shirt that I fail to see the way he stares at me. It's not until he disappears and reappears at my side that I take notice.

He fingers the hem of the shirt. "This looks good on you."

I freeze.

Des is all coiled purpose. His eyes flick to mine. We're just moths circling a flame.

It's right then that a yawn slips from my mouth.

Worst—timing—ever.

I'm not tired. I mean, I am—it's been a long day, from waking up early to the hours-long training session to watching a man get eaten by a living nightmare—but I'm not tired enough to miss out on this.

Des's eyes drop to my mouth. Whatever passion took him over a moment before, he tucks it away.

I want to cry out when I see him slip on the respectful mask he used to wear back when I was in high school. For all his wicked tendencies, he can be surprisingly chivalrous.

He tugs on the edge of my shirt. "We're not done with this yet," he says, his voice still rough with promises of sex.

He drags me to bed, and I almost think the man hasn't been deterred by my yawn.

Des's wings disappear so he can roll on his back. A moment later, he pulls me half onto his chest. The way he holds me...the dude has definitely shelved getting frisky for the moment.

I could probably make him reconsider, but damn, there may be nothing comfier than curling up against Des.

"Tell me a secret," I whisper.

"Another one?" He looks so legitimately put out that I laugh.

I can't even remember the last "secret" he told me—was it about his friendship with Malaki?

"Yes, another one," I say.

He groans and pulls me tighter. "Fine—but only because I like you."

I smile a little against him. *Can't believe asking him actually worked.*

Des smooths a hand over my feathers. "The only thing I dislike about your wings is that they hide your ass—and I *really* like your ass."

The room is silent for all of three seconds, and then I can't contain my laugh. "*Des,* that's *not* what I meant when I asked for a secret."

"And yet you received a secret nonetheless. Consider yourself indulged." He squeezes my backside for emphasis, and I let out a little shriek, which causes him to chuckle. And that rumbly chuckle leads to kissing...lots and lots of languid, delicious kissing.

When I finally break away, I lay my head against his chest. The room falls silent, the only sound the thump of Des's heart beneath my ear. I close my eyes.

I can get used to this.

What a terrifying thought.

"For two centuries you've been nothing but a whisper of a possibility," Des says, breaking the silence. "And then I met you." He pauses, like an entire story begins and ends with that sentence. Like life was one thing before he met me, and it became something else afterward.

It's enough to make me ignore the fact he's all but admitted to being over two centuries old.

"You were everything I never knew I wanted. You were chaos. You were desperation. You were the most mysterious secret I'd ever come across. Everything about you drew me in—your innocence, your vulnerability, hell, even your tragic life. You were the most captivating creature I'd ever met."

My throat works at his words. There's a gravity not just to *what* he's saying but that he's saying it at all. I asked for a secret, and he gave me a revelation, something I can hold close to my heart late at night.

"Seven years apart," he continues, "and the woman you became was a world away from the girl I met." He tilts my head so he can look me in the eye. "That only made me want you more. You were both old and new, familiar and exotic, within reach and forbidden. And I wanted you so badly, for so long, I was sure it would kill me.

"And when I look at you even now—*especially* now—I see one simple truth." He stops speaking.

I sit up a little. "What truth?"

In the darkness, I see him staring back down at me. "You are magic, love."

CHAPTER 6

There's blood everywhere. In my hair, on my skin, splattered around where I lie. I push my torso off the ground, glancing around.

No.

Not this place.

Not again.

I take in the rotting leaves that cover the floor, the dead vines that climb up the walls of the long room, and the chair of bones that looms large among it all.

Karnon's throne room.

"Pretty, pretty bird."

My blood runs cold at the voice at my back.

It can't be. The Fauna king is dead.

"Do you like your wings?"

But that voice... A shiver ripples down my spine. Karnon's voice is deep and rough, just like I remember it.

Leaves crunch under his feet as he comes around to my

front. First I see his twisting antlers then his strange, mad eyes and wild hair. God, it *is* him.

"Now you're a beast like the rest of us."

I pinch my eyes shut. He's *dead*.

"You'll never be free," he says…only, Karnon's voice is no longer his own. It's another voice I know all too well.

My eyes snap open, and I stare at my stepfather. The same man I accidently killed eight years ago. Why have these ghosts come back to haunt me?

I only have seconds to gape at him before the room darkens.

The air shifts to my left, stirring my hair. I glance over, but I cannot see anything, the darkness is so complete.

On the nape of my neck, I feel someone's breath, so close that they must be leaning over me, but when I spin around and reach out, my hand only grasps air.

In the dark, there's a faint echo of laughter, which raises the gooseflesh along my arm.

Responding to my fear, my siren comes out, making my skin glow softly.

"Who's there?" I call out.

A woman's voice rings out, coming from everywhere and nowhere all at once. "Secrets are meant for one soul to keep."

"Who are you?"

"He's coming for you." This time, it's a child's voice that speaks from the darkness.

"Who?" I ask.

Karnon is *dead*.

Laughter echoes all around me, growing louder and louder. In it I hear the woman's voice, the child's, the Fauna king's, and my stepfather's. I hear them and so many others laughing at me.

All at once, it ceases.

"*Who?*" I repeat.

The air rumbles like thunder, thickening as some strong magic builds and builds, gathering power. With a crack, a booming voice breaks through the magic—

"*Me.*"

I gasp awake. My wide eyes gaze into Des's concerned ones. His hands cup my face, his worried gaze searching my expression.

That dream felt too real. My stepfather and Karnon are both dead and gone, and yet on nights like tonight, it's as though they never died.

I suck in air, my chest rising and falling far too fast.

Of course, those evil men only starred in a portion of the dream. There were other equally chilling presences calling out to me from the darkness. Intuitively, I know who they belong to—the sleeping women and their unnatural children.

And then there was that final voice… I don't know what to make of it.

His brow pinched, Des kisses me fiercely. As quick as it begins, it's over.

"You wouldn't wake," he says.

I shiver. It might've been just a dream, but the truth is that the warrior women still sleep, and the male soldiers are still missing. Karnon might be dead, but his work isn't.

I stare into Des's eyes. "I want to see the casket children again."

For the second time in my life, I willingly visit the little monsters the sleeping soldiers birthed. I might very well be

41

the stupidest woman out there for seeking them out again. But there's something I have to see.

"Remind me again why I agreed to this?" Des says next to me, echoing my thoughts.

Today Des wears the T-shirt and black pants combo I'm so used to seeing him in, his hair tied back with a leather thong and his sleeve of tattoos on display. He looks broody as hell, probably because he's not exactly thrilled to be bringing me back to the royal nursery.

"I'm helping you solve this mystery," I say, heading down the hall.

He doesn't say anything to that, but a muscle in his jaw tightens.

I feel it, low in my belly, the fear that whatever happened to me and those women wasn't the end of this. Death should lift magic—even fae magic. That rule is the same both here and on earth. But it didn't.

My thoughts shift to the dream I so recently had of the Thief—

Fee, fye, foe, fum. I'm not done, siren. Oh no, I've just begun.

I shiver before forcing the thoughts away. They won't do me any good for what I'm about to do.

When we enter the nursery, a wave of déjà vu washes over me. Many of the younger children lie in cribs or beds, eerily still, and the older ones stand at the far side of the room, staring out the large windows. It's all nearly identical to how I found them before.

The only thing different about the nursery is that more beds and cradles have been brought in to accommodate the influx of children from Karnon's prison.

I try not to shudder as I stare at the kids. They were frightening before, when they were simply strange children who drank blood and prophesized, but now, knowing how they were conceived... The horror washes over me again.

Even after the nurse announces us to the kids, none of them move.

The hair along my arms rises.

There's something deeply unsettling about these kids, this place.

Taking a deep breath, I head toward the window. Des is right at my side, his heavy boots thudding with each step, his jaw tight.

"You came back," one of the children says, her back to me.

I falter for a moment before pulling myself together. "I did."

"You weren't supposed to," another says.

I'd forgotten these kids act as a single unit.

As one, they turn, watching me with wary eyes as I approach them.

Des steps in front of me, and several of them hiss at him.

"Any of you touch my mate like last time," he says, speaking over their hisses, "you'll find yourselves banished."

Surprisingly, the threat works, and their hisses die off.

I catch Des's eye as he steps aside, and I give him a look. Threatening kids, even creepy ones, is not kosher.

He meets my gaze with a steely one of his own.

All right. Banishment it is.

The children split their attention between cagily watching Des and shrewdly studying me.

I crouch in front of the closest child, a girl with flaming-red hair, my eyes scouring her features. No horns, no claws, no slitted pupils. She looks nothing like Karnon, save for the fangs she must have in order to drink blood.

"Slaves live such short lives," she tells me as I assess her.

Slaves, the official classification of most humans living in the Otherworld.

Ever heard of human babies being swapped with fae changelings? Ever wonder what happened to all those human babies? Enslavement is what happened to them.

The Night Kingdom deemed the practice illegal some time ago, but the other kingdoms still allow it.

"Why do you say that?" I ask the girl, trying to hide that I'm majorly creeped out.

"They are dirty and weak and ugly," the boy next to her says.

I'm acutely aware of the fact that, in these children's eyes, I am one of the humans they're degrading.

Out of the corner of my eye, I see wispy, curling shadows form at the edges of the room, a clear indication of Des's rising anger.

I focus on the boy. "Who told you that?"

"My father," he replies. His mouth curves into a small secretive smile. "He's coming for you."

I straighten and take a step back, my eyes glued to his face. Blood rushes between my ears.

They're just words. They don't mean anything.

But my bones believe they do mean something. As do my instincts. As does that little voice in the back of my head. They're all telling me what I feared the moment I woke from that nightmare: it's not over.

I feel Des's hand on my stomach, gently backing me away from the children. Dazedly, I let him do so, all the while I stare at the boy. He and the rest of the children follow us with their eyes, and I get the distinct impression they're tracking me the same way predators track prey. Finally, I turn away from the boy, making a beeline for the exit.

I feel myself trembling. How absurd that a child could frighten me so much.

Des and I are just about to the door when I hear the boy's voice at my back. "These are dark times."

My wings tense, hiking up, and thank goodness the castle is full of large doors, otherwise I'd be wrestling with my unwieldy wings to get out of that room.

As soon as the door clicks shut behind me, I draw in a shuddering breath.

How could that boy know to say that line? It's the same line I heard whispered in the air when I visited the sleeping women weeks ago.

"Karnon's dead," Des says.

I nod. "I know." I run a hand over my mouth.

My fear doesn't abate. If anything, it grows. The thing is, I didn't come to see these kids because I was afraid Karnon was alive.

I came here for another reason altogether.

"Do all Fauna fae have animal features?" I ask as we leave the nursery.

My jailers had animal features. As did Karnon. As did the unfortunate Fauna messenger I saw yesterday.

Des stops. "Most do."

"And Karnon's children?" I say. "Would they share his features?"

The Bargainer's mouth tightens. "At least some of them would, yes."

"Those children didn't share any of his features," I say.

By Des's expression I see he's already aware of what I'm only now realizing—

Karnon is not their father.

CHAPTER 7

Karnon is not their father.

Karnon is not their father.

But...how? He was the one imprisoning those women. He was the one sexually assaulting them.

Beside me, Des begins walking again, like this revelation doesn't change everything.

That's when I realize—

"You *knew*," I accuse as we head down his palace halls.

Rather than appearing surprised or guilty or ashamed by my accusation—rather than any of those normal responses— Des appraises me with one of his typical devil-may-care looks.

He lifts a shoulder. "So what if I did?"

So what...?

I slap a palm to his sculpted chest and halt him in the middle of the hall. "Oh no, amigo, our relationship doesn't work like that."

He glances down at my hand, and I can tell I'm getting close to riling up the King of Night.

"Our relationship doesn't work like *what* precisely, cherub?" he asks, his gaze going shrewd.

"You can't just keep secrets like that from me."

He has the audacity to look amused, though it doesn't reach his eyes. "I assure you, I *can*."

My eyes narrow. "*Des*," I warn.

He removes my hand from his chest. "Is that supposed to be a threatening tone?" he asks, raising an eyebrow. He clucks his tongue and brings my hand up to his mouth. "Because if it is," he continues, "then you've got to work on your intimidation game. I mean, you gave it a decent try, but I'm more turned on than anything else."

Des proceeds to kiss the tips of my fingers, which is totally distracting. Who knew fingertip kisses were even a thing? Because they so are. I'm declaring it here and now.

Focus, Callie.

"Let me show you something," he says softly.

So much for focusing. Rather than picking up our argument where we left off, I let Des lead me through his palace. We eventually enter what looks like a grand library, the arches of it inlaid with decorative tile. Between several bronze chandeliers hang a myriad of colorful lamps. And that's not even mentioning the books.

Shelves and shelves of them line the walls and fill aisles of the room, each one bound in cloth or leather. There are also heaps of scrolls stacked along the shelves, the handles they're wound around made of carved wood and bone, some even inlaid with mother-of-pearl and semiprecious stones.

I spend a solid minute turning in a circle and taking the whole place in.

"*Wow*," I finally say.

It smells like leather and paper and something else I'd

say was cedar, but who knows? I have the urge to walk up to each shelf and pull out the books and scrolls one by one, letting my hands trail over the dried ink and soft paper. This place feels like magic and wisdom, and I might be having a spiritual experience right now.

I feel Des's eyes on my face. Eventually he peels his gaze away to take in the place as well.

"Is this the royal library?" I ask.

The corner of Des's mouth curves upward. "One of them."

"One of them?" I repeat.

"This one is where many of the realm's official documents are kept. The main library is on the eastern grounds of the palace."

I can't wrap my mind around the sheer magnitude of that.

He leads me to a table, and one of the chairs magically slides out for me. Des takes a seat across from me, and for a second, he just appraises me. When he looks at me like that, I feel acutely exposed.

"What?" I finally say, tucking a lock of hair behind my ear.

He gives me a soft smile. "My mother would have loved you."

Just saying those words, he's invited ghosts into this place. I barely remember my own mother, and I don't have any memories of her being especially loving to me. It's a beautiful gift to imagine Des's mother might've loved me.

"You think so?" I say.

"I know so." He says it so steadfastly that my one objection— that I'm human—dies before it ever leaves my lips.

Before I can ask more about the subject, Des lifts his

48

hand and flicks his wrist. Off in the distance, I hear paper sliding against paper.

A scroll rises above the aisles and floats toward us. The Bargainer's hand is still in the air, and the scroll lands softly in his open palm.

"This is the report taken from the victims who recovered from their imprisonment," Des says, changing the subject. He places the scroll on the table.

I get up and drag my chair closer to him.

"These were taken from the survivors of Karnon's prison?" I ask.

"Just the Night fae survivors," Des says. "The other kingdoms are recording the interviews of their victims. At the next summit our kingdoms hold, we'll compare notes, but until then, we only have my subjects' testimonies."

I know without looking that I'm one of those testimonies. It was optional for me (perks of being the mates of a king), but I did it anyway. I've worked enough cases to know how helpful testimonies can be.

"Why did you want me to see this?" I ask, lifting the edge of the parchment between us. I catch a glimpse of my name, and my stomach dips a little.

Des had been in the room when I gave my testimony, so he knows what happened to me, but seeing it written out next to all the other victims still makes me squirm.

Des slides the parchment over to me. "I thought you might like to read what the other prisoners had to say about their experience."

His words sound almost like a challenge, and I eye him a bit circumspectly before I glance down at the scroll.

The paragraphs are written in an elegant scrawl. My heart grows heavy at the sight of the words—at the reminder of what happened to myself and all the other imprisoned women. But these testimonies are also a marvel. Des had been unable to get any fae to talk about the Thief before now. I assume it was because those individuals had something to lose.

As for the survivors of Karnon—well, there's hardly anything left for us *to* lose. We've already lived through our darkest fears.

I skip over my own testimony, focusing on the other women who escaped.

I read about nine different fae soldiers, each who'd been kidnapped in her sleep. They had languished in Karnon's prison between one and eight days.

Apparently, they—like me—managed to recover from a week's worth of the Fauna king's black magic. Those who were captives for longer than eight days...they now lived far below us in glass caskets.

The more I read, the more Callie the PI surges back to life. I've missed this: digging into cases, solving problems.

It takes me only a little longer to stumble across what Des must've wanted me to see.

I tear my gaze away from the scroll. "All but two were sexually assaulted by Karnon," I say.

The two who escaped that fate hadn't been sexually assaulted at all. This wasn't due to the Fauna king having a change of heart; they just happened to be the two most recently abducted. Karnon hadn't had enough time to incapacitate them with his magic. He liked violating women when they couldn't fight back.

Des nods. "And?" he probes.

I return my attention to the parchment. It takes only seconds for the rest of the pieces to fall into place.

"And all but two confirmed they were pregnant," I say.

Seven women are raped solely by Karnon; seven women end up pregnant.

I meet Des's gaze. "So Karnon *is* the casket children's father?"

Des leans back in his seat, his legs splayed. One leg jiggles restlessly. "So it seems."

I want to pull my hair out. None of this makes sense.

"But I thought…" I thought Des believed Karnon *wasn't* the father.

Before I can finish the thought, someone knocks on the library's doors.

Des waves away the scroll, and it floats back onto the shelves. Another flick of his hand, and the library doors open.

In saunters Malaki, looking just as rakish as usual. He bows to both of us then straightens, focusing his attention on Des.

"Sorry to interrupt," Malaki says by way of greeting, "but duty calls."

Des straightens in his seat. "What's on the docket?"

"There are Borderland issues to deal with, two fairies you'll be honoring with war cuffs and brunch—oh, and a Solstice invite you need to respond to."

I'm already beginning to stand. I really need to figure out what I should do with my free time now that I'm marooned in the Otherworld.

"Wait," Des says to me.

I turn to look at him.

"Would you like to join me?"

After what I saw yesterday in his throne room? I shake my head. "Have fun."

I head out of the room, leaving the King of the Night and his oldest friend to run the realm without me.

CHAPTER 8

I almost cloister myself away in Des's chambers. Almost. But the prospect of hours and hours of boredom keeps me from getting too comfortable in his rooms.

So, after changing into the most badass outfit I can find (leather pants, knee-high boots, and a wing-friendly corset top that I get hopelessly tangled in because *straps*), I decide to explore the palace. I might not have my emotional armor back in place, but damn, a good outfit does half the job.

Today's stop: the Night Kingdom's main library. After stumbling around asking for directions, I finally find it. Like the rest of Somnia, it's made from distinctive white stone, its roof the green blue of oxidized copper.

I climb up the grand stairs leading to the building, the pale stone glittering in the moonlight. The lamps that line the stairs spark with warm light.

And inside...oh, inside. The arched ceilings are lined with painted tile, copper chandeliers hanging between them. Everywhere I look in the cavernous room, beautiful fae objects are on display, from a huge tapestry that seems to shimmer different colors in the light to a marble sculpture of two winged fairies locked in battle.

Correction: a *moving* marble sculpture. The statues make grinding noises as their stone muscles move.

I walk up to the sculpture and stare at it. Several seconds in, one of the statues turns its head, scowling at me.

"They don't like being gawked at."

I nearly jump at the voice. A man stands at my side, gazing at me rather than the sculpture.

"If they don't like being stared at, why are they on display?" I ask.

He presses his lips together, and for the life of me, I can't tell if I've just irritated or amused him.

"Do you need any help?" he asks.

"Uh, no, just looking."

He bows his head. "Please find me if you need assistance, my lady, and welcome to the Night Kingdom Library."

I watch as the fairy walks away.

That was…nice. He called me *lady* and didn't ogle at my wings the way I feared he might.

Tentatively, I pass the sculpture and move deeper into the library. Here there are rooms upon rooms and floors upon floors of books. Fairies sit at tables between them, flipping through volumes.

Like the library I was in earlier, this one smells like old parchment, leather, and cedar.

Choosing a room at random, I pace the aisles. Out of sheer curiosity, I pull a book bound in light-blue silk from the shelves before flipping it open.

I don't know what I expected to find, but another

language wasn't it. I skim through several pages, but they're all written in the same archaic script.

"It's Old Fae."

I let out a squeak, nearly dropping the book.

The fairy who greeted me earlier is back, lurking just over my shoulder.

"Are you spying on me?" I accuse, my voice a whisper.

He gives me a shrewd look, standing even taller. "The King of the Night has requested I make myself indispensable to his mate."

Uh-huh.

"He doesn't even know I'm here."

Way to go, Callie. Tell your would-be stalker that no one knows where you are.

He tilts his head. "But doesn't he?"

Fairies have this weird doublespeak I'm starting to get the hang of. This one is pretty clear. Translation: Better check your facts, lady, because he totally does know where you are.

So Des is keeping tabs on me, and he sent Would-Be Stalker to help me.

I reassess the fairy at my side. "Callie," I finally say, holding out my hand.

He stares at it for a beat before delicately clasping it in his own. "Jerome." His gaze moves to the book in my other hand. "Are you looking for anything in particular to read?" he asks.

"Just browsing," I say. I wouldn't even know where to begin.

"Perhaps you'd enjoy a different section of our library— unless you're worried about curses."

"Curses?" I repeat.

Stoically, he says, "The book you're looking at deals with

curse-caused ailments—particularly those that cause hemor-
rhoids, unexpected bowel movements—"

Jesus.

I close the book and return it to its shelf.

A thought comes to me. "Do you have any books on
the king?"

Several hours later I sit at one of the tables, a stack of biogra-
phies and histories of the realm next to me.

Some of the books were originally written in English,
the colloquial language of the Otherworld, but the book
I currently have open was originally written in Old Fae.
When he pulled it from the shelves, Jerome spelled it to read
in English. It's a strange sight; every time I turn the page, Fae
letters dance and morph into English ones.

As for the content of the book…it is equally intriguing.
I feel like a thief in the night, learning Des's family history
without his knowledge.

He would've done the same thing had roles been reversed.

My finger moves over the text. It describes yet another
battle Des fought in. Like most of the others, this one took
place on the Borderlands, the area where, according to this
book, "day meets night."

And like all the other battles mentioned, the book
discusses how swiftly Des cut down his opponents and how
courageously he fought.

I begin to skim over the battles. It's not that I'm
unimpressed, but after reading about the umpteenth person
getting brained, the glory of the fight is a little lost on me.

Several pages later, I close the book. I'm not sure what
I expected to find—perhaps some insight into who Des the

Night King really is—but I should've known better. So far, all the books seem scrubbed of all interesting and relevant information.

All I've really learned is that Des has been a revolutionary king, dragging the Kingdom of Night from the dark ages (pun unintended) to be not just one of the leading realms but also one of the most enlightened, a title that had traditionally belonged to the Kingdom of Day.

I've also learned that before Des was a king, he was a soldier, as the last book so eloquently (*graphically*) described.

Other than that, there's precious little about my mate.

I grab the next book from the pile, a small worn volume that fits neatly in the palm of my hand.

There's something about this book, between the soft, faded leather cover and its humble size that makes me think this one will be different.

As soon as I open it, I can tell I'm right.

Chapter 1: Desmond Flynn, the Forgotten Child of Night

The next line I come across, I have to read twice.

Like most fae kings, Desmond Flynn was born from the royal harem.

Harem?

That one little word makes me go hot and cold all over. Kings have *harems*?

Des never told me this. I find I care less that Des came from one and more that this is a normal practice in the Otherworld.

It's unnaturally hard to concentrate after that, and my eyes drift over most of the text.

At some point, the atmosphere of the library changes. Where it was quiet before, now the place is deathly still. It's like silence itself becomes muted. The hairs along my forearms rise.

And then, from the silence, the sound of heavy footfalls.

I glance up in time to see Des striding into the room, his body sinuous as it moves. He has eyes only for me, and it's here in this grand setting that I realize just how much Des commands the space around him. I'm used to him moving among the shadows. Seeing him stride through this huge, cavernous room like he owns it (technically, he does) is sort of hot.

And by sort of hot, I mean really fricking hot.

Harem.

The word slides into my mind, souring my sexy thoughts.

Des disappears a moment later before reappearing at my table. He perches himself on the edge, tilting his head to read the spines of the books next to me.

"Doing some light reading, cherub?"

"Some."

Harem, my mind whispers. *Harem. Harem.* Harem.

He lifts the cover of the top book and raises his eyebrows. "You want to know about the history of my kingdom?" His eyes go soft when he glances back at me.

He's making my intentions seem *way* too noble. He should know better—he *must* know better. But he looks sincere, and that's enough to throw me off.

"Do you have a harem?" The question just slips out, my voice hoarse with emotion.

Des's expression freezes in place. "I'm sorry, what?"

"Do you have a harem?" I repeat.

A crease forms between his brows. "Why do you ask?"

That's not a no.

My heart is in my throat, my pulse thundering in my ears. "One of the books mentions you were born into one."

His eyes flick to the open book. "I wasn't," he says

57

smoothly. He lifts the small volume. "Desmond Flynn, the Forgotten Child of Night," he reads. His gaze moves to me. "So my inquisitive siren hasn't *just* been reading about my kingdom after all."

"Do you have a harem?" I press.

Around us, other fairies have fallen back into their books. Either they're no longer interested in our spectacle, or—more likely—Des is using his magic to cloak our words.

He leans forward, a lock of his white hair falling loose from the leather tie holding it back. "And if I did? What would you do?"

I'm weak in so many ways, but not in this one.

"I would leave you." Even though it would ruin me, I would.

Shadows begin to coil and twist at the edges of the room. Someone doesn't like my answer.

Des raps his knuckles against the table. "As you rightly should."

I don't know what I expected him to say, but it's not that.

He straightens, sliding off the table. "Come." He holds out his hand.

"You still haven't answered my question," I say, staring at his palm.

He sighs. "No, Callie. I do not have a harem—I never have."

My body relaxes, and I take his hand.

"Why not?" I ask as he leads me out.

He glances down at me, a brow raised.

"It's an honest question."

"And one that has many answers," he responds smoothly as we leave.

"Answers you want to tell me," I nudge.

He smiles a bit. "I do…" he admits, "but at some other time."

We exit the library and cut across the palace grounds. Before we can so much as enter the castle proper, Des releases my hand and halts.

I stop a few paces in front from him, turning to glance over my shoulder.

The look he wears… Des is no longer being playful or doting. He looks so very *fae*. Hungry for things he wishes to possess. I know that sly, calculating look. It's the same one he gets when he has something in mind that I might not entirely like.

"What?" I ask.

"You've been reading about me and my kingdom." That does not at all explain his expression.

His gaze cuts to my bracelet.

I take a step back, the skin of my wrist prickling. I know *that* look. It's the look he gets right before he has me repay a debt.

"Don't." I give him a warning look. I have no idea where his mind is, and that, more than anything, frightens me.

He strolls forward, his heavy boots thudding against the stone. "Funny that after all I've demanded of you, cherub, you still think you can sway me with your protests." Des steps in close. "You still owe me many, many favors."

Hundreds of them, I know.

"Forcing me to do things against my will won't make me like you more," I say.

He leans in close. "I've tricked, hurt, and killed men in front of you. I'm confident a few debts *that you owe me* won't damage my chances."

I narrow my eyes at him. What am I supposed to say? I

do owe him favors, favors I bought fair and square. And I *am* the sucker who loves Des even at his worst.

"Let me see that pretty wrist," Des coaxes.

I don't have time to react before his magic wraps around my arm, lifting it. He steps in close, inspecting the remaining rows of beads.

His eyes move from my bracelet to my face. "Several weeks ago you mentioned you wanted to see my kingdom," he says. "Were you being serious?"

First he comments about me reading up on his kingdom, now this?

I bite the inside of my lip, not sure where he's going with this line of questioning. Eventually I nod. I meant it; I do want to know everything there is to know about this man, including the kingdom he rules.

"Good." He looks all too pleased. "Then you and I are going on a little trip—"

Should I be worried? A trip doesn't sound too bad.

"—and we'll be flying there. Together."

CHAPTER 9

I glare at Des for the millionth time as we step out onto the highest balcony of his castle, rubbing my arms against the slight chill. Right now, we're out at the witching hour, stealing away in the night like criminals.

I can't believe I'm about to do this.

Fly.

Back on earth, flying means boarding a plane. Here it means flapping your wings, which—shocker—I'm not too thrilled about. I mean, even birds can screw up this flying business, and I am no bird.

I glance down at my bracelet, where two beads are missing, the price Des paid for taking me on this trip.

Two. Beads.

He catches me glaring at my bracelet and, capturing my jaw, steals a kiss that definitely wasn't his to take. "Cheer up, love," he says. "This will be fun."

Fun, my ass. The only thing remotely pleasant about this experience is that Des is wearing an Iron Maiden shirt, his tattoos are on full display, and his leather pants are hugging the shit out of his backside.

I mean, I can be mad at him and still enjoy the view.

Over his shoulders, his wings expand, taking up a staggering expanse of the balcony on either side of him. They shimmer in the moonlight, his curved talons gleaming along their edges.

"Stretch your wings," he commands.

"I'm still annoyed at you," I say, even as I comply.

The sensation of them unfolding is both uncomfortably foreign and inexplicably satisfying—like taking off a bra at the end of the day. Since my wings appeared, I've kept them closely pressed to my back. I didn't realize until now how good stretching them would feel.

"I'm aware of that," Des says, his voice a silken caress.

He disappears. Before I can so much as swing around to look for him, his warm hand runs over the upper ridge of my wings. He strokes them the same way he strokes the rest of my flesh, the touch oddly erotic.

"They're breathtaking, you know," he says, his fingers skimming over my feathers. "Just one more tempting thing about my enchantress."

"Enchantress?" The question slips out before I remind myself he's supposed to be receiving my ire right now.

"That's what fairies have started to call you—an enchantress."

I can't decide whether I'm more flattered or flustered by this detail.

"We don't have sirens here in the Otherworld," Des continues, "but from time to time, we do have magical beings—enchanters—who can enthrall others with their magic. It's a very coveted power."

He circles back in front of me, his gaze moving to my wings. "Try beating them."

I groan. I forgot for an instant that I was out here learning how to fly.

I do as he says, the action stirring my hair. Des watches my wingbeats shrewdly, nodding like an instructor.

"Now try jumping," he says. "See if you can keep yourself in the air for any length of time."

"Want me to juggle while I'm at it?" I feel like a circus sideshow.

He folds his arms and just waits.

I sigh. "*Fine.*" I jump, beating my wings. Nothing impressive happens.

"Again."

I try again, and like the first time, my wings are useless.

"Again."

I try again. And again. And again. After doing it a couple dozen times, I begin to understand there's a timing to it. And then, after a few more dozen tries, my wings successfully fight gravity, if only for an extra second.

Des nods, his face serious. "Good enough."

He takes my upper arm, leading me to the edge of the balcony.

"Goo—good enough?" I look over at him skeptically. "Good enough for *what*?"

The Bargainer steps onto the balcony railing.

"What are you doing?"

He steps over the ledge and turns to face me, securing his feet between two delicately carved columns on the stone balustrade.

"Cherub, it's all right." He says this like he's the most reasonable guy in the world and not in fact the dude balancing precariously on the edge of the highest balcony in Somnia. He slaps the top of the marble railing between us. "Step up here."

A disbelieving laugh slips out. "No way."

"Callie," he says, sounding disappointed, "I'm wounded. I would never lead you astray."

Says the man who taught me to drink and gamble. I think he needs to tighten up his definition of *astray*.

When I stay rooted in place, he says, "We can do this the easy way or the hard way."

I fold my arms over my chest, not budging.

His eyes brighten with excitement. There are few things Des enjoys more than my defiance. Unfortunately for me, it never gets me very far with him.

I feel the breath of his magic at my back, forcing me forward and then propelling me onto the edge of the balcony in front of him.

"You are such a bastard," I say as I climb onto it. Up here the wind is blustery enough to shake my body and whip my hair about.

From the other side of the railing, Des grabs my waist, bracing me. He grins up at me like a pirate. "Sticks and stones, Callie. Now"—he gives my sides a squeeze—"open those wings for me again."

Ignoring all my better judgment, I do as he asks. A gust of wind blows against me, lifting my wings.

"You feel that?" the Bargainer asks, studying my every reaction. "That's an air current. We'll be using them to travel."

"Can I get down now?"

Des's lips quirk mischievously. "Cherub, the next surface your feet touch will be in a different city."

I pale and shake my head. "I'm not ready."

"Yes, you are."

Des's wings spread wide behind him, and wind tugs at his T-shirt and hair.

Right now, in this moment, I'm sure I'm in a dream. He's too wild, too beautiful, too fantastical to be mine, and what he's asking me to do is too strange and unbelievable to be real.

"*Fly,*" he says, releasing my waist. Power rides his words, pulling my wings into position.

Before I can object, he spreads his arms to either side of him. It happens in slow motion, his body tipping away from me and the balcony, the night poised to swallow him whole. His feet slide off the ledge, and then he's falling.

"*Des!*" I reach for him reflexively.

My body pitches forward, and I lose my balance. Suddenly, there is no more balcony railing to perch on. There is nothing but empty air beneath me.

Des smiles as he stares up at me, completely at peace with the fact that *we're falling*. And then, right in the middle of our descent, he vanishes.

Vanishes.

I'm left staring down at the palace grounds a hundred feet below, and Des is nowhere to be seen.

Oh God, I'm fucked. So, so fucked. This isn't flying, this is the art of dying, and the one person who got me into this mess is gone.

I guess I now have my answer to that stupid "rhetorical" question: If a friend asked you to jump, would you?

Apparently, twat-waffle that I am, I would.

Des's magic still encircles my wings, tugging at them. I grit my teeth and follow their lead, angling them to catch some of the wind. The force of my descent makes it difficult to control my movements.

Floor after floor of the palace blurs by me, the ground quickly zooming up. I continue to fight the wind trying to fold up my wings, Des's magic aiding me. Just as I'm beginning to think it's hopeless, my fall begins to slow.

I let instinct take over, tilting my wings to level me out. I go from falling to cutting into the wind, my body beginning to glide over the ground rather than plummet toward it.

I'm pretty sure I'm no longer going to fall to my death, but I'm still not exactly flying. I'm more like that autumn leaf that gets blown about by a gust of wind.

Out of nowhere, Des manifests beneath me, his hands moving to my waist. "*Beat your wings, love.*"

I can barely hear him over the whistle of the wind, but I force my wings up and down, up and down.

I wobble, and for a few seconds, I worry I'll lose whatever gains I've made and plunge the rest of the way to the ground. But now Des is beneath me, making sure I don't do exactly that.

Slowly, steadily, my wings propel me up. Des releases me as I break away from him, rising higher and higher in the air.

Holy crap, I'm *flying*.

A shocked laugh escapes me. It's more exhilarating than I could've imagined. I hit a warm air current, and then I'm gliding, the thermal carrying me on its own.

A shadow with wicked-looking wings swoops in next to me. I glance over at the Bargainer, his white hair rippling in the air. He smiles at me, and it lights up his entire face.

"*Follow me!*" The wind snatches away his words, but I read his lips.

He pulls ahead then banks right, his body arcing across the sky, those giant wings of his gleaming dangerously in the moonlight. If I thought he was fantastical before, it has nothing on him now. Des is magic, and somehow, through some odd twist of fate, I get to be a part of that magic.

I follow his lead, adjusting my wings to curve through the air like his do. I laugh again, my heart so much lighter now that I'm officially flying.

Des is still on my shit list for scaring me almost literally to death, but this might be worth it; it might even be worth the fear and self-loathing I endured in the days after I received my wings.

I follow Des until he drops back, and then the two of us glide next to each other. There's nothing quite like the silence up here in the sky. The wind is too loud for us to talk, and yet everything has a quiet pall to it.

Every so often, Des points to something or other. Once, it's a troop of pixies; another time it's the faintest pattern of lights far, far below us where I imagine another kingdom of the Otherworld—a kingdom that doesn't float in the sky—is located.

He even gestures to a fae couple I glimpse out in the distance, their bodies largely hidden in the clouds. I can only just see a mismatched pair of glittering wings and two intertwined legs, and then the clouds move, obscuring them from view.

I notice one or two more of these couples as we fly. Judging by their embraces, they're lovers who've snuck away to be together under the starlight and clouds.

After what must be an hour or two, I make out a giant landmass ahead of us blocking out a segment of the night sky.

Another floating island! Just like Somnia.

As we get closer, I notice the city lights, which twinkle in pale pastel colors. Des begins to descend, angling himself toward the floating island.

It's only once we're flying over it that I truly get a sense of the place. It's a land of turrets and moats, towers and bridges. They flash by me as we glide across the landscape. Interspersed between the buildings are huge swaths of foliage. This far away, I can't tell whether they're fields or forests, jungles or manicured parks.

When we're nearer, I note the idiosyncrasies of this island. Buildings seem to change size and shape the moment you peel your gaze away; streets lead to nowhere. Even the colors of this place are somehow both brighter and duller than they should be. It looks like a fairy tale and a carnival all wrapped into one, and yet…it's as though everything is not quite as it should be.

No one looks at us as we begin to land. We're just two more fairies in this strange land.

Des glides to a stop, gracefully lowering himself to the ground.

There's nothing graceful about my landing. I slam into the Bargainer, nearly bowling us both over.

He catches me around the waist, holding me high off the ground, his eyes wide, and then he begins laughing. Presumably at me.

The elation that flying brought me is bubbling up my stomach and out my throat, and I can't help but join in.

I just *flew*. With Des. All those years of me hoping to be a part of his world, of despairing that it would never happen—they led me right to this moment. The irony is that it took a madman to make one of my deepest wishes come true.

Eventually our laughter dies off, but I can still see it twinkling in Des's eyes.

"I like your hair when it's windswept," he murmurs, touching a lock of it.

The same can be said for his hair. I've always had a weird obsession with his nearly shoulder-length locks, and right now they look especially sexy.

"Was flying everything you hoped it would be?" he asks.

This would be the perfect time to rip him a new asshole for tricking me off a ledge. But I find I don't want to ruin the moment. Not when I enjoyed myself so thoroughly in the sky, and not when he's holding me like he's not sure he ever wants to let me go.

"It was amazing," I say breathlessly.

His eyes spark with excitement, and Des lets my torso slip through his hands until we're face-to-face.

He presses a hard kiss to my lips, his mouth demanding. And then I slide the rest of the way through his arms until my boots touch the ground.

Des steps aside to give me a better view of our surroundings.

"Welcome to Phyllia, the Land of Dreams," he says.

My eyes devour the shop-lined street before us. Each store is more spectacular than the last.

Hanging in the window of the clothing shop closest to me is a dress that looks made of actual sea-foam. Next to it is a man's suit made in a hue of blue I swear I didn't know existed. There's a cloak that seems made of the night sky, small dots of light flickering in the dark fabric, and a wristlet that looks spun from clouds.

Next to the clothing store is a curiosity shop filled with furniture and decorations as unusual as they are alluring. A table made entirely of rose quartz seems to glow from within. Beside it is a glass vial filled with a swirling mist; the sign for it says it's a Dream Come True.

Farther down the street are restaurants whose tables spill

onto the streets, the aromas drifting out from them foreign and appetizing.

I feel Des's attention on me. He places a hand on my lower back, leading me forward.

"Here on Phyllia," he explains, "you'll find doors that lead to nowhere, people you recognize one moment and don't the next, places you're sure you've visited before, though you can't say when or how. Phyllia is the place where every one of your fantastical thoughts can come true."

The Land of Dreams. It's some strange love child of the Otherworld and what I imagined Wonderland might look like. Everything has that elegant, fae touch to it, but nothing is quite what it appears.

We pass a bubbling fountain that people are gathered around, vials in their hands.

"The waters here can make humble wishes come true," Des says next to me.

I watch in fascination as a fae woman with golden hair dips her glass container into the water. I'm tempted to try the water myself, just to see what small wish might come true.

We stroll by several cafés, and my attention lingers on the low lighting and the soft conversations drifting from within.

"You have restaurants here in the Otherworld," I say.

"You're surprised?" Des looks amused.

I am. I assumed the Otherworld was essentially flowering fields and impossible architecture. Restaurants seem so... *human*.

Suddenly, Des is steering me toward one of them.

"What are you doing?"

"Taking you out to eat—unless, of course, you aren't hungry."

My stomach chooses that exact moment to rumble. I

don't know how many calories flying burns, but the number must be staggering.

"I could eat."

His lips twitch. "Good. So could I."

The restaurant we walk into is done up in shades of silver and periwinkle—from the place settings to the mounted mirrors to the walls. Near the top of the high ceilings, plumes of clouds hang, and in the center of each table is a vase full of a type of delicate white flower I've seen all over Somnia.

As soon as Des and I are seated, I surreptitiously scan the room.

Even at first glance, the people around us don't look quite normal. For most, it's simply small details: eye color that's a little too bright to be human, or hair too long to be grown by a mortal head. But then, there are a few fae who especially stand out. Like the man with lavender-gray skin and a mouth full of sharp, pointed teeth. Or the woman whose limbs are long and slender, her skin the shifting color of deep shadows.

In contrast to my gawking, the restaurant's patrons ignore us completely.

"Do these people know who you are?"

"They do," he says.

"Why aren't any of them…?" I look for the right words.

"Fawning over me?" he says, filling in my sentence for me.

"Yeah."

He lifts a shoulder. "I've cloaked our appearances."

"Cloaked our…?"

"It's a small illusion meant to subtly alter our features—to prevent recognition." He leans forward. "I figured neither of us wanted the extra attention."

Damn, but that was thoughtful of him.

My attention drifts around us again. It's not just the people here who are unusual. Partway through the meal, the other half of the building suddenly morphs into a Gothic cathedral, the pews and pulpit currently empty.

"Dream logic," Des explains.

I glance back at him only to realize someone has already served us drinks and bread.

I blink at the sight. "This place is really"— *unnerving*—"magical."

Des leans back in his seat, a sardonic smile spreading across his lips. "What do you want to eat?" he asks.

I furrow my brows. "We haven't received menus yet…"

I haven't even fully finished speaking when a plate of ravioli drops to the table in front of me.

Now, how the *hell* did that happen?

Des laughs at my wide eyes.

"Is this even safe to eat?" I ask.

He leans forward, his sculpted forearms resting on the table. "Would I lead you astray, cherub?"

I give him the stink eye. "Last time you said that, you tricked me into falling off a building."

"*Flying* off a building."

I roll my eyes. "Semantics, Des."

"Semantics are everything, Callie, or have you learned nothing from me?"

I pick up my fork, eyeing my pasta, which is covered in some mystery cream sauce. "No, you're right. You've taught me exactly what it means to be a slippery bastard."

Des lounges back in his seat, a smug expression on his face. "I'm taking that as a compliment."

I cut into one of the ravioli and take a bite. Somehow, it's everything I didn't know I wanted.

"Good?"

I close my eyes and nod, savoring the taste a little longer.

"And look, it didn't even kill you."

Des just had to go and be Des.

"*Yet*," I tack on because I can be snarky too.

I open my eyes, and—I shit you not—a *churro* shimmers into existence in front of Des, plopping onto the table a moment later. It even has that cheap waxy paper wrapped around its base, just like what you'd find at a carnival.

I raise my eyebrows.

Des picks up the churro and kicks one foot then the other onto the table. Shamelessly, he bites into the dessert.

I'll give him this: he's owning this moment.

Crossing his ankles, he says, "Tell me, love, what's a dream of yours?"

"A dream?" I repeat, another bite of ravioli midway to my mouth.

"Something you want out of life?"

I take my bite of the ravioli and chew slowly. Once I swallow, I shrug. "To be happy, I guess."

"C'mon, cherub," he says, pointing the churro at me, "Don't make me take a bead. I know you've got something more specific than that."

I stare down at my pasta, sucking my cheeks in. "I don't know," I eventually say. "Two months ago I would've told you I wanted a husband and a family." I'm surprised the confession comes out as freely as it does. Des might not be the only person learning how to be vulnerable.

The truth is, before Des came roaring back into my life, I was lonely—painfully, achingly lonely, the kind of lonely that comes from feeling like your life is passing you by and there's no one there to witness it.

The Bargainer squints at me, his face inscrutable. "You no longer want that?"

I meet his eyes. It's so hard to read him when he's like this. I take a deep breath. "No, I still want that, but..." It takes only a few extra seconds to pry the words loose. "But now I'm not scared it won't happen."

That's what happens when you discover you have a soul mate. The fear of a lifetime of loneliness evaporates.

Des's eyes heat at my admission, and I swear if we weren't in a restaurant full of people, he'd sweep the place settings off the table and make love to me right here.

I clear my throat. "What's a dream of yours?" I ask, feeling like my skin is lit.

He watches me, his body so still, I feel like he's waiting for a moment to strike.

Finally, he says, "We share similar dreams."

"You want a husband too?" I can't help but tease him.

He flashes me a wolfish smile, choosing that moment to take another—very suggestive—bite of his churro. "Perhaps," he says, "but you'll do."

I all but roll my eyes. "I'm *thrilled* to be your booby prize."

His lips curve up. He stares at me for a beat; then, coming to some sort of decision, he kicks his feet off the table. Tossing a few coins next to my plate, he reaches for my hand.

"But I'm not finished..." I complain. I've barely touched my ravioli, and I planned to eat the crap out of it. I'm a girl who can throw back her food.

"Want something to go?" he asks.

My lips part, but before I can respond, another churro drops to the table, nearly falling into my ravioli.

Now it's Des's turn to raise his eyebrows. "Looks like someone has a little case of food envy."

I totally do. He made his churro look *good*.

I grab mine and let Des lead me out of the restaurant. Outside, the sky is still as dark as ever. I stare up at it as I take a bite of my churro, feeling oddly exhilarated.

Our boots echo along the street as we walk. I don't know where we're going, but I don't much care. Nights like this are familiar to the two of us. Countless times Des took me to some foreign metropolis, and together we'd wander the streets. Sometimes he'd ply us both with alcohol, other times coffee and pastries.

"This reminds me of our past," I murmur.

Des takes my hand before bringing it to his lips and giving it a kiss.

I feel my heart expand. I get to have this man forever. A lifetime of Des at my side. It's such a wild thought, I'm not sure I'll ever fully get used to it.

We get to the end of the block of shops. Here the street opens into a grand plaza. Right in the center of it is a sculpture of a winged couple holding each other in a tight embrace. The sculpture floats several feet in the air.

I pause in front of it.

"Who are they?" I ask, staring at the couple. The woman seems made of the same dark stone my beads are, her skin drawing in the light. The man she embraces is made of some shimmering sandstone, his skin seeming to glow from within.

"The Lovers," Des replies. "Two of our ancient gods." He points to the man. "He's Fierion, God of Light, and she's Nyxos, Goddess of Darkness."

Nyxos…why does that name sound familiar?

"In the myths," Des continues, "Fierion was married to Gaya, Goddess of Nature, but his true love was Nyxos, the woman he was forbidden from ever being with. Their love for each other is what causes day to chase night and night to chase day.

"Here in the Land of Dreams, they're finally allowed to be with each other."

I stare at the sculpture a long time, finishing off my churro. Even though it's just a myth, the tragedy of it still gets to me. I hate doomed love stories. Life's filled with enough heartache as it is.

My eyes drift past the statue to an enormous stone bridge the length of at least two football fields that branches off the grand plaza. Halfway across it, its lamps fade into the misty darkness.

Beyond the bridge, I can just make out another floating island.

"What's over there?" I ask, nodding in that direction. There's something about it, something insidious and compelling that calls to my darker nature.

Des frowns. "Memnos, the Land of Nightmares."

"Memnos," I repeat, staring at it. I remember Des listing off the names of all these floating islands weeks ago. "Are we going to visit?" I ask.

The Bargainer hesitates. "Do you remember the bog?"

How could I forget?

I nod.

"That's just one of the many creatures that call Memnos home."

I shiver a little. Point taken.

"Eventually, I'll show you the island, but right now…" He takes my hand, giving me a deep look. "Right now this trip is for us."

CHAPTER 10

The next morning, I wake inside our suite in Phyllia to the tickle of Des's hair against my back and the press of soft kisses down my spine, between my wings.

I stretch languidly, a small smile spreading across my face.

After a magical evening exploring Phyllia last night, the two of us checked into a hotel just off the main plaza boasting rooms that change color and theme.

When we're outside the room, Des will surely still be camouflaging our appearances. Staying at a hotel like a normal person is just not something a king can usually get away with.

The kisses down my back now pause. A moment later, Des nips my ear. "Have I mentioned how well you wear bedhead?" he says, his voice low and husky.

I laugh into my pillow, reaching out with a hand and pushing away his meaty body. He rolls, dragging me on top of him, stealing kisses from my lips. I blink my sleepy eyes open and stare down at his face.

"This is my favorite thing," he says.

I'm still trying to drag myself awake.

"What is?" I ask.

"Waking up to you each morning." He taps a finger to my nose. "Especially when you're sleepy and adorable."

I suppress a yawn. "How are you so...*awake*?"

Rather than answer, he slides out from under me. I plop onto the mattress, my eyes already beginning to close.

Once again I'm roused by his touch, his hand warm on my back. And then I smell it.

Deliverance—a.k.a. coffee.

I pry my eyes open, and there it is: the steaming mug of coffee is only inches from my face.

I reach for it.

"Ah, ah," Des says, moving it out of my grasp. "If you want it, you're going to have to get out of bed."

As if to encourage me further, my covers slide off my shoulders of their own accord, slipping down to my ankles.

I grab the edges of them and haul them back up.

They slide off again.

More forcefully this time, I yank the covers back up. *Screw Des and his coffee.*

Just as I'm tucking the blankets under my arm, they begin to slip away once more. I grapple with them, playing some ridiculous game of tug-of-war with an inanimate object.

"Oh my God, Des, *seriously*?"

He leans against one of the bedposts, sipping what's supposed to be my coffee. "I have no idea what you're talking about."

That lying bastard.

"*Fine*," I growl, rolling myself off the bed. "I'm up."

I stomp over to him. Studiously ignoring the fact he's

gloriously shirtless and his hair is tied back in a stupidly sexy man bun, I snatch the mug of coffee from his hand and head out onto the balcony that branches off from our room.

"A thank-you would be nice," he says, following me out.

"So would an apology," I retort over my shoulder.

Big surprise, he has nothing to say about that.

Breakfast is already laid out on the tiny mosaic table that occupies a good portion of the balcony, and it smells so good.

I take a seat, careful to drape my wings over it, before I bring the coffee to my lips and take a sip. Lord, does it taste good. It's almost worth losing sleep over.

Across from me, Des sits, his large frame dominating the little bistro chair. He picks up his espresso cup, sipping delicately from it.

Normally the sight of that tiny cup in his hands would make me laugh. Right now, however, I just glower at him over the rim of my mug. It doesn't help that he has a painfully pretty face. Or that his massive chest and corded arms are on display.

Why does he have to always look so goddamn good? Especially when I'm pretty sure I look like roadkill.

This is just one more reason why the world isn't fair.

Des stares pointedly at my plate, where a steaming breakfast burrito sits. "Aren't you going to eat?"

"Why did you make me breakfast?" I ask suspiciously.

He sets down his espresso, his eyes guarded. "Is this a trick question?"

"It seems unusually nice," I say.

"Now you're just trying to be mean."

Maybe I am. In the past, Des would take me out to breakfast, and there were never any strings attached.

So why do I feel as though this time there *are*, indeed, strings attached?

I take another gulp of my coffee before placing it on the table. "Did you seriously wake me up early just to feed me?"

"It's not that early," Des says, sidestepping the question.

He may be right. The stars twinkle above us just as they did last night when we fell asleep.

"Why did you make me breakfast?" I repeat.

"Because I love you," he says. "Does everything have to come with a price?"

My gooey heart melts a little at his admission, but I've known him just a little too long and a little too deeply to trust those wide silver eyes of his.

I look at him skeptically. "With normal people, no. With you? Absolutely."

He smirks over the rim of his espresso, the first sign that I'm right. He does have something up his sleeve.

"So what is it?"

"You'll find out soon enough."

I do find out soon enough. The moment we reenter our suite, my training leathers appear on our bed.

I groan. "But I thought we were on vacation?"

"Your enemies don't care about your vacation."

He does have a point.

It's no use fighting him on this; I already feel Des's magic compelling me onward. Grumbling, I don the clothes as best I can, Des helping me secure the top around my wings, and the two of us head out of the room.

We leave the hotel and trek toward the dark wilderness that borders the city center. And it *is* wilderness, pretty as it is. I trip over loose roots and have to push ferns and exotic flowering plants out of the way as we bushwhack a path through the overgrowth.

The farther we walk, the more sluggish my movements

become. I think it's simple exhaustion from last night until the sensation becomes so extreme that it feels like I'm in a slow-motion action sequence. Des, meanwhile, seems to be moving just fine.

The wilderness opens to a clearing, and Des stops, turning toward me. He tosses me a sword, and it takes a ridiculous amount of effort to lift my arm and snatch it out of the air.

Mirth dances in his eyes. "Sword up, Callie."

I tug the weapon from its sheath, my limbs heavy. It takes forever for me to lift my sword, and by the time I do lift it fully, he's already coming at me. It's all I can do to duck and dodge his blows. And he's going easy on me. So pathetically easy.

"Faster, Callie."

There is no way in heaven or earth that I can move any faster. I can barely *move* as is. It's like trying to swim through honey. Not even the kick-ass leather outfit I wear makes up for the particular torture of training today.

Des, meanwhile, doesn't seem afflicted by the same issue I'm having. Whether it's because the place doesn't affect him, or he's using magic to counteract its effects, he moves swiftly, coming at me so much faster than I can defend myself.

I don't know how he does it with such accuracy, but each time Des nicks me with the sword, he strategically slices into my outfit, making little cutouts in the leather. I now have dozens of tiny triangles speckling my upper chest and my outer thighs. And not once have I landed so much as a blow on him.

Not once.

Finally, after what feels like an eternity, Des announces training's over for the day.

I fall into a heap, the sword clattering to the ground next

to me. From the ends of my hair to the tips of my toes, I'm tired; my outfit looks like a cutout snowflake; and right now, I don't give a damn about pretty much anything.

Day: 1. Callie: 0.

"You did good," Des says, coming over to me. "This place is enchanted to move slower than the rest of the world—it's said to mimic a slow-motion dream."

That would've been helpful to know beforehand.

Of course, it doesn't affect Des the same way it does me. Sneaky fairy.

I lay my cheek on my knees, exhausted from the training.

He crouches next to me, his knuckles stroking my face. "We can't rest just yet. We've got to move on to the next island." His voice sounds half-apologetic.

There's just no way I'm dragging my butt off this patch of grass.

Des must see that because rather than try to coax me back to my feet, he slips his arms under my wings and the backs of my knees.

He lifts me against his chest, cradling me to him. His talon-tipped wings spread wide around us, and then he leaps into the air, the two of us ascending into the night sky.

As the cool air whips my hair about, Des cups my face to his chest, shielding me from the worst of the wind.

I lean my head into him, breathing in his masculine scent. I don't understand how even out here, in the middle of a foreign world's night sky, I can still feel right at home pressed against this man. But I do.

My eyes drift close, and I let the beats of his wings rock me to sleep.

My stomach dips, and I wake with a start. A thousand stars sparkle around me as I blink my eyes open.

When I try to sit up, Des's arms tighten around me. It takes me a moment longer to realize two things: one, we're still in the sky, and two, Des makes for a surprisingly good bed.

I glance beneath us and notice we're beginning to descend onto yet another floating island that is not Somnia.

Now Des's earlier cryptic questions about my interest in his kingdom become clearer. *He's taking me on a tour of his realm.*

I try to remember just how many floating islands he rules over, but I'm totally drawing a blank. All I manage to piece together is that we're going to visit several of them.

This one looks fun. Even from far away, I can already see that. Everywhere I look, there are strings of colorful lights illuminating the buildings—not like the lights you might see at Christmas but the kinds you might find outside a cantina.

The bright flowering plants and trees that grow here have a tropical feel to them—as does the balmy night air.

It's not until we get closer that I make out a series of bar fights happening in the streets. The fairies who aren't fighting are drunkenly staggering on and off the pavement—except, of course, for the lovely couple that may or may not be getting it on against the side of a building.

Allll riiight.

We land outside what looks to be a gambling hall, the fairies inside clustered around several tables where more fae are rolling sets of dice.

I slip out of Des's arms, looking around me. "What is this place?"

"Barbos, the City of Thieves."

Barbos. This is where he first met Malaki and joined the Angels of Small Death.

I gaze at my surroundings with new appreciation. I could easily imagine the Bargainer haunting these streets, making deals with drunks, thriving in the night.

We start walking, and oh God, everything hurts. I mean *everything*. Whatever that horrible place was where we trained in Phyllia, it worked me over good. I groan as we walk, rubbing my backside. "Des, I think you broke my ass."

He shoves his hands into the pockets of his leather pants. "Cherub, you'll be making different moans when I break your ass."

Sweet Lord of heaven and earth. Blood rushes to my face. To my horror, my skin begins to brighten.

Bad, siren. Bad.

I guffaw. "*That* will only ever happen in your dreams."

Des stops and catches my jaw in his hand, forcing me to look in his eyes. "You know, the endearing thing about you is that you still say things like that, even though I know you're more than a little intrigued." His thumb strokes the side of my face.

Intrigued at the thought of anal play? Traitorous heat blooms low in my belly that has nothing at all to do with my siren.

Still, I manage to say, "I'm *not*."

The Bargainer's gaze drops to my lips, a smile curving up the corners of his own mouth. "Is that so?" he says, his voice more serious than before. "Perhaps I should sacrifice one of your beads to pull this truth from you."

I swallow, not sure if the thrum in my veins is from indignation or a perverse sort of anticipation.

Rather than make good on his word and take a bead, Des releases my face, strolling forward once more.

All the tension that drew my body taut now releases.

I stand in place for several seconds before I pull myself together.

"I want to renegotiate this bond," I finally declare.

"Sorry, cherub," he says over his shoulder, "but that sore ass of yours is mine whether you like it or not."

I make a face at his back.

"Saw that."

"Good," I say, and then I proceed to ignore him.

I don't know whether Des is still working his illusory magic because people aren't fawning over him, but me…me they're checking out.

Their eyes linger on my wings and my forearms, but I don't see fear or pity in their eyes. If anything, they look… *mesmerized*.

Self-consciously, I reach around myself and run a hand over one of my wings.

"They don't see your features as you do," Des says, still not turning from where he strolls ahead of me.

I furrow my brows.

He stops, waiting for me to catch up to him. "Fae come in all shapes and sizes," he explains. "Seeing someone who looks as you do does not seem strange to us. You're a beautiful human with wings, and that's both strange and appealing."

I glance down at what I can see of my dark wings, the iridescent feathers shimmering green under the light. It's hard to wrap my mind around what he's saying and even harder to try to reframe how I see myself.

Beautiful. Appealing. Those words are a far cry from the ones that come to mind when I look in the mirror: *Monstrous. Mutated.*

I'm ashamed to admit those appreciative stares soothe a part of my broken self-confidence.

"You should really remember that, cherub," Des says, "especially when you meet some of the elites from other realms. They'll find you just as attractive as all these fairies do—perhaps more so because you're mine—but they will try to mask whatever they feel with disgust or some other emotion to make you feel small."

These fae sound like charming people...

Wait.

I glance at Des. "*When* I meet other elites?"

CHAPTER 11

No, I'm not about to meet other elites.

Yes, I likely will at some point in time.

No, not tonight.

Yes, Des cares about my feelings.

No, caring about my feelings won't get me out of meeting said elites when the time comes.

Apparently, meeting important fae is part of this whole soul mate package I signed on for.

Bleh.

If I could live my life without meeting another high-powered fae, I'd consider it a win. Des is more than enough.

Des stops me in front of a tavern, and I give it a good once-over. It looks just like the others. Same carved-wood façade, same bright lights strung up over its awning, same gummy look that suggests the place has endured decades of beer spills.

Honestly, this is my kind of bar. Fun, no frills, good alcohol. The only drawbacks to this situation are: one, we're in the Otherworld, not earth; and two, I can't drink, thanks to a repayment Des took from me weeks ago—oh, and three, I'm walking into a bar still wearing my training leathers. At this point, the outfit is more cutouts than actual leather.

The Bargainer opens the door for me, and the two of us step inside the pub.

One by one, the rowdy patrons notice us. Within seconds, the place goes deathly silent.

"Um, was that supposed to happen?" I whisper to Des. He doesn't bother responding.

At the far end of the room, a chair scrapes back, and a huge, hulking fairy steps forward—though it's a bit of a stretch to call him a *fairy*, at least by my own definition of the word.

The man's scarred face, torn leathers, and wild red hair make me think he's less a fairy and more a pirate.

His golden-brown eyes are harsh as he stalks toward me and Des. No one else in the establishment moves, all eyes riveted to us.

"What the hell are you doing here, Bastard?" he asks, his voice gravelly.

My eyebrows shoot up. I don't think that, aside from me, I've heard anyone insult the Bargainer to his face.

A different sort of unsettling silence now cloaks the room, like someone lit a match over a pile of gunpowder and everyone is preparing for the explosion to come.

And then, like something from a movie, both men laugh and embrace each other in a bone-crushing hug.

Whaaa?

I stare at them incredulously. For the life of me, I'll never understand men, no matter what world they come from.

The roguish fairy pulls away to look my mate over. "How the hell are you, Desmond?"

Desmond. No wonder the whole room went still. These people recognize their king. He must've lifted whatever enchantment he placed on himself right before we stepped inside the bar.

Des nods, a sly smile spreading across his face. "Real good, my brother. Real good."

"Ha! I know that smile," the redheaded fairy says, clapping him on the back. "Whose fortune have you swindled this time? Or"—his eyes swivel to me—"is it a wife you've stolen? It's been a while since you last brought a girl here, you scoundrel."

Oooh, cringey-cringe. I could've lived without knowing that.

To me, the redheaded man says, "Beware of this one." He shakes Des's shoulder. "He likes to ruin his women before he cuts them loose."

Ruin his women? A hot wave of jealousy rises in me.

Des's expression sobers. "It's not like that. At all." His eyes land heavily on mine, and I think he's trying to beam me an apology.

I suppose this situation is only fair. After all, Des had to quietly endure seven years of me hooking up with other men while he waited for me to unknowingly repay my final wish. I can grit my teeth through a little of Des's own dating history.

The redheaded fairy reassesses me. This time, he must notice something he hadn't before because he says, "She's not just any girl, is she?"

"No." Des is still flashing me an intense, heated look.

The other man stares at the Bargainer for a moment longer, and then he lifts his eyebrows. "Oh—*oh*," he says, "this is the girl you've been searching for?"

Des nods.

The fairy turns to me again, and he sweeps me into a hug that practically chokes the breath out of me. "Welcome to the family, then," he says, his voice rumbly. "My sincerest apologies to you for getting stuck with the Bastard for a mate."

He finally lets me go, looking from me to Des like a proud father.

This is *so* weird.

"Ah well," he says, sucking in a deep breath through his nostrils. "This changes things for the better." He claps Des on the side of his arm. Then, seeming to remember that the two of us are just standing there in the threshold of the bar, he says, "Well, c'mon, let me get the Bastard and his bride a drink. It's the least I can do."

I'm no one's bride, but I don't bother correcting Redhead. I'm living with Des, making love to Des, and I'm bonded to Des. A ring and a piece of paper seem like super-fluous details at this point.

"Why does he keep calling you 'Bastard'?" I ask Des when his roguish friend leads us toward one of the grimy tables.

The noise of the tavern escalates once more.

"Because I am one," Des says.

"I thought you knew your father," I say. In the book I'd read, hadn't it stated the King of the Night was born into the royal harem? Wouldn't he have known his father if this were the case?

"I found out who he was when I was a teenager," he says. "Before that," Des continues, "I was referred to as *the Bastard.*"

Blood drains from my face. "I've called you that," I say, mortified. I had never considered the term as an actual label.

Des's friend stops at a table, and Des and I slide in.

"Cherub," he says, his voice low, "I assure you, it's fine."

I don't feel fine about it.

The Bargainer's redheaded friend sits across from us, thumping the table. "Three meads," he calls out to the bartender at the back of the room.

When his attention returns to us, his eyes twinkle. "Desmond, my old friend, you've not officially introduced me to your mate."

Des leans an arm on the sticky wooden surface. He looks over at me. "Callie"—he gestures to Redhead—"this no-good son of a bitch is Phaedron. Phaedron, this is my mate, Callypso."

Phaedron takes my hand. "It truly is a pleasure," he says, his voice turning serious.

Not knowing what else to do, I nod, giving his hand a squeeze. "It's nice to meet you."

Phaedron is clearly another of Des's old friends, which is baffling to me. I'm still getting used to the fact someone like the Bargainer *has* friends—and technically more of them than me.

That's somehow really depressing.

A new group of fairies enters the bar. Most are women, though there are two men among them. They walk through the room, their outfits low-cut and largely transparent. All of them move from table to table, their hands gliding over the shoulders and arms of many patrons.

Phaedron sees me staring. "Prostitutes," he says.

I give him a look. "I wasn't born yesterday."

I swear I have a filter. I just don't always use it.

Phaedron breaks into a smile, eyeing me up and down. "And the Bastard found his match." He leans forward. "Tell me, Desmond, are all human women this feisty on earth?"

91

Des flashes him a rakish smile. "Only the best ones."

"Aye!" Phaedron laughs. "And they're firebrands in bed!"

I raise my eyebrows at that.

The conversation is interrupted by the bartender, who drops off our drinks. I make a moue of disappointment as I stare at the glass of amber liquid set in front of me.

Still can't drink.

On the other side of the room, one of the patrons whistles. "My king!" he calls out, leaning back in his seat. "When are you going to come over and greet an old friend?"

A slow, lazy grin snakes across Des's face. "I was hoping to avoid that fate," he shouts back.

I watch all this in wonder. I'm seeing yet another side of Des, one that's crude and raw and rough around the edges. I don't say it, but right now he reminds me of all the Politia officers and bounty hunters I worked with as a private investigator. I'm not surprised to find I like this side of him a great deal, despite his crassness.

The fairy lets out a cackling laugh. "Aye, you still might. My arse is too ancient to leave this seat."

"But not too ancient to get you here," Des notes.

The fairy cackles again, his friends joining in.

I can tell Des wants to go talk to what appears to be yet another friend, so I bump him with my shoulder. "Go." I nod to the laughing fairy.

Des hesitates, and then decision made, he stands, grabbing his drink. "I'll just be a minute," he promises.

I watch him as he saunters away before kicking out a spare chair next to the fairy and straddling it backward.

"What have you done to my friend?" Phaedron asks.

I give him a quizzical look. "I have no idea what you're talking about."

Phaedron shakes his head. "He waited until you gave him permission before he got up to talk. And since you two entered, there have been at least two different opportunities Desmond could've—would've—bargained something away from you if he wanted to."

I furrow my brows. "He's known for making bargains here too? In the Otherworld?"

"Oh, aye. Does it the fooking time. Well, less now—because he's king. But back when he still lived here, he could rob the green from grass, he was that good."

I know just how good Des can be.

"I think he already has plenty of leverage over me." I hold up my wrist, showing Phaedron the rows and rows of my black beads. "Each one of these represents a favor I owe Des."

He squints at the bracelet. "So *that's* how he caught you. Sly devil."

I lean forward, laying my hands flat on the table. "That's how *I* caught *him*," I correct.

Phaedron barks out a laugh. "Desmond is more of a scoundrel than I give him credit for if he let you believe that. No way in hell he'd let so many favors go unpaid unless he planned on keeping you—either with your consent or against your will."

Against my will?

My thoughts must be written on my face because Phaedron explains, "You must not know much about our kind. No fairy would let his mate get away just because she put up a little protest."

That's more than a little horrifying.

"Des isn't like that."

Phaedron snorts. "The King of the Night?" Our eyes

move to where Des sits, laughing and slapping the back of some fae with several tattoos on his face. "He's the worst of them."

"I don't believe that," I say. There have been a few times where Des's fae side got the better of him, but he always snapped out of it, and always for my sake.

Phaedron eyes me up and down. "Maybe you just haven't resisted him enough to push him to the edge."

That shuts me up. I never was one for playing hard to get when it came to the Bargainer. It had always been Des for me, and he and I both knew that.

"Trust me," Phaedron continues, "the man is desperate for you. He might not say it, but..." His eyes return to Des, whose own gaze has inadvertently found mine. The Bargainer gives me a wink when he notices me staring. "Put up some true resistance," Phaedron says, "and you'll see. He won't let you go."

How is it that one sentence can fill you both with such satisfaction and such dread? More than anything, I love the idea that Des wants to be mine every bit as much as I want to be his. But to think he'd force me to stay at his side—that part of him would cast aside my own wants and needs—that's frightening.

That's *not* Des. It's not. But I decide I don't want to argue Phaedron on this point all evening.

"How do you and Des know each other?" I ask, changing the subject.

Phaedron takes a swig of his mead before responding. "He joined the Angels of Small Death when I was its leader."

My eyebrows hike up. It's not like I'm surprised Phaedron was the leader of a gang or that Des became close with him. I think I'm most surprised about the fact Des, a fae king, and

I are here in this bar on Barbos, hanging out with Phaedron, who is probably a career criminal.

Hell, I'm probably sitting in a room full of criminals. And the King of the Night isn't punishing them, he's *catching up* with them.

Phaedron leans forward. "Now tell me: Do you have a sister—?"

Someone screams, thankfully interrupting us. The table in the corner topples over, mead splashes everywhere, and the previously seated fairies now lunge at each other.

Everyone who's not in the fight swivels their gaze to Des.

In response to the growing eyes on him, Des raises his glass in a silent toast to the room.

A triumphant shout goes up, and suddenly, it's not just the corner table of fairies who are fighting. Fae from nearby tables get involved. Glass shatters, tables break, and fists fly.

Those involved in Barbos's sex trade scream, slipping off laps to escape to the edges of the room.

"It's not a truly successful night until at least one fight breaks out," Phaedron notes, grabbing his drink as he stands.

Des comes over. "Time to go, cherub."

"You both are welcome to come over to my place. I'll be heading there in another hour or so," Phaedron says.

"We've got plans, but thanks, my brother."

"You take care of your little mate," Phaedron says to Des, winking my way. "Don't give me a reason to come after you. I can still kick your ass. And for Gods' sakes, man, next time stay for a bit longer. I barely had time to start corrupting your girl."

"Fair enough," Des says, clasping his hand. "Take care of yourself."

We part ways with the redheaded fairy to the sounds of breaking glass and shouting.

The streets of Barbos are just as rowdy. More fairies in the sex trade are out, flirting with disreputable people. There are a few more fights on the street, a group of fairies catcalling a woman who blows them a kiss, and another fairy who's standing on a rooftop, breathing fire from his lips, the inferno taking the shape of a dragon. And then there's everyone else: fairies dancing on balconies, flying drunkenly from building to building, or passed out on the city streets.

We pass by torches—the closest thing this city has to gaslights—and the flickering firelight dances along Des's face, making me feel like I'm in another time as well as another place.

Des takes a deep breath of air. "There's nothing quite like Barbos," he says, sounding invigorated.

If Des were a city, he'd *be* Barbos. The lights, the chaos, the criminality, the *sexuality*, the excitement. It's all part of who he is.

Most of the businesses we pass are bars, brothels, or gambling halls. On the sidewalks in front of them are street vendors selling their wares. Des stops us in front of one.

I glance down at the items laid out.

"Knives?" I ask, raising an eyebrow.

"Daggers, swords, maces, axes," he corrects, pointing to each different weapon. Like there's some sort of difference to them. "I figure now that I'm teaching you how to fight, you should carry your own weapon."

My eyes slide from him back to the blades. I've never exactly been a weapons kind of lady, and looking at all those sharp objects now, I find I'm still not really one.

The woman selling the weapons begins explaining the

pros and cons of different grips and blade lengths. It all turns into background noise. When I look at them, I see blood and violence and memories I've been running from.

Des leans in close. "You are no victim, cherub," he reminds me. "Not even here in the Otherworld. Pick a weapon. Make the next person who crosses you regret it."

Those are the devil's words, wicked words, but the siren in me rallies at them. Hell, the broken girl in me rallies at them.

I am *no one's* victim.

I study the weapons in earnest, comparing the leather handles to the metal ones, the curving blades to those with jagged edges.

"Move your hand over them," the fairy behind the table suggests. "The right one will call out to you."

I shake my head, ready to tell her I'm not a fairy and that their magic will be useless on me, but Des takes my hand and steadies it over the table, my palm facing down toward the weapons.

His meaning is clear: *Give it a try.*

When he releases my wrist, I take a deep breath. *This is not going to work.*

I begin to move my arm anyway, sweeping it over the table of wares.

"Slower," the seller instructs.

Setting my skepticism aside, I slow my movements.

At first, nothing happens.

Surprise, surprise.

Just as I'm about to turn to Des to tell him so, I feel it. It's just a little tug, but it draws my attention back to the table.

All right, so this brand of fae magic might work on me after all.

Like a magnet, my hand moves to the right side of the table. It slows then stops. I move my hand away to see what weapon I unwittingly picked out.

The dagger is no more than a foot and a half long from hilt to tip. The handle is made from labradorite stone, and carved into the blade itself are the phases of the moon.

For a weapon, it's awfully pretty.

"A wise choice," the seller comments. "The blade is made from the mines closest to the Kingdom of Death, and its metal is infused with the blood of titans. The hilt is crafted with the Stone of Many Faces. A powerful weapon made for a worthy individual."

Cool beans. I'm just glad my hand didn't land on the huge battle axe on the other end of the table.

"We'll take the set and a belted holster," Des says, stepping up to my side.

From behind the counter, the seller pulls out another blade—the twin of the one I picked out—as well as the holster.

I hesitate. "I don't have money for this."

Des looks at me like I'm precious before handing coins to the woman. "It's a gift."

I'm used to gifts from Des. Back when I was a teenager, he bought me all sorts of trinkets. But I'm no longer a teenager, and these blades are no trinkets.

Still, I accept them.

I take the daggers and holster from the woman, running my hands over them.

"Put it on," he urges.

I don't need much more encouragement. I may still have my reservations about owning a weapon, but I'm not going to lie, securing the belted holster to my waist and arranging those daggers onto either side of my hips makes me feel powerful, dangerous. For the first time since I arrived in the Otherworld, I feel like myself again.

All it took were a couple of weapons.

CHAPTER 12

By the time we leave Barbos for Arestys, the smallest of the Night Kingdom's floating islands, Des hasn't told me much about it, so I don't have any expectations.

I fly next to him, heedless of his mood. The night air ruffles my hair like a lover, the warm current carrying me and Des across his realm.

Flying is still just as thrilling as the first time I took to the sky, and I briefly wonder how I'll ever return to earth. Before Des taught me to fly, all I wanted was for my animalistic features to disappear. Now I don't know whether I'll ever be willing to give them up to be normal. Sure, the wings make things like getting through narrow doors and sleeping on my back nearly impossible, but they've also introduced me to a whole other side of myself, one that's wilder and freer than Callypso Lillis, the lonely PI.

It's a fairly long flight to Arestys, and when I finally do see the island, I'm surprised by how dark it is. Most places we've visited so far have been brightly lit. Only Memnos, the Land of Nightmares, appeared anywhere near this dark, and that sends a wave of trepidation through me.

I catch a brief glimpse of the underside of the island, where hundreds, if not thousands, of caves dot the rocky surface. A few minutes later, Arestys is beneath us, and I get my first good look at the Night Kingdom's poorest island.

I see a series of homely cottages clustered along a shallow stream, the water sparkling under the starlight. Strange plants grow in and around the edges of the riverbed, but outside of that, the place is a desert.

Des is quiet as the two of us land in the shimmery sand covering much of what I can see. The island is small, proba-bly only ten miles across or so. Some of the other floating islands seemed massive, but this place...this place feels like an afterthought, forgotten by most of the Otherworld.

Maybe that's why I like it. There's something about how lonely and overlooked it is that appeals to me. And out here, so far away from any city light, it feels like it's just me and Des and an endless ocean of stars.

"This is where I spent my early childhood," he says, so softly that I almost miss it.

My attention snaps from the barren landscape to him. "You did?"

It seems impossible that someone as beautifully complex as Des came from this strange, desolate place.

His eyes have a faraway look to them, like he's lost in a memory. "My mother worked as the town scribe." He points to a cluster of buildings in the distance. "She used to come home smelling of parchment, her fingers stained with ink."

I barely breathe, afraid anything I say will halt this story in its tracks.

"We were so poor that we didn't live in a proper house."

Des looks both pained and happy as he recalls it. "We lived in the caves of Arestys."

"Can I see where you lived?" I ask.

All expression wipes clean from Des's face. "It no longer exists." His eyes meet mine. "But I can show you the caves."

I duck my head as I move through the caverns beneath Arestys's surface. The rock here has formed into a maze of honeycomb-like structures. There's a sad beauty to this place, like a rainbow in an oil slick.

The tunnels are cold and drafty, claustrophobic and wet.

Des *lived* here.

My mate, the King of the Night, spent days—years—in these caves. It seems an unusually cruel existence in a place as magical as the Otherworld.

"So your mother raised you here?" I ask.

His mother, the scribe. The same woman Des claimed would've liked me. The same woman who must've once been part of the royal harem.

Des nods, his jaw hard as we wind our way through the tunnels.

I glance around at the gloomy caverns. There's a dark sort of magic here, deep within the rock. It's made of desperation and wishes, of unfulfilled desires and dreams locked away.

How is it that a son born into a royal harem ended up here? And how is it that a boy who grew up here became king?

"What about your father?" I press, sidestepping a puddle.

"Funny you should ask that..." The way he says this makes me think it's not funny at all.

He lets his words fade into nothingness, and I don't press him for more.

Ahead of us, the tunnel opens into a crater the size of a football field. Up until now we've been belowground, but here the stars twinkle overhead, shining down into the bowl-shaped depression.

Des steps ahead of me, his huge boots kicking up dust as he heads across it.

Near the center of the crater, he kneels.

It's all I can do not to stare at him. His white hair, his broad muscular back, his tattoos, and those wings he stubbornly refuses to hide all look so very appealing—so very appealing and so very tragic.

He's my own personal brand of salvation, yet right now I get the impression he's the one who needs saving.

I come up behind him, placing my hand on his shoulder.

"This is where my mother died," he says quietly.

My stomach drops at his confession.

There are no words.

Des's eyes move to mine. It's rare for him to wear his thoughts on his face, but right now he doesn't bother keeping me out, and I get an acute glimpse of all that pain bottled inside him. "I watched her die."

My throat closes.

I can't begin to imagine. It's one thing to witness your monster of a stepfather bleed out on your kitchen floor, another to watch someone you love die.

I circle around to Des's front, and his arms come around my waist. He lifts the hem of my shirt to press a kiss against the soft skin of my stomach, his thumbs rubbing back and forth over my skin.

I run my hands through his hair, loosening the locks from the leather band holding them back.

This tragedy might've happened years and years ago,

but right now it looks like it's all playing out in my mate's memory as though the events are fresh.

"What happened?" I ask softly. I almost didn't ask at all. God knows there are so many memories I hate sharing.

He looks up at me, his white hair loose. "My father happened."

CHAPTER 13

My father happened.

If that's not foreboding, I don't know what is.

Des stands, his wings expanding behind him. He clears his throat. "Enough of this." He takes my hand. "There's one more place I want to take you to before we return to Somnia."

I'm still burning to ask Des about his parents, but it's clear from his body language that he's done sharing secrets for the night. Perhaps for many nights.

Reluctantly, I take to the sky alongside him. I have no idea where he's leading me, but when Arestys falls away beneath us, I realize that'll be the extent of our visit. There will be no tour of the island's remaining highlights, no further exploration of its topography, no more discussion about Des's life here.

It's that last one I want to know about most. I keep gleaning pieces of Des's past from various sources, but I've gained more questions than answers.

What I know: Des was born into the Night Kingdom's

royal harem but raised on Arestys. He moved to Barbos and joined a "brotherhood," and at some point, he became a medaled soldier and a king. He watched his mother die, and he blames his father.

Oh, and during all this time, he was building a career for himself on earth as the Bargainer, for whatever reason.

What I don't know: pretty much everything else.

The wind ruffles his hair and clothes as we fly. Out here in the middle of the night sky, he looks completely at ease. I can't tell if it's a carefully crafted mask or if he really did leave his agony back on Arestys. I can, however, finally see that the enigmatic Bargainer has demons of his own.

This flight is quite a bit longer than the others, and by the time we descend, my body is exhausted.

The floating island we come upon seems made up of glowing pools and moonlit meadows. Scattered here and there are elaborate villas and a few temples, some length away from one another.

Off in the distance is a shimmering city, its white walls lit up with lights. Des heads straight for it.

As we close in on it, the scattered homes begin to cluster closer and closer together, gradually changing from rural to urban. The city itself sits on the edge of the island, the white buildings built along its cliffside.

Winding through the island is a glowing river, its waters a luminescent aquamarine. It spills over the side of the island, the waterfall turning to mist hundreds of feet below.

We circle past the city center and follow the river upstream before doubling back toward the interior of the island. We soar over hills, the river a glowing ribbon far below us. Soon the hills become mountains, their sides covered in dense flowering foliage.

We only begin to descend when we come to a particularly large mountain peak. Here sits a palatial white stone
home, adorned with all the Moroccan accoutrements Des's
palace has.

Des and I circle around it before landing in its front
courtyard. The only sounds around us are the soft calls of
cicadas and the hiss of rushing water. I spin, taking in the
impressive building and the mountain beyond it.

"Welcome to Lephys," Des says, "the City of Lovers."

He takes my hand, leading me through the home with
its cathedral ceilings and tiled floors, the only light coming
from the dozens of brightly colored lanterns that hang from
the ceiling above us.

The edges of arched doorways are inlaid with more
painted tiles, the colors emerald, indigo, and persimmon.
Thick painted columns hold up the sweeping ceilings,
making the place feel even vaster than it already is.

Much as I want to drink in this place, we don't linger
inside for long. The two of us exit from the back of the home.

Out here rests a huge gazebo, its gauzy curtains blowing
in the night air. Beyond the gazebo, the river we followed
here glows a pale blue green.

The luminescent river cascades into the shallow pool in
front of us. On the opposite end of it, the water pours off,
slipping farther down the mountain.

Des releases my hand before reaching behind him to
pull the back of his shirt over his head. His magic parts the
material as it passes around his wing joints, reforming once
more when it's above them.

He shucks the shirt, cutting across the gazebo and toward
the water. He lifts a foot, tugging off one of those huge
boots of his and then the other.

Des looks over his shoulder. "Need any help, cherub?" he asks.

Before I can respond, my own clothes loosen, magically peeling away from my body like the skin of a banana.

I let out a little yelp as they slip from me and fall into a pile of rags at my feet, leaving me exquisitely bare.

Des strides back to me, the last of his clothes sliding off him. Am I ever going to get over the sight of him in all his glory or the way he looks at me?

He pauses, then takes my face in his hands and kisses me deeply.

"I've imagined bringing you here for years," he admits when he breaks away.

"You have?" I ask.

He clasps my hand, walking backward through the gazebo and toward the river. "Many times."

I take in the scenery with new eyes. It's dizzying to think he imagined bringing me here when I could not have imagined a place like this even existed.

His voice drops low. "Over our time apart, I've gotten *very* imaginative when it comes to you."

Jesus. Just him saying that sends a bolt of heat through me. The way he's looking at me doesn't help either. He stares at me like I'm his starlight and he's the darkness preparing to devour me.

"Perhaps"—he backs up to the water's edge, his first foot dipping into the water—"if you play your cards right tonight, I'll even share a few of my more creative ideas—for a price, of course."

I'm pretty sure whatever price he asks for, I'll be more than willing to pay.

First my toes dip into the water, then the tips of my

wings do. Inch by inch, my naked body submerges into the water.

There's something about this place, with the heavy scent of jasmine and moist earth in the air, and the intoxicating sensation of Des's full attention on me that has my breath hitching and my eyelids lowering. My breasts feel heavy, and my core aches. Perhaps it's this island—the City of Lovers—or perhaps it's just the strange magic between us, but he has me fully under his thrall.

I want him to drown me in the madness of this. Us.

Des watches me the entire time, the glow of the water reflected in his eyes. It's a strange sensation, letting someone you trust see you bare. It's frightening and exhilarating all at once.

My eyelids flutter. The siren is calling out for me to dive deep into the pool and soak in its waters. My eyes briefly flick to the moon above us. Here, in this small glowing pool, our primordial natures are satisfied—mine and Des's. I'm guessing that was no mistake on his part.

I step up to Des, our damp chests brushing. Idly, I trace the tattoos that cover his arm, the action sending a small shiver through him.

"Keep doing that, love, and I'm not going to be able to draw this evening out like I want to," he says, his voice rough.

One glance at his face lets me know he's serious. I also know it's not helping my own willpower. Maybe I don't want this drawn out. Maybe I want the King of the Night to be fast and fierce rather than slow and exquisitely cruel.

Des wraps an arm around my waist and pulls me closer. He leans in and gives each side of my neck a kiss, his deliciously damp hair dripping against my skin.

"I could get lost in you," he murmurs.

He wraps my legs around his narrow waist, and I feel the brush of his cock, already hard and ready. The sensation of it makes my face flush.

"What's this?" he whispers between kissing my reddening cheeks. "Is my siren...bashful?"

I let out a husky laugh. He's such a scoundrel, even when he's being endearing.

He nuzzles the side of my face. "I would steal the stars from the sky for you," he whispers into my ear. "Anything to hear you laugh like that."

"You wouldn't have to steal them, Des," I say. "I bet you could strike a deal with them and they'd come down for you."

His eyes crinkle with amusement. "You give me far too much credit."

Rather than answer, my mouth finds his, taking it roughly, my hand splayed along his cheek. Let that be answer enough.

His hold tightens on me, pulling my pelvis closer even as his lips match my passion. He groans into my mouth, and I move against him, my body impatient for his, my skin illuminating.

It's been so long. Far too long. Suddenly, I don't have a decent reason why that is. Our bodies have a lot of catching up to do.

He breaks away from the kiss long enough to lean his forehead against mine, and he searches my eyes, looking for permission. I move against him once more, silently encouraging him on.

He shifts my body ever so slightly, lining us up, and then he slides into me, his head resting against mine, his eyes devouring my expression.

It's all I can do not to moan as I feel him enter me. And yet this is so much more than just sex. It's him and me and this place.

If I could drink him up, I would. He's my guilty conscience, my nightmare, my mate. The man who drinks espresso out of tiny cups and sometimes wears his hair in ridiculous man buns. The same man who likes the wild, wicked parts of me that even I'm not always comfortable with.

I roll my head back, staring up at the stars. There are thousands upon thousands of them, and their light kisses my skin. Between each one of them is unfathomable darkness. It's all around me, inside me, making love to me.

Des pistons in and out of my core, his cock stretching me in the most exquisite way. I wrap my arms around him, pressing myself in close.

It's no longer just the water that's glowing. My skin is lit up, the siren thoroughly enjoying the water around us and the man inside us.

Right in the middle of the act, he moves us near the waterfall, where the rocky mountainside creates a wall of sorts. He presses me gently against it, being careful about my wings.

"Truth or dare?" he rasps, still thrusting in and out of me.

Wait, is he kidding?

When I don't immediately answer—because my brain shut off several minutes ago—he slides out of me.

I make a pained sound, feeling empty without Des between my legs.

I should know my wily fairy better by now.

He dips underwater, moving my legs over his shoulders. And then, right in the middle of the pool, his lips press against my core.

Now I let out the moan I held back earlier. And thank God Des is underwater; it's one hell of an embarrassing sound.

As I lean back against the rock wall, panting, I piece together that *this* is Des's dare. For once, I'm not complaining about the Bargainer's sneaky fae games. Especially when they involve his incredible mouth.

He sucks first one lip into his mouth and then the other. I buck against him, his ministrations driving me wild.

His tongue finds my clit, and an unexpected orgasm rips from the depths of me. I cry out as I move against him, my fingers buried in his hair.

How the clever man knows I've come is beyond me—like I said, my brain shut off long ago—but my legs slide from his shoulders as he rises. And then, in one smooth thrust, his cock is back in me, working me from the inside out.

"Ready for number two?" he asks. He doesn't even sound breathless.

Before I have a chance to respond, he begins moving harder, deeper, and like a puppet master, he's pulling the strings of my body, dragging me back to the edge.

I tighten my grip on him. It's rough and it's sweet, relentless and coaxing. I'm almost regretting that I wanted this to be swift and fierce. With Des, I could stay like this forever.

Hypothetically.

Realistically, the moment he kisses me, I'm done.

Like a dam breaking, I find my second release. I'm gasping into his mouth, holding on to him like he's the only thing keeping me from floating away. And then he's coming too, his lips still moving firmly against mine, his thrusts becoming even deeper and harder.

It seems like we spend an eternity in that moment, locked together, and there's no beginning or end to us.

But, at some point, the moment does end. We break off the kiss, and Des eases out of me. Neither one of us let go of the other, our breathing heavy, our bodies plastered together.

"Never want to leave," Des rasps against me.

My grip on him tightens. "Neither do I."

I don't know how long we stay like that. Long enough for my skin to dim and our breathing to quiet.

"Cherub," Des eventually says, "there's something I wanted to show you."

With a good amount of reluctance, I slide out of his hold.

After taking my hand, he tugs me toward the waterfall, my feet skimming over smooth river stones as we move beneath the cascading waters, the river pounding against my head and shoulders when Des leads me through it.

On the other side, the glow of the water illuminates the outlines of a cave. Des snaps his fingers, and all at once, there's light.

Hundreds of flickering candles are piled on almost every surface of the cavern, glittering softly in the darkness. The light from the water and the flames dances along the ceiling and the glow of it is hypnotizing.

"*Wow*," I breathe. The place is like something out of a dream.

Right in the middle of all the candlelight is a soft pallet piled with blankets, a tray of food sitting next to it.

Des swims to the edge of the pool and pushes himself onto the rocky lip of the cave, then runs his hands through his hair as he slicks it back. He turns and reaches for me, every inch of his glorious body glistening.

I take Des's hand and follow him out of the water, my wings heavy. Before I can look for a towel, he reaches around me and runs a hand over my feathers.

A warm brush of magic tickles my back, and in an instant, my wings, skin, and hair are all dry. When I glance at him again, I notice he too has dried himself.

Des and I are still naked. It's both odd and oddly enjoyable to be laid bare like this in front of each other. There are so many firsts I'm only now experiencing with this man.

I step up to the pallet and fold my knees under me, stretching my wings out. In here, the churning sound of the waterfall echoes. This feels like some primitive temple, and Des is the god it pays homage to.

The Bargainer sits next to me, the tips of his wings lifting to rest themselves on a nearby rock. He takes in our surroundings. "After all this time, I find myself back in a cave," he says wryly. His words remind me of those caverns back in Arestys.

There's a vulnerability to him in this moment.

Even now he struggles to let down his guard.

I want to tell him that this place is perfect, that *he's* perfect. That I cherish every broken bit of him.

But I don't say any of this. He is, at his core, just as uncomfortable with emotional intimacy as I am.

Instead, I reach out and run my hand over his wings.

He closes his eyes, like he's savoring the sensation. After getting up, I circle behind him, studying the silvery skin of the wings as my hand passes over each talon and joint.

Beneath my touch, he shivers. His wings stretch in response, the fine veins of them clearly visible even here in the dim lighting.

"I always assumed fairies had butterfly wings," I admit.

"You're not wrong," Des says, his back still to me. "Mine are particularly rare."

He turns long enough to wrap his arms around my waist

and pull me back to the soft pallet, his hands then drifting down to cup my ass. This, naturally, makes my skin come to life as the siren wakes up.

Des's expression, of course, is one of complete innocence.

I give him a look that says, *I'm onto you.*

His eyes crinkle, and he laughs. "So suspicious of my motives. It's like you think I'm just trying to get into your pants."

As if he's not. He's a slippery fucker. "You say that as though you didn't literally strip me of my pants five minutes ago," I say.

"I think it was a *little* more than five minutes ago."

I barely manage not to roll my eyes. Apparently, human or fairy, men's egos are still very much the same.

Des spreads his body out next to mine, his hand lingering on the dip where my waist is. The warm, humid air of the place caresses my skin and curls my hair.

Propping myself up, I reach out and continue to trace what I can of Des's wings.

"So all fairies have insect wings but you?" I ask.

He shakes his head. "Most do, but not all," he says, running his hand up my waist and over my rib cage. "There are other wing types too. Some fairies have avian wings like yours."

"Why are yours different?" I ask.

He stares off into the distance, his thumb absently stroking my skin, drawing out goose bumps. "Some say my line's descended from dragons," he murmurs, the candlelight dancing over his body. "Others say we come from demons."

Dragons? Demons? *Damn.*

I'm not going to pretend I understand how fairy lineages work.

"I always thought they looked like bat wings," I admit.

"*Bat* wings?" Des raises his eyebrows, his gaze refocusing on me.

I'm pretty sure I've offended him once again, but then he throws his head back and lets out a laugh.

"My family history is long and lurid, but I can safely say it did not involve bats."

I think about Des's mother, the scribe, telling a small boy with white hair all sorts of stories—and among them, tales of his heritage.

I smile a little at the thought. I can't imagine being told dragons existed…and that I might be descended from one of them.

"What is it?" Des asks, touching a finger to my lower lip like he wants to steal my smile for himself.

I shake my head. "I'm just imagining you as a boy listening to stories from your mother about your ancestors."

Immediately, Des's expression loses its lighthearted playfulness.

I've said the wrong thing, I know it. I expect him to pull away and run like all those times he used to. I'm steeling my heart against the possibility.

But he doesn't run, he doesn't leave.

He simply says, "The stories are from my father's side of the family."

The same father who had something to do with his mother's death.

Yikes.

I reassess Des's wings. I hadn't realized they might represent something terrible about his past—the same way mine did. It's odd to look at his wings and see something very different than what he must.

I ask softly, "What do you think: Are you descended from demons or dragons?"

"Knowing my father? Demons."

My throat works. I really, *really* want to ask him about his father, but I can't bring myself to form the words. There's clearly an ocean of bitterness and anger buried beneath that relationship.

"Well," I say, running a hand over the fine bones of the wing closest to me, "whatever their origin, I think they're perfect."

Beneath my touch, a tremor runs through Des's body.

"That doesn't scare you?" he asks. "That I might have a little demon blood running through me?"

I shrug. "You met me the day I killed my stepfather." I finger one of his talons. "And I've seen you execute men. I think we're past that."

At my words, Des's eyes deepen. He pulls me in close, one of his wings covering me like a blanket. He kisses the tip of my nose, then rests his chin against the crown of my head.

"Thank you, cherub," he says softly.

I'm not sure what he's thanking me for, but I nod against him anyway, stroking his face. Eventually, my eyes drift closed, my body warmed by Des's.

And that is how we spend our first night on Lephys. Not in the palatial home beyond the pool, but in this humble cave, our naked bodies tangled.

CHAPTER 14

When Des and I finally return to the city of Somnia, something about me is noticeably different.

I no longer hate my wings…or my scales or claws. Somehow, during my trip through the Night Kingdom, I found the very things that frightened me about myself now…*empower* me.

I can fly. I can slice my enemies with my bare hands.

There's strength in that, whether Karnon intended it or not.

My training with Des has also bolstered my courage. I swear my arms and legs are more defined, and even though I haven't been able to land a blow on Des yet, I'm fighting with more confidence.

I won't admit this to Des, but I'm glad he forced me to train with him. I might hate the process, but I kind of dig the results. I'm also coming to love the sweet pair of blades strapped to my hips. They clink against my clothing now as Des and I walk down the familiar hallways of his palace.

The tower room Des leads me to is one of the coolest places in the palace. Made of floor-to-ceiling glass windowpanes, the tower room gives me a bird's-eye view of Somnia, from the castle grounds to the city spread out beyond it.

Aside from the lanterns hanging overhead, the only piece of furniture in the room is a massive table currently set for two. Spread out on it is what looks and smells suspiciously like Indian food, my favorite.

Des swaggers over to the table, wearing the same dark pants and shit-kicking boots that he regularly did back on earth, his hair tied back with a leather cord.

The only fae additions to his attire are the three bronze war cuffs that ring one bicep, and that pretty much just adds to his sex appeal at this point. I stare at the thick bands of muscle and the inked skin of his arms as he pulls out a chair for me.

I slide into the seat he offers, watching him take his own.

Before I can even begin to serve myself, he does it for me. A plate of *aloo gobi* and another of rice lift into the air and meander over to me. While I begin to scoop out a helping, a teapot moves to the mug in front of my plate, and it pours me a cup of chai.

"How did you even get your hands on this stuff?" I ask as I finish serving myself.

Des leans back in his seat, looking all too proud of himself. "There are perks to being a king."

He spends a good five minutes watching me eat before he joins me. I know the man likes good Indian food himself—he's the one who introduced me to the cuisine—but he seems more interested in my enjoyment than his own.

"Mind mixing a little business with dinner?" Des asks eventually.

I shrug. Now that we're back in Somnia, it's back to work for Des and back to finding things to occupy myself with. There's pretty much nothing worse than boredom, so I'll take a little business with dinner if it gives me something to do.

I wipe my mouth with my napkin. "What's up?"

Des snaps his fingers, and a sheet of parchment appears in midair before fluttering down in front of me. I don't reach it before it lands on the plate of chicken tikka masala, the food's oily orange sauce bleeding onto the paper.

Leaning forward, I grab the sheet of parchment and use my napkin to dab the sauce off it.

"Was that really necessary?" I ask, frowning when my efforts to clean the paper only end up further smearing sauce all over it.

On the parchment is a chart of sorts, one column containing a list of names, another containing gender, another containing dates and times, another containing locations, and then, finally, a column containing what looks to be notes.

The Bargainer nods to the paper. "That's a list of all the fae who've disappeared within the past three months," he says, taking a sip of his chai.

I raise my eyebrows, looking at the chart all over again. The sight of so many names is staggering, and this list includes not just missing women, but missing men as well.

So far, Des and I haven't talked much about them, mostly because, unlike the women, the men who vanished have not reappeared, giving us no clues as to what happened to them.

"Notice anything unusual?" Des asks, watching me from over the rim of his cup.

I continue to skim the chart. "You know, if there's

something you want me to notice, you could just come out and say..." My words dry up when I get to the dates.

Since Des killed Karnon, no women have disappeared... but five men have.

I glance up at the Bargainer. "The men are still vanishing."

Des looks out the window at the twinkling city below. "Many men disappear in the Night Kingdom," he says conversationally. "It could be nothing."

I can practically hear the *but* that follows his statement.

"What is it?" I ask, lowering the parchment.

He takes another sip of his tea. "Four of the last five men who've gone missing are soldiers."

Too many disappearances to be a coincidence, which means...

It's not over.

The paper rustles a little as my hand begins to tremble.

"But you killed him," I say softly.

Des's eyes soften as he gazes at me. "I killed *Karnon*."

It takes me a few more seconds to put together what Des isn't saying. When I do, my eyes widen. "Someone else is taking the men."

CHAPTER 15

Karnon only ever took the women. Now that Des killed him, those disappearances have stopped. The paper in my hand says as much.

But the men…

"So you think there's more than one person behind this." I stare at Des across the table, dumbfounded. "But…why? And how?"

Des runs a hand through his white-blond hair, his arm muscles rippling. "I'm working on that."

Just then, Malaki comes into the room, his strides long and powerful, looking every inch the pirate with his eye patch and scruffy cheeks.

He drops a large waxy leaf on the table. "Solstice invite— the third one they've sent, for the record." He crinkles his nose. "Ugh, what's that smell?" he says, grimacing at the plates of Indian food scattered across the table.

Did he just scorn my dinner?

Des leans back in his seat, crossing his arms over his chest. "We're not going to Solstice this year."

Malaki takes a seat, a plate and place settings appearing in front of him. A moment later he reaches for the tray of samosas.

"Really?" I say derisively to him, raising my eyebrows. He hated on my dinner, and now he's about to eat it. "That's how you're going to play this?"

He gives me a confused look as he adds the samosa to his plate. Turning his attention to Des, Malaki says, "That's a really bad idea."

Des lifts a shoulder. "Last time Callie visited another kingdom, she was someone's prisoner."

"And then you killed that kingdom's king," Malaki says smoothly. "I think everyone knows not to fuck with your mate."

"We're not going," Des repeats.

"Being a mate does not mean you stop being a king."

"*Careful.*" Des's words cut through the room like a whip, his power riding them.

Malaki sits back in his seat, bowing his head. "Apologies, my king."

The Bargainer's body seems to ease, and the power that thickened the air moments ago now recedes.

"*Loi du royaume,*" Des says quietly.

Malaki mouth goes grim. "I know."

I glance between the two men. So far, I've been somewhat able to follow the conversation, but now they lost me.

"What's that?" I ask. "That phrase you just said."

Des nods to his friend. "Tell her, Malaki. If she's to go and subject herself to Solstice because you think it's a good idea, then you tell her what she's going to have to sacrifice."

Malaki sighs then turns his attention to me. "You know the human saying, 'When in Rome do as the Romans do'?"

I squint at him. "You actually know that phrase?" He doesn't strike me as the kind of fairy who hangs out on earth.

"Do you know it?" he presses.

Looking from him to Des, I hesitantly nod.

"That's the law here in the Otherworld."

I'm still not following.

"When in the Night Kingdom," Malaki explains, "a fairy must follow their laws. Des here doesn't want you to leave the Night Kingdom because you'll both be subject to another fae kingdom's laws."

"That's pretty much how it works on earth," I say, confused as to why this is an issue.

"The Flora Kingdom enslaves humans," Des cuts in.

Ah. And therein lies the true probl—

BOOM!

The room shakes as a wave of magic washes over us, throwing me back into my seat. Our plates and utensils rattle on the table, a few falling off the edge and crashing to the floor. In the distance, I hear muffled gasps.

The three of us look at each other.

What in the—?

All at once, we're moving, my chair toppling behind me in my haste to figure out what's going on. Malaki, Des, and I rush from the room—dinner, missing men, and enslaver kingdoms forgotten.

Out in the halls, fairies are dashing around, trying to find shelter. One of the palace officers runs to us, bowing hastily to Des.

"There's been a security breach," he explains, his voice breathless. "One of the portals is down—something's crossed over and collapsed it."

"Gather a hundred of my best soldiers and have them meet us in the air."

As soon as Des gives the order, the officer is off, running back the way he came.

We move again. Rather than head down to the main floor of the palace, I follow Des and Malaki to one of the castle balconies.

My eyes scour the horizon, looking for something, anything to explain that violent wave of magic. It had felt so familiar…

Des tears his gaze from the horizon to look at me. His lips part, and I'm pretty sure this is where he tells me to get back inside.

Instead, he closes his mouth and squares his jaw. After striding over to me, he clasps the back of my neck. "Do you wish to join me?" he asks.

"Always." It's less thought than it is instinct. Where my mate goes, I go.

"Desmond—" Malaki protests.

"This will be dangerous," Des warns me, ignoring his friend. "Either of us could die. Are you still sure?"

My heart thumps like mad. Had I ever thought Des's love would be stifling? That it would coddle me like a security blanket? Because this isn't stifling or coddling. It's dangerous and all-consuming, and right now it leaves a taste in my mouth like blood and smoke.

"I'm sure."

Behind us, Malaki throws up his hands.

Des nods to me, his face foreboding. "Follow my lead and keep yourself safe. That's an order."

His wings unfurl behind him, blossoming like some twisted thorny flower. In response, my own wings stretch wide.

With a burst of magic, he leaps into the night air, his wings propelling him up. My own takeoff isn't nearly so graceful, but several seconds later, I too am airborne, trailing after the King of the Night, Malaki at my back.

I don't see what caused the commotion until well after Malaki, Des, and I have joined with Des's soldiers.

Far below the floating island of Somnia, on the main landmass that makes up the Otherworld, a massive fireball is unfolding, thick inky plumes of smoke already rising from it.

Flakes of smoldering ash drift around us the closer we get. I squint down at the flames as the smoke burns my eyes.

My brows furrow.

Right in the center of the inferno, right where I'd assumed the heat would be the hottest and the fire would burn the brightest, there's a blackened pathway the flames don't dare touch.

One of the guards points to something along the singed trail, and I follow his finger. There, amid the charred earth, are what appear to be two figures.

It's not until we're about a hundred feet away from the ground that I recognize one of them.

Well, fuck me good.

Temperance "Temper" Darling, my best friend and colleague, is striding amid the blaze like she controls it, dragging a very frightened-looking fairy along with her. Her dark eyes glow like coals, bolts of electricity snapping from her.

Uh-oh.

She's officially lost control of her power. I've only ever seen her like this two other times, and neither of which ended well.

Around me I feel fae magic building in the air. I don't know if it's all coming from Des or if his soldiers are also adding to it, but throwing power at Temper when she's like this only ever leads to one thing—destruction.

I glance over at Des, who's studying Temper. There's no recognition on his face, and why should there be? For all I've told him of her, he hasn't met Temper in the flesh.

Sometimes I assume my mate is omnipotent and infallible, that he knows everything and everyone at every moment in time. That nothing can truly sneak up on him.

But it can and it obviously has.

He begins signaling to his men, who adjust their positions, their bodies tense and ready.

If I don't do something now, they're going to firebomb my friend, and that's going to end badly for everyone.

Coming to a hasty decision, I tuck my wings close to my back. My body dips, beginning to dive for the earth.

"Stop!" someone shouts behind me.

There's no way I'm stopping.

I glance over my shoulder. My eyes meet Des's, and for a moment, all we do is lock eyes. Right now I'm neither following his lead nor keeping myself safe like he instructed. He has every reason to use his magic to stop me in my tracks, but he doesn't.

That small show of faith bolsters my courage.

There's no way for me to communicate to him that this woman is my best friend or that I might be the only one who can salvage the situation before someone gets hurt. The only thing I can do is nod to Des. *I know what I'm doing*, I will him to understand.

Even though he can't read my thoughts, I think he must glean them from my face. He stares at me for another moment, and then he puts up a fist. In response, his soldiers hold steady, their bodies still poised.

That's all I have time to notice before I face forward again.

Beneath me, Temper stares up at the group of us, her normally warm eyes foreign and blistering as they land on mine.

This is the Temper people feared at our boarding school, and here is the power that ostracized her. The terrifying reality of her existence, the one she stares down each morning when she wakes up and closes her eyes to each night, is that she is capable of this carnage. She's capable of it, and a part of her craves it.

There is a seductive power she can tap into, and it lures her in whenever it can. It's a struggle I understand all too well. Most days, she tells it to fuck off.

Today, she gave into it.

I know what the soldiers looking down at Temper are wondering. It's the same question that's plagued many of our clients.

What is *she?*

I stare at my friend through the haze, the heat waves making her form shimmer and bend. There's only one type of supernatural whose magic is this powerful, this frightening, this intoxicating—

A sorceress.

CHAPTER 16

Temper and I stare at each other across the expanse of space, her skin sparking as magic dances along it. Her brimstone eyes and electric skin are a world away from her normal expressive self.

My friend is a rare breed of supernatural, one most people should hope to never encounter. Sorcerers and sorceresses wield magic like witches, but unlike witches, they have a nearly limitless amount of power they can tap into on a whim. The only trouble is every time they use their magic, it eats away at their conscience until there is nothing left.

Using small amounts here and there makes no real difference. But power like this? It can cleave away large bits of Temper's morality.

The worst part of the whole thing is that Temper's power coaxes her to use it the same way my siren coaxes me to give in to my own inner darkness. It's always there, waiting for a moment of weakness.

My friend came for me. I disappeared, and she hunted

me down, working herself up into a frenzy until her power swallowed her whole. She gave up a bit of her morality for me.

It's a totally messed-up show of friendship, but one that moves me nonetheless.

I begin to lower myself to the ground, the heat and smoke of the inferno suffocating.

Callie. I sense more than hear Des's voice in the sky above me. I glance up at him from where he and his men linger several dozen feet away.

His expression says it all. He's not okay with me getting closer. Not one bit, and he's getting ready to intervene.

I turn away from him. Temper is my biggest concern.

She watches me the entire time I descend, the fairy she holds struggling to get away even though he's definitely not going anywhere.

I land on the smoldering ground, the heat like an oven around us.

"You grew wings," she says, her voice toneless.

Not *hi*, not *how are you?* or *why haven't you called?* Just *you grew wings.* Temper's as far gone as I've ever seen her.

"That bastard made you grow wings," she says, the heat around me rising with her voice. Her gaze moves from me to Des.

She shoves the fairy she's holding away from her, nearly managing to chuck him into the fire. He staggers away from the blaze just in time, and then he's bolting, taking to the sky, muttering all sorts of obscenities that Temper doesn't hear. Her wrath is focused on my mate.

"Whatever you're thinking Temper, *don't*," I say, my voice low.

If she touches a hair on Des's head, then friend or not, I'm taking her down.

Temper's attention swings back to me, her eyes thinning menacingly. She tilts her head, trying to figure me out. "What has he done to you?"

It's obvious she thinks I'm the crazy one.

On a whim, I take a step forward. "Put out the flames, release your magic, and I'll explain everything."

Her eyes still look as haunted as ever, and those little bolts of lightning are still jumping from her skin, but I swear I'm getting through to her.

But then she smiles at me, and it's positively sinister. "What if I don't want to?"

There it is, the monster that consumes Temper.

My siren surfaces, illuminating my skin. "Don't make me glamour you," I state, my voice menacing.

"You wouldn't *dare*," she says.

She's right. In any other situation, I wouldn't. But right now, things are different.

"He's not my betrothed, Temper. He's my soul mate." I never had the chance to tell her.

It's an explanation of sorts—that I'm not being held here against my will and that I will stop her if she tries to hurt my mate.

For one long moment, Temper doesn't react at all. Then, slowly, her eyes drift up to the Bargainer, her face expressionless.

In the sky, more fairies have joined him, not all from his kingdom by the looks of them. Temper's gathering a crowd, and if this doesn't end soon, either my friend is going to get hurt or a bunch of innocents are.

Temper's gaze returns to me. "He's your soul mate," she states, her voice almost trancelike.

I nod, my skin still bright. *Protect our mate*, my siren whispers, cajoling me to glamour my friend.

I keep my mouth adamantly shut.

Temper closes her eyes, and I tense. For all I know, she's about to ignite the skies and every fairy in them.

I could stop her right now. All it would take is a little of my own magic. I have every reason to do so, and my siren wants it badly.

But I don't.

Des gave me the benefit of the doubt only minutes ago. I can do the same for Temper. So I hold my tongue and wait for her to act.

My friend's eyes snap open, and all at once, the flames of the explosion extinguish, as though they were nothing more than birthday candles being blown out.

Temper's irises dim, and the glowing red lines that streak through them now begin to recede. Her skin stops sparking, and that hot, overbearing power of hers finally reels itself in.

One moment she's a savage sorceress, and the next she's just my friend.

She lets out a faltering breath. "*Callie*," she exhales.

That's all I need to hear. I close the last of the space between us, wrapping Temper in a hug. Her skin feels like sunbaked sand under my touch. She grips me tightly.

"God, I was worried about you," she confesses.

"I'm so sorry," I say. I have valid reasons for vanishing on my friend, but I never meant to distress her.

"You're going to tell me about the wings," she says as we hug, "and how you're a soul mate, and how the hell you ended up here. Then and only then can I promise you I won't fry your boyfriend."

Now that the imminent danger is gone, I hear the drumming of my pulse. What would've happened if I hadn't come along with Des? What would've happened if Temper hadn't listened to my pleas?

I squeeze her tighter. "Fair enough," I say into her shoulder.

Around us, fairies are beginning to drop to the earth before cautiously creeping closer. I don't know how many seconds we have left to ourselves.

I pull away from her. "I can't believe you blew up a portal to the Otherworld."

She flashes me a devious smile. "That's just called making an entrance."

CHAPTER 17

Several hours later, after many death threats (both to and from Temper), a near incarceration, and a whole lot of explaining, Temper and I are with Des and Malaki in one of the Bargainer's private rooms.

Temper crosses her heels over the armrest of the wingback chair she's in, her back resting against the other armrest. "So let me get this straight: you two"—she points to me and Des—"are soul mates, but you couldn't get together for a stupidly long time because this one"—now she points to me—"made some ridiculous wish. And right after you both finally got together, she"—me again—"was thrown into a fae prison, and some psycho king decided to give her wings"— and scales and claws—"and you"—she points to Des—"killed that asshole, but now you"—me again—"are stranded here."

"She's not stranded here," Des says darkly. He sits in another chair, his forearms resting heavily on his thighs.

Temper guffaws. "Like she can just waltz her feathery self around LA."

Malaki steps forward. "Why don't we talk about the

pressing issue at the moment? You obliterated one of the Fauna Kingdom's portals and held a fairy hostage."

Temper folds her arms, eyeing the fairy up and down. "If you want an apology, you're looking at the wrong girl, compadre."

A knock on the door interrupts the conversation. Des waves his wrist, and the door opens.

The fairy on the other side bows. "My king," he says. "Lord, ladies." He dips his head to each of us before returning his attention to Des. "There are Fauna fae soldiers at the palace gates. They're demanding the sorceress's arrest."

And that marks another attempt at incarceration.

Des rubs his chin. "I refuse to hand her over," he says.

"My king—" the fairy begins.

"The sorceress is an honored guest and thus has my protection and that of my kingdom," he says. His eyes flick to mine. "Any damages her arrival incurred will be paid in full from my personal coffers."

My breath catches. He's so obviously doing this for me. Just when I thought it was impossible to love him more…

Malaki's eyebrows go up. He assesses Temper, who's giving him a considering look.

The fairy standing in the doorway hesitates then bows. "Very well. I'll let them know."

After the door closes, the room falls into silence.

Finally, Temper clears her throat. "I suppose you want me to thank you," she says, picking at a stray piece of lint on the chair.

The fact Des offered Temper his protection… I'm not sure he realizes that's kind of a big deal for her. Temper is used to being judged and condemned, not given the benefit of the doubt.

"Now you *must* make a showing at Solstice," Malaki interrupts. "You're going to need to prove to the other kingdoms that you're still a faithful ally. Otherwise, this could mark the beginnings of war."

Des rubs his face. For once he seems like a weary king.

Sensing that he has sway over Des, the Lord of Dreams steps forward. "If you attend Solstice and show them you are the same ruler you've always been, it will go a long way to cooling tensions."

Des doesn't say anything for a minute, just ponders Malaki's words.

Those hypnotic, silver eyes of his meet mine. I can tell he's torn between protecting me and protecting his kingdom. It shakes me to my core to matter that much to someone.

"I don't need protecting," I say.

"From these fairies you might," Des mutters. Finally, reluctantly, he nods. "All right, I'll go—we'll *all* go." His eyes sweep over the room, touching on Malaki, then me, then—shockingly—Temper.

She's coming too?

Temper looks pleased. "Sounds good to me. Consider me this one's rib," she says, jerking her chin in my direction.

It hits me, really hits me, then: Des means to take me and my best friend to a place where mortals are enslaved. We'll have to respect their archaic laws, laws that subjugate humans.

I suppress a swallow. What have we gotten ourselves into?

CHAPTER 18

"Callie, what is going on with you?" Temper asks.

The two of us stand inside her guest suite. Like the rest of the Night Kingdom's palace, this room has a Moroccan feel to it, with arched doorways, tiled columns, and hanging lanterns.

I lean back against the door. "What do you mean?" I say.

She begins to poke around the room. "Seems an awful lot like you're getting comfortable here while you test drive your fairy prince."

I *am* getting comfortable with this realm and my mate, something the old Callie would've not been chill with. In her eyes, the Otherworld was too frightening and Des too flighty.

"What do you want me to do, Temper? You said it yourself earlier—I can't just head back to earth." I gesture to my wings. "I'm a freak."

Freak. The word tastes like a lie when it leaves my lips. Maybe it's all the things I've discovered I can do, maybe it's that everyone in this realm looks a bit like me, or maybe it's that the King of the Night seems to think I'm perfect even with all these additions. Somewhere along the way, I decided *different* no longer equaled *bad*.

"There are ways to undo what happened to you," Temper says.

Something uncomfortable slides through my stomach. To undo Karnon's magic... How many times have I wished for these scales on my forearms to disappear? For my black nails to return to their normal fleshy color? For my wings to disappear?

It's a familiar feeling. There was a time I wished to wash away my flesh and live in someone else's skin.

I'm only now accepting that I want *this* skin, imperfections and all. And Temper is suggesting I can get rid of those imperfections. That I should.

I don't expect to be hurt by the offer, but I am, just a little. I want her to accept all of me the way Des has.

"I don't want to undo it," I say.

Temper stops poking around to arch a sculpted eyebrow my way. "Seriously?"

Self-consciously, I reach around and drag the edge of one of my wings forward, the dark iridescent feathers shimmering.

Releasing my wing, I sigh. "Is that so hard for you to believe?"

"You and I both know you can't come back to earth looking like you do. Don't you want to come home? You have a whole life waiting for you."

A lonely, empty life. That's not to say I want to abandon it, but I don't also want to have to change myself to return to that life.

I open my mouth to tell her this, but then I stop. I'm not going to defend myself to her. We've always had each other's backs, and I want her to be okay with this.

I shake my head. "Forget about it." I turn to leave.

"Wait." She heads back over to me and catches my wrist. "Callie, you know I only care if you care." Her warm brown eyes search mine. "It's just that I know how much you didn't want to be a werewolf when you were with Eli, and now after being with another guy for three point five seconds, you look like a fairy."

I give her an exasperated look. "I haven't been with him for 'three point five' seconds."

She squeezes my hand a little tighter, reading my features. "Fine," she says, making some judgment call, "you have a long and sordid history with him. I only needed to make sure this is truly what you want."

It might not have originally been what I wanted, but—

"This is truly what I *am*." A siren. A creature who can beguile humans, one who is not quite human herself. Karnon might have manifested my scales, claws, and wings, but now I'm starting to embrace them. I'm now starting to embrace it all.

Temper looks at me, really looks at me, and I swear the air turns heavy. The two of us are having one of those moments that come up every so often in our friendship, when we cannot just joke our way out of the reality of what we are. She sees the raw, harsh truth of my supernatural ability, and her eyes soften.

"You are perfect, Callie," she admits. "Just like this."

My throat swells at her absolute acceptance, and I pull my hand out of her grip so I can give her a hug. "Thank you," I whisper. "I love you, Temper."

Her arms come around me a second later. "I know. How could you not? I blew up a portal for you."

Right there, in the middle of the hug, I begin to laugh. "I still can't believe you did that. And the look on that fairy's face…" I say, referring to the fairy she held hostage. That dude probably needed a change of pants after the experience.

"You mean my guide?" she says. "That's what he gets for overcharging me."

Now the both of us crack up, and it's so messed up, but the two of us can be like that.

Temper pulls away, her laughter trailing off. "Okay, now where do these fairies keep the liquor?" she asks, glancing around the room. "I'm going to need a drink or three if I'm to stay here in the freaking Otherworld."

"I thought you were all about fairies," I say, moving deeper into her room.

"Yeah, back when I was *seventeen*. I was also all about orange lipstick then too." She shudders at the memory, kneeling in front of a hutch pressed to the side of the room. "At least I'm now a whole world away from that odious Leonard Fortuna," she mutters under her breath.

I make a face at the name. Leo, a sorcerer whose notoriety is widely known in supernatural circles, has been relentlessly pursuing my friend for years, despite Temper making it clear she wants nothing to do with him. Leonard, however, seems to see her lack of interest as more of a minor hiccup than a nonstarter.

Seriously, the dude is odious. But, like Temper said, she's a world away, so he's shit out of luck for now.

"Aha!" she says, interrupting my thoughts as she opens the hutch's doors. "Here we are." She grabs a bottle with shimmery lettering. Uncorking it, she sniffs.

She winces a little. "Ugh, smells like leprechaun piss, but it'll do."

Not even going to ask about the leprechaun comment.

She takes a swig straight from the bottle before offering it to me. I wave it away.

"So"—she plops down on an ornate side chair—"Mal-a-ki." She stretches out his name, waggling her eyebrows.

I groan, falling onto her bed. "*Nooo.*"

"No, what?" she says.

I grab one of her pillows and tuck it under my chest. "I already know how this will play out: you're going to screw him then screw him over, and then he's going to be huffy, and he'll take it out on me because I'm your best friend."

She gives me the side-eye, taking a swig from her bottle. "It would serve you right, you know. I've had to deal with Eli since you broke things off with him, and that man has had a bone to pick with me ever since."

Oops. Temper has a point. Our business, West Coast Investigations, contracted some work out to Eli, who was a supernatural bounty hunter. I assumed our relationship—or lack thereof—wouldn't affect our work.

Clearly, I assumed wrong.

"So," Temper continues, "does he have a girlfriend?"

"Eli?" I lift a shoulder. "I wouldn't know."

She gives me a look. "*Callie,*" she says emphatically, "you and I both know I'm not talking about Eli. *Malaki.*"

Poor, poor Malaki. Seems he's going to have more to do with Temper in the coming days whether he knows it or not. She's charming as hell when she wants to be.

"No clue," I say.

I don't even know if fairies *have* girlfriends or boyfriends. They seem like the kind of creatures to have courtships rather than dates, and betrotheds rather than significant others. And apparently, if you're a ruler, *harems*.

I suppress my shudder.

"Hmm…" Temper takes another swig from the bottle, completely oblivious to where my mind is.

The urge to drink rises in me. Damn Des for forcing me to be sober. I could use a little liquor for this conversation.

"Is the eye patch real?" she asks.

I just give Temper a look.

"It is, isn't it?" She says this like it's some great revelation. "I want to see what's under it."

"Has anyone told you you're seriously disturbed?"

"Says the girl who loves to fuck bad men. How *is* the Bargainer in bed? I bet he's got really good tongue game."

I could *definitely* use a little liquor for this conversation.

"Temper, I don't want to kiss and tell."

"What? You *always* kiss and tell."

That was back when the men didn't matter, and it was fun to laugh about some sexual situations I got myself into. But intimacy with Des…it feels different, *sacred*.

"It's the best I've ever had," I admit primly, "and that's all I'm going to say."

Temper eyes me over the bottle. "The best you ever had?" She whistles. "And here I thought this guy was a bad influence."

"Oh, he's still a bad influence," I say, my eyes going distant.

Des may be my soul mate, but he's still the man who tricks me into jumping off buildings, who kills remorselessly, who still intends to collect repayment from me.

"Whatever you say."

The two of us talk for a bit more. It's only once the

alcohol hits Temper's system and makes her sleepy that I tuck her into bed and steal away from her room.

I spend an extra few seconds quietly closing her door.

"You have some explaining to do."

I cover my mouth to muffle my yelp.

Leaning against the hallway wall is Des.

He strides toward me, and like a fool, I back up. When his eyes glint the way they do now, he's right on the edge that separates sanity and madness, humanity and fae cruelty.

He's on me in an instant, pinning me to the wall.

"Let's try this again," he says, nipping my ear. "You have some explaining to do." He presses a leg between mine, the movement rubbing against my core. "Now, do you want to start with the fact you did not listen to my instructions when we were on the balcony earlier or the fact you nearly got yourself killed by facing down an angry sorceress?"

I swallow delicately. I knew this was coming.

"I could've—" His voice breaks. "I could've lost you," he says harshly. "If you had been hurt…I wouldn't have even had time to administer lilac wine."

Lilac wine?

My mind lingers on the term for only a second or two before focusing on the more pertinent issue at hand.

This is where I apologize for frightening him, and it's where I thank him for his faith in me.

Only, I never get the chance.

Des's face bricks itself up until the suave, cunning Bargainer stares back at me. "Or perhaps," Des continues, "we should skip the explanations and move on to reconciliation."

Reconciliation?

Suddenly, the Bargainer no longer has me pinned to the

wall. He lifts first one of my legs, then the other, wrapping them securely around his waist.

"Des—" I say, now nervous. Just what exactly does he have in mind?

He begins to walk, holding me to him. "Let's try listening to instructions all over again: this time, when I give them to you, you're going to follow them."

I narrow my eyes at him. "What are you planning?"

He flashes me a dark, smoldering look. "You'll see soon enough, cherub."

He heads up the hallway and down another, all the while, I'm trapped in his arms. I don't bother trying to squirm away, mostly because I know he wants me to and because last time I tried to get out of this position, he used his magic on me.

So I let him carry me. I'm no featherweight. If he wants to exhaust himself lugging me around, he can be my guest.

Eventually he kicks open a set of double doors leading out to yet another one of the palace's many balconies.

Cool evening air blows in at my back, ruffling my feathers and stirring my hair. "If you toss me off the balcony…" I warn.

He doesn't wait for me to finish my threat. One moment he's on solid ground, the next, the two of us are spiraling into the air, me still in his arms.

All right, so Des wasn't planning on tossing me from a balcony… He's planning on dropping me from the sky.

Only, he doesn't let me go.

I stare him in the eye, the two of us locked together. "What now?" I ask.

His eyes glitter.

That's about the time I feel my clothes loosen, just as they did in Lephys.

What in the…?

My fae attire essentially melts off my body. I let out a squeak, trying to grab at the remnants of my clothes. It's no use; they slip through my fingers like grains of sand.

Good thing I already stowed away my daggers; otherwise, Des's little gifts would be long gone.

I glance below us, watching the shimmering fabric fall to Somnia. Already, we're too high to see where it lands.

The night air caresses my bare skin. It feels like skinny-dipping, the sensation strange and new and not altogether unpleasant. I'd be embarrassed over the exposure, except we're too high in the sky and the night is too dark for anyone to see us.

I turn back to Des, my flesh bare. Like me, his clothes have long since peeled away. I run a hand over his biceps, my thumb tracing one of his war cuffs.

We slip through a layer of wispy clouds, the mist prickling my flesh. It's the clouds that remind me of the first time I flew. Des had pointed out the couples hidden in the darkness, each caught in a lover's embrace.

I suck in a breath, realizing what Des means to do. What *we* mean to do.

Of course, the King of the Night, the man who rules over sex and sleep, violence and chaos, means to take me up here, where the stars and the great vastness of the universe are our audience.

"I told you I had many, many demands," he says softly, his words harkening back to what he told me when he first reentered my life. Back then, his demands had made me nervous, but now, as he gazes at me with those expressive eyes, it's clear his *demands* aren't anything but the wishes of a man who was kept away from his love for too long.

As the two of us hover in the heavens, our hair rustling in the gentle breeze, I can feel Des's magic settling around us. It's not pushy or uncomfortable like it sometimes can be. Rather, I feel as though I'm bathing in his essence—shadows and moonbeams.

Slowly, his hands slide down my back. They feel like a sculptor's touch, molding me into some pleasing form. They slip under the backs of my thighs.

My hands are clasped loosely around Des's neck, and I play with the soft ends of his hair.

"I thought you wanted me to follow your instructions," I say, my breath a whisper.

He lifts my body a few inches, and then slides me onto him. My lips part as I stare at him, my skin beginning to glow. I look like just another star in the sky as our flesh meets.

"I do," he says, nuzzling my cheek, "but I find I prefer you a bit untamed too."

With that, the two of us begin to move, our bodies quickly turning feverish. And we spend the night as two more lovers hidden among the clouds.

CHAPTER 19

The next day, Des and I are back out in the training yard: me a little bedraggled from my evening, Des looking just as sharp as always.

If I thought that after the closeness of last night, the Bargainer would go easy on me today, then I thought wrong.

I clutch my brand-spanking-new daggers, feeling every inch the amateur as Des comes at me.

"Block—*block*," he barks as he begins his attack.

My arms come up belatedly, barely holding him back.

"My flank is open, Callie," he says.

"How am I—?"

He spins out of my grip, and then I feel the press of his blade against my neck.

"How many times have I killed you today?" he asks, his breath warm against my cheek.

"Twenty-three." He's been making me count. Like I don't already feel supremely shitty about my combat skills.

He clicks his tongue. "You can do better."

I don't *want* to do better. I want to go back inside the palace, find the royal kitchens, pillage their pastries, and then take a nice long nap.

But wishes, I've decided, are little bastards that always bite you in the ass—at least if you have them around the Bargainer.

Des swipes out, knocking one of my blades from my grip, the metal clattering against the ground.

Okay, seriously, my suckiness is starting to piss me off.

"Your blade is an extension of your arm," Des says, beginning to circle me. "You wouldn't let someone cut off your hand—don't let someone divest you of your weapon."

I lunge for my fallen dagger, just barely missing another swipe of my mate's weapon as I roll out of the way.

"Finally, my siren shows potential."

"What I would *give* for you to be quiet," I mutter. Much as I love his voice, there's something particularly unpleasant about receiving instruction from someone you're sleeping with.

"You would give me something?" Des says, looking intrigued. "Cherub, I'm *always* open to that sort of bargain."

Beyond Des, Malaki and Temper exit the palace, heading right for our training grounds. Never have I been so happy to see them. Surely this will get me out of training for the day.

The tip of Des's blade is suddenly poking my breastbone, his silver eyes intense. "Don't take your eyes off your enemy for a second."

"Temper and Malaki are here," I say, nodding to them.

"Good," he says, not turning from me. "Perhaps you can impress them with your skill."

"We're not stopping?" Temper's presence is a whole

lot less welcome. I don't want everyone and their mother watching my ass get handed to me. I sort of have a reputation to maintain. There are also the tatters of my dignity to consider. I'd like to keep those.

Over Des's shoulder, I can just make out my friend giving Malaki fuck-me looks.

Des swipes my feet out from under me. I land on my hip, my weapons clattering out of my hands.

"Concentrate," he growls.

You'd think for a dude who got repeatedly laid last night, he'd be in a slightly better mood.

I scramble for my daggers just as he kicks one out of the way. *Screw this. Seriously.*

"Callie!" Temper calls out, "I know you can give him better than that!"

I throw her a nasty look, but it's a wasted one. She's already moved on, leaning into Malaki and whispering something to him that makes him laugh. I'm pretty sure it's at my expense too.

The Bargainer swats my butt with his weapon, making me instantly livid. "If you don't like the way I talk to you, then show me."

I grab my remaining dagger and lash out, the tip of my blade cutting through the leather covering Des's calves. He pauses, his eyes flicking to the tear in his protective gear. A smile breaks out along his face.

"Well done!" he says, sliding his weapon back into its sheath. "I'll make a warrior out of you yet." He reaches for my hand. "Training's officially over for the day."

I give his hand a skeptical look before taking it, half thinking this is another trick. But it isn't. Apparently, I get to finish training early if I make progress. Score.

"Aww, you guys are done already?" Temper asks, sauntering over with Malaki.

As if she even cares about me ending practice. She's just bummed her impromptu date with the Lord of Dreams is coming to a swift end.

"Don't look so sad, Temperance," Des says. "I have plans for both of you."

Both of us?

I flash him a quizzical look, my belly squeezing uncomfortably.

"You two will spend the day getting ready for Solstice."

———

"I hate this," Temper says to me.

The two of us are locked away in the royal dressmaker's shop with a series of fairies taking our measurements and holding swatches of cloth up to our faces. The air is thick with the scent of sandalwood and burning oil. We've already gotten our nails (or, in my case, claws) filed and our hair trimmed.

The fairy measuring Temper sniffs.

I only barely manage to contain my smile at her words.

"I thought you liked getting primped?" I say. Lord knows Temper's always going on about improvements I could be making to my own wardrobe.

"Yeah, I like it when I do it myself. It only takes five minutes, and most importantly, I don't have to strip down to my lacy bits while some random fairy paws at me." Temper yelps as said random fairy sticks her with a pin; then my friend glares pointedly at the woman.

"Perhaps if you stopped moving…" the fairy says.

"I've been holding still for an hour. I'm not a statue."

Another fairy intercedes. "My lady, we are terribly sorry for the inconvenience. We're working as fast as we can."

The tailor working on me pats my arm. "All finished," he whispers, letting me step off the pedestal I've been standing on.

"Wait, you're done?" Temper looks aghast. "How is that fair? I'm not even an important part of this Solstice thing."

"Don't worry, Temper," I say, heading over to our things. "The tailors will be finished soon enough, and I'll be right here in the meantime."

"Actually, my lady," the tailor interrupts, "the king has asked that you join him once you're finished."

Oh. Well, then.

"Callie—" Temper begins, a desperate look in her eye.

I shrug, gathering my things. "Sorry, Temper. King's orders," I say. "I can't disobey them." I head for the door.

"You and I both know he can—" The door closes on the last of her words as I slip out of the dressmaker's shop.

Do I feel bad running out on Temper?

Not nearly as bad as I probably should. But she'll be done soon enough, and she can more than hold her own against a few fae dressmakers.

Outside, a soldier waits for me. "My lady." He bows. "I'm here to escort you to the king."

I nearly roll my eyes. Of all the pomp.

The two of us wind our way through the palace grounds, heading to one of the towers. The soldier stops at an ornately carved wooden door braced with bronze fittings. He knocks twice, then, bowing again to me, moves into formation against the hallway wall.

Silently, the door swings open, and I step inside. It's another library—a tower library, judging by the curving walls of books. Several tables take up the center of the room, and on one is a stack of tomes, a partially painted canvas, an abandoned set of paints, and a paintbrush.

But no Night King.

I head over to the table, my footfalls echoing throughout the room. Curious, I pick up the canvas. At first, all I make out is the curve of a waist, the indent of a belly button, and the beginnings of a dusky nipple. But then I notice the forearm lying languorously near the corner of the painting, distinct for its rows and rows of golden scales.

I nearly drop the painting.

This is me. *Naked*. Sure, it doesn't show my face, but it doesn't need to. There's only one person I know of who has scales on their forearm—me.

This is so obviously Des's doing.

I take in the painting again, and oh my God, there's my nipple! My *nipple*. He'd been in the midst of painting it when he was called away from his work.

And the fiend isn't even here for me to confront him.

My eyes move to the pots of paints. On a whim, I grab the paintbrush and dip it into a pot containing black paint. Once I've coated the brush, I systematically black out the painting.

Do I feel guilty about ruining good art?

Not as guilty as I feel about walking out on Temper— which is to say, not guilty at all.

After I finish, I set the wet canvas aside, my hands now covered in smudges of black paint.

Satisfied at my payback, I move on from the canvas to the stack of books. A note sits on the stack.

Callypso,

In case you wanted a little extra knowledge on Solstice.

—Jerome

It takes me a moment to place the name, but finally I do. Jerome was the librarian I met a week ago.

Intrigued by the books he pulled for me, I take the first one from the stack and set it on the table. After pulling up a chair, I open the cover.

Before I can look at the title page or the table of contents, the pages flip themselves then settle on a chapter titled "Solstice."

My eyes skim the first page, and then the next...and the next. I lose myself in the words, my curiosity about the festival only growing the more I absorb.

From what this chapter says, Solstice is a gathering of all four major kingdoms—Night, Day, Flora, and Fauna—which occurs on the week surrounding the longest day of the year. It's a renewal celebration hosted in the Kingdom of Flora, and its whole purpose is to celebrate the regeneration of life. Bitter rivalries and old enmities are set aside during this week so the four main kingdoms can meet, discuss issues of the realms, and revel together.

Apparently, from a side note I found in one of the books, not attending Solstice is a pretty big taboo, hence why Malaki hounded Des so doggedly to attend.

As soon as I finish the chapter, the book snaps shut.

All riiight.

I grab the next book in the pile, this one on the Kingdom of Flora. Like the last book, this one flips to a specific page.

On it is a painting of a beautiful woman with curling flame-red hair and green eyes, vines of bloodred poppies coiling up her arm.

"Mara Verdana," the description beneath reads, "Queen of Flora, and her consort-king, the Green Man."

My eyes flick back to the image, surprise coating my features. There's a second person in the photo?

But now that I look, there is—he just happens to blend with the foliage in the background. Off to the Flora Queen's side is literally a green man, his skin a soft shade of the color, his hair and beard a darker, wilder hue. His eyes sparkle with mischief.

I stare at the image for a long time. Mara Verdana is all bright, blooming colors, like a flower in its prime, and the Green Man is the thicket of shrubs and the down of wild grass; he's all the bits of plants that go overlooked and underappreciated.

These are the rulers who'll host Solstice. The same ones who enslave humans.

The thought unsettles me greatly, particularly because these two rulers don't *look* evil or unjust. Just like my stepfather didn't seem like a man who'd abuse his daughter.

I push the book away.

Where is Des?

I've been waiting for nearly half an hour, and he still hasn't shown up. Absently, I wind my bracelet 'round and 'round my wrist. My eyes move to the beads as a thought comes to me.

I don't need to wait for him if I don't want to. He has a calling card that's particularly effective.

"Bargainer," I call out to the empty room, "I would like to make—"

"Love?" Des's voice is like smooth scotch, his breath fanning against my cheek.

I look over my shoulder at him. His body is a wall of very appealing muscle, blocking out the rows of books behind us.

He leans a heavy arm against my desk, his eyes dipping to my mouth. "Because if that's what you wish, cherub, I'd be happy to arrange that."

He looks so thrilled to see me, his eyes twinkling. I almost feel bad for being impatient.

"Why did you bring me here?" I ask, glancing around the room.

"I assumed you'd want to know more about Solstice."

I stare at him a beat longer. "It's sometimes uncanny how well you know me."

"I *am* the Lord of Secrets."

His eyes flick to the remaining stack of books. "Oh, you haven't even gotten to the books with the really juicy information," he notes.

His eyes move from the stack to his now blacked-out canvas.

He sucks in a breath. "You naughty, naughty thing," he says, his lips curving up. He flicks his fingers, beckoning the canvas forward. Then he snatches it from midair, studying the tarnished image. "Trying your hand at painting?" he asks, raising an eyebrow.

"You were painting *me*," I accuse.

Had I hoped to make him feel guilty? If so, I'm barking up the wrong tree.

He sets the painting down. "Censorship, you know, is the death of creativity."

"I don't care."

Des levels his face close to mine. "Oh, but if your moans

155

last night were anything to go by, then I think you do care about creativity—in all its forms."

I flush and then glance at the pile of books again. "When are we leaving for Solstice?" I ask.

"Tomorrow."

I nearly fall out of my seat. "*Tomorrow?*"

Now Malaki's insistence really makes sense. Talk about coming down to the wire with a decision.

Des pulls up a chair next to me before sliding into it and kicking his heels up on the table. He folds his arms over his chest, his war bands catching the light. "If you had read the books, you wouldn't be so surprised."

"I don't even know what *day* it is," I say. It's not like the Night Kingdom has calendars posted throughout the palace. "Or, for that matter," I continue, "how many days are in an Otherworld year."

"The exact same number as yours."

I let out an exasperated sigh. "That's not the point."

"It's June seventeenth," Des says.

"That's also not the point."

He gives me an indulgent look. At the flick of his wrist, one of the books slides off the stack before drifting through the air and settling into Des's waiting hands.

I look at him quizzically. "What are you doing?"

"Story time, cherub," he says. "You want answers, and I'm feeling particularly indulgent, so for today, I'll spoon-feed them into that sinful little mouth of yours."

I purse my lips, which only causes Des to grab my jaw and kiss me before returning his attention to the book.

He opens the first cover, and the pages begin to rapidly flip. "Ah, yes," he says when the pages settle. "A Brief History of the Four Kingdoms," he reads.

He narrates the chapter to me, his voice taking on a cockney accent just for the hell of it as he explains the old rivalries between Flora and Fauna, Night and Day. I stare at him, utterly mesmerized by his voice and charisma.

"Each fights for the Borderland they believe is theirs, even though the Great Mother and Father spoke of the earth, sea, and sky belonging to all fae creatures. Greed was seeded at the dawn of time, and with the cycle of the seasons, it has grown in fairy hearts."

What should've been a dull read is enlivened by Des's narration. One by one, he moves through the remaining books, taking on various accents as he does so—sometimes it's an Irish or Russian accent, other times it's German or French, and once (to my utter delight) he impersonates a Valley girl.

Des was right: some of the later books he reads don't need fanciful narration at all; they are quite a bit more engaging than the earlier reads.

From these later tomes, I learn the Day King's father had a harem full of men, that it was considered a miracle that he fathered Janus, the current King of Day, and his now deceased twin brother, Julios.

And that Mara Verdana, Queen of Flora, wasn't heir apparent—her older sister, Thalia, was. However, before she ascended to the throne, Thalia fell in love with a traveling enchanter posing as a minstrel. He bewitched Thalia into believing the two were mates, and she gladly gave him most of her power. It nearly tore the kingdom apart. Eventually, the enchanter was put to death, and Thalia, in her heartache, fell on her own sword.

I stiffen when the text moves on to tales from the Kingdom of Fauna and, more specifically, Karnon.

Apparently, according to the author of the text, he was a "softhearted" youth.

"Fear stirred in the kingdom's breast. Kind souls make for poor rulers, especially in a realm of beasts," Des reads.

Absently, my thumb moves over the scales of my forearms.

"But Karnon grew to be both soft and strong, the way a bear might be tender with her young but vicious to outsiders. Under his rule, he brought true harmony to a realm that had waged many civil wars throughout the long centuries."

Des closes the book. My eyes flick between it and my mate. "Wait, that's it?" I say. "That's all it says about him? Nothing about his madness?"

"His madness is too recent to be included in such an old book."

"How could they say he was a gentle ruler?" I ask. He raped and imprisoned women.

"Callie," Des says softly, "you and I both know monsters aren't born, they're nurtured into existence."

I know that's true, but right now there's a bitter taste at the back of my throat. "History should remember him how he was." I pick at one of my scales, the book's words getting under my skin.

"It will."

The heat of my anger dies down a little at Des's words, but I can't get the image of Karnon's mad eyes out of my head. *Pretty, pretty bird*, his voice echoes in my memory.

Now that I think about him, the mystery I'm supposed to be solving comes bubbling back up.

Karnon *isn't* solely to blame; there's someone else out there doing who knows what to the missing men. And as for the King of Fauna, what of him and his blackened heart? Where did his death get anyone?

The women still slept, and their children still terrorized other fairies. Whatever dark spell Karnon cast, his death didn't break it.

"Death undoes enchantments?" I ask Des.

He searches my face, probably trying to figure out just where my mind is. Only seconds ago I might as well have been carrying a torch and a pitchfork.

"It does," he finally says.

"Karnon's death hasn't undone the enchantment."

"It hasn't," he agrees.

We're back to where we were over a week ago, when I stared into those casket children's eyes and saw no evidence of Karnon's paternity in them.

Only now, knowing there's more than one perpetrator out there, and hearing about the Fauna King's gentle disposition...

What if Karnon *wasn't* behind the dark spell?

Just the thought of lifting any blame from Karnon's shoulders has me nauseous. But I push past all my hatred and my twisted memories of being a captive, and I try to see it through a clearer lens.

When I visited the Fauna King, there seemed to always be two Karnons: one who was wild and strangely gentle and another who was calculating and sinister. The former liked to pet my skin and whisper promises about wings and scales; the latter would force dark magic down my throat. Karnon could slip from one version of himself to the other in an instant, like putting on or taking off a coat.

I was disturbed by the wild Karnon, the oddly tender ruler who was still very much insane, but I feared the sinister Karnon—he was both cruel *and* lucid.

I'd always assumed these sides of him were two aspects

of the same man, but perhaps…perhaps there was something more going on there. Could it be possible Karnon wasn't two different personalities residing within the same flesh but two different beings taking up space within one body? Maybe Des killed the primal, wild man who gave me scales and claws but not the man who was trying to subdue me with his dark magic…

I can barely follow my own thoughts, mostly because the idea of two different beings residing in one body is so impossible to me.

But *impossible* is not a term fairies subscribe to.

I stare down at my scales and claws. Hell, these features should be impossible. People don't just transform the way I did.

The longer I stare at my animalistic features, the more another traitorous thought bubbles its way up. Scales, claws, and wings are *sirenic* features. Even when I hated them, my siren hadn't. She'd felt more powerful than ever. And the man who brought these features out in me wasn't the king trying to suck me under with his magic—he was the one who'd pet my skin and mutter nonsense about my latent wings.

My breathing slows.

"What is it?" Des asks, reading my expression.

I look up at him. "What if…what if Karnon hadn't been trying to punish me that day in his throne room? What if"—I can't believe I'm about to say this—"he was trying to save me?"

It's a wild thought.

Des leans forward, kicking his feet off the table to brace his forearms on his thighs. "Explain," he commands.

"I was about to die that day. I could sense it." The whole

day is rearranging itself to fit this new possibility. "Karnon transformed me, and it did nearly kill me—but it also brought you to him.

"What if he knew what he was doing? What if he knew something was wrong with him? What if he deliberately baited you?"

Des's eyes narrow. "I'm not following."

I run my hands through my hair. My thoughts are all jumbled. "I always thought there were two versions of Karnon, but what if there weren't two versions of him—what if there was a completely separate entity inside of him?"

Okay, saying that out loud sounds way more ludicrous than it did in my head.

Des reels back.

Seconds tick by. He's not saying anything, and I'm beginning to think my theory is Grade A crap.

"You think this is why the spell hasn't lifted?" he asks. "Something or someone else was living inside Karnon, and it escaped his death?"

When he puts it like that...

I lift a shoulder, feeling like a teenager all over again. I don't know jack about fae magic and its limits.

Hesitantly, Des nods his head, his brows furrowed. "It's possible."

I don't know whether I'm more relieved or frightened by his agreement. Because on the one hand, I'm happy he doesn't think I sound crazy, but on the other hand...if what I suggested is true, then there's some malevolent fae creature that can body hop...and it's still out there.

Still hunting, still killing, still *living*.

CHAPTER 20

The next day, the palace is in a flurry of activity. Fairies throughout the royal grounds seem to be cleaning, primping, and packing—all, I assume, in honor of Solstice.

I head down the hall, toward Temper's suite. Before I can get there, she pokes her head out, taking in the fairies rushing down the halls.

"What the hell is going on?" she says. She's still wearing yesterday's makeup, and she looks like she got very little sleep.

I scrutinize her a bit more. "What were you up to last night?"

"You mean after you abandoned me to the wolves?" she accuses.

I roll my eyes. If anyone's a wolf, it's Temper. "Did you kill anyone at the dressmaker's shop?" I ask.

"No, but I gave that nasty fairy measuring me split ends and dandruff."

Take it from Temper on how to punish with subtlety.

Back in high school, she had a whole notebook of crafty little hex ideas.

"Temper, she was just doing her job."

She makes an indignant sound. "She was sticking me like I was a pincushion! On purpose! Anyway..." She eyes me again. "What's going on?" Her gaze drifts back to the bustling hallway.

"Solstice," I explain.

"What about it?" She stifles a yawn.

"It begins today."

"*What?*"

"We're leaving in, uh..." I reach for my phone before I remember we're in the freaking Otherworld, where electronics are nonexistent. If I want to rattle off the time, I'm going to have to learn to chart the stars.

Ugh.

"We're leaving soon."

"How soon is soon?" she asks.

I shrug. "I'm heading off to get changed."

"Changed? Into what?" Temper is glancing around the hall like clothes will materialize out of thin air.

"A flour sack—the outfits tailored for us, what do you think?" I edge away. "I got to go. Just get yourself ready and meet me in the courtyard."

She lets out a frustrated growl, then closes her door.

I head back to Des's rooms, feeling oddly nervous about the week ahead. From everything I learned about Solstice, there'll be balls and meetings and schmoozing, none of which appeals to me. And then there's the fact I'll have to rub elbows with fairies who believe humans are nothing more than forced labor.

This is going to be super-duper fun.

When I slip back inside Des's chambers, there's a package waiting for me on the bed, my name scrawled across it in looping script. After hesitating just a hairbreadth away, I flip the lid off. Resting inside the box is a gown unlike anything I've seen before. I'm not especially girly, but I have a healthy appreciation for nice clothing, and this is so much more than nice.

The pale material glows—*glows*—a soft blue color. The lacy neckline plunges in a deep V. I run my fingers over the material, and it's both incredibly soft and quite delicate. Nestled next to the dress are two coiled flowering vines, which also give off the same pale glow as the dress. The fittings Temper and I stood through—they hadn't been for *this* unearthly gown.

Des comes out of the bathroom then, fiddling with his own outfit, which is made of the same luminous material as mine.

He's a far cry from the rough-edged Bargainer I'm used to seeing, clad now in fitted pants, knee-high boots, and a shirt that lovingly molds itself to his wide shoulders and trim waist. Topping it all off is his hammered bronze circlet.

Before I laid eyes on him, I would've assumed such attire would make Des look less dangerous, but instead, it serves to sharpen the slant of his eyes and the painfully beautiful cut of his jaw and cheekbones.

Here is the monster all those fairy tales warned me of. A man too beautiful to be real, one who rides out on dark nights to snatch up wayward maidens.

"Do you like it?" he asks.

I nod at him, thinking he's referring to himself, until I realize he's gesturing to the package.

I drag my attention back to the dress, noticing the corner of his mouth twitch.

"It's…breathtaking," I say, staring down at my own outfit. And I mean it. I rub the luminescent cloth between my fingers. "What is it?"

"Spun moonlight," Des says, looking pleased by my reaction.

"Spun *moonlight*?" I repeat. I'm trying to wrap my mind around the fact that, in the Otherworld, this is perfectly normal. "And I get to wear this?"

His lips twitch again. "That is the idea, cherub." He steps in close and strokes away the hair from my face. "I've waited years to see you dressed as the queens of my world are dressed," he says.

I touch his shirt. "Sometimes, I forget you're a fairy," I admit.

It's ridiculous to think this happens to me; there's nothing about Des that's particularly humanlike, but he has a disarming nature about him that makes me forget. It's only now, when I see him dressed in his fae attire, that I remember.

"I know," he says softly.

There's so much in those two words that he leaves unspoken. Not for the first time, I wish he'd spill more of his secrets.

I pull away from him. "Will you help me put the dress on?" Now that I have wings, clothes are a struggle.

His hands slide down my back. In response, the clothes I currently wear slide off my body, leaving me in just a skimpy pair of panties. Of all Des's magic tricks, I'm beginning to think this one is his favorite.

My dress lifts from the box to drift above me. All at once it slips downward, the material cascading over my body like water. I don't even need to lift my arms; it settles seamlessly onto me.

Des's hands smooth over the lacy material that covers my arms.

"Tell me a secret," I say softly.

I hear the smile in Des's voice when he says, "Greedy thing. I can see you won't be pleased until you know all my secrets."

I grin a little, mostly because what he says is true. I want to share every secret of his, simply because they're part of him.

His hands slip down my arms. "Fine, here's one for my demanding mate: normally, you'd have a retinue of ladies to dress and bathe you."

"How is that a secret?" I ask, turning to face him.

"I eliminated that tradition the moment you came to my kingdom so I could tend to you myself."

Wicked man. Not that I'm complaining.

But now that I think about it...

I raise my eyebrows and look over my shoulder. "You would *bathe* me?"

Des's silver eyes deepen. The answer is written all over his face. "Would you like a bath?"

Jesus, I swear this room just got five degrees hotter.

I clear my throat. "Rain check."

"It's a *deal.*"

A shiver runs down my back. I forget this man will make binding agreements out of common language.

Des's gaze lingers over me for another second. Then he shakes his head, takes my hand, and leads me out of his chambers. I stare down at my outfit as I follow him through his palace, Malaki and more guards joining us on the way. The tight, lacy bodice flows into a wispy floor-length skirt that trails behind me as we walk.

Those flowering luminescent vines that came with the dress now wrap up my wrists and forearms, becoming some strange cross between gloves and jewelry. The flowers blooming from them are the same ones I've seen across Somnia. I run a finger over the delicate petals. They feel real. More impossible fae magic at work.

We head out of the castle and across the extensive gardens, each one lit up by floating fairy lights and those glass-encased sparklers.

"Callie, there's something I need of you," Des says next to me.

"It's going to cost you," I respond without missing a beat.

He walked himself right into that one.

His eyes brighten. "You saucy thing. You've clearly learned my tricks." He doesn't look at all upset by this. "A bargain it is."

"What do you want me to do?" I ask.

Des looks ahead of us, and I follow his gaze. Waiting in a neat, orderly line that winds through the palace grounds are rows of foot soldiers and mounted horses. The soldiers all wear black uniforms embroidered with the same luminous thread my entire dress is made from.

Behind them, sitting astride the horses, are all sorts of fairies, from royal guards, to political aides, to what must be some of the kingdom's nobility. Some of them hold instruments, while others carry lanterns from tall poles, and still others prop up banners with the image of a crescent moon, which I suspect is the royal crest.

"I want you to let your siren out and keep her out until after you're introduced to Mara, the Queen of Flora," Des says, drawing my attention away from the sight in front of us.

His request immediately puts me on edge. "I can't control her."

"You don't need to control her, cherub. You are the

Night King's mate. We represent all deeds better done in the dark."

The way he says that has my stomach tightening.

All right, so the dude's giving me free rein to let my siren out. I stare at all the fae men and women ahead of us, thankful for once that my glamour can't control other fairies. Because if it could, my siren would consider it open season.

"I'll agree to it on one condition," I say.

Des smirks, seeming to thoroughly enjoy the bargain I'm striking. "What do you want? You already have my balls—"

"Lift my sobriety."

That wipes the amusement clean off his face. "No."

"Then forget about the siren," I say with false bravado.

Des stops to pull me in close. "Careful, little mate, how you play your hand." He strokes my spine. "Tempting as your bargain is, you're forgetting one simple truth."

"And what's that?"

"I could simply coax your siren out," he says, his voice dipping low.

If the King of the Night decides to seduce me, there's not a whole lot that can stop my body from giving in to him. Being a siren, I'm not hardwired to resist sexual overtures, especially not when they come from my mate.

"You'd regret it," I say, my voice equally low.

He eyes me, weighing my words. "Fine," he finally says, a fair bit of amusement returning to his eyes. "I agree to your terms. You can drink alcohol—for now." He gives me a quick kiss on the lips, and as he does so, I feel a thread of his magic lift from me.

I can drink again. Yasss.

He pulls away from my lips, his eyelids heavy as he gazes at my mouth. "Your turn, cherub," he says.

It doesn't take much for me to draw on my own magic. My skin glows as I feel her take over. I roll my shoulders a bit, my gaze moving from Des to the fairies ahead of us.

Those who catch sight of me appear captivated. It's a different look than the one humans wear; human eyes always appear a little glazed, their minds willing to be bent. These fae don't look as though they're about to be dragged under by my glamour; they just seem fascinated by my appearance.

I relax further, letting the siren loose in a way I rarely did on earth. I begin walking again, an extra sway to my hips, my entire body now glowing. A sinful smile tugs at the corners of my mouth.

Tonight is going to be *fun*.

So many people wait for us—far more than I assumed were coming. I feel their mounting gazes on me as our group joins theirs. My claws sharpen, and my wings perk up a little.

Des's hand falls to my back, and now my attention goes to him, my eyelids lowering. If there is one person who, even now, has power over *me*, it's him.

His white hair is swept away from his face, the color of it nearly matching his outfit. It looks as though someone plucked the moon from the sky, made it into a man, and then gave him to me. All I want to do is fill myself with him. I *will* fill myself with him.

He takes notice of my interest. "Give me just this evening, Callie. Then everything you want, I will give you," he promises.

"Everything I want?" My eyes move to his mouth, and I click my tongue. "You know better than to make such an open-ended deal."

His eyes alight. "I'm eager to see what you'll do with it."

We're interrupted by the clomping of hooves. A soldier

holds the reins of two sleek black steeds. "Your mounts," he announces.

"We're riding *horses*?" I say.

The horse closest to me bumps its head into my shoulder, snuffling my hair.

"Do you have an objection?" Des asks.

I look at the beast again, feeling the siren beginning to fade away. Apparently, no sex and no violence means no service.

It's an unusual task, trying to keep her visible; I'm so used to repressing her whenever I can. I wrestle with my strange power, finally managing to wrangle her.

"It's fine," I say.

With that, Des grabs my waist and helps me mount my steed. I wait for it to nervously nicker, but it never happens. Either these are exceptionally well-trained horses, or Otherworld steeds are made of sturdier stuff.

Next to me, Des smoothly swings himself onto his own mount, and the rest of Desmond's closest men do so as well.

Our horses trot back into line, moving into some sort of formation. I glance behind me, catching sight of Temper astride another horse. The dress she wears is a deep burgundy color.

Looks like she found one of her new outfits.

Malaki moves over to her on his own steed, and the look he gives her...good God, he's already smitten.

Someone whistles, and the musicians in our procession begin playing their instruments, the sound soft and ethereal.

I turn back around as we move, the line of soldiers and mounted steeds heading around the castle and toward the palace's front gates. I find I don't need to steer my horse; it moves as one with the group.

Ahead of us, the gates open, and then there are Somnia's residents, cheering for us as we pass them by.

Des leans over his horse to speak to me. "Fairies have begun exposing their wings," he says, nodding to the crowd.

I follow his gaze. He's right. Many of them do have their wings out, their thin membranes glittering under lamplight.

"Why are they all out?" I ask. Fairies usually only bare them when their emotions run high.

"Because ours are," he says.

Indeed, Des, who once studiously hid his wings from me, now proudly bares them. And I have no choice but to show off mine.

"Why would they imitate us?" I ask.

"Because we're royalty."

"*You're* royalty," I correct. "I'm not."

Des gives me an unreadable look then nods distractedly.

The procession winds through the city streets, and just when I think our pretty line of horses and soldiers intends to walk right off the edge of the island, we double back to the palace.

I'd love to dismount already, but something tells me that's not going to happen any time soon.

My glowing hands tighten on the reins as I glance at the Bargainer, who watches the crowd like a wolf among men. He's going to have to pay me steeply in sex before I consider this a fair trade—

The arrow comes out of nowhere, whistling as it bears down on me.

Des's hand shoots out and snatches it just inches away from my breast.

Holy shit.

We both stare at the flimsy bit of wood and stone that might've very well killed me.

My breath catches.

Someone tried to kill me.

My mate *saved* me.

Des's eyes flick up, tracing the trajectory of the arrow back to its source. His gaze homes in on the figure hopping down from a nearby building.

"Guard her," the Bargainer commands to the soldiers nearest to me, and then he disappears.

A split second later, I see him on a rooftop, his wings spread wide. He grabs a fae man and pulls him close, pressing a blade to his throat. It only takes a moment for me to notice the feathers growing in place of the captive's hair and the bow and quiver still strapped across his body.

A Fauna fae tried to kill me.

My wings unfurl as adrenaline belatedly surges through me.

Des spins the man so he faces the crowd. And then, in front of hundreds of his subjects, my mate drags his blade across the fairy's throat. A waterfall of blood cascades from the wound.

Fucking Methuselah, that is one way to handle your enemies.

With a booted foot, Des kicks the fairy off the building.

The crowd below parts as the dying man pinwheels through the air before landing on the ground with a sickening splat.

For several seconds, the Bargainer remains on the rooftop, his chest heaving. He sheaths his weapon then jumps into the sky, his wings fanning out around him. The crowd gasps as they watch those talon-tipped wings—dragon's wings, *demon's* wings—soar above them.

He glides over the stopped procession before landing smoothly into his saddle, his wings folding behind him.

The crowd's earlier cheers have been replaced with an ominous silence. The only one who doesn't seem affected by it is Des. He reaches for me, pulling me into a savage kiss.

Des tastes like blood and love and death. He kisses me like he's pillaging my mouth, and I don't mind one fucking bit. I kiss him back greedily, drinking in my Night King's essence.

He might be death on wings, but he saved me.

Right in the middle of our kiss, a cheer goes up through the crowd. It's a little more feral, a little less forgiving, than our audience's previous roars.

Des pulls away from my lips, his hand on my neck still holding me close. In his eyes I see a spark of fear, a dash of adoration—but most of all, I see a deep and endless well of fury. Here's the monster behind the war cuffs and pretty fabric, the monster I don't want to tame, the one I want to *unleash*.

I am the darkness, his eyes seem to say, *and you are my lovely nightmare. And no one will take this away from us.*

He blinks, and the swirling chaos in his eyes dies down. "Are you okay?"

I nod.

"Good."

He releases me, and already my body aches from the absence of his violent touch and his malevolent eyes.

Some soldiers are coming up to us, asking questions, while others are pushing the crowd back. Where the Fauna fairy fell, there's now a thick cluster of fairies fighting among themselves. Things are turning ugly, and the crowd is getting heated.

Waving away the people who come to talk to him, Des lets out a whistle, signaling for the procession to resume. Rapidly, fairies fall back into line, some mounting their steeds, others resuming their position as foot soldiers.

This time when the convoy moves, it doesn't meander. My steed begins to gallop, its shoes sparking against the stone road as it races up the streets, following the line of horses and soldiers back toward the palace.

Next to me, Des's face is set into uncompromising lines. It's not until we're through the gates that his expression relaxes—though his hands still grip his reins like he's choking the life out of them.

Eventually, our group heads toward a building I've never seen before. The circular annex is massive, its large double doors thrown open in invitation. Our procession doesn't slow as it barrels toward it.

Excitement and a thread of fear move through me. I can't see anything beyond the marble structure's shadowy entrance, but I can tell there are too many horses and too many fairies to possibly fit into the building.

No one else seems to share this concern. Not even Des, who's still brooding from where he sits next to me.

The first of the foot soldiers who head up our convoy storm through the doorway, their bodies disappearing within. Then the next row disappears, and then the next.

And then the first of the mounted guards head inside. There's thirty feet remaining between me and the door, then twenty, then ten...

Des and I pass through the double doors, our horses' hooves echoing as we enter the vaulted room. I only have time to see the air ripple like cloth ahead of us before Des reaches over and grabs my hand.

A portal, I realize. *Of course.*

Seconds later, we're dashing through it, my stomach bottoming out as my body is forced through time and space.

My horse hits the ground on the other side of the portal, not missing a single stride.

I blink several times, squinting at the bright light I'm suddenly doused in. *Sunlight.* I drink it in like it's sex or carnage, feeling my magic swell.

I close my eyes again, enjoying basking in it. I almost forgot what it felt like. When I open my eyes, my gaze goes to the endless rolling fields that stretch out in all directions, the small wildflowers that speckle them swaying in the breeze. It's only ahead of us that the hills give way to forested mountains and purple peaks.

"Welcome to the Kingdom of Flora," Des says next to me, releasing my hand. His earlier fury is completely gone.

Though we've left the danger behind us in Somnia, my horse doesn't slow. Our entire procession moves at full speed. Even the foot soldiers are running, and I can't help but think that all the wishes in the world couldn't convince me to run with a herd of galloping steeds at my back.

But maybe that's just me.

The sun begins to set as we ride, giving my skin a rosy hue and making my glowing dress dance in all sorts of colors.

After some time, the grasslands give way to woodlands, the hills growing steeper the farther we travel. Eventually, our group slows, my horse falling back from a gallop to a canter and then finally to a leisurely trot.

A few bends in the road later, I realize why.

Up until now, the trees have been big, but ahead of me, they utterly dominate the scenery, their trunks far bigger than even the giant sequoias I've seen back in California. And as

I stare, I realize these trees are *homes*. A staircase twists up one, and another two are connected by intricately wrought bridges made of branches and vines. Built around and inside these trees are elaborate fae structures. Currently, hundreds of Flora fae gather along their treetop bridges and balconies or on the edges of the footpath to watch our procession as it passes them by.

The path we follow curves, and the trees part. Ahead of us, a castle made of gray stone and covered largely in flowering vines stands amid a ring of Goliath trees.

The Flora palace.

The closer we get to it, the more fairies gather along the sides of the road. Many of their gazes are pinned to Des, the King of the Night, riding in on his dark steed, but a good number of them focus on me, their eyes taking in my glowing skin, my face, my wings.

Let them know that this is what it means to be human, the siren whispers. *I am no thing to be trifled with.*

There are no gates to divide the palace grounds from the rest of the land, but as we cross onto them, the air feels viscous for a split second, like I'm moving through honey. Whatever this magical barrier is, it's meant to keep most people out.

On the other side of it, the crowd that waits for us is noticeably wealthier. Their clothes are more ornamented, their hair more elaborately coiffed, their jewelry more intricate. Many of them touch their fingers to their foreheads as we pass, which I'm assuming is a sign of respect.

At the foot of the castle, our procession stops, and the music our group has been playing up until now fades away.

Next to me, Des vanishes from his horse, earning several gasps from the crowd of onlookers. He reappears at my horse's side.

"Time to disembark, Callie," he says. Des reaches for me, helping me off the horse. He's completely unaware of himself—his beauty, his strength, his magnetism. However, he's not oblivious of *me*. He holds me close for a beat longer than necessary, his eyes moving from my eyes to my lips.

"I'm still holding you to your promise," I say softly, my glamour making music of my words.

A secretive smile lights his face as he remembers his vow to give me everything I wanted. "I haven't forgotten."

He finally releases me, and the two of us move forward with our group once more, this time on foot, while our horses are led away. We head through huge double doors made of heavyset wood.

I try not to stare as we enter the palace, but it's hard not to. The forest seems to have made its way into the castle: The floors are covered with wild grass and dotted with spring flowers. Vines crisscross the stone walls, each strand heavy with blooms. Even the chandelier hanging over our heads is an extension of the natural world, the frame made almost entirely of what appears to be living wood and moss. The only things not alive appear to be the dripping wax candles that dot the chandelier.

We cross the entryway, and all but a few of Des's soldiers break away, lining up on either side of the door that leads deeper into the castle.

Des takes my hand. "Time for introductions," he quietly explains.

Now for the most curious part of the entire evening.

We all wear pretty masks, pretty masks that hide depraved thoughts. Mine's hidden behind glowing skin and a melodic voice. Des's lurks deep in the shadows. What will this queen and her consort-king show me?

Our now much smaller group heads through the door in front of us. On the other side of it is a throne room, this one packed with fae of all shapes and sizes. Most look like normal fairies, but then there are some who look more like plants than people, a few I'm pretty sure are hobgoblins, and one with an uncanny resemblance to a troll. All of them are attired in sumptuous outfits. Clearly, these are the most privileged of the Flora Kingdom's citizens—most privileged and probably the most fickle, their allegiance as pliant as my body under Des's touch.

The Bargainer and I walk down the aisle, our bodies still glowing—in my case partly because of the clothing and partly because of my skin. I feel the room's eyes on me, their gazes like a touch. Their curiosity, their envy, their yearning fills me.

I'm intrigued by all these alien creatures, creatures I barely understand and cannot control. They, in turn, stare back, their eyes mesmerized by my skin and face. I know I look like a strange angel, my black wings shimmering under more of those odd chandeliers.

When we reach the end of the aisle, the guards in front of us step aside, unveiling the raised dais behind them.

Leaning back on a throne made of vines and flowers is Mara Verdana, the Queen of Flora.

Her wild red hair cascades down her shoulders and chest, her eyes the same sharp green color as the plants we're surrounded by. Her skin is alabaster pale, and her mouth is just as voluptuous as the rest of her appears to be.

There are flowers in her hair and woven into her dress, and her crown is simply a wreath of them. But she is the loveliest flower of them all. I want to touch that skin of hers and see if it's as petal soft as I imagine it to be.

She watches us with narrowed eyes, a slight amused smile on her lips. She might be the lovely Queen of Flora, but just like Des, she looks to me like a panther, something beautiful and dangerous that will strike when you least expect it. For all her magnificence, she must be a deranged thing.

Next to her, in a throne noticeably smaller, is her husband, the Green Man. True to his name, he is green from head to toe. His hair is the dark hue of evergreens, and his skin the pale color of spring grass.

I expected a brawny bearded man, but compared to the Bargainer, the Green Man is more of a dandy, his face pretty without that roughened edge Des's has. Unlike the portrait I saw of him, he has no beard, his face as smooth as his body is lithe.

The siren in me finds that she has no interest in him. There's no power to coax from him and no danger to feed from. All I feel toward the man right now is...*pity*. Such a creature has all the trappings of a wild, violent thing, but next to his vibrant wife, he's docile, compliant, *defeated*.

Des and I come up right to the edge of the dais. I don't know what the fae etiquette for this situation is, so I touch my fingers to my forehead like I saw other fairies do to us.

"Queen of Flora, Green Man," Des says, inclining his head to both of them, "as always, it's a pleasure."

Mara stands, her sage-green gown swaying as she does so. Her face splits into a smile. Her happiness is like an arrow to the heart. I wonder just how many people have given up all they hold dear to bask in this woman's smile.

She spreads her arms. "Welcome, my Emperor of Evening Stars."

My emperor? My hands curl.

Mara descends the steps, her eyes not once traveling to

me. My hackles are rising. *I am not someone to be ignored*, my siren hisses.

The queen comes in close to Des and kisses him on either cheek. Behind her, the Green Man steps down from his throne, trailing after her, his amber eyes on me. Just from the way he's staring, I feel his longing. I feel *all* their longing. It hangs in the air like perfume; I am something enviable, something strange and taboo.

How many hands wish to stroke my flesh, how many faces wish to bury themselves in my hair? Mara can have her moment with Des. The King of the Night is mine, and the Flora Queen's subjects might as well be under my spell.

"Mara," Des says, "this is my mate, Callypso Lillis, one of the last sirens."

Reluctantly, Mara turns her gaze from Des to me. Genuine interest flickers in her eyes. "What a *beauty.*"

The compliment is a balm to the bloodlust thrumming beneath my skin. Beauty is one of the few powers I still wield in this foreign place. But somewhere deep inside me, the compliment sours.

Nothing defangs a woman quite like being called beautiful, my rational mind whispers.

Resting her hands on my upper arms, Mara pulls me in close and kisses each of my cheeks. Behind me, I hear her subjects suck in air, and I get the sense Mara just broke etiquette.

Because I am human…

She releases me and straightens. "Desmond is lucky to have found himself such a gem. And you are lucky to have found yourself a mate in a king."

Slippery, slippery woman. Her words are not quite an insult, but they're phrased so that they toe that line.

I give her a slow smile. "You are too kind." This is the first time I've spoken directly to her, and the room goes quiet as they listen to my harmonic voice.

Mara waves over some of her people. "Please show the king and his consort to their rooms," she orders them, not bothering to let the Green Man greet us. To me and Des, she says, "The feast begins in an hour in the Sacred Gardens. I look forward to seeing you both there."

CHAPTER 21

The two of us stand inside our guest suite, finally alone.
Nearly every surface around us is covered with flowering plants. They grow from pots, they wreath the walls, and they hang from the ceilings. The smell of them is almost too powerful.

The suite itself is alive, situated inside one of the colossal trees that ring the castle. Above and below us are more rooms, where Temper, Malaki, and the rest of our group are staying.

My skin dims as I force the siren back to her watery depths before locking her away. I rub my arms, remembering the siren's egotistical, screwed-up thoughts.

Des raises an eyebrow. "I still owe her," he says.

And my siren still plans on pillaging the promised sexual favors from him. "She'll be back to collect from you at some point." I run my hands through my hair, reclaiming my body. "Why did you want the siren out?"

"Fairies are always aware of power dynamics," Des says,

folding his arms as he leans against a side table. "I wanted Mara to meet you at your wickedest."

And who better to pit her against than my siren?

I let out a shaky breath. We're not even an hour into the visit and already I'm being sized up.

This is my welcome to Solstice. Let the festivities begin.

By the time we make it to the Sacred Gardens, the sky is dark, and I feel more like myself.

"Sacred Gardens," I murmur as we walk under a flowering trellis and enter the wooded clearing. "That sounds like something teenage me would call my vagina."

Next to me, Des smirks. "Undoubtedly, cherub." His eyes turn a little sad, and I wonder if, like me, he's thinking about all the time we missed together between then and now.

As soon as we enter the garden, which isn't so much a garden as it is a flowering meadow surrounded by hedges and trees, the crowd's attention moves to us. A sea of strange faces stares back at me and Des, and there are only two I recognize—Temper's and Malaki's. The two must've arrived here shortly before we did.

Des leads me deeper into the Sacred Garden. The area is lit by dancing fairy lights and several bonfires. Out here it smells like jasmine and smoke, and as the fire hisses and burns, the scent drifts into the star-filled sky above.

Des leans into me, his breath tickling my ear. "It would behoove you to know—"

"Did you just say 'behoove'?" I interrupt him. "How old are you, eight hundred?"

"—that as King of the Night," he continues without

183

missing a beat, "I'm expected to help lead this evening's festivities, and as my mate, you're expected to be at my side."

"Because I have so many other places to be," I say. I catch sight of a giant urn of fairy wine. Stop numero uno once the party begins.

Des's eyes brighten, his lips curving into a pleased smile. "Word of warning, cherub: sass is a turn-on, so if you expect me to keep my hands off you and your precious beads, you might want to work on being pleasant."

I raise an eyebrow. "If you think I'm going to be some docile, agreeable girlfriend, you're—"

Before I can finish, an invisible hand pushes me forward into Des's arms. He still has that smug-ass smile on his face. "*Mate* is the correct term," he says, his voice pitched seductively low. "I'm not your"—he makes a face—"*boyfriend*. I'm neither a boy nor particularly friendly." He ends his little speech by kissing me on the nose.

I realize the mistake I made only once Des's lingering hands finally release me. He baited me *deliberately*, knowing I'd mouth off to him and he'd get his opening to pull me close.

Wily man.

I glance around us. The spit of the flames and the glow of the flickering lights play with my vision. Now fairies are flashing us sweet smiles; now they're leering at us suggestively.

The whole thing is discomfiting, like Des and I are some drama unfolding purely for their pleasure.

But just as soon as I notice the unnatural attention, it gets diverted. The crowd goes quiet, and from the darkness emerges Mara, the Green Man on her arm. The train of her dress drags behind her, leaving a trail of flower petals in its wake.

Following the Queen and King of Fauna is a group of

beautiful men, each dressed in a deep green tailcoat and breeches, and behind them are a set of musicians carrying harps and lyres, fiddles and flutes.

Mara breaks away from the fairies around her to approach the middle of the gathering.

"Welcome, welcome all," she says, spreading her arms out wide, "to the first evening of Solstice."

All around us I spot Fauna fae, Flora fae, and Night fae. There's only one set of fairies that's noticeably absent.

"Where is the Kingdom of Day?" I whisper to Des.

"They don't usually come until the first morning light."

I make an O with my mouth like that makes some sort of sense to me, when it really doesn't.

Whatever.

"This is a week of revelry," Mara continues, "when even the Mother and the Father embrace deep in their earthen tombs. When water and wine, soil and sun, men and women all come together.

"This week, let us set aside our woes and vendettas"— some Fauna fae cut their gazes to me and Des—"and let us drink deeply, eat heartily, love fully, and revel thoroughly."

A cheer goes up from the crowd, several fairies whistling their approval.

Mara waits until her audience quiets before she continues. "Deep from the womb of the night, we were born, and deep into the night do our spirits return when the body has died and the flesh has cooled.

"And so we shall begin this week of festivities with that which came first, before the flickering of the first light: the primordial darkness. Turn your gazes to the Lord of Secrets, Master of Shadows—Desmond Flynn, the King of the Night."

She gestures across the clearing to where Des and I stand. The stares of the crowd were unnerving before, but they're nothing to the heated focus of the gathering now.

My wings hike up at the attention, but Des is as calm as ever. Placing a steadying hand on my back, he maneuvers us toward Mara and her makeshift stage.

This is not exactly what I had in mind when I agreed to stay by the Bargainer's side this evening.

Once we reach the Queen of Flora, Des's gaze sweeps around the clearing. For a moment, the only sounds are the sputtering hisses of the bonfires.

And then Des begins speaking. "There are a few things all fae are born knowing: That the night is dark, and the flesh is warm. That our lives might be long, but someday even they must eventually end. Tonight, and for all of Solstice, let us bring forth life from the darkness."

His words sound old, like this verse has been recited long enough to have a sort of magic to it.

"Only in the shadows and dark spaces do we find our truest wishes and deepest desires," he continues, the audience watching him raptly. While he speaks, his thumb draws small circles on my lower back. "Only in the night do we let go of our civility and loosen the ties that bind us during the day. Only then do we reach for soft skin. Only then do we dare to dream.

"So release your inhibitions, give in to my pull, find a willing partner, and sow yourself deep."

I glance at Des. Is he suggesting what I think he's suggesting?

The music strikes up, distracting me from my thoughts, and fairies take to the clearing, grabbing waists and hands. People begin to spin, and all that expertly coiffed hair and

186

all those tightened bodices loosen themselves as people are sucked in by the music.

Even I'm not immune to it, my hips swaying from side to side, my hand going to my own hair, which hangs in waves down my back.

"You managed to keep me waiting this year, Desmond." Mara's voice is deceptively sweet as she comes up behind us. She places a hand on his shoulder, and he turns to face her.

"I thought," she continues, "that perhaps you wouldn't show."

"Ah, how fun it is to keep you guessing," Des says, his eyes sparking with mischief.

The men who followed Mara now come up to her—one proprietary hand goes to her hip, another grips her arm. One of them leans in, whispering something into her ear, his dark eyes pinned to me as he speaks. She leans back into their touches.

The whole thing has my skin prickling uncomfortably, especially when she flashes Des a wanton look. "Enjoy your evening, my Night King," she says, and then she turns away into the group of waiting men.

They close in on her, and a moment later, I hear her peeling laughter as they begin to twirl her between them.

I swivel to Des, and we have an entire conversation with our eyes.

That was fucking weird, my gaze says.

I know. It's only going to get worse.

Des steps in close. "Would you like to—?"

Before he can finish his question, a fae noble cuts in, the man's dark brown hair plaited into an intricate series of braids that spill down his back. "Desmond, Desmond, Desmond, you're a hard man to get ahold of..." He pats my mate on the shoulder, angling him toward a waiting group of similarly dressed people.

Des resists, reaching a hand for me.

His companion pauses, noticing me for the first time. Or maybe the fairy was aware of me but didn't want to acknowledge my presence. Despite their interest in me, I feel the subtle rebuffs coming my way. No fairy seems terribly eager to elevate a mere human to a status of importance, a king's mate or not.

"You go on," I say to Des. "I'll meet up with you later."

He frowns. "Later," he reluctantly promises, looking unhappy about my decision to slip away.

I get that he wants me by his side, but it's clear his audience wants him and him alone. And I'm not all that eager to stand next to him and play docile little mate while the rest of the fairies ignore me.

I back up, sensing that the crowd gathered here is still watching me. And that's the irony of the situation. Pull me into a group, and I'll probably be ignored for the conversation, but let me roam free, and every eye will be fixed on me.

Ignoring the looks, I back away, moving into the crowd until I find the woman I'm looking for.

"Finally, I get you to myself," Temper says. "I was thinking I'd have to hex someone to get three freaking minutes with you."

"I wish you had," I mutter. At least then I'd stop feeling like the most unfortunate person at the party.

Temper arches a brow, beginning to smile. "Good to know…"

"I need something to drink." As soon as the words are out of my mouth, my eyes dart to the fairy wine.

"I have you covered." Temper takes my hand and tugs me toward the table of wine. "I thought you were taking a break from drinking?" she says over her shoulder.

Errr, I never actually admitted my sobriety was more Des's idea than my own. "Break's over."

"Praise Jesus and all the baby angels," she says. "Things are much more fun with a little bit of rum," she sings, reciting a stupid song we came up with once upon a time in Vegas.

We get to the table and ladle ourselves each a glass of wine, carrying our bounty off once we each have a full cup. The two of us stick to the edges of the clearing, not fully in the party but not fully out of it either. We're still those two misfits who met back at Peel Academy.

"Ahhh," Temper sighs after she takes her first swallow. "Now this is good wine."

I take a sip myself and—*yum*. Fairies make excellent wine. The two of us sip our drinks in silence, people watching.

"I hate this place," Temper finally says. "I never thought I'd say that about the Otherworld," she admits a bit quieter. "I built this realm up in my mind so much as a teen, and it looks even more beautiful than I could imagine it. Yet..." She exhales. "It's like eating stale cereal. It seems fine on the outside, but once you bite into it, you have all the regrets."

That's...an apt way of putting it.

After a moment, Temper nods to the fairies mingling about the field. "Look at the way they stare at us. It's worse than high school."

In the darkness, I see the firelight flickering in their unnatural eyes. Their gazes indeed keep coming back to us.

"They've been staring at you too?" I ask, my brows rising.

"Since we rode in," she says. "You'd think they'd never seen a human before."

To be fair, I doubt they've ever seen a sorceress—or a winged siren.

Not that those are the reasons they stare.

Here we are, the two enigmas among them, the humans who managed to outmaneuver the rules of their realm to end up in the highest echelons of fairy society.

"Did you notice?" Temper nods at the servers moving in and out of the crowd like ghosts.

I watch the humans, the changelings of this realm. Either they, or their ancestors, were swapped at birth with a fae baby.

"Notice what?" I ask, following her gaze.

"Look at their wrists." I hear the horror in her voice.

I take another look at one of the nearby waiters. It takes several seconds to see it at just the right angle, but when I do...

I suck in a breath. The raised, mottled skin of their wrist is a raspberry color, and it's styled in the shape of a leaf. "They're branded."

CHAPTER 22

Branded like livestock. I'm reeling from that realization long after Malaki joins our group, his eye patch silver tonight. He only lingers long enough to invite Temper to dance, and then my friend is gone, dancing about the field like she belongs to these people, her earlier words be damned. I can't help but wonder if this is Temper's defiant response to this land and its awful treatment of changelings. That she will not allow herself to feel small or outcast, even as a human.

And here I am, still the same wallflower I was in high school.

I stare down at my wine. This is why I really shouldn't drink. Pity isn't flattering, no matter how well you wear it.

My eyes sweep over the gardens, taking in the revelries of Solstice.

This isn't a party; it's a bacchanal. Everywhere I look people are dancing, their forms illuminated under the moonlight. They're laughing and spinning, their loose hair whipping about them.

Those who aren't dancing are on the outskirts of the

dance floor, chatting and drinking. Well, they're either chatting and drinking or else slipping away. Couples are disappearing into the woods, and I've seen at least one fairy leave with one partner and return with another.

Everyone's eyes are too bright, their smiles too wide, their cheeks too flushed.

Tanked out of their minds.

The revelers all managed to let go of their cares for the evening. The only people who haven't are me and the human servants, the latter keeping their eyes downcast most of the time.

"Enjoying yourself?"

I jump at the voice, my drink spilling over the cup's rim and onto my hands.

"*Shit*," I curse under my breath.

The Green Man is at my side, and I have no fucking clue just how long he's been there watching me as I've been watching everyone else.

"Sorry," he says, his eyes trained on my face, "I didn't mean to scare you."

"No, you're fine," I say, shaking off my hand.

"We were never formally introduced," he says, holding out his hand. "I'm the Green Man, king-consort to the Flora Kingdom."

I take his hand, mine still a little sticky with wine. Rather than shake it, he brings my hand to his lips and presses a kiss to the back of it, his amber eyes trained on me.

His eyes, I decide, are too intense, too mischievous, too covetous.

He releases my hand. "So are you enjoying yourself?"

The man is too perceptive. He knows I feel uncomfortable and out of place.

"No," I say, going with the truth.

The Green Man's face lights up with my admission. "It's a rare treat to come across honesty within these walls." He glances around us.

Technically, there are no walls, but the ones he's talking about are invisible. They divide peasants from nobility, humans from fairies.

I give him a tight smile, my gaze moving to the crowd. They're watching me again, probably because the Green Man is at my side.

"It's awful, isn't it?" he says.

I glance to him. "What is?"

"The eyes that both see you and don't. The posturing. The studied gaiety."

I hide my swallow. This man *is* reading me, and I don't like it that he can do it so easily.

I make a noncommittal sound, searching the crowd for Des. There's an ever-increasing cluster of fairies around him, vying for his attention. I'm tempted to elbow my way back to his side, but I don't want to be in that dogpile any more than I want to be right here.

My eyes then land on Mara, who's laughing among her group of men and some fawning nobles. She's the sun, and they're all planets revolving around her, eager for her smile, her touch, her gaze. The only one missing from her group of admirers is the man at my side.

"Will you dance with me?" said man asks.

That makes me turn my full attention to the Green Man.

Fairies in general, and male fairies in particular, make me nervous. Karnon and his men are to blame for that.

But when I look at the Green Man, I don't see a predator—I see a kindred spirit.

Why not dance? Tonight is a festival, the Green Man looks eager, and it's high time I stopped clinging to the edges. If Temper can do it, so can I.

"Sure," I say.

He smiles at that, and I reel back at how staggeringly handsome he is when he's happy. It's not that I hadn't noticed earlier—all fairies seem to be attractive. It's just that Mara's presence eclipses him.

He takes the wine from my hand, sets it on a side table, and leads me into the crowd of dancing bodies. And then we're moving, spinning just like all the other couples.

The alcohol warms my stomach, and the dancing throws away the last of my caution. I find that as soon as I move my feet, I'm caught up in the music's haunting rhythm.

"So you are the Night King's mate," the Green Man says, staring a little too intensely at me.

"Mm-hmm." It's hard to focus on him when the music, the wine, and the dancing all want to pull my attention up and away.

"You have our kingdom fascinated by you," he says, his hand moving to the small of my back. "A human with supernatural powers, a mate to the King of the Night. Not to mention that you are lovelier than many of our women."

Why are we talking? And why about this? "What does being lovely have to do with anything?" I say, distracted.

I guess it's a stupid question to ask here in the Otherworld, where beauty is a point of fixation and ugliness only ever lurks beneath the surface.

"Everyone thought the merciless Desmond Flynn had gotten himself shackled to some ordinary slave," the Green Man says. "We had pitied him until we met you."

The wine sours in my stomach, the music begins to

grate, the dancing starts to dizzy me. I push away from the Green Man, no longer interested in dancing with him.

"Is something wrong?"

He says this as though he didn't just refer to my people as slaves, as though he didn't just insinuate that he holds them in such low regard. It's his casual bigotry more than anything that's off-putting.

"*I* am an ordinary human," I say as the couples around us continue to twirl.

"No, Callypso Lillis, enchantress of mortals," he says, "you are not." With that, he begins to back away. "Try to enjoy yourself tonight," he recommends. "You have a week of festivities ahead of you."

With that, the crowd swallows him up, and I'm alone once more, warm twisting bodies brushing against me from all sides.

The thought of a week here, surrounded by these fairies, is suddenly terribly daunting.

On the edge of the dance floor, a thick shroud of darkness cuts through the brightly clad fae, and right at the center of it is the Bargainer. He strides toward me, the night clinging to him like a cloak.

I head over to him, noticing that for once this evening, he's free of an audience.

His eyes are pinned to someone in the crowd. "That little fool is right," Des says when he reaches me. "You are not ordinary."

"You were listening to my conversation?" One day I'm going to figure out just how he comes by his secrets. There's no way Des could've just overheard what the Green Man said to me.

"Are you surprised?" he asks, turning my question into one of his own.

I shrug. Now that he's here, his presence like a drug, I find I don't really care about whether he was snooping or the fact that he might've left his fan club just to make sure another dude wasn't poaching me.

I drape my arms around his neck. Suddenly, I understand what's gotten into everyone else. It's the smell of the smoky bonfires, the thrum of the music, the tingle of the alcohol in my veins. It's all coaxing me to fall into this night and this man. To give everything to magic, if only for a single evening.

He cups my cheeks, and I see him drinking in my expression. I imagine I must now look like all the other revelers—flushed cheeks, dilated eyes, easy smile.

Making some decision, he kisses me hard. He tastes like fairy wine and dirty thoughts.

"Dance with me," I say when our mouths part.

His thumb strokes my cheek. "I don't want to dance with you." The pitch of his voice hits me right in my core.

He doesn't want to dance, but his pale smoky eyes want something else, something that's waking up my siren. My eyes move to the edge of the clearing, where fairies have been disappearing and reappearing all night.

He pulls me in tighter. "I would make it worth your while…" he whispers, knowing where my thoughts are.

I could just give in. I mean, why not?

But I shouldn't. Right?

His hand moves to my wrist. "Or I could simply make the decision easier."

My breath catches as Des holds my wrist between us, the black beads seeming to suck in the light around us.

"*Truth or dare*, cherub."

If I choose truth, the two of us will have a little

heart-to-heart, and then we'll go back to dancing and drinking. But if I don't...

My gaze moves up his imposing frame to that pretty, hardened face of his.

"Dare."

His hand squeezes my wrist tighter for a moment as a slow devious smile spreads across his face. "So be it." His hand slips down to my palm, his magic smoothing along my skin like a thousand light caresses.

The Bargainer warned me about this before I bought my first favor off him. That with a siren, he wouldn't just ask for secrets.

There'd be sex too.

Only then, he'd been saying that to scare me off. But now...being mates, well, sex often comes hand in hand with love. And none of this feels like I'm paying back favors, but more like Des has found a loophole in his magic that feeds my siren and brings me so much pleasure.

Des pulls us toward the dark woods that border the clearing, his silver eyes smoldering.

I feel the sly looks of other fairies as we slip away, and I can't help the rising heat in my cheeks. They all know what we're about to do.

We leave the music and the dancing behind us, the forest eerily silent.

"What are you thinking?" Des asks, his voice smooth like scotch.

That just the thought of your skin pressed to mine is making my knees weak.

"That you're a sly devil," I say instead.

His laugh echoes through the night, unfettered, abandoned. He pushes me against a nearby tree, the trunk slipping between my wings. "You're as wild as I am, Callie. I know what you crave—what your siren craves." He nuzzles my neck. "Let me show you."

Between that soft touch and his seductive words, my siren surfaces, brightening my skin.

I arch into him, throwing my head back.

Yes.

This is everything I want. Him and me beneath the dark sky. Primal. Passionate.

I reach for his pants just as he reaches for my skirts, gathering them in his hands. Our hands are deft and hurried, our movements jerky. I hear my own breath hitch.

With our clothes still halfway on, that hard, delicious flesh of his presses against me.

"My mate," he murmurs, his hair tickling my cheek as he leans into me.

There's an urgency both to the magic that's demanding, demanding, demanding and to our own fevered passions.

The Bargainer's shadows blanket us, darkening our surroundings until it's just him and me, a single point in the dark universe he rules.

His wings come around us, further shielding our bodies.

Next to the glowing skin of my hands, I see his neck muscles clench, and with a powerful shove, he enters me.

One of his hands cups my breast through the fabric of my dress, and then his head dips, his hot mouth kissing the exposed skin of my chest. My fingers dig into his shoulders.

He's moving in and out of me, our bodies hot and wet where we're joined. They make slick, wet noises as we come together.

"Meant…to take this slower," Des rakes out.

It's almost painful, the force of his thrusts. This joining

isn't something sweet. It's wild, primal, and it calls to all my darkest corners.

I thread my fingers in his hair and force his head to the side. Minutes ago, all his white-blond hair had been elegantly swept back from his face. Now it's fallen victim to my touch.

I tighten my grip on his hair. "I don't want *slow*," I say, glamour entering my voice. "I want everything the King of the Night can give me—and then I want more."

With a growl, Des gives me exactly that.

Again, and again, and again.

CHAPTER 23

I wake to the rustle of oak trees and the cold chill of dew on my skin. My hip bone hurts from sleeping on a hard surface, and the scent of moist earth fills my nostrils.

Where am I?

Blinking sleep away, I sit up, running my hands through my hair and pulling out several leaves and twigs. My dress still glows softly, and at my back is the tree Des and I thoroughly sullied earlier.

Des.

I glance around, but he's nowhere in sight. I rub my temples, trying to remember through the beginnings of a hangover just how the night ended and why I'm now alone.

Off in the distance, a branch snaps.

I go still.

What are the chances that's my Night King?

Zero, my mind whispers.

I rise to my feet, trying to be as silent as possible. Not that I'm doing a great job being innocuous. Kind of hard to go unnoticed when you're in a dark wood wearing a glowing dress.

I begin retracing my steps. I think I can figure out a way back to my suite; I just have to get out of this forest.

Another branch snaps, and I jump at the sound.

Is someone following me?

And where's Des?

Just when I'm sure I'm heading in the right direction, the forest seems to deepen rather than give way to the Sacred Gardens.

I massage my forehead. Did I really get it all backward? The smoky remnants of the bonfires seem stronger here than where I woke up...but there's no music, no laughter, no sounds of any revelers.

I'm utterly alone.

Behind me, leaves crunch.

I tense.

Maybe I'm not alone...

Slowly, I swivel around.

Off in the distance is a broad-shouldered man with a shock of white hair.

"Des!" I instantly relax. I head to him, first walking, and then, when he doesn't come any closer, I begin to run. "Des!"

Before I can get to him, he disappears.

That stops me in my tracks.

He's coming for you...the trees whisper.

"Des?"

I feel the press of metal against my throat, and from the edge of my vision, I can just make out Des's white-blond hair.

"What are you doing?" I ask.

If this is his idea of training…

But it's not training. It's not. I sense the malicious intent in the rough grip he has on me and the way the blade digs into my flesh, like it wants my skin to split.

The Bargainer's supple lips skim over my cheekbone. "Fear me, mortal," he whispers, "for I will be your undoing."

Des brushes a kiss against my skin and then drags his knife across my throat.

———

I wake with a choked cry, holding my neck.

Not dead. Just a dream. Just a dream.

Des has my body cradled in his arms.

"Callie," he says when he sees I'm awake, relief coating his words. He pulls my head in close. "Callie, Callie, Callie," he murmurs—more, it appears, to reassure himself than to get through to me.

The Bargainer and I are tangled in soft sheets, our bodies naked.

I pull away from him long enough to look into his eyes. He has no idea that right now I'm coaching my mind to not see him as a threat. The bite of that blade felt *so* real.

I swallow.

A nightmare is all it was.

I draw in a shuddering breath, the last of the dream sloughing away. "I'm okay—it's okay."

Early morning light filters through the window of our room, the sun making the scent of flowers come alive around our suite. At some point last night, the two of us slipped away to our rooms, finishing here what we'd started in the forest.

I stretch myself back out along the bed, dragging Des

down with me. Reluctantly, he lets me pull him to the mattress, tucking me against his side.

I'm not ready to wake up, but I'm not sure I can fall back asleep either.

"Tell me a secret," I murmur.

He plays with a strand of my dark hair, not saying anything for a long time. Finally, "My mother's hair was exactly this color."

"It was?" I ask, tilting my head to peer up at him.

He smooths the lock of hair back down. "Sometimes," he says, lost in his own thoughts, "when I'm feeling particularly superstitious, I think that's no coincidence."

I don't know what he means by that, but the confession raises the gooseflesh along my arms. This was the woman who raised Des, the scribe whose death he blames on his father.

"Tell me about her—your mother."

He holds me close. "What do you want to know, cherub?"

I draw circles onto his chest. "Anything—everything."

"Demanding thing," he says fondly. His tone sobers when he speaks again. "Her name was Larissa, and she was someone I loved deeply…"

Something thick rises in my throat. It's not so much what he says as how he says it, like his mother fashioned all the stars in his sky.

His chest rises and falls as he swallows. "It was always my mother and me, ever since my earliest memory."

I notice he conveniently skirts any mention of his father.

"She was my guardian, my teacher, and my closest confidante. Perhaps it shouldn't have been that way—I'm sure she didn't want it to be that way—but in Arestys…my mother and I were seen as oddities."

My finger pauses on his chest.

Des, an oddity? And in the Otherworld of all places?

"Even by Arestys's standards, we were poor," he says. "We couldn't afford lodgings, so we lived in the caves I showed you. And under my mother's roof, I had to live by two hard-and-fast rules: one, I must never use my magic, and two, I must control my temper."

I don't know where Des is taking this story, but his eyes are far away. For once, he isn't mincing his words.

"Naturally, I worked my way around both rules."

The Bargainer bent someone's words to fit his needs? How shocking.

"I couldn't wield magic, so I learned to bargain with magical creatures for bits of theirs."

So *that's* where Des came by his affinity for deals. I never stood a chance against him.

"There are few things that will get you ostracized in the Otherworld as quickly as being poor and being weak. And growing up, that's what people thought of me and my mother—that she was a scribe because she could only wield weak amounts of magic and her son couldn't wield any at all."

My heart is beginning to hurt. I didn't expect this when I asked about his mother.

"Being seen as poor and weak made us targets," he continues. "For my mother, it came in the shape of bad men. There were several fairies who went missing on our island after they encountered my mother. She never breathed a word about what happened, and I didn't know better at the time, but...I don't doubt my mother did something to them."

"And what about you?" I ask.

"What about me?" Des responds.

"How did you get around being a target?"

Des smiles, but it's a little malicious. "I didn't, cherub. I just got around my mother's second rule."

Rule number two: Des must control his temper.

"Fairy children love nothing more than picking on the vulnerable," he says. "My mother couldn't stop the bullying, and she couldn't prevent me from defending myself, so she coached me on how to fight and how to separate my emotions from a battle."

Who was this woman who was once a part of the royal harem before she became a lowly scribe? Who made her son control his magic and his temper but still taught him to fight?

"I don't understand," I say, "why hide your power in the first place?"

Des strokes a hand down my back. "That is a question for another time. But for now, I will tell you this: ill-fated mothers, cruel fathers, and friendless childhoods—you and I, cherub, really do share similar tragedies."

CHAPTER 24

"You're going to have to roll me out of here," I tell Des.

The two of us sit in a large atrium among a throng of other Solstice guests, all dining on tea, fruit, nuts, and breakfast pastries as the sun glitters in the large glass windows.

I lean back in my seat, kicking my feet up on the edge of the table before I realize I'm wearing a dress.

Whoops. This is why I don't usually do dresses. They're not terribly versatile. Also, this bodice is totally constricting my stomach.

I pull at it as I take in the fairies around us. Des and I are at our own private table; his guards and the nobles of the Night Kingdom sit at the tables surroundings ours. Farther out, members of the Flora and Fauna kingdoms also feast.

On the whole, the crowd looks just a smidge worse for the wear. There might be lazy smiles and casual touches, but I've seen several fairies hide a yawn behind their hand, and the conversations are somewhat muted.

Noticeably absent from the group breakfast are Mara and

the Green Man. Their raised table sits at the far end of the room, looking lonely.

I'm about to ask Des what's up with the Flora rulers' relationship when, out of nowhere, my training leathers materialize in midair, falling to the table a split second later. They knock over a container of cream and the last of my coffee, most of the outfit landing in a bowl of honey.

Oh God, please tell me I'm hallucinating. "Seriously, Des?"

The two of us are garnering attention from other tables.

He stretches, completely unbothered by the stares, the smallest sliver of his abs peeking out beneath the edge of his fitted shirt. "Training begins in thirty minutes," he announces.

You've got *to be kidding me.*

"Training freak," I mutter under my breath.

"What was that?" he asks.

"Nothing."

An hour later, I'm clad in my leathers, my daggers at my sides and a sword in my hand.

The two of us spar in one of the gardens near the great cedar tree that houses our rooms. The monstrous tree looms high above us, the stairs that wind around it currently filled with Night fairies who are coming and going.

In the gardens, wisteria and roses grow along trellises, while heather and lilac grow in thick clusters beneath them. Well, that and about a billion other plants, some I recognize and some I don't.

I stomp on a hyacinth blossom as I back away from Des.

"You sure it's okay to be training here?" I huff. "I'm destroying the queen's gardens."

Des strides toward me, his sword clutched in his hand. He smirks, hopping off a rock as he stalks forward. "Don't pretend like what you're doing is an accident."

All right, so I haven't been too careful with my footwork; I might still be a smidge bitter about the proprietary way she interacts with Des.

"And no," he adds, "the queen is quite fine with us training here, destroyed flowers and all. The only place she cares about protecting—other than her cedarwood guest houses—is her sacred oak grove."

A.k.a. the place where I boned Des last night.

I glance over at the edge of the gardens, where part of the oak grove butts up against its outskirts. In the light of day, I can see the vast wooded forest circles the palace grounds.

Why, out of everything here, some ordinary oaks are worthy of protecting, I'll never know.

Des swipes at me.

I yelp, hopping back to dodge the blow.

"Release your siren." The order comes out of nowhere.

"Why?" I pant, ducking another swing of his sword.

"I'm curious about something."

I carve my own blade upward at him, but he springs away before I can make contact.

"Leave her alone," I say. She had a busy evening last night. Even evil bitches like my siren need their rest.

The Bargainer disappears. A moment later his breath, fans against my neck. I go rigid, remembering my dream.

"We can do this the easy way"—he slides the hair off my shoulder, his lips skimming my skin—"or the fun way."

He doesn't know just how effective he's being at the moment. Nothing gets my siren stirring quite like fear and arousal, and I'm feeling a bit of both at the moment.

"I could undress you slowly and lay you out on the grass," he breathes. "I'd spread your legs apart and give you the most sacred of kisses."

A flush creeps up my cheeks.

His hand smooths down my torso. "I'd savor that sweet pussy of yours right until you were on the edge, but I wouldn't give you that release," he says. "Not until you wrapped your pretty legs around my waist and begged me to bury myself in you."

I push away from him, my body crying out at the sudden distance between us. My siren batters against the walls of her cage, and my control on her is slipping.

"I'd take you right out here, right where anyone might find us, just as my ancestors used to do."

Jesus, that is dirty.

He circles around to the front of me, one side of his mouth curving up. "I would want them to find us, to see me claiming you."

Fuck it. I give up.

My siren surfaces, turned on by all his taboo suggestions.

"There she is," he says, backing up, and I hear the glee in his voice.

I pace restlessly, my eyes trained on him.

All of that, all of what he just said, was to release the siren. The thing is I don't like being teased, *manipulated*. I like doing the teasing and the manipulating.

I roll my neck, power thrumming through me, and I swing the sword in my grip a few times.

Des raises his sword. "Hello, lovely." I slit my eyes, and he must understand my look because he says, "Do you know why I brought you out?"

I don't bother answering him.

"I want you to fight me," he explains.

That's not going to be a problem.

Casually, I saunter toward Des, my earlier reticence gone. It's been replaced by a primal need for vengeance and bloodlust.

This time, when I get close to him, I swing my blade without the same hesitation as before. Des parries it then moves forward, his own sword brandished.

I block the next blow, our swords locking together. Beyond them, Des's eyes dance with mirth.

"Does it bother you, love, to be toyed with?"

I flash him a lethal look, my nails sharpening. Gritting my teeth, I shove his sword off mine, slashing out with my claws. He spins out of the way, just avoiding the kick I aim for his crotch.

"Silly fairy," I say, mocking him. "You know better than to toy with me. I'll always make you pay in the end."

If anything, Des looks more exhilarated than ever, which only serves to rile me more. With a growl, I come at him again.

The two of us block then strike, block then strike. At some point our battle feels less like a collection of steps and swings and more like a dance. I move fluidly, my instincts guiding me, my courage making each of my blows sure and swift.

The more we fight, the harder he makes me work for it, and the harder he makes me work for it, the more I want it. Blood. Sex. Fighting. Fucking. Any of it. All of it. His violence and his passion are mine to use. Mine to exploit. Mine to savor.

I swipe low, my body rolling with the motion. As I follow through with the swing, I hear the whizz of Des's blade and then a snip. A lock of my dark hair tumbles to the ground.

"Oops," Des deadpans, looking remorseless.

In response, I smile at him, and then I attack. I feint left but then go right. Blocked. I kick out, aiming for his solar plexus. He dodges and spins away. Lunging forward, I strike again, aiming for his face.

I miss his jaw by inches, but my blade sheers off a stray lock of his white-blond hair. The two of us pause, watching it flutter to the ground.

Des's expression is caught somewhere between shock and awe.

"You got me," he says. "You actually got me." He straightens and smiles. "You know what this means, cherub?"

Warily, I take a step back. I'm still high off my small victory, but I'm not yet too prideful to not know when I should retreat.

"I need to make this harder." He moves his weapon from his left hand to his right.

Shit.

I hadn't even noticed.

I back up, moving into the queen's sacred oak forest. The leaves brush against me, whispering, whispering…

Des comes at me, looking oh so eager.

I move deeper into the forest, sap from an overhanging oak dripping onto my neck, then against my bare shoulder.

"Evading me will do you no good," Des says. One moment he's standing in the middle of the garden, the sunlight brightening his pale features, and the next, he's gone.

I rotate around, searching for him among the trees.

"Looking for me?"

His voice tickles my ear, but when I spin to face him, no one's there.

"You're never going to find me if you're looking for where I should be." This comes from deeper in the wooded grove.

"Come out and fight fair!" I call, my voice ethereal.

"Fairies don't like to play fair," he says from directly above me.

I glance up just in time to see Des crouched on one of the branches high above me, his body poised to spring.

I tense, readying myself for an attack, savoring the possibility of it. But it never comes.

The Bargainer's expression changes in an instant as he takes me in. "*Callypso*—" He disappears before materializing in front of me a moment later, his hands brushing away my hair. "You're bleeding."

My skin dims at the concern in his voice.

I'm bleeding?

My hand goes to where his eyes are trained. Immediately, I feel warm wetness. The sap that dripped on me.

Except, when I pull my hand away and stare at my crimson-coated fingers, it looks less like sap and a helluva lot more like blood.

"Ugh," I say, wiping it off as the last of my siren slips away. "It's not mine."

"Then whose is it?"

"It came from the tree." It only takes a couple of seconds for my words to register.

Trees don't bleed.

Des is already two steps ahead of me, scouring the oaks for more signs of blood.

Speckled around several nearby trees are dark spots on the ground, glistening stains I assumed were sap. But are they?

Des scuffs a patch with his boot then glances up at the tree's canopy. I follow his gaze up, now noticing the strange rivulets of the dark liquid running down the tree trunk.

The Bargainer vanishes and reappears on a branch above us before disappearing again. Higher and higher, he moves.

Less than a minute later, he's back at my side, wiping his hands off.

"No body and no signs of an attack," he says. "The fluid seems to be coming from the tree itself."

I think that makes me feel better. "So...it's sap," I say.

Des shakes his head, his mouth a thin line. "No, it's blood."

CHAPTER 25

The trees are bleeding.

I suppress a shudder.

"Is that normal?" I ask, wiping what I can of the—*cringe*—blood off me as the two of us exit the oak forest.

It wasn't just that one tree. Several surrounding oaks had bits of blood trickling from their trunks.

Des shakes his head, his brow furrowed. "No."

Why would a tree bleed? And is it just the oak trees right where we were training, or is it the whole forest of them?

I think back to last night when Des had me pressed up against another oak. That one had been fine...

One of Des's guards comes striding out to us, his eyes wide. "Your Majesty—" His voice cuts off abruptly when he sees me.

"You may speak freely," Des commands.

The guard's attention returns to Des. "Two of our soldiers are missing."

Two soldiers are *missing*?

Des raises an eyebrow. "It's well past noon. Why am I being informed of this now?" Des demands.

The guard shakes his head. "The festivities... They had the morning off... They were supposed to check in for roll call at twelve. When they didn't, several soldiers went looking for them. Their beds are still made, their bags still packed. We don't think they made it back from the celebration last night."

Des's mouth tightens. His gaze briefly moves to me, his expression inscrutable.

"Continue searching for the men," he finally says. "There's still a chance they're sleeping off the effects of last night."

Des's grim gaze meets mine, and his eyes say what his mouth won't: there's still a chance, but it's an infinitesimally small one.

Bleeding trees and missing men.

And we haven't even been here a day yet.

Training for the rest of the day is canceled. Des and I part ways at the garden—him to check on his men, and me to take a shower. Wearily, I climb the staircase that wraps around the giant cedar, passing room after room.

Going to have buns of steel before this week is through.

Des and I are on something like the thirty-seventh floor.

I pause when I see Temper's room ahead of me, giving myself a moment to catch my breath. As I lean against the railing, enjoying the view, the door to my friend's room opens.

I raise my eyebrows when I see Malaki slipping out.

Whelp. Temper bagged the Lord of Dreams all right.

As soon as he sees me, he ducks his head, running his hand along the back of his neck, clearly uncomfortable.

I lift my hands. "None of my business."

But it's going to become my business the moment Temper corners me. She loves divulging all the juicy details of her sexploits.

He clears his throat then nods sheepishly as he passes me. His footsteps are fading down the stairs when I think of something.

"Wait"—I swivel around—"Malaki."

He stops on the stairs below me and turns around, his eye patch glinting in the sun. In the harsh light of day, the scar that stretches out from beneath the patch is even more gruesome.

"Is there any way I could see the Flora Kingdom's sleeping women?"

His brows furrow. "I could ask…"

I suck in my lower lip. "Would you?"

He studies me for a moment longer. Finally, he nods. "Consider it done."

―――――――

By late afternoon, Malaki's made good on his promise.

I stand inside one of the Flora Kingdom's expansive greenhouses, Temper at my side. The hot conservatory is filled to the brim with sleeping women, each one laid out in her glass coffin. Like in the Kingdom of Night, there are hundreds if not thousands of them, their caskets spread throughout the building.

"My God," Temper says next to me. "This is…"

I nod. "I know."

Considering that solving cases is what Temper and I do

best, I brought her along to help me, filling her in on the mystery during our walk over here.

My gaze moves from woman to woman. I'm still not used to the sight even after all this time. It's the little details that get to me—how one's pointed ears peek through her hair, how another looks like she might have dimples if she were to wake up and smile.

I still remember Karnon's terrible kisses, how he forced his dark magic down my throat. Being a lowly *human* benefited me then. Whatever tainted spell he put these women under, I escaped it.

The door to the conservatory opens, and in strides the Green Man.

"I heard I'd find you here," he says, his footsteps echoing throughout the room.

"What's this little pipsqueak up to?" Temper asks under her breath, watching the Flora fae head our way.

I shrug. "I think he finds us curious."

"Hmm..."

The Green Man reaches our side, introducing himself to Temper, who looks less than impressed.

"So you plan on solving the mystery?" he says, turning to me.

I hear the subtle scorn in his voice. Why wouldn't he be scornful? For ten years this mystery has plagued the Otherworld, and all the king's horses and all the king's men couldn't stop the disappearances from happening again—and again and again.

"I plan on trying."

His eyes move over the women around us. "I knew some of these women...*personally*."

The way he says this makes me want to scrunch my nose.

I think he was more than just friends with some of these soldiers.

Temper and I share a knowing look. God, I *love* having my best friend here with me.

"Where are the children?" I ask, turning my attention back to the Green Man.

"They are sleeping a different sort of sleep," he says cryptically.

My brows furrow in confusion.

"Mara has them killed," he explains.

Temper sucks in a breath.

"'Poisoned fruit'—that's what she calls them," the Green Man elaborates. "They're removed as soon as they enter the kingdom—rot spreads quickly."

I fold my arms across my chest. "The queen's trees seem to be rotting as well—why aren't they too being removed?" I ask.

The Green Man assesses me. "What are you talking about?"

"The sacred oak grove. The trees are bleeding."

"What? Fucking hell," Temper says under her breath.

"You must be imagining things," he says. "The oaks are fine."

Imagining things?

"No, I'm not—"

Temper puts a hand on my arm. "There is no use trying to talk sense to this man. He and his wife *kill* kids."

The Green Man's expression turns patronizing as he looks between the two of us. "Don't tell me you have a bleeding heart when it comes to those creatures?"

"It just seems hypocritical," I say. To protect a plant but smother a fae life.

"It would be hypocritical *if* the trees were afflicted the same way those children are," the Green Man says.

Ugh, why did I even bring this up? Fairies can be so tedious to talk to.

"Forget about it," I say. I bump Temper's shoulder. "There's nothing here to see."

We move between the aisles of coffins, heading for the door.

"Even if the trees have developed rot, they didn't start out that way," he says to our backs. "The children did. You can cure an illness, not a permanent state of existence."

I ignore him.

"They say a specter haunts this place," he adds, changing the subject.

I stop.

"He's just trying to reel you in, Callic," Temper says, grabbing my arm and urging me on. "Be better than his tricks."

But I remember something I heard a month ago, about a shadow watching over the children in the Night Kingdom's nursery.

I turn around. "What do you know?"

He smiles. "The slaves are usually the ones who see him. They say that during a full moon, you can see him move about the coffins."

"'Him'?" I say, stepping a bit closer. "How do you know it's a man?"

He tilts his head. "Because there's only one person who attends these women now—

"The Thief of Souls."

CHAPTER 26

I stare up at the stars, Des next to me, the two of us quiet.

Both of us have been plagued by worry: him for the Night soldiers, who still haven't turned up, and me for what the Green Man told me.

The creep's just trying to get a rise out of you, Temper said when we left.

Maybe he was, and maybe he wasn't. I haven't yet figured out the motives of fairies. Not even those of the one who sleeps next to me.

The King of the Night and I have returned to the Sacred Gardens. Last night this section of the palace grounds was teeming with activity. Now it's utterly abandoned; the only evidence of the previous evening's revelries is the wine-stained ground and the piles of ash where the bonfires burned out.

Des reaches out for my hand. Wordlessly, he brings it to his mouth, pressing a kiss to the skin there.

"I'll be happy to leave this place," he says.

I sigh. "Me too."

My eyes move from star to star. The constellations are foreign to me but no less beautiful than they are on earth.

Out of nowhere, one of the stars begins to fall from the sky. I blink a few times, just to make sure I'm seeing things correctly. One moment it sat up in the heavens, the next it descends, dropping from the sky as though gravity were pulling it to the horizon.

I'm still trying to make sense of the falling star when another one slips from its perch, leaving a faint, shimmery trail of light in its wake.

"Des!"

"Hmm?" he responds lazily.

Then another star falls…and another and another, each one leaving its place in the canopy above us, dropping to where sky meets earth.

"The stars are falling from the sky!" That's definitely a phrase I never imagined saying.

Now dozens are dropping from the cosmos, making the night look as though it's crying the most exquisite tears.

I sit up, unable to tear my gaze away.

Just before any of them hit the horizon, they alter their trajectory, moving…*toward us*.

My brows knit. I glance over at Des, who still hasn't responded. He's watching the sky too, but he doesn't look alarmed or surprised. He reaches out for the heavens, the air wavering a little with his magic.

Then, in perhaps the strangest moment I've ever seen, the fallen stars gather one by one into Des's outstretched hand, looking as tiny there in his palm as they did in the canopy above us.

I don't breathe as he lowers his arm then holds his hand

out to me. Cupped in his hand is starlight. But I know stars aren't this small. I reach out and touch them with my finger. They feel like grains of sand, and they're warm to the touch.

I still can't contain my surprise. "How did you…?"

"I borrowed their light for an evening," Des explains, starlight reflecting in his eyes.

I let out a surprised laugh, remembering our late-night conversation on Phyllia, the Land of Dreams.

I would steal the stars from the sky for you.

You wouldn't have to steal them, Des.

"You made a deal with the stars?" I ask, incredulous.

"I asked nicely." He says that as though there's some distinction.

Now I throw my head back and laugh. He talked the stars out of the sky.

When my laughter finally dies away, Des is still staring intensely at me. "I told you I'd give you the stars for that laugh."

He did.

He leans forward, bringing his cupped hand to the top of my head.

"What are you doing?" I ask, beginning to lean away.

"Be still, cherub."

Reluctantly, I do as he asks, my body motionless.

All at once he pours the starlight onto the crown of my head.

I raise my eyebrows, still not moving. "Why did you just do that?" I ask, afraid of what will happen if I shake out my hair.

"The stars agreed that, for an evening, they'd hang the night sky in your hair."

He's still giving me that intense look. It makes me want to shyly tuck my hair behind my ear.

A small handheld mirror shimmers out of the ether and into Des's palm. He hands it to me, and I take it, tentatively glancing down at my reflection.

I suck in a breath.

Hundreds of pinpricks of light glitter from my hair, the starlight clustered into constellations. I shake my head, and the starlight moves with it. It really does look like I'm wearing the night sky in my hair.

"It's beautiful," I say, tearing my eyes away from my reflection to look at Des.

It's more than beautiful. It's breathtaking, surreal. I glance above us to make sure I'm not imagining this, but I'm not. The dark sky overhead is missing its twinkling companions.

Des leans forward and kisses me, just the softest brush of his lips, before he stands. He straightens his fitted shirt, picking off a stray blade of grass. "I hate to cut the evening short, love, but we ought to get going. We do, after all, have another dance to attend."

CHAPTER 27

Apparently, there will be dances every day and night, each one called some fancy name that distinguishes it from the others. There's the Solar Celebration, the Midsummer's Eve Ball, and—oh, my personal favorite—the Fecundity Formal. If that doesn't make you cringe, then I don't know what will.

I'm not exactly surprised by all the balls—I sort of figured as much—but the true horror of a week's worth of dancing, drinking, and schmoozing with fairies is finally starting to set in.

Not to mention the fact that for seven days straight, I'm going to have to wear *heels*.

Ugh, the bane of my existence.

The silver lining is that, being associated with the Kingdom of Night, I'm not required to participate in some of the Solstice dances and mixers hosted during the day. Apparently, many Night fae like to sleep during that time, so I'm off the hook as far as official Night King–mate duties go.

My shoes click against the stone walkway as Des, his retinue, and I all enter the Flora Kingdom's royal palace.

I touch my hair for the millionth time, oddly self-conscious that the night sky now glitters from it. I feel like the cosmos personified, my dress tonight the deep midnight blue of the dark heavens.

We head down flight after flight of stairs, and the farther we go, the more claustrophobic I feel.

Just how far down is this ballroom?

The answer: far enough to make my already sore ass even sorer.

When we finally reach the bottom, the room we walk into utterly takes my breath away. It might be underground, but it doesn't feel that way.

Intricate soaring arches hold up the cathedral ceilings, the pale stone faceted. The pillars throughout the room are carved into images of fairy maidens, flowers strewn in their hair.

Hundreds of glass lanterns hang from the walls and from several enormous candelabra, the dripping candles illuminating the room in bright flickering light.

Most surfaces are covered with plants and flowers, some arranged in pots, others growing up the various walls. More ferns cover the food-laden tables that line the sides of the great ballroom.

In the very middle of the room is an enormous tree, its trunk extending all the way to the ceiling, where its canopy spreads. From it, petals of some strange fae flower rain on us.

Des sees me staring at the tree. "It's said that the first Queen of Flora is buried beneath that tree. That rather than dying, she chose to be buried alive so her body and soul could continue to nourish her land and people for thousands of years."

"That is fucking hard-core," I say.

The giant tree, the fae maidens carved into stone, the

high cathedral ceilings... I spin in a circle. "It's just like your drawings," I breathe.

Back at Peel Academy, Des drew me several pictures of the Otherworld. At least one was of this great hall, I'm sure of it.

"You remember that?" he says, surprised.

"Of course." *I remember everything.* "I was desperate to know about your life."

He doesn't respond to that, but he doesn't need to. It's all in his expression. *It's yours to take.*

"It's almost as dark in here as it is outside tonight," one of the guests murmurs to her companion as they pass us.

That one little sentence interrupts the moment Des and I were having. A laugh bursts out of me, and the Bargainer's lips spread into a secretive grin, his eyes crinkling at the corners. Little do those fairies know that the man next to me is responsible for the unusually dark evening.

Des pulls me in close, the action not going unnoticed. For the second day in a row, we hold the room's attention. It's not as obvious tonight, more like something I feel rather than see, their gazes warming my skin. I imagine there's something particularly alluring about the King of the Night—the ruler of secrets, sex, dreams, and violence— enjoying a human.

Des runs a finger along my exposed collarbone. "Have you noticed?" he asks.

"Noticed what?"

Des's eyes flick across the room. "The wings."

I turn my attention to the fairies around us.

He's right. Just like in Somnia, there are several individuals with their wings out. Not many, but definitely more than last night, and back then the fairies were toasted.

It's nearly an hour after we enter the ballroom before Mara makes her appearance, a group of men around her, none of them the Green Man.

The sight is unsettling, and I can't quite put my finger on why until, a few seconds later, she cups the chin of one of the men and kisses him.

My eyebrows hike up.

"The queen's harem," Des explains.

So fae queens have harems too.

"But she has a mate," I say, my eyes riveted to her.

Today, her dress is a vibrant scarlet, her bodice cinched with gold ribbon. Her lips are bloodred, and they look particularly savage when she smiles.

"She does." Des grabs two flutes of champagne from a passing waiter before handing me one.

Distractedly, I take it. "But I assumed..."

I had assumed soul mates couldn't sleep with other people, but what had I been doing all those years Des and I were apart? Just because my heart couldn't move on didn't mean I avoided dating other men—or being intimate with them.

Des is gracious enough not to mention this. Instead, the two of us spend several more seconds staring at Mara.

"What does the Green Man think of this?" I ask.

Des lifts a shoulder. "I imagine he's not too keen about sharing his mate. But she's the queen, and he's a coward."

Ouch.

Before either of us can continue, we hear rhythmic stomping just outside the hall, coming from the staircase leading down here.

Ever so slowly, the room quiets, hundreds of gazes going to the huge double doors that lead into the ballroom.

The echoing footfalls quiet, and the doors to the ballroom

are thrown open. Two rows of fae soldiers wearing uniforms of gleaming gold file into the room, their movements choreographed and precise.

Eventually, they stop and pivot, creating a makeshift aisle of sorts. Another uniformed fairy heads down the aisle, pausing at the end of it.

"It is my eminent honor to present, from the radiant heavens above, His Majesty Janus Soleil—the King of Day!" he announces.

I cover my eyes against the brightness that flares at the entrance of the ballroom as someone strides down the aisle before coming to a full stop in front of the soldiers. It takes several seconds for the glare to die away.

When it does...

All I see is golden hair, tan skin, and eyes the clear blue color of Caribbean waters.

My flute of champagne slips from my hand, shattering against the ground.

It breaks whatever spell was cast over the room. Fairies turn from the fae king to stare at me, their frowns deepening when they realize it's the human, the one who shouldn't be here, who's causing the commotion.

I'm too distracted to care, my gaze pinned to the fairy.

The King of Day.

I begin to shake, my mind screaming, screaming.

Des moves his hand, and under his magic, the glass pieces itself back together, the champagne refilling into the cup. Surreptitiously, he looks between me and the man who was, only seconds ago, glowing like the sun.

"He took me," I whisper. "He was the one who took me. From your house. He took me to Karnon."

The person who delivered me to my attacker, the person

who could very well be the Thief of Souls himself, is another fae king.

I feel more than a little nauseous.

Des's gaze is on me for a hot second, and then, in the blink of an eye, Des disappears, both champagne flutes he held a second ago falling once more to the ground. They shatter, glass and bubbly wine soaking the floor and the hem of my dress.

Des reappears in front of Janus, the air around my mate cloaked in shadow, his talon-tipped wings splayed out. Shadows billow about the room, beginning in the far corners and creeping between fairies' legs like some sinister dark fog.

The room is still silent, still frozen, when Des grabs the King of Day by the collar and cocks his arm back. His fist slams into Janus's face with a meaty smack, the sound reverberating.

Whatever strange reverie overtook the room, that single action breaks the spell. The hall erupts into shouts, and people begin to move.

Des's arm is like a sledgehammer, pummeling the Day King over and over. Janus's uniformed soldiers close in on Des, while Night Kingdom soldiers run into the fray.

Before I know it, soldiers have turned on soldiers, guests on guests. The room is suddenly in an uproar as fairies fight each other. The Fauna fae are pointing to me, and several of them begin to weave through the crowd, heading in my direction.

Aw, shit, I almost forgot the little vendetta the Fauna Kingdom has out for me and the Bargainer.

A little distance away, Malaki, Temper, and several Night Kingdom soldiers are now trying to shove their way toward me.

In all directions, wings unfurl, each more beautiful than

the last. They shimmer in all sorts of colors, and it would be breathtaking if it didn't mean hundreds of fairies were losing their shit.

The cavernous room no longer feels quite so large, and oh, am I developing a massive case of claustrophobia.

I did this. I set Des off. And even though the cruel, vicious part of me savors his retribution, the rest of me is horrified that I set these events in motion.

I push my way through the crowd, determined to get to the two kings.

If anyone is going to have their vengeance, it will be me, my siren purrs.

Fairies are taking to the air, ripping at each other. Meanwhile, Des and the King of Day are still tussling, one bright as the sun, the other dark as the night.

The Fauna fairies are almost to me, and the Night guards coming for me are still too far away to offer me any sort of protection. I'll have to take these fairies on my own. The thought sends a shiver of delight down my spine, and I smile.

My nails are on the brink of sharpening when Mara's voice cuts through the noise. "*There will be no death in my house!*"

All but Des and Janus, the King of Day, pause, no one willing to cross the queen hosting them.

The Bargainer doesn't appear to give a flying fuck what Mara thinks. He has the King of Day pinned beneath him, and he keeps hammering into the man's face.

"*Desmond Flynn, King of the Night, by law of my kingdom, I order you to stop,*" Mara's voice booms.

Arm pulled back, Des hesitates, his breathing heavy and ragged. His hair, which he'd previously worn combed away from his face, now hangs in wild tendrils. I've seen my mate when he's all coiled rage, but I have only rarely seen him like this: messy with his anger. There's something so very...*raw* about it.

Reluctantly, he drops his fist. Leaning in close to Janus, he whispers something into the King of Day's ear, and then Des stands, his eyes moving about the crowd. They still when they land on me.

He looks like a hurricane contained in a man. He has speckles of blood on his face and a small line of it at the corner of his mouth. But it's the leashed fury in his eyes and the deep shadows swathing the room that are the true indications of how upset he is.

The King of Day pulls himself up to his feet, giving Des a murderous look.

Mara begins to clap, and the attention suddenly swivels to her. She swaggers across the room toward the men, the crowd parting for her. "Ladies and gentlemen," she says, "I present to you the first mate challenge."

Mate challenge?

Everyone else in the room stirs, their assessing gazes moving between me and the men. Mara follows their lead, her eyes finding mine. She smiles at me, her lustrous lips making her look equal parts lovely and wicked. The rest of her face is flinty with anger.

"Congratulations go to the King of the Night and his siren mate," she says. "Now, everyone, sheathe your excitement, and please, carry on as before."

I don't quite understand how she does it, but Mara manages to bring this place back from the edge of chaos. One by one, fairies' wings disappear, and people smooth down their rumpled outfits. While a few dirty looks pass between the guests—several thrown my way by some disgruntled Fauna fairies—conversation and bits of laughter begin to bloom across the hall.

Des wipes the blood off his mouth, glowering at the King of Day, who glowers right back. But Mara isn't done with them. The Queen of Flora leads the two kings away from the room and out a side door.

My heart stutters a bit at the sight. Without Des, I'm acutely aware that I'm a lamb in a den of lions.

"Get out of my way. Get *out* of my way—if you step on my dress, I swear to the saints, you're not going to have toes." Even among the rising noise of the crowd, Temper's voice carries over to me. "Who do I have to hex for a little room? *Move!*"

Malaki follows on her heels, his face set into severe lines.

"What the hell was that?" Temper says when she gets to my side, glancing back at where the two fairies tussled not a minute ago.

I shake my head, my throat working.

"Are you okay?" Malaki asks, coming to stand next to Temper.

I nod and swallow. Now that the fight's over and the adrenaline is subsiding, it hits me—the man who took me is a fae king, and he's *here*. I'm going to have to be around the King of Day for the rest of this visit. I might even have to interact with him. The thought sends a wave of nausea and nerves through me.

"I'll say this for the Bargainer," Temper says, "he throws a mean right hook. That pretty-boy king went down like a boner in church."

Temper, ever the eloquent one.

"What's a mate challenge?" I ask Malaki.

He frowns. "If a rival fairy disputes a bond, they can

232

challenge a mate to a duel. It's an old tradition, mostly used to either show off the worth of the mate being contended over or as an insult if an outside fairy doesn't think one of the mates is worthy of the other. Most of the time it's simply a way for mates—usually male ones—to work off their aggression and establish their claim."

Have I mentioned fae traditions are weird? Because they *so* are.

"Never thought I'd see you again," a familiar voice says at my back, shaking me from my thoughts. The sound of it raises all sorts of pleasant goose bumps along my skin.

Aetherial.

I turn just in time to see the fae soldier dressed from head to toe in a buttery-gold uniform, a sun emblem emblazoned on her breast. She languished in the cell next to me when we were Karnon's prisoners.

"Aetherial!" It's shocking to see her in the flesh, her angular face glowing and her blond hair cropped short. I'd been blindfolded when I was escorted in and out of the cell, so I had only my imagination to go on when I talked to her. She's taller and leaner than I imagined, her lips soft and pouty when I expected them to be thin and fierce.

Probably breaking all sorts of etiquette norms, I pull her into a hug.

Rather than edge away, she hugs me back. When she does eventually release me, it's to take me in.

"I have to admit, cleaned up, you're even lovelier than the few glimpses I caught of you," she says. Her eyes move to my wings. "Though I don't remember those. Has Des given you the wine?"

"The wine?" I furrow my brows. "No, this"—my voice catches—"this was Karnon." I swear his ghost must be here tonight because the dead king seems to be everywhere and in everything.

"Karnon managed that?" She raises her eyebrows. "I guess I shouldn't be surprised."

I want to ask her what she means by that, but an even bigger question plagues me. "How did you...?"

"Survive?" she fills in.

I nod. Last I remember, she was all but catatonic.

She shrugs. "Apparently, I wasn't beyond the point of no return when they found me. I hear I have your mate to thank for that." Her eyes drift to where she last saw Des. "He seems...intense."

I let out a hollow laugh.

"I heard," she continues, "that after he finished with Karnon, there wasn't a spare tooth left of the man."

Unwelcome memories of that final encounter flit through the back of my mind.

"I was going to try to thank him tonight," she admits, her features hardening. "I've had dreams of gutting that horned bastard."

"Who's your friend?" Temper, who's been hanging on the periphery of our conversation, now inserts herself into it.

"Aetherial, Temperance—Temperance, Aetherial," I say, making introductions.

Aetherial takes Temper's hand. "You must be the sorceress everyone's talking about." She brushes a kiss to the back of Temper's hand. "Enchanted."

Nothing takes the wind out of Temper's sails quite like a little flattery.

"Who are you?" Temper asks, a touch nicer than she would've otherwise been.

"A fellow former captive," Aetherial says.

Our conversation trails off when the noise in the room dies down. Dozens of fae look to the side of the room. I follow their gazes in time to see Mara, Des, and Janus filing out of the side door they previously entered, Des wearing a dark expression.

I tense when I see the King of Day behind him, my palms beginning to sweat. He might not have abused me, but he delivered me to my abuser. In my mind, there's hardly a distinction between the two.

"I need to get back to my duties," Aetherial says, excusing herself. "Temperance, a pleasure to meet you." She dips her head. "Callie, I hope to see you again soon." And then she melts back into the crowd, working her way back to the very man who made it possible for her and me to meet.

As soon as Des catches sight of me, he disappears and reappears at my side. His wings flare wide around me, pushing away everyone nearby—including Temper.

"I will go to war with him for this," he growls. "I swear it to you."

It takes me a second to catch up with the trajectory of Des's thoughts. War. Janus. The Kingdom of Day. Revenge for my abduction.

"I won't stop until I've toppled his throne and captured him," Des continues. "I'll imprison him in the Catacombs of Memnos, where my monsters will cut out his innards and feed them to hi—"

I press my hand against Des's mouth.

Holy shit. I mean, ho-ly *shit*.

"Okay, so that's super vivid, and I really appreciate where this is all coming from—"

He removes my hand. "Clearly, I've been too soft and you've been too lenient if you don't believe—"

Hand back on his mouth. "—but I'd really just like to get through the week without any other incidents," I finish.

This time when Des pulls my hand away from his lips, he's gentler, clasping my hand between both of his. "I cannot undo what's been done, but I want to make things right for you." His voice drops low. "I don't want you to ever have to go through that experience again."

He's legit going to make me choke up.

"I won't," I say, my voice hoarse.

It's an empty promise. Neither of us managed to stop my abduction from happening once before, so who's to say we could stop it from happening again? But sometimes you just need to make those stupid empty promises for the benefit of everyone. "I can deal with the Day King for a week."

A blatant lie because I'm pretty sure I can't. I'm a chicken when it comes to facing the bad men who've victimized me.

But somehow I'm just going to have to deal—both for Des's sake and for mine.

CHAPTER 28

That night, I lie in Des's arms, the stars back in the sky where they belong, my hair spilling around us. A few fairy lights hover in the air above us, giving the room a soft glow.

Des strokes my back, his movements stirring the feathers of my wings. My cheek presses against his warm chest. If ever I had a home, it would be right here.

"Tell me about your father," I say, my own fingers idly tracing the muscles that run down his torso.

Des lets out a laugh devoid of mirth. "Did I scare you that much earlier?"

I lift my head and give him a quizzical look. "What are you talking about?"

His hand on my back pauses. When it resumes, it's to draw idle pictures with his finger. I wonder, if he were handed a pencil and paper, what, exactly, those idle drawings would be of.

"They say I get my temper from my father," he admits.

"Who says this?" I ask quietly.

"It's known that the Night Kingdom's royal bloodline is quick to anger," he says, sidestepping the question. "It's why my mother made me work so hard to control my anger, and it's what made me particularly ruthless when I was with the Angels of Small Death."

I find I want to ask about his brotherhood, but I bite back my questions, afraid they would derail what I really want to know tonight.

"Even now," he continues, "when I've had so much time to work on it, it can still take over."

Like earlier tonight.

I want to tell him he's not giving himself the benefit of the doubt. When I think about Des and control, I think about all those months I spent back in high school trying to whittle my mate down to no avail. Or how, when he found me in Karnon's throne room, bloody and broken, he still kept a leash on his anger up until the very last moment.

But I don't mention any of this.

Instead, I ask, "Would your father lose control?"

Des's hand moves to my hair. He runs his fingers through it, letting it slide through them. "Sometimes—from what I've heard," he says. Des's eyes grow distant. "Usually when something unpleasant surprised him."

I lay my head back down on his chest. "You still haven't exactly answered my question."

There's so much I don't know about Des—centuries' worth of memories he hasn't bothered to share. And I want to know each and every detail about his life, but this particular detail, his father, is one that seems especially important.

"Then perhaps"—his finger taps my nose—"you should be more precise with your questions."

"Des."

I hear the sigh of air that leaves his lungs. "Out of all the fun, wicked little truths you could ask me, you had to choose this one..."

He's squirming, I realize. It's so very human, and so very unlike my mate.

"I don't like talking about him," he admits.

I get that. God, do I get that.

"He was killing off his children," Des says out of nowhere.

I tense in his arms.

"When I was conceived," he continues, "he was killing off all his children. The adults, the kids, even the babies."

I don't breathe for several seconds.

The first ludicrous thought I have is that Des once had siblings.

The second is that they're all ghosts now. Every one of them. All because of his father.

I can't wrap my mind around that. It's too cruel, too evil, too unconscionable.

"Why?" I finally ask. My question seems to echo in the quiet of the room.

I don't expect an answer, not just because Des isn't forthcoming with them but also because I've found as a PI that the most twisted cases hardly ever have an explanation. Sometimes people do atrocious things just because they can.

The Bargainer's hand slides from my hair, down my arm.

"Some prophecy he received forewarned him that his legacy would lead to his downfall."

It sounds like a Greek drama.

"I don't know if he ever cared about his children, but if he did, he cared about his power more."

Now I understand why, as frightening as the casket children are and as soulless as they seem, Des won't harm them.

No child deserves to be slaughtered because of their bloodline.

"My mother was a favorite concubine of his. When she found out she was pregnant, she fled the palace. Eventually, she ended up in Arestys. I didn't know it until later, but throughout my entire childhood, we were living in hiding."

I wondered how Des could've come from the royal harem and still have led the life he did.

Now I know.

My wicked king. He wouldn't have existed if his mother hadn't done what she did.

Trying to imagine a world without Desmond Flynn is even harder to fathom than a world in which a father kills off all his heirs.

What would life be like if there were no Bargainer to save me from my past, no Des to comfort me in the night, no mate to stake his claim after seven long years of waiting?

Just the thought hurts.

I stroke my fingers down his skin. *It didn't happen.* The man beneath me is more than dreams and wishes. He's flesh and blood, skin and bone, muscle and magic.

And he's mine.

"Did it come true?" I ask. "The prophecy?"

For several seconds, all I hear is Des's breathing. Eventually, he lifts his hand, and the fairy lights above us wink out.

"That's enough sharing for one evening," he says.

In the darkness, I'm left to my own thoughts. And I can't help but wonder—

What is Des still keeping from me?

CHAPTER 29

The sounds of clinking silverware echo in Mara's private breakfast nook.

"Well, last night was more than a little thrilling," Mara says, breaking the silence.

The three fae rulers, I, and the Green Man all are seated around a table, enjoying an awkward-as-fuck breakfast.

The diplomatic talks that occur this week are a cornerstone of Solstice, and apparently today's breakfast meeting is the first of them.

To be honest, I don't have high hopes about how this year's talks are going to go. The Fauna King is noticeably absent while his kingdom is scrambling to find a replacement ruler. Des and Janus, meanwhile, have been glaring at each other the entire meal, Des rolling his knife around his hand like I've seen him do with daggers. And Mara has glanced at me a few times, but she hasn't quite been able to make the leap to addressing me properly.

All I'm hoping for is to keep breakfast down and not

freak the hell out. I shouldn't be docilely sitting at a table with the man who abducted me from Des's house. If he were a human man, I'd have already been elbows deep into my revenge, using my glamour to get him to do anything and everything I willed. But, alas, he's a fae king, both immune to my powers and staggeringly powerful himself.

The only one who seems to be enjoying himself is the Green Man. He's been tucking into his eggs like it's a profession.

This is the weirdest diplomatic meeting ever.

"So, remind me again," Mara says, glancing between the King of Day and the King of Night, "what tiff was it again that almost ruined two millennia of peaceful Solstice gatherings?"

Des leans back in his seat, folding one leg over the opposite knee. "Janus kidnapped my mate."

Janus slams his silverware on the table, making the plates rattle. "For the last goddamn time, I didn't touch her." His eyes flick to me. "I've never even *seen* her before."

Liar.

I don't know what he's playing at, but I could never forget the corona of light that shines around him or that face of his, which would make sculptors weep.

He must read my thoughts from my expression because his eyes flick away in annoyance.

Mara's gaze moves to me. "Did Janus kidnap you?" she asks, folding her hands under her chin.

It takes me a second to respond because, oh my God, she actually addressed me, a mere mortal. I set down my fork. "Yes." My voice is steely.

Janus lets out a huff, throwing his hands in the air. "I did *not.*"

"So Janus was working with Karnon?" Mara asks the room.

My eyes are trained on the King of Day.

No one answers.

"Well?" she presses, her attention turning to Janus. "Is it true?"

"Of course it's not. I can provide an alibi—not that I'm inclined to." He levels Des with another glare.

"Well, there we go," Mara says, smiling tightly. "He can provide an alibi. Perhaps Callypso here was just confused."

"I wasn't," I say. Only, my voice sounds a touch defensive because...what if? What if the King of Day could prove he wasn't on earth that morning he abducted me?

What then?

"Now can we all move on?" Mara says, ignoring my response. She gives everyone a hard look—me in particular—and I quickly realize we've come to the last of her good graces.

Put up and shut up, that's what she's demanding of us.

"*Please,*" Janus says, exasperated.

Shadows seep into the corners of the room. I haven't glanced over at Des, but just from those shadows alone, I can tell he's not going to agree to anything.

Des leans back in his seat. "N—"

Swallowing down my cowardice, I place a hand on his thigh, stopping him. "*Yes,*" I say, my voice hoarse.

Des drags his attention off Janus long enough to give me a stormy look. Whatever he sees on my face has him working his jaw. Ever so slowly, the shadows recede.

Folding his arms over his chest, he gives a hard nod.

"Fabulous." Mara picks up her flute of champagne. "Now, on to the real news: Desmond, you killed Karnon?"

Next to me, the Bargainer says nothing, looking both savage and insolent.

"Desmond," Mara presses. She appears almost predatory, waiting on his answer.

Idly, he picks up my hand and plays with it, a small gesture that draws our audience's attention. "Yes, I killed him. He hurt my mate."

"Hmm." Mara takes a sip of her drink. Her eyes move to me, calculating, curious. "What was it like, being Karnon's prisoner?" she asks me.

My heart's racing. I take a steadying breath. "It was hell. Absolute hell." I'm proud that my voice doesn't waver. I might feel like a mess, but I sound sure of myself.

Mara leans forward, a sick light to her eyes. "Did he rape you?"

"*Enough.*" Power rides Des's voice.

The Flora Queen sits back in her seat, taking another sip of her champagne.

My skin crawls at her question, at her disturbing interest.

"I believe Karnon was behind the women's disappearances," she says, "but the fact remains, the spell hasn't lifted. Someone else is still out there pulling strings."

A chill runs through the room.

"Our investigation has assumed as much," Des says.

"As has mine," Janus adds.

The two rulers' eyes meet. I'm pretty sure oil and water do a better job of mixing than these two.

I get the impression this rivalry predates me. Light and darkness, constantly battling each other.

"What I find interesting," the Green Man cuts in, "are the casket children."

All eyes move to him. So far, he hasn't added much to the conversation.

He tosses his utensils onto his cleaned plate. "Those

children drink blood and prophesize—traits closely associated with the Night Kingdom."

He lets that little revelation linger in the air.

Traits closely associated with the Night Kingdom.

His meaning is clear: whoever fathered those children was a Night fae, and the only Night fairy powerful enough to wield the kind of magic the Thief of Souls does would be...

Des's mouth curves into a vicious smile, his whole face turning sinister. "So you believe it was me. That I raped those women and fathered those children?"

The idea isn't just ridiculous, it's abhorrent.

"It wouldn't have to be rape," Mara says contemplatively. She eyes Des, her gaze disrobing him. My hackles rise at the sight. "I've heard tales of your conquests. Who can resist the Night King with all his charms?"

My fingers curl around the edges of my seat, and I fight to keep my anger at bay.

"Surely you guys can't be serious?" I say. "Any of the women taken can tell you—Karnon and Karnon alone touched them."

"And yet my mate's point remains the same," Mara says. "The casket children have Night fae—not Fauna fae—traits."

This is the same conundrum I grappled with when I went to see the children in the royal nursery. I hate that it's now being twisted to incriminate my mate.

Des, meanwhile, is doing nothing to dispel the accusations against him. He just continues to stare at Mara with that malevolent grin on his face, unaffected by her words.

"Why should we not believe it was you?" Janus says. "I heard it took you nearly a week to rescue your mate from Karnon's palace. Why so long, Flynn?"

That question…that question hurts. Forget the fact these rulers are spinning tales out of shadows. Why *did* Des wait so long?

Des leans back in his chair, looking haughtily at the other rulers. "And what if it is me? What if I, in my infinite power, staged the whole thing so the mad king would take the fall? What would you do? What *could* you do?"

Mara and Janus share a look.

Janus leans forward, his eyes intense. "Whatever needed to be done."

I feel the depth of Des's power then, sitting in that room. It's as vast as the universe and as dark as the night.

If he were cruel, if he were evil…there'd be no stopping him.

If he were cruel and he were evil, our bond wouldn't care one way or another.

Like it or not, I'd still be his.

CHAPTER 30

The casket children have Night Kingdom traits.

My skin prickles, even though it's warm outside.

"Why did it take you so long to find me when I was Karnon's prisoner?" I ask Des as he and I head back to our room. I don't want to sound hurt or accusing, but a part of me feels both.

Des stops, turning to face me. He tilts his head. "Are you actually considering their words?"

I don't know what to say, caught between my own uncertainty and Des's secrets. "I just need to know," I say, my voice quiet.

Des's mouth flattens into a grimace. He glances around us, looking at the fairies who stroll the gardens. His meaning is clear: this is not a private place. He nods to the huge cedar we're rooming in, his wings unfolding behind him. "Follow me."

Before I can ask him what he's doing, he leaps into the air, his massive wings looking out of place in the bright light of day. Around us, people stop and watch.

Releasing a sigh, I take a running leap, letting my wings lift me into the air.

Des lands on one of the highest branches of the cedar. Clumsily, I join him, nearly overshooting the branch and falling off. He catches me around the waist, letting out a husky laugh I feel to my core.

He can't be bad, he *can't*. We might both be fucked up, and sure, Des has killed a few people, but he can't be *evil*—more like…wicked lite.

I situate myself on the branch so that my legs are hanging off, the backs of my ankles brushing my wings and my shoulder brushing Des's. From this high up, fairies look like tiny bugs.

I breathe in the crisp forest air, the treetop swaying slightly in the breeze.

"That morning, the morning you went missing," Des begins, "you can't even—" His voice breaks, and I swivel my head to stare at him. He's a far cry from the cocksure fae king he was back in Mara's breakfast nook. Now I feel the heat and pain in his words.

"At first, I thought you walked out on me," he says. "I thought you took off the way I had so many times back when you were in high school. In the days that followed, I *wished* you had.

"It was the full cup of coffee that changed everything. It was just sitting there on the patio table, still full. You of all people wouldn't just leave a cup of coffee untouched."

I smile a little because it's true; I'd never let good coffee go to waste.

"That's about the time I realized you hadn't left; you'd been *taken*.

"The anger I felt, the fear—" He shakes his head. "I

scoured the earth for you, and then I scoured the Otherworld. Every minute that passed, the dread deepened. And it—" He runs a hand through his hair, letting out a choked laugh. "It was so much worse than those seven years of waiting. So vastly worse.

"I cashed in years of favors for bread crumbs, and still it took me days to find myself in the Fauna Kingdom."

My heart squeezes as I watch Des recall those days I was missing. I hadn't known any of this.

"I should've been able to find you. I should've. The way my power works…the secrets I hear—the voices that tell me what I need to know—they were ominously quiet."

Secrets? Voices?

He reaches for my hand before pressing the back of it to his mouth. I feel the slightest tremor in his touch, like the memory is still visceral to him.

"What about our bond?" I ask. "Couldn't you have found me through it?"

I've heard tales of soul mates tracking each other down, their bond like a compass directing them to the location of their mate.

Des tears his gaze from the horizon. "There is something about our bond that I haven't admitted to you…"

I don't know how a single sentence can fill me with such foreboding, but this one does. My gut squeezes.

"What is it?" I can barely force the words out.

"Cherub, our bond…has issues."

CHAPTER 31

When I find Temper back in her room, she's picking out what to wear. Today, the braids in her hair are woven through with crystals and spirals of gold thread.

"What's up?" she says after I plop onto her bed.

I watch her change, propping my head on my hands. "Nothing..."

Everything.

"Not going to lie, these fae outfits are cute as hell," she says, tossing one next to me.

I make a noncommittal response.

Why did I come here? Temper is practically humming under her breath. Clearly, things between her and Malaki are going well. She's a sorceress in lust, which means she's in no mood for a sad story.

"What is it?" she asks as she begins undressing.

"Nothing."

Temper snorts. "Callie, we've been friends for nearly a decade. Stop beating off the bush—"

I wince. "*Around*, Temper. Beating *around* the bush."

She turns to me. "I know. I'm just not going to miss an opportunity to say *beat off* when it presents itself. Now spit out whatever's on your mind."

"Des and I aren't officially soul mates." It comes out as a whisper.

She pauses in the middle of changing. "What do you mean?"

I grab the bra from the pile of clothes next to me and throw it at her. Distractedly, she begins to put it on.

I can hear Des's words up in that treetop. *Cherub, our bond...has issues.*

"When I was Karnon's prisoner, Des couldn't find me because even though we're technically mates...our magic is incompatible."

"Incompatible?" Temper says, looking bewildered. "That's the stupidest thing I've ever heard. How can it be incompatible?"

"I'm a human. He's a fairy. Our magic comes from different worlds." It's the same reason why my glamour doesn't work on the fae and why Karnon's dark power never worked on me.

It's not like human and fae magic is completely incompatible—Des can obviously use his own powers on me—but when it comes to the melding of our two essences...our bond is imperfect.

Soul mate bonds are always described as a magical thread tethering two people together. I never actually felt our bond—not as an actual, physical thing—but I never thought to worry about it either. Des has always felt like mine, even during all those years when I lived without him.

"And yet you're still soul mates?" Temper says.

I nod, my chin rubbing against the backs of my hands. That was the one thing Des emphasized over and over.

You are my mate.

"All right, so then suck it up," Temper says, slipping on her outfit. "At least you *have* a soul mate. The rest of us have to do this whole love thing the old-fashioned way."

I grab one of her pillows and bury my face into it. "Ugh, you're right," I say.

"Of course I'm right." She sees the pillow in my hand. "Oh, uh, you don't want to be cuddling that. I'm pretty sure it was used as a prop last night when Malaki—"

"Eugh!" I toss the pillow away while my friend laughs her ass off.

"Your face was deeper in that pillow than Malaki's dick was in me."

"I don't want to hear this for *so* many reasons."

So. Many.

"He's *huge*," Temper says, flopping onto the bed next to me. "But, you know, just the right amount of huge."

I groan. Really, why had I come here?

"And when he starts going at it," she continues, "he's like a jackhammer"—okay, that visual is way too vivid—"I just have to hold on for dear life."

I push myself off the bed. "All right, story time's over."

"Don't act like you didn't want to know."

"There's knowing and then there's *knowing*," I say.

No one needs Temper's level of detail.

"Are you ready?" I ask her when she adds a pair of earrings to her ensemble.

"Gah, you're so impatient," she says. She shakes out her braids and grabs her things. "I'm ready."

The two of us leave Temper's room and head for the

gardens below us. We cut through the palace grounds then stop when we come to a table and chairs. We take a seat, and for a minute or so after we sit down, we don't talk, instead watching the fairies stroll.

"So," Temper says, finally dragging her attention off the fairies around us, "where is everyone's favorite criminal?" she asks.

"You're going to have to be more specific than that." She and I know a lot of criminals.

Temper sighs. "The Bargainer."

"Oh—more meetings." Ones that are strictly for rulers. I should be there; I know the discussions will include the reports of Karnon's captives. But tradition forbids me from joining, so here I am, twiddling my thumbs with Temper.

A human woman comes up to us carrying a tea set and a plate of little sandwiches, the crust removed from them. I tense when I see the branded skin of her wrist as she sets the tray on our table.

She's enslaved.

Being served by her feels wrong. If she chose to be a waitress, that would be one thing, but this is something else entirely.

Her eyes are downcast as she begins to set teacups in front of us.

I try to wave away her efforts to serve us. "It's all right," I say. "We've got this. Thank you for bringing this out."

She won't look at me, even as she nods. And damn it, I feel bad about everything I'm doing and not doing right now because enslavement twists it all up into something ugly.

She turns to leave.

"Hey, wait," Temper says to the woman.

The human woman pauses. Then, hesitantly, she turns back around.

Temper pats the empty seat next to her. "Sit down."

The woman looks like sitting is the last thing she wants to do, but reluctantly, she does in fact sit down.

"What's your name?" As Temper talks, she begins fixing the woman a plate of sandwiches and a cup of tea.

"Gladiola." The woman fidgets, glancing around us nervously.

"Hi, Gladiola. I'm Temper and this is Callie," she says, introducing us.

Gladiola's eyes dart to me. "I'm not supposed to talk with you."

"Why not?" Temper asks. "We're all humans here."

I stare warily at my friend, trying to figure out what she's playing at.

Gladiola lets out a shaky breath. "The fairies are uncomfortable that a human woman is going to become the next Night Queen. They're afraid you'll put ideas in our heads."

"About equality?" Temper says. "What a terrible thing indeed," she says sarcastically.

The woman presses her lips together and glances down at her hands in her lap. I assume that's all she's going to say, but then she admits, "They also don't trust the Night King. He killed another king, and the Fauna fae want revenge. And—" She hesitates, as if realizing she's doing the very thing she wasn't supposed to.

"And what?" Temper encourages.

Gladiola's hands twist in her lap, and her eyes move from Temper to me then back to Temper. I see her swallow, but then something resolute enters her features. "People have been saying the Night King is behind the disappearances," she confesses. Her chin shakes a little.

My stomach drops. That's the second person today to say such a thing.

"They say," she continues, "that he's the last person they see."

Unease skitters up my back.

It's just a rumor.

Gladiola glances at me, and it's as though she's only now realizing who she confessed these rumors to. "I'm sorry," she whispers softly, looking horror-struck. "Can I leave?"

Before either Temper or I can respond, Night soldiers come running through the gardens.

Several of them flash past us before I snag one by the shirtsleeves. "What's going on?"

He almost doesn't stop. It's not until he sees who caught him that he pauses.

He takes a deep breath. "Another soldier has disappeared."

CHAPTER 32

Another soldier disappeared. That's all I can concentrate on that evening as fairies enjoy yet another dance inside the Flora Kingdom's castle.

Since we arrived in the kingdom, three Night soldiers, four Fauna soldiers, one Day soldier, and two Flora soldiers have disappeared from the outskirts of the palace grounds. The numbers are staggering, even for the Thief of Souls.

Whoever he is, he's growing bolder—or more desperate.

The whole thing casts a dark pall on the festival. Even this evening's ball is a more somber occasion than the last two. The conversations are subdued, and I swear I see fairies looking over their shoulders, like the boogeyman might jump out and snatch them when they're not looking.

This evening, rather than enjoy himself, Des ping-pongs from one official to the next, receiving updates, offering suggestions, and listening to worries. Even now, even when he's supposed to be enjoying the evening, he's working. I watch him, his arms folded across his massive chest as he leans down to listen to a Flora fae.

"I'm surprised he left you alone." Janus steps up to my side, looking like the morning sun.

Almost immediately, I feel my panic rise.

He's not going to take me, I try to calm myself. *Not here at least.*

Then an even sharper thought lances through me. *What if he's behind the recent disappearances?*

Sure, he wasn't here that first evening when two of our men went missing, but he did take me, that I'm sure of.

"I'm surprised you're not alongside him offering aide and advice." I'm proud that my voice doesn't tremble as I speak.

"I wanted a drink"—he lifts his glass—"and a break." He swirls his wine. "Besides, I find the King of Night insufferable—no offense."

He glances at me, and I hold his gaze. Everything about him is made to be warm and inviting, from his tan skin to his golden hair to his bright blue eyes. And yet I find him cold, so very, very cold.

You took me. We both know it.

"You must hate me," he says softly, not looking away.

"Are you admitting to what you did?" I can't believe I'm having this conversation.

"I *didn't* take you."

"You and I both know that's not true," I say.

"Gods above," he says, glancing heavenward, "it is."

My skin is crawling. Every second I stand here talking to this man, I feel like I'm one step closer to death.

"Listen," I say, leaning in, "I don't know if you're the Thief of Souls or if you simply work for him, but I *will* fucking pin this on you, you sick son of a bitch."

I'm shaking, and I'm frightened, and I'm hopped up on enough adrenaline to lift a car, but I just looked my abductor in the eye and told him off.

Goddamn, I feel like a badass.

I'm about to leave when he catches my wrist. "Wait—"

"Do *not* touch me," I warn.

Des snaps his head up from his conversation across the room, his attention homing in on us.

Janus releases my wrist like it burned him. "I was giving a speech to my people when you were taken. I have proof."

Shadows creep up the edges of the room.

"I don't believe you," I tell him. But not for the first time today, I hesitate. Am I remembering things wrong?

Suddenly, none of that matters because Des materializes in front of me, coming between me and the King of Day.

"Janus, you need to step the fuck away from my mate." Des's wings begin to unfurl, his talons looking particularly lethal. "Don't talk to her"—he takes a step forward—"don't look at her"—another ominous step—"don't come close to her." The two are almost nose to nose. "As far as you're concerned, she doesn't exist."

Around us, the room has gone quiet. I'm pretty sure everyone is expecting a repeat of last night's brawl.

Janus appears unimpressed. "You've forgotten your place, Flynn. It's within my rights to speak to any of the subjects here, mated or not."

Des's voice drops low, so that only we can hear it. "Have I told you how easy it was to kill Karnon? His bones broke like twigs, his body burst like overripe fruit." Des smiles, the action cruel. "Ending him was the easiest thing in the world.

"Don't make the same mistake he did. Stay the fuck away from my mate, or I will kill you, just as I did the mad king."

Des's warning is enough to keep Janus at bay.

I rub my arms as I watch the Day King move into the crowd, downing his wine and snagging another flute from a nearby table.

Slowly, the Bargainer's wings tuck back into themselves, and the darkness recedes.

"Are you all right?" Des asks, his hands moving to my upper arms. He looks me over, like Janus might've done some damage to me while we talked.

I nod, taking in a shaky breath. "I'm fine. He just...he unnerves the shit out of me," I say, my eyes wandering to the Day King, who's now talking with Mara and the Green Man, the three watching Des and me carefully.

The Bargainer lets out a husky laugh, some of his dangerous edge dying away with it. "And to think I once worried that you'd like the asshole."

I remember Des telling me about the King of Day, that he was a lover of truth and honesty and beauty, and yadda, yadda, yadda.

I let a very real shudder course through me.

Des's hand cups my face. "We can leave. Right this second. My men will pack our bags and follow us. Janus cannot step a foot into my kingdom without me knowing, and he's aware that if he does, death awaits him." The Bargainer's eyes glint with malice.

Perhaps Des does descend from demons. I see something in the back of his gaze that craves violence far more than even my siren.

"All you have to do is say the word," he says.

His offer is so very tempting. If I stay, I'll have several more days of this.

But if we left...

If we left, it would make Des look weak or, worse, guilty. I shake my head. "Let's see this through."

He stares at me for several seconds before nodding. "If you change your mind—"

"I'll tell you," I finish for him.

The next hour is filled with discussion after discussion as Des and I move about the room. Now that the Bargainer is at my side, I've gotten roped into talking with fairies. Bleh. It doesn't help that these are the same fairies desperately trying to ignore my existence. It would actually be fairly entertaining if it weren't so grating.

I'm a human, not a human-shaped dump someone took on the floor. No one has to pretend I don't exist.

Despite Des's best efforts, I eventually manage to slip away. As I move away from him, he gives me a look that has me clutching my bracelet of beads.

Methinks I'm going to pay later for leaving him to suffer his fate alone.

I mosey over to the table where row after row of wineglasses sit, ripe for the taking.

Don't mind if I do.

I snag one, sighing a little after I take my first sip.

So dang good.

Several minutes into my escape, I realize I have no conversation to join. Both Malaki and Temper are suspiciously absent. I search the crowd for Aetherial, wondering if she's here tonight. If she is, I don't see her.

I take another sip of my drink. The only other people I've come to know here are the rulers. Eff no am I talking to Janus, who's currently schmoozing with some Fauna fae officials, and Mara is on the dance floor, in the middle of the closest thing to an open orgy that I've ever seen. Her harem of men clamors around her, their hands and lips pressed against her skin. It's weird to see them all gyrating together while a string quartet plays in the background, and it's even weirder that I'm watching.

I desperately want to unsee this...but I also can't look away.

Damnit, where is Temper when you need her? She'd have a whole commentary on what's going down.

But instead of Temper, I get the Green Man. He sidles up next to me, and I suppress a groan.

Not him.

He follows my gaze to Mara and her harem. "You get used to it," he says.

I take a healthy swig of my drink.

Jesus, Joseph, and Mary, am I glad I can drink again. Fairies, I'm quickly learning, are best dealt with while buzzed.

"Flora fae are not usually monogamous—not even mates," he continues.

Don't care and don't really want to know. "Huh," I say.

"The past kings of the Night realm have not been either. Not even your mate's father."

The Green Man stands a little too close, and my hand twitches with the need to push him away a few feet.

"I know."

Drop the subject, Green Man. Please, for the love of baby angels, drop the subject.

"I would think that, as future queen of the Kingdom of Night, you would be open to...hedonistic pursuits."

I don't know if he's propositioning me or just feeling me out, but ugh, this guy is creepy.

I grimace. "I'm not."

Mara grabs one of the men nearest to her, kissing him deeply on the dance floor while another man squeezes her breast.

And her mate stands at my side, watching the entire thing go down.

The ick factor of this situation is off the charts.

"Once you get past the unusual nature of it, I think you'll find it can be very liberating. I've had many, many lovers—though never a human woman."

All right, that was *definitely* a proposition.

I down my wine, and when that doesn't make the situation immediately better (it was worth a try), I push the Green Man back several steps. "You need to back up, buddy."

And I need more wine. I need *all* the wine.

"So what does the King of the Night intend to do with you, a mortal?" he asks, smirking at me, his chest still pressed against my hand.

I look at the Green Man, really look at him. "Excuse me?" What kind question is that? I'm Des's *mate*, not some new hire.

"Producing heirs," the Green Man muses aloud, "that would be at the top of his mind, especially given his age and your fertility…"

Producing heirs?

Producing—*heirs*?

I feel like I'm pressing the fast-forward button on my brain, my thoughts racing by at warp speed until they stop on one very poignant realization.

Des and I have been having unprotected sex.

Des and I have been having unprotected sex.

Oh God, oh God, oh God.

There's suddenly not enough wine in the world for this conversation.

My hand drops from the Green Man's chest.

I haven't been using birth control. Des hasn't been wearing condoms.

Fuck, fuck, fuckity *fuck*.

What sort of loser just *forgets* about these things?

It's a trick question because obviously this bitch right here is the loser who does.

Des and I have never talked about the subject of children, aside from one confession he forced out of me weeks ago, where I admitted I wanted to have children with him.

But not this *second*.

What if, oh God, what if…*what if I'm pregnant?*

The Green Man's voice drifts in. "…fae aren't particularly fertile, but humans are."

Gah, this dude won't shut up about it. Where is the *eject* button for this conversation?

I catch sight of Temper, who is entering the ballroom, self-consciously straightening her dress.

There is my escape.

"Temper—*Temper!*" I call out, the panic clear in my voice.

She whips about, searching the crowd until she sees me. My best friend takes one look at my expression and another at the man next to me, and bless her to the ends of the earth, she begins to slip through the crowd, a determined look on her face.

"Are you all right?" the Green Man says, his eyes bright with excitement rather than concern.

As if he's unaware of the effect his words have on me.

My eyes search the crowd, falling on Des, whose back is

to me. He's the one I should really talk about this with, but he's trapped in discussions, and more importantly, I don't really want to have *that talk.*

Temper swoops in then. "Back up, Green Man, my friend needs more wine."

Before either me or the Green Man have a chance to react, Temper slides her arm through mine and forcefully escorts me away.

"Oh my God, I love you," I say.

"I know. I love you too." She gives my arm a squeeze.

"I need to get out of here," I say, not bothering to comment on the fact Temper has a healthy glow to her or that her hair is a little sex shaken.

"What's wrong?" she asks, eyeing me up and down. "You look like you accidently saw your grandparents getting it on."

I swallow. "I'll tell you, just—" I glance around us at all the fairies crowding the room. Dropping my voice, I say, "Not here."

She eyes me again but nods.

We're just about to the door when I hear Mara's voice. "*Callie!*"

I close my eyes.

We nearly made it.

"Wanna just pretend we didn't hear that?" Temper asks.

"*Callie!*" Mara calls again, more insistent this time.

I sigh and shake my head.

The two of us turn. The Queen of Flora is no longer on the dance floor, instead drinking a refreshment from where I stood a moment ago with the Green Man, who is now no longer in sight.

"You must come here." She beckons me over, her crowd of men eyeing me curiously.

"Have I mentioned I don't like that woman?" Temper says next to me. "Look at that smug smile of hers. She looks like the kind of snake who befriends you just so she can steal your boyfriend."

This is precisely why Temper and I are friends. The girl gets it.

"Ugh, I should probably go over," I say.

Being mates with a fae king has its drawbacks. I spent my teen years being a wallflower and the years following that making people forget they'd run into me. But now, being Des's mate, I'm as far from anonymous as I can be.

Temper dips her finger into her wine, stirring it contemplatively. It's a look she gets right about the time she's concocting a spell. "If she pisses you off, give me a signal, and I'll rescue you again, no questions asked."

I nod. "Thanks for having my back, Temper."

"Anytime—oh, and later I want to hear what you were about to tell me," she says as she backs away.

I swallow uncomfortably, the Green Man's conversation bubbling back up.

I could be pregnant.

I nod and part ways with her, taking a deep breath as I head over to Mara, who's giggling with her harem. Her gaze moves to me, and her eyes sharpen.

"So, tell me," she says, "how *did* you and Desmond meet?"

I glance around at the men watching us. Everyone looks so goddamn predatory. This is exactly why I wanted to stay far, far away from the Otherworld in the first place. These people will eat you alive.

She sees where my attention is. "Don't worry about them. Now, I've been dying to hear this story."

I have a knee-jerk reaction to lie, as I have in the past

when it comes to how Des and I met, but before I can, I reassess my audience.

You know what? Why not give them the truth?

"The first time I met the King of the Night was the evening I killed my father. He helped me hide the body."

For a moment, no one speaks.

And then, one of the men begins to laugh. One by one, the rest join in. Even Mara cracks a smile.

"What have I told you about humans?" one man says to another. "They are vicious little things when they want to be."

I frown at the man before the Queen of Flora drags my attention away.

"My, my," she says, "how *much* you and Desmond have in common. No wonder he's so smitten with you. A woman after his own heart."

I furrow my brows. "What's that supposed to mean?"

She waves the conversation off, taking another sip of her drink. "That's not my story to tell. But, speaking of stories, I imagine you have quite the tale from your time with Karnon."

Yeah, that's not exactly a tale I want to share during cocktail hour at the Flora Queen's palace.

"It must've been a shock," she says when I don't respond, "coming here to the Otherworld—and being kidnapped no less! I can't imagine being trapped in Karnon's palace. That awful place had long since gone to seed by the time you arrived."

Bones breaking, blood dripping, endless agony.

I give her a tight smile.

She leans forward. "I hear Desmond arrived *just* in time. It seems uncanny almost. I wonder how he found you so quickly..."

I narrow my eyes at her, seeing exactly what she's getting at. Had I not talked to Des about this earlier, her words would worm their way under my skin.

She lightly touches my arm. "Well, it's no matter now. You're safe, and thanks to those wings of yours, Desmond has ensured you cannot leave his side to return to earth."

As soon as that last sentence registers, my heart seems to skip a beat.

Thanks to those wings of yours, Desmond has ensured you cannot leave his side...

"*Callypso?*" Mara's voice echoes, as though from a distance.

I blink several times, the Flora Queen's face coming into focus. Her expression is pinched with concern, though I know it's all an act. Just like the casual way she managed to plant those bits of doubt in my mind.

"Are you all right?" she asks, reaching for my arm.

Des's words up on the treetop return to me. How, despite our weak connection, he felt my need and my pain through our bond. That my agony at the hands of Karnon had to be as intense as it was for the Bargainer to sense my distress and, through it, my location.

That was how Des found me when he did. *Not* because he wanted to keep me here in the Otherworld like some caged bird. He doesn't think like that, even if the Flora Queen does.

The moment Mara's fingers touch my elbow, I jerk it out of her reach.

Around us, I hear a few muffled gasps from fairies who must've caught sight of the action. Apparently, not letting a queen touch you is some sort of faux pas.

"You're wrong." I take a step back. I can feel my wings ruffling in agitation. "So, so wrong."

I need to get away from these creatures, with their fake smiles and duplicitous words.

"Wait, I hope I didn't upset you," she says.

A lie.

"I called you over because I've been meaning to give you a gift in honor of your bond to the King of the Night."

I feel the first tendrils of apprehension. I've learned from Des that when it comes to gifts from fairies, there are always strings attached.

The Flora Queen's harem presses in around me, boxing me in while Mara gestures to someone over her shoulder. A human servant weaves through the throng of guests carrying a silver tray. Resting on it is a delicate metal wineglass filled with light-purple liquid. She stops at the queen's side.

Carefully, Mara removes it from the tray. "Do you know what this is?" she asks.

I shake my head, bewildered by this newest turn of events.

"I would've thought that perhaps...but never mind." She hands me the goblet, and it's only as she does so that it clicks. This is her gift—whatever this actually is.

Reluctantly, I take the silver cup, staring down at the liquid with a slight grimace.

When I don't take any further action, some of Mara's men laugh at me like I'm a simpleton. To receive a drink but not to taste it!

"You must try it," the Flora Queen insists.

There's no way in hell I'm going to try it. Not a drink given to me by this broad.

Before I can commit some further faux pas, the air shifts and the shadows deepen. Everyone else must feel it too because conversations hush.

And then, out of the shadows, Des appears, as though from a dream. He's light and darkness, from the shadows that curl around him to the moonbeams that seem to illuminate him from within.

Fairies step out of his way, making an aisle of sorts for him to stride down. Silently, he heads for me, his white hair brushed away from his face, his jaw firm. Just like the first time I saw him, he takes my breath away.

"What is this I hear of a gift?" he says when he reaches our group.

He gently takes the delicate chalice from my hand. "Is this it?" he asks, pacing several feet away, his eyebrows raised. He brings the glass to his nose.

"*Lilac wine,*" he says.

Several people throughout the room gasp.

He gives Mara an approving smile. "Cunning as ever, dear queen."

Ever so deliberately, he overturns the liquid, letting it spill onto the floor as he paces.

The room goes utterly silent.

I glance from person to person, trying to figure out what's going on.

"You trod on my hospitality?" she says, an edge entering her voice.

"Perhaps you should think twice before you try to con my mate. Someone could get the wrong idea," Des says, looking remorseless.

I *knew* something was up with that drink.

Now Mara smiles. "And perhaps you should explain to your human mate why you refuse this most sacred and arcane of lovers' rights. Or why she will die a mortal when she could've lived at your side for eons."

CHAPTER 33

"All right, what is lilac wine?" I ask.

The two of us are back in our rooms, Des's jacket thrown haphazardly across the table, his shirtsleeves rolled up to reveal his corded forearms, and my heels are kicked off, my hair cascading wildly down my back.

He leans against the wall, watching me, his arms crossed over his chest. "A drink."

Awesome. Forthcoming Des has gone into hiding.

"You've got to give me more than that." Both Mara and Des had almost lost their shit over the wine.

"Contrary to your opinion, I actually don't," he says, his eyes glinting in the dim room.

Frustrating man!

"Listen," I say, "if you don't tell me, someone else will. This is your chance to set the record straight."

His arms drop to his sides, and he prowls forward. "Fine, you want me to set the record straight? Here it is, straight and clear: I have imagined giving you lilac wine a *thousand* times." He comes right up to me, and something about his agitated mood has me backing up. "I imagined slipping it to you just as Mara did, coaxing you into drinking it when you didn't know any better."

My back hits a wall, and Des pins me in with his arms.

"I've even had it prepared before," he says, reaching out and stroking the column of my throat with his thumb. "I had it in my fridge back on Catalina Island, and I've had it on hand in my palace."

"What is it?" *And why do you have to be deceitful about it?*

His jaw muscles clench as he wages some internal war between telling me or not. Eventually, he gives in to my questioning.

"Somewhere deep in time, fairies found a way to make their mortal lovers immortal," he says.

His eyes look piercing, *eager*, as he speaks.

"They gave their human lovers lilac wine, and flesh that should've aged became ageless, and magic that was once imperfect became perfect. Two species became one."

"I don't understand," I say. "Why keep this a secret?" It's not like I have anything against lilac wine now that I know about it.

"Maybe I didn't want to know your opinion. If you wanted to be immortal, it would mean you were okay forsaking all those things that make you so delightfully human—things I happen to love."

Awwww.

"But if you didn't want to be immortal, it would mean you expected me to stand by and watch you age—watch you die."

His gaze scours my face, deepening with sadness. Because I *am* aging. Without the lilac wine, I will die long before he ever does.

"So you thought slipping me the wine was a better idea than getting my opinion on the matter?"

See, this is why couples need to talk about things. Healthy option versus unhealthy option here.

"If you notice, I have slipped you *nothing*," he says.

"But you've considered it," I counter.

"How many things have you considered? Does consideration make it wrong?" His lips brush my cheek.

I swallow. "What stopped you from giving me the wine?"

He pulls away a little, frowning. "The same thing that stopped me from taking you away the night of your prom and making you mine forever. I have enough broken humanity to know it's wrong and enough self-control to fight my innate nature."

"And what's your innate nature?" I say, my words whisper soft.

"To take what I want, when I want, and to apologize to no one for it."

Yeesh.

"You want to know a secret?" He doesn't wait for me to answer. "Only if you drink the lilac wine will our bond be complete. Only then can we freely share our magic."

CHAPTER 34

This lilac wine is sounding better and better the more I hear about it.

"Remind me again why you don't want me to drink the wine?" I ask.

Des gives me a small smile. "It doesn't matter what I want. I waited eight years for you, cherub, and now you're here, warming my bed and weaseling my secrets out of me. This is more than enough."

"Why would Mara give lilac wine to me?" I ask, now curious about the Flora Queen's motives. It's obvious enough that she's no fan of mine, so why give me such a gift?

Des tilts his head. "Let's strike a deal: I'll answer your question if you'll answer one of mine."

Everything just has to come down to a deal with the Bargainer.

"Fine," I say. It's not like he can't just take a bead and force the truth out of me anyway.

I feel a subtle shift of magic in the air as Des binds me to the agreement.

His smile spreads before he tucks it away. "To answer your question: Mara probably had several motives when she gave you the lilac wine. She'd want the room to see her being generous to a human and accepting of our bond—that's just good for politics. She was also making a point that you'd be more accepted if you were made to be more like us. And finally, she was probing our relationship for weaknesses."

"Why would she do that?" I ask.

"Leverage," Des responds. "It's quite easy to control people once you understand them."

It's dizzying, the layers of schemes fairies are pursuing at any given moment. Just when I think I might understand such creatures, I hear something like this. I couldn't even keep such intrigue straight in my mind.

"Now," Des says, "I believe it's my turn."

Ah, yes, my turn to answer a question.

"What were you talking about with the Green Man earlier this evening?" he asks.

My face pales.

He noticed that conversation?

The man is way too perceptive.

My throat works. I *really* don't want to have this talk.

The longer I hesitate, the stronger the pull I feel from his magic. It wraps around my windpipe, forcing me to speak.

"We've been having unprotected sex," I finally say.

The magic doesn't release me.

Ugh.

Des waits for me to finish.

I take a deep breath. "I could be pregnant," I whisper.

His eyes widen at my confession.

274

I rub my neck and watch him warily as his magic dissipates.

He studies me, and for the life of me, I can't tell what he's thinking. Finally, he says, "What is this about, cherub?"

Huh?

"It's about that, Des. Having a baby." Just saying it makes it that much more real. I need a pregnancy test, stat.

"I thought you wanted to have my child?" Des says in his dangerous voice.

I do want to have his child—this isn't a matter of if; it's a matter of when.

"This whole thing is just moving too fast," I say.

"Moving too fast?"

Those are clearly the wrong three words to say. I see it in his eyes. That foreign flicker of something alien, something fae.

"Haven't you had enough of moving slow?" His hand presses gently against my stomach, cradling it.

I stare at him, well aware that I'm facing down fae Des, dark Des, Des who craves things I can't understand.

What was it Phaedron had mentioned?

No fairy would let his mate get away just because she put up a little protest.

Hasn't that been the theme of the evening? The possibility that I want things that will take me away from Des rather than bring me closer to him?

"Perhaps I want you to have my child," he says, moving his hand from my stomach to my bracelet. "Perhaps I want us to begin right now..."

I swallow, my mouth dry.

All at once, he releases my wrist and backs away, running his hands through his hair. That dangerous spark extinguishes from his eyes.

Des sits heavily on a nearby chair, and now that edgy Des has retreated, I feel my own knees weaken with—what? Relief? Disappointment? Des's feral side is nearly as appealing as it is frightening. And that might make me sick, but screw it, I've known I'm twisted for a long time.

"Forgive me," he says into his hands. "This bond comes with its own set of barbaric instincts."

I smooth down my dress, stepping away from the wall.

"I shouldn't have reacted that way." He rubs his mouth and chin. "It's just…it's particularly difficult to conceive fae children. We don't see them as burdens. *I* wouldn't see a babe as a burden."

I feel hot and cold and confused, like someone's pulled the rug out from under me.

"And I'd hoped," he continues, "that you wouldn't see it that way either."

I search his eyes. "I wouldn't ever consider a child with you a burden," I say fervently, "and I *do* want that future with you." The very *idea* of it sends a bolt of yearning through me. "Just not yet," I add. Not when our relationship has only just begun, and there's so much of him—of us—that I want to discover.

Des's gaze softens, and I see that hope he spoke of clear on his face.

I clear my throat. "Is that part of the reason you won't give me the lilac wine?" I ask. "Because it would…affect my fertility?"

This is all conjecture on my part; I have no real idea if the wine would make me like fae women in this regard.

He laughs. "Gods, no. I already stated my reasons for not giving you the wine. And if I were determined to get you pregnant, cherub, I don't think a little thing like immortality would get in the way."

The way he's looking at me has my core heating up.

I let out a breath. "But you do want children?" I ask.

Those shocking silver eyes meet mine. They remind me of light and darkness and everything in between.

"With you?" he says. "Of course."

I don't know why that gets to me, why what he says and how he says it tightens my throat, but it does.

Sometimes I forget I really do get to have this life, with all its horror and beauty. With all its messy entanglements. I can reach out and take it whenever I want. More than that, Des *wants* me to reach out and take it.

I head toward Des as I face down all my raw, raging emotions.

"I don't think you're pregnant," he says, tilting his head up from his seat as I approach him, "though if you are, we'll deal with that, cherub, just like everything else—"

I take his face in my hands and silence him with a kiss.

This love between us is bigger than him, bigger than me.

"From flame to ashes, dawn to dusk, for the rest of our lives, be mine always, Desmond Flynn," I whisper against his lips, reciting the same words that first took him away from me.

They still hold the same wonderful, fearful power they did when I first spoke them, even after paying my tithe for them.

Des draws me closer, pulls me in tighter.

I keep forgetting that beyond his cockiness and power, there's a part of him that's vulnerable, unsure. I said those words to him seven years ago, but seven years is a long time to go without hearing them—an eternity for two soul mates.

I feel him shudder against me as he responds, "Till darkness dies."

CHAPTER 35

It's late morning when Des and I enter Mara's sitting room.
So far today, I've managed to eat breakfast...then nearly
upchuck said breakfast while training with Des.

Oh, the joys of becoming a weapon of mass destruction.

Mara is already reclining on a couch, waiting for us. She
looks impossibly regal with her lilac dress draped around
her, revealing just the right amount of leg from one of its
slits.

"Ah, there you are," she says, raising her hands in greeting, like yesterday never happened.

I'm still sweaty from the workout, inconspicuously
picking at the training leathers now sealing themselves to my
skin. Des for his part looks far more badass, his gear molding
to his body like a lover.

We were right in the middle of a scrimmage that I swear
was going my way when Mara's soldiers interrupted us,
telling us the Queen of Flora requested my presence.

Des sort of took it upon himself to join me despite

not receiving an invitation himself. And now here we are. Completely out of place in this dainty little sitting room.

Around Mara, several servants move about. I catch sight of the upraised red skin on their wrists.

Humans. *Enslaved people.*

Mara's eyes follow mine, and her expression seems to grow excited when she realizes what I'm looking at. In her world, regardless of titles and relationships, at the end of the day, I am one of *them*. A shadow, a servant, an inferior being.

Mara's attention slides to Des, and she flashes him a sly smile. "Didn't trust me alone with your mate?"

"The last time my mate was alone with a ruler, she nearly died. It's nothing personal."

Mara clicks her tongue. "So *very* protective." Her eyes slide to me. "But you don't need protecting, do you?"

On earth, no.

In fact, if Des pulled something like this back home, it would royally irk me. But here, where my glamour is useless and I'm surrounded by immortals who like blood sport even more than my siren does, I'm inclined to let Des be protective.

"What did you want to talk to me about?" I ask instead, taking the lead and heading deeper into the room. Des follows behind me.

I sit on the green velvet armchair adjacent to her, and Des takes the matching seat across from it.

"Tea?" Mara offers, gesturing to the delicate tea set in front of her on the coffee table.

I shake my head.

"Don't mind if I help myself," she says.

The vines that have taken over the room now slither up the coffee table before wrapping around the teakettle and a delicate cup. They lift the porcelain containers into the air, and then, ever so gently, the vines tilt the kettle, and tea begins pouring into the cup.

"Have you enjoyed your stay so far?" Mara asks, settling herself into the seat.

I can't quite rip my eyes away from the sight of all those plants pouring a cup of tea.

Magic will *never* get old.

"Mm-hmm," I say, watching as more vines join the production, one to add some cream to the cup, another to add a cube of sugar.

"I hear that during the first night of festivities, you and the king slipped away to the forest for a bit."

Now I tear my gaze away from the tea.

I flush as I remember being pressed to that tree, Des's chest pinned against mine as he pistoned in and out of me.

Of course, the queen knows we made love under the canopy of her forest.

"Oh, there's no reason to be embarrassed," she says, noticing my reddening cheeks. "We celebrate the cycle of seasons by coming together. It's an honor to have the King of the Night and his mate sanctify the celebration by joining in. I myself disappeared into the forest several times that evening alone."

Really, I could've lived without knowing that.

My eyes slide to Des.

He lounges back in his chair, one ankle thrown over his knee, his thumb rubbing his lower lip while he watches me. Judging from the heat in his eyes, he's vividly remembering that evening as well. And unlike me, he doesn't seem the least bit embarrassed by it.

One of the vines extends the cup of tea to Mara. She takes it, sipping daintily from it.

"So," she says, "festivities aside, I've also heard you are actively looking for the Thief of Souls." Mara watches me over the rim of her teacup.

I nod. I mean, technically, Des and I are investigating this together, but when I look at him again, I get the impression he wants me to take full credit for this.

"So you're aware guards from all four kingdoms have gone missing during the Solstice festivities. All men."

Again, I nod.

"I was hoping to avoid this situation." She takes a sip of her tea and shakes her head. "I wanted to discuss with you the testimony of the last people to see these soldiers alive. I think you'll find it most interesting."

Deliberately, she leans over and picks up a silver stirring spoon from the tea tray then dips it into her cup. "You see, many of them say they last saw their comrades with a single individual. The *same* individual."

I grip the edges of the armrest, already dreading, already *knowing*, what she's going to say.

"Who?" I ask anyway.

"Your mate, Desmond Flynn."

CHAPTER 36

Des continues to languidly sit in the chair across from me. One of his eyebrows arches. "You thought to tell my mate about this *alone?*"

Nothing about this situation makes any sense. Not the testimony, which I can barely wrap my mind around, and not Des's unruffled reaction to it.

Mara ignores him. "Can you account for your mate's whereabouts over the past several evenings?"

Wait, seriously? She wants me to give an alibi for Des?

My eyes move between Mara and Des—Mara, who looks like a shark who's scented blood, and Des, who's not giving away anything.

"Yes," I say, my voice unfaltering. "He's been with me. You're looking at the wrong man. Janus was the one who took—"

"Desmond was with you the entire night?" Mara probes, talking over me.

My siren stirs at my agitation, wanting out. If I were

back on earth, I'd repress her, but here in the Otherworld, where my magic is mostly useless, I don't have to worry about my power getting out of hand. So I let her out.

My skin begins to shimmer. "Do you *really* think I would let the King of the Night out of my bed once he was in it?" I say, glamour riding my voice.

I am *not* one to be interrogated.

Across from me Mara smiles a little, her eyes shrewd.

Glass shatters, interrupting the moment.

A pretty, young servant stares at me, her eyes wide, a shattered vase at her feet. She steps closer, glass crunching beneath the soles of her shoes.

Mara rolls her eyes. "Insolent thing," she says under her breath. "Clean that up now," she orders.

But the servant doesn't clean up the vase. She's not listening to the Flora Queen at all. Her eyes are trained on me, completely under my spell.

My dark, seductive power laps beneath my skin.

Finally, someone to bend to my will.

Mara sets down her cup of tea, the vines around her beginning to slither and snap in agitation.

"Do you want a lashing, woman?" she says, her voice turning shrill.

I smile as the servant comes closer, enjoying the power, the control.

"Congratulations, my queen," Des says. "You're one of the first fairies to see what my mate can do to humans," Des says.

Mara glances away from the servant to cast a baffled look at the Bargainer. She then reappraises me, something like reluctant approval in her eyes. Meanwhile, her servant is still heading toward me, her glassy gaze fixed on my face.

I turn to face the human woman. "Clean up the vase you broke, and then return to your normal duties," I say.

Immediately, the servant turns around, returning to the broken glass and beginning to pick the largest pieces of it up.

"*Amazing*," Mara breathes.

I frown as I watch the servant girl, catching a glimpse of the reddened skin near her wrist where she was branded.

Mara did that to her. Marked her.

"How much easier it would be to control them if we had someone like her," Mara muses. "Are there more of her kind?" she asks Des.

My fingers curve into the arms of my chair.

Human. Prisoner. *Victim*. That's what I once was, what this servant *is*. And the fairy queen at my side is her captor, her tormentor. *She's* the one who deserves my wrath.

I turn to Mara, feeling wild. I stand, the thrill of power coursing through me. Here is an evil to vanquish, a queen to conquer, a soul to break, and a body to bleed.

In my periphery I can just make out Des tensing. My unshakable king is on edge for once. How *delightful*.

My body rolls as I move over to Mara. Slowly, I lower myself onto her lap.

"Do you mind?" I ask as I do so. I don't care what her answer is.

Her mouth curves into a smile. "You have a mate, enchantress," she says.

"He's not protesting." *Yet*.

She raises her eyebrows. "Then by all means."

I see desire stoking in her eyes. Fairies, I'm coming to find, are a bit more sexually fluid than most humans.

I place my hands on either side of her head, boxing her in. I lean in close. "Why do you keep them?" My gaze

284

travels to her neck. Her delicate neck. Such a fragile part of her body. I cannot control this woman, but I can seduce her. I can hurt her.

My nails sharpen, pricking the fabric of her couch. She has no idea that her words will determine what I do next.

"Who?" she asks, her wicked lips forming a perfect O.

"Humans," I say. "You mark them and keep them. Why?"

A heavy hand snakes under my arm. "That's enough fun, love," Des says, hoisting me out of Mara's lap.

I nearly fight him. I can practically feel her blood between my fingers.

Quieter, he whispers, "Save your vendettas, cherub."

Rather than set me back in my seat, Des settles us both on his, pulling me into his lap. My vengeance is only curbed by the slow strokes of his hand against my side.

Mara's low-lidded eyes watch us. "Have you heard the story of my sister?" she asks, staring at me contemplatively.

She doesn't wait for me to respond.

"Thalia Verdana," she says, "the most powerful Flora heir to be born within this millennia. No great beauty, but what is beauty to power?" Mara's eyes go distant. "Of course, to Thalia, beauty *was* everything. She coveted what she didn't have."

The Flora Queen's eyes drift over me and Des. "One also knows you don't need beauty if you've found love instead— and she found it in a traveling minstrel of all things. At least, that's what we assumed he was."

Mara stirs her cup of tea idly. "Our parents were scandalized by the match, but that didn't stop Thalia from seeing him.

"Did you know fairies can bargain away their power?" Mara says to me. "They can share it, they can gift it, but they cannot bequeath it—death severs all deals."

She takes in my glowing skin. "He ended up being an enchanter—a fairy who could ensorcell other fairies with a wish and a kiss. Thalia fell under his spell…"

She clears her throat. "My parents killed him before he could destroy our kingdom. Of course, by then Thalia was too far gone. She followed him to the Kingdom of Death.

"That's how I became heir to this kingdom."

Mara gives us a tight smile. "It has been a long time since I've met an enchanter—and never a human one. I find that despite all my reservations, you hold me captivated." Her eyes flicker with desire as she takes me in.

"Yes, Callie does have that effect on people," Des says, his voice a touch possessive. "Now, what were we talking about?" Des looks first to me then to Mara. He snaps his fingers. "Ah, yes, now I remember. Mara, you were insinuating that I was behind the recent disappearances."

She rearranges herself in her seat. "When several witnesses all see the same thing, one has to wonder…"

This is the second time in two days another royal has cast doubt on Des's innocence.

I want to lash out again.

"It's not him," I growl. The sound that comes out of my mouth is harsh yet melodic. "Janus took me. Either you must cast suspicion on both kings or on neither of them."

The Flora Queen reaches out to one of the vines, and it begins to twine itself up her arm. "None of the other captured women have complained that the Day King has abducted them," she says. "Only you, the mate of the Night King, have. How do I know you aren't just protecting him?"

Only Des's ironclad grip across my waist keeps me from throttling the fae queen.

"Furthermore," she says, "those captured women have

all said they were taken once they dozed off. Sleep, as you know, is ruled by the Night Kingdom."

It all leads back to Des. Why does *it all lead back to Des?*

My skin dims as I consider this worrying thought.

"And yet here we are, sitting and talking as civilized people." Des leans forward. "You haven't sanctioned my kingdom nor kicked me out of the festivities. You haven't barred me from any part of the celebration, even though I broke the neutrality agreement two nights ago when I fought Janus. Your actions—or lack thereof—don't strike me as those of a concerned queen."

The vines around Mara begin to whip about. "Do *not* presume to know my intentions, Desmond Flynn." The room fills with her power, the air nauseatingly thick with the smell of flowers.

Des's eyes spark. "Send me and my mate away, Mara. We will leave, Solstice can continue, and you can test your theory concerning my guilt," he challenges, his voice hypnotic.

The Flora Queen's power still fills the room like a rain cloud poised to break wide open. But rather than unleashing her wrath, Mara appraises Des. "Give me your oath that you are innocent, and this can end," she says.

The Bargainer, a man who makes half his living striking deals with fools, doesn't hesitate now. "I will give you an oath in exchange for one."

"I beg your pardon?" Mara says, looking affronted.

"I will swear you an oath of innocence, if you, in return, promise me fifty years of an unbreakable alliance between the Flora and Night Kingdom."

A swell of anger rises at the back of Mara's eyes, the floral smell once again thickening the air. "You would dare to leverage my good graces?"

"I would have you as an ally, not an enemy."

And to think that only minutes ago, I was about to lose it on this woman.

Des's words seem to pacify most of her anger. She leans back in her seat. "Fine."

Using one arm to still hold me in place, the Bargainer reaches out with his other, and Mara grasps it.

The moment they clasp hands, the air around them wavers, rippling like waves.

"I swear to the Undying Gods, I am not behind the disappearances."

The queen's body seems to relax. She nods. "I swear to the Undying Gods on behalf of my kingdom that we will ally with the Night Kingdom for fifty years."

The moment the words are spoken, the magic rippling around them implodes, sucking itself back into their clasped hands.

And then it's over.

CHAPTER 37

"Enjoying yourself, slave?"

I spin, looking around the Flora Queen's dark forest for the man who spoke. The sacred oaks around me shiver in the night air.

That voice...

So familiar.

But there's no one here in the forest—no one but me.

I rub my arms, not sure how I ended up in the queen's sacred oak grove.

No matter, I'll just fly back to my room.

At my back, my wings open, beating a few times to loosen up.

Something drips onto my arm. Another wet drop splats against my hair.

I lift my forearm to my eyes. In the darkness, I can barely make out the fluid, only that it's dark.

Dark and warm.

I suck in a breath.

Blood.

Another drop hits the crown of my head. I glance above me at the latticework of branches. The bark is oozing blood, and the longer I look, the heavier it flows down the trees. I hear drops of it hitting the leaves of the forest floor. It sounds like the beginning of a storm, the blood first coming in soft patters then faster and faster. The droplets hit my skin and my clothes.

A voice cuts through the darkness. "Life and death are such intimate lovers. Wouldn't you agree?"

A man steps out of the woods, his irises and plaited hair as dark as the night.

He's everything I ever imagined a fairy to be before I met Des. The upturned eyes, the expressive pouty mouth, the straight, narrow nose, and the pointed ears. He has the sinister beauty I've read about in fairy tales.

The man's lips curve ever so slightly, his eyes brightening in that manic way that fae eyes do.

"Kill her," another man says from behind me.

That voice! So painfully familiar. Any other time I'd whip around, but my gut is telling me the true menace is staring me down, and I will not turn my back on him.

"Her soul is not mine to take," the black-eyed man says, still staring at me with a dark intensity.

I feel the bite of a blade at my throat, and from the corner of my eye, I catch sight of a lock of white-blond hair.

"You're right," the familiar voice at my back says. "It's mine."

All at once the realization slams into me.

Des. It's Des's voice at my back.

"Enjoy each small death you have left," he whispers into my ear. "I'm coming for you."

And then he slits my throat.

I gasp awake, my body tangled in sheets, a strong set of arms around me.

Predawn light filters into the room through the window, casting everything in shades of blue. It's so very different from the darkness of my dream.

I glance up, into Des's soft silver eyes, and my heart nearly stops.

My ear still tingles where he spoke to me seconds ago, and I swear I still feel the phantom prick of pain across my throat from his blade.

His eyes widen just a smidge at my reaction. "Cherub, are you...*afraid* of me?"

I swallow down the lump in my throat, not wanting to answer.

It was just a dream, and yet...and yet it felt *real*.

What had Des told me a while back? *Dreams are never just dreams.*

He searches my face a bit more. "You *are*."

Des runs his hand over my bracelet. "Why are you so scared of me?" The moment he asks the question, Des's magic settles over my shoulders, and I don't need to look down at my wrist to know that yet another bead is now missing from it.

I get up from the bed, dragging a bedsheet with me.

"It was just a dream," I answer.

Not good enough. The magic is still there, still pressing down on me.

"And?" Des says, also aware I'm under the grip of his magic.

I clutch my throat. "And in it, you killed me." The answer is good enough to release me from Des's power.

He lounges back in our bed, his face brooding. My eyes drift to his sleep-tousled hair and his bare chest. It's an odd sensation, to be both frightened by and drawn to someone at the same time, but I am.

"Callie," he says, seeing me fighting my impulses, "come here."

I hesitate, and I swear that momentary pause breaks something in my mate.

His voice drops lower. "It's okay. I would never—" He falters. "I would *never* harm you," he finishes.

And now I feel like a royal schmuck. I know he would never harm me. He's the part of my soul that lives outside my body.

I pad over to him. He gets up from the bed, all six plus feet of him staggering, *intimidating*.

He steps up to me then folds me into a hug. The presence that in my dream had felt so hateful now feels immensely loving. The muscles that were used to kill me are now here comforting me.

"Tell me everything about your dream," he says.

And I do.

By the time I'm done, my unshakable mate looks... worried.

"What is it?" I ask.

He shakes his head, frowning. "Nothing good. Normal dreams, I'd be able to wake you from. These ones...these ones don't release you until they're ready. I assumed I'd lost my touch for waking you up, but now I wonder..."

I search his face. "What?"

"Controlling dreams is a Night Kingdom trait. It's possible someone's targeting you while you sleep, perhaps the same someone who's taking soldiers."

He's coming for you.

"The Thief of Souls," I whisper.

CHAPTER 38

Who exactly is the Thief of Souls? And why would he invade my dreams? That's what I wonder as the two of us head to Mara's throne room.

If my dreams are more than just idle nightmares, then who was the black-haired man? And was Dream Des anything other than an illusion meant to scare me? Or could it be possible my dreams have nothing at all to do with the disappearances?

All these questions are making my head hurt.

Des and I head into the Flora palace, the walls awash with living, blooming plants. Part of Solstice entails sitting near the Queen of Flora in her throne room as she holds an audience with her subjects, so we're on our way.

"What Night fae, aside from you, has enough power to enter my dreams?" I whisper as we head through the castle.

"Many."

Er, that's unsettling.

Des shakes his head. "But," he continues, "none should

have enough power to keep me from waking you. If I had any living siblings, perhaps they'd be strong enough to perform that kind of magic, but my father killed them all off."

That's interesting to know—that power moved through bloodlines.

"And your father?" I ask. "Could he—?"

"He's dead," Des says, his face stoic.

Whelp, guess that takes care of that.

I quiet as the two of us enter Mara's throne room and join the throngs of other fairies.

The throne room is the same place we met the queen when we first arrived. I look around it again, taking in the vaulted ceilings, the vine-covered walls, and the chandeliers with their dripping candles as Des leads me down the aisle.

My stomach drops when I see Janus at the end of the room, standing off to the side of the queen's throne, looking like the morning sun.

How does *he* factor into this mystery?

As soon as the two kings see each other, the tension in the room ratchets up. Others must sense it too because fairies glance around. The air begins to thicken with magic, making it hard to breathe.

This is what happens when two juggernauts come together.

I touch Des's arm. "It's okay."

If only I were half as brave as my words. I steel my spine.

I am someone's nightmare, I tell myself.

Sure, that someone is probably the next macaron I come across, but hey, we all start somewhere.

We end up standing near the King of Day, much to the frustration of both Des and Janus.

But Janus isn't the only fairy who has beef with us. A dozen different Fauna fae sit or stand throughout the throne room, and most of them throw me and the Bargainer dirty looks.

Guess they still haven't gotten over the fact Des offed their king…

It doesn't help that the whole shebang starts what feels like an hour late, and even after it does, it's been about as interesting as watching paint dry.

The only saving grace is Des, who's busy whispering secrets in my ears about the audience members sitting in the pews.

"He is one of the most vocal opponents of equal rights and protections for changelings, largely because he was spurned by the human he fell in love with."

"She's sleeping with the entire royal guard, and everyone knows it except her husband."

"She has a servant who she secretly calls Daddy*, and she regularly has him punish her."*

He leans in again now. "All morning I've been fantasizing about spreading those soft thighs of yours and fucking you until you're begging me to come."

I stagger a little on my feet, and my siren nearly bursts forth; it's all I can do to keep her caged.

Mara's eyes flick over to us before returning to the subject in front of her.

I give him an incredulous look. He decides to dirty talk with me *now*?

"Just making sure you're still paying attention," he says.

From behind us, a side door opens, and Malaki, along with two Night soldiers, step up to Des, Malaki whispering something into Des's ear.

The Bargainer nods then leans into me. "Another soldier has disappeared."

Another one?

"I need to step out briefly to talk to my men. Malaki will be here in my stead until I return."

He kisses me on the lips, and then he's gone, retreating through the side door with the Night soldiers.

I blink at Malaki, who gives me a tight smile before openly glaring at Janus.

Mara excuses her latest subject, leaning back against her throne, her fiery hair cascading down her chest. Today white roses are tangled in those bright locks of hers.

Next to her, the Green Man's gaze flicks to me, his gaze intense.

Gah, that fairy is unnerving.

The double doors at the far end of the room open, and a manacled woman is brought in. Her arms are exposed, and I catch sight of a branded leaf peeking out from beneath her shackles.

Human.

Her eyes are swollen, but her face is dry, and her chin is defiantly lifted. All eyes watch her as she's led down the aisle, her footsteps and those of her guards echoing throughout the room.

Up until now, the fairies who've had an audience with the queen have been nobles squabbling over petty matters. This, however, I can already tell will be different.

When she comes to the edge of the dais, her fae guards force her to her knees.

"What are her crimes?" Mara asks lazily.

"She was caught fornicating with a fairy," one of the guards reports.

Wait, *seriously*?

The girl is in shackles because she boned a dude with wings?

"Witnesses?" Mara asks, bored.

"Two," the guard says.

The two witnesses are brought forward, both human judging from their rounded ears. Each in turn attests to the fact that they caught the servant out on the palace grounds playing hide the salami with a soldier.

In the middle of the second testimony, the human girl begins to silently sob.

I shift on my feet. This whole situation feels wrong to me. This woman is on trial because she did exactly what Des and I have been doing.

Next to me, Malaki clears his throat uncomfortably.

He too is guilty of what this woman's on trial for.

"Do you have any words to say in your defense?" Mara asks the human woman once the witnesses leave.

"Please," she says, her voice roughened with tears, "he grabbed me. I tried to push him away, but he overpowered me…"

Oh God.

My blood runs cold. I feel my nausea rise, my stomach twisting sickly at the woman's words.

This doesn't sound like some illicit tryst in the woods. This sounds like rape. And now this woman is getting punished for it.

"Where is this man?" Mara asks.

The bone-deep sickness that consumed me a moment ago is transforming into something hot and uncomfortable.

Do something.

"He's on his way," the guard says.

"Very well." Mara rearranges her skirts. "Give the slave twenty lashings, and if she conceives, abort the offspring."

"*No.*"

I don't realize I've spoken until all the occupants of the throne room are staring at me.

Shit, all right, I'm doing this.

"I beg your pardon?" Mara looks half-skeptical, half-amused.

"No one is hurting this woman," I say, stepping forward.

My power builds beneath my skin. My body doesn't illuminate, but I feel my magic right there. I didn't go through hell just to watch something like this happen to another woman.

Mara's eyes flick to Malaki. "General," she says, "handle your king's mate."

My hands fist, the siren stirring restlessly. She's not even addressing me, like I'm beneath her notice.

The room's attention swivels from me to Malaki.

He folds his arms across his chest. "*No.*"

A ripple of whispers rises from the crowd.

My gaze finds Malaki's, and I find it hard to breathe. Des's oldest friend is putting himself on the line for me.

Mara raises an eyebrow. Turning from both of us, she announces to her men, "Proceed with the punishment as planned. Bring the headsman out."

A fairy peels away from the wings of the room, approaching the dais with a whip in hand.

That sick sensation rises in me all over again.

"Mara, you cannot do this," I say.

Another wave of whispers spreads through the room, even as the Flora Queen ignores me.

The headsman approaches the girl, centering himself behind her. Someone else brings in a curved bench of sorts, and the guards on either side of the servant now force her body to bow over the bench, locking her cuffs at the base of it so she's completely restrained, her back bared to the headsman and the crowd beyond him. I hear her sobs and see her back shaking.

The headsman unravels the whip, and oh God, oh God, this cannot be real.

The metal tip of the whip glints in the room, and it's that one detail that forces me into action.

I'm moving, the fierce need to protect this woman singing through me. Now my skin begins to glow, and I hear the dark, whispered thoughts of my siren.

Spill their blood, make them pay. Protect the girl.

I push my body between the human woman and the headsman.

"Touch her and you'll regret it," I say, my voice just as savage as it is melodic.

If I didn't have the room's attention before, I certainly have it now.

"For the sake of the Undying Gods, Callypso," Mara says, finally addressing me, "remove yourself."

"No."

Malaki takes a step forward, presumably to join me.

Mara's hand snaps up to stop him. "*Ah*-ah," she says. As she speaks, the vines on the wall behind Malaki slither up and around him, shackling him in place. It's the first real sign that I've pissed off the Flora Queen. "If Callypso is to be a ruler one day," Mara says, her gaze returning to me, "then she can fight her own battles. Can't you, enchantress?"

Both Mara and the Green Man watch me with fevered expressions, lapping up my anger, waiting for me to react.

I stare at her, regretful that I didn't rip out her throat when I had a chance.

"Anyone who hurts this woman will have to go through me," I say to the room.

Mara grins, the expression malevolent. "So be it." She flicks her wrist. "Headsman, carry out the punishment."

Behind me, the headsman shifts nervously. I hear the slick sound of the whip unraveling and the startled gasps of the audience.

Smoldering anger burns low in my belly as I drop to my knees, my hands going to the woman's shackles. She stares at me with wide, red-rimmed eyes as I work at the locks.

Fuck, I need a key.

The headsman takes position behind me, giving a few practice cracks of the whip.

I quake when I realize I'm not going to be able to release this woman in time. These chains need a key, and the key is in the pockets of soldiers too far away and too unwilling to help. My only ally, Malaki, is being restrained. I'm on my own, and if I leave this woman, she will be whipped.

There's fire in my soul and poison in my veins.

If my glamour worked, I would make them pay—every last fairy who stood idly by. But all I have is my body and my beliefs.

Making a split-second decision, I drape myself over the woman, my winged back now exposed to the headsman.

She's shaking with her fear; it only fuels my vengeance.

"I'm not going to let anything happen to you," I whisper, my voice ethereal.

I hear the headsman step back. Beyond him, Malaki is shouting.

I look up at Mara, my wrath in my eyes.

You will *pay.*

I'm still staring at her when the snap of the whip echoes throughout the room. I feel the laceration a moment later.

With a sickening crunch, the delicate bones of my wings

break under the blow. I gasp as pain floods my system. I can barely see through it.

Several bloody feathers float to the floor.

When I hear the headsman draw back his arm again, I have to tighten my grip on the shaking woman beneath me to keep myself between her and the whip.

Beneath me, the servant is still shaking.

"It's going to be okay," I whisper, glamour thick in my voice. I'm not going to let them get to her.

I hear the whip hiss through the air once more. This time, when it splits my flesh and crushes bone, I can't hold back my scream, the sound horrifyingly harmonic.

Warm blood drips down my back as more feathers fall to the floor.

Twenty lashes. Eighteen more to endure.

At this rate, I will have no wings by the time the headsman is done with me.

Through my pain, I begin to laugh, feeling the horrified gazes of the crowd around me.

Isn't that what I wanted? To be rid of my wings?

Suddenly, the once brightly lit room darkens. Leaves curl up and vines retreat, as though they're repelled by the shadows. Darker and darker, the room grows. The vines binding Malaki now dry up and waste away, allowing him to break his bonds.

The crowd was silent before, but now they're quiet in the way dead things are.

I hear the whip hiss through the air a third time.

It snaps as it strikes flesh, and I flinch, waiting for the pain. It never comes.

I glance up, and there Des is, the end of the whip in his fist, a line of blood sliding from his palm and down his wrist.

He yanks the weapon out of the headman's hand before tossing it aside.

"What is the meaning of this?" he says, his voice deceptively engaging. He spins in a circle, looking about the crowd. His power fills the room, the space growing darker by the second, and the once blooming plants are now shriveling and dying.

I slide off the human woman's body, slumping to the side. I can't move either of my wings; it feels like they're one giant open wound.

"What grand fun you all have had while I've been away," Des says to the room, his gaze lingering on Mara and the Green Man, both still seated on their thrones, "allowing my mate to be flayed alive."

He is my vengeance. He is my violence. He is winged death come to deliver all these fairies to their fates. I nearly smile.

"Malaki," he says, "take stock of who's here. Make sure the Lord of Nightmares sends them his regards."

"Gladly," Malaki replies, shucking off the last of the dead vines that once bound him.

"And you—" Des turns to the headsman, his footfalls echoing ominously in the room as he approaches him. "You stupid fool. What were you thinking? Surely you know the rules: an injury deliberately inflicted on a fairy can be avenged by their mate."

Des grabs the man's arm before twisting it behind the headsman's back. My mate leans in close. "And I'm avenging."

It doesn't matter that it's Solstice and there's a neutrality agreement. The Bargainer is out for blood.

For the third time in that many minutes, I hear the sickening snap of breaking bones as Des shatters the headsman's arm. He doesn't stop there either. He breaks the man's other arm and then his legs. In between blows, he whispers things into the headsman's ear, and they must be horrible, for the fairy cries louder in response to them than he does the pain.

Just then, the double doors open, and a man with pointed ears is led inside by two Flora guards. Unlike the human woman dragged in earlier, this fae wears no cuffs.

All three of their steps falter at the sight in front of them—me with my bloody, broken wings, the mangled headsman, and ruthless Des, who looms over the fairy. And then there's the captive room who neither speaks nor moves as they watch everything unfold.

"Who is this?" Des asks, peering at the fae man being escorted in.

My voice is entirely human when I respond. "That's the man who abused this woman." At least, I'm pretty sure that's who it is. They said they were bringing him in.

Desmond glances at me for several seconds, and I can see how hard it is for him to make eye contact. Every moment he takes me in like this, with my wings bashed in, his fury and hatred seem to double. His gaze goes to the shackled woman next to me, and he must understand a little of what's going on, even though he missed the trial itself.

Finally, his eyes cut to the fairy being escorted in.

There are few beings who hate crimes against women as much as I do, but Des is one of them.

The Bargainer stalks forward and grabs the man by the neck. The guards around Des protest, their gazes darting to Mara. But if they think she'll intercede, they are sorely mistaken. The Flora Queen looks content to let the events play out as they will.

Des pulls the fairy in close, again whispering something

into his latest target's ear. Whatever Des says has a sobering effect on the man. Even dozens of feet away and distracted by pain, I notice the fairy's eyes widen and his face pale at whatever my mate is saying.

And then Des begins dragging him past the guards and toward the dais. The Bargainer all but throws the fairy to the floor in front of Mara's throne.

"Tell your queen what you intend," he demands.

The fairy mumbles something, his head bowed.

"Louder."

"I will take the slave's remaining lashes as punishment," he says.

Mara leans forward and places her chin in her hand. "As punishment for what precisely?"

I'm not sure whether Mara's confused about what this man did to the woman or if she's just toying with him.

"For slee—" The fairy chokes. I've experienced the sensation enough to know just what—or rather *who*—is behind it.

I glance at Des, who stands over him, his arms crossed and his jaw locked. Dangerous beauty—that's what he is.

The fairy tries again. "For having se—" He begins to stutter, avoiding the one word he's going to be forced to say.

Five seconds later, he gives up the fight. "For...raping her."

The previously silent room now breaks out into scandalized whispers.

Mara raises her hand. "Silence!" she says, quieting the room.

Des levels his attention on Mara. "The only thing—the *only* thing—saving you from death is our oath," he says, his voice quiet.

With those final words, Des stalks back to me, his wings fanning out behind him menacingly. With his heavy boots and massive frame, he looks like some dark prince who crawled out of the abyss.

Oh so carefully, he scoops me up and strides down the aisle and out of the room.

CHAPTER 39

Des is silent as we leave the throne room, his footfalls echoing in the cavernous halls. The two of us are cloaked in his shadows. With every step he takes, the candles nearby him snuff out and Mara's precious plants wither away.

"What happened." He doesn't ask it.

I feel him shaking with anger, fighting some impulse to rip and render and destroy. His body practically hums with the need.

"They were going to punish that human woman. She'd been raped." I have to steady myself for several seconds through the pain in my back before I continue. "I couldn't let that happen."

His eyes, his stormy, tormented eyes, move down to me, and I see that a big part of him is fighting to stay mad. That if he doesn't keep his anger right where he can see it, then he'll have to let in all those other pesky emotions.

"So you took the punishment instead." His words have no intonation, so I have no idea what he's thinking.

I nod, and his mood continues to worsen.

Des carries me out of the castle, crossing the palace gardens as he heads toward our guest suite. The darkness he's been dragging along with him now shadows the palace grounds, dimming the sky and choking the life out of the plants it touches.

Fairies stop what they're doing to watch us, the wrathful Night King and his mate, the latter dripping blood along the stone pathways.

My sight's becoming a little unfocused, spurred on by either pain or blood loss, and damn, but my wings hurt.

As soon as we near the giant cedar that houses our rooms, we catch the attention of several Night soldiers who man its perimeter. Once they see us, they come running.

"Get a healer," the Bargainer orders them.

As quickly as they arrive, they dash off.

Des storms up the staircase that winds around the tree. When he reaches our rooms, he kicks open our guest suite's front door, splintering the wood frame. Inside, he heads to the bed before laying me out on my stomach, his touch gentle.

"We're going to heal you, love," he promises me, moving some of my hair away from my face.

I nod to him, swallowing my emotions. I feel shattered and vulnerable, and I'm so unused to being taken care of. I forgot how nice it is to matter to someone and how tender the ferocious Bargainer can be.

He straightens, and a moment later, I hear him curse under his breath, presumably after getting a peek at the damage to my wings. And then his hands are on me, smoothing down my skin. I feel his magic soak into me, dulling the sharp bite of my injuries.

I sigh out my relief, the churning in my stomach settling now that the throbbing of my wounds has dulled.

"This will numb the pain, cherub," he says, "but I do not have an affinity for healing." He crouches next to me, taking my hand. "What you did…" He searches my face. "No one will forget it. Not that woman you protected, not the room full of fairies, not the Flora Queen and her consort—and not me. Mara might wear a crown, but everyone in that room saw who the true queen was today."

My throat tightens. He's going to make me cry.

"I couldn't just stand by while—"

He silences me with a kiss. "I know."

Just then, someone knocks on the remnants of our door. I hear several footfalls as soldiers file into our suite, bringing with them a fae healer.

Des slides away from me to speak with the group. For a minute, all I hear is low murmuring, and then the Bargainer and the healer come back over to me.

"But she's a human," the healer protests when she sees me.

The shadows in the room deepen. "She is." Des says it like a challenge.

"Surely you know our magic doesn't work on—"

"Heal her, or consider your life forfeit," he orders the woman.

The room is quiet for several seconds. Then I hear a shaky exhalation of breath. "I'll do my best, Your Majesty."

Des comes to my side a moment later.

"Stop picking on innocent fairies," I breathe.

"No one here is innocent," he says darkly.

I shiver a little, my skin chilled. I don't know if it's heavy blood loss I'm experiencing or just shock. Des rubs my arm, and his magic is at work once again, trying to warm me.

"Do you want to know a secret?" he whispers, threading his fingers through mine.

"Always," I whisper back. I don't mention the fact we're in a room full of fairies. Knowing my mate, what he's about to tell me is either no great secret, or else he's muted the world to our conversation.

"Before my mother was a scribe, before she was even a concubine, she was a spy," Des admits, smoothing my hair back as he talks.

I know he's only trying to distract me, but it works. I settle in for the story as the fae healer begins to lightly run her hands down my wings. I can tell she's straightening the bones out, but Des's magic is so potent that what should be agonizing is merely uncomfortable. And I can ignore that discomfort while Des holds my attention captive.

"How did she go from a spy to a concubine?" I ask, my voice soft.

"She thwarted a conspiracy against the king." He stares at our entwined hands.

I can still feel his ungodly anger in his trembling grasp, and I see it in the dimness of the room, but I don't say anything. The King of the Night might be frightening to the rest of the world, but he isn't to me.

"I sometimes wonder just how badly she later regretted doing her job that particular day," he says. "My father called her into his throne room to personally thank her for saving his life. Whatever words were exchanged is a mystery, but he must've been quite taken with her because by the end of the encounter, he had her removed from her post and placed in his royal harem."

That has me raising my eyebrows. "And she was okay with that?"

Des lets out a breathy chuckle. "No. Not in the least. She was what you'd call an *unwilling* concubine. But at that time in my kingdom, things were different, and my father… he was a very different ruler than me."

The more I learn about my mate's mother, the more I wish I knew her. And the more I learn about his father, the more I dislike the man.

"After she died, I never imagined I'd come across another woman like her," Des says. "Someone who'd lived through much and still inherently knew right from wrong. Someone strong and brave."

His hand squeezes mine. "And then I met you."

I blink my eyes several times, my throat thick.

Des sobers, his grip on my hand tightening. "When I saw you lying there, your wings broken…" He shakes his head. "It brought back memories from that night in Karnon's throne room, and *that* night…that night brought back memories of my mother's death."

I had…no idea.

No wonder he's so fierce about punishing those who prey on women; he's been sculpted by his experiences.

Story time ends shortly after that, and a half hour later, Des has left my side, his heavy footfalls pacing up and down the opposite end of the room.

His boots come to a halt. "Well?" he finally demands.

The healer hovering over me straightens, throwing yet another bloody rag into a washbasin.

"That's the best I can do," she says. She's managed to fuse my wing bones back together and partly seal up the split skin, but it's obvious the injury isn't close to being healed.

The shadows in the room shift and thicken. Today is really taking Des's mood to task.

I don't know how empty Des's earlier threat was when he ordered the fairy to heal me, but she's done her best. It's not her fault fae and human magic aren't terribly compatible.

"Temper," I murmur.

Des comes over to me. "What was that, cherub?"

"Get Temper. She can help."

You wouldn't think a sorceress so inclined to evil would be good at healing, but Temper is. Proof the Fates are ironic bitches.

As it turns out, we don't have to tell Temper at all; the broken door to our guest house is thrown open before Des has so much as left my side.

"*Callie.*" Power rides Temper's voice.

Gingerly, I raise one of my hands and wave it weakly.

She rushes to my side, her eyes landing on my back. She inhales sharply. "What *happened*?" I hear the panic in her voice. I must look worse than I think I do for Temper to have that kind of reaction.

Des comes up behind her. "I need you to heal her." And now he too has an edge of panic in his voice.

"Obviously," she says, laying her hands on my wings. She closes her eyes, humming low under her breath.

Almost immediately, I feel Temper's magic at work. Where Des's magic is sultry darkness and coiling shadows, hers is like heat from a furnace.

When she opens her eyes again, they glow. She continues to hum, the low bars of her voice sounding eerie.

"Bargainer," she says, "tell me what happened."

He and I share a look. The last time Temper was pissed off on my behalf, she blew up a portal.

"What do you already know?" Des asks.

"Only what Malaki told me—"

Malaki told Temper about this? That fairy is officially smitten.

"That Callie was injured and we might be leaving soon."

"Whoa," I say, beginning to sit up. "We might be *leaving* soon?"

Temper pushes me firmly back down. "What else did I miss?" she asks.

Before Des can explain, I cut in. "They wanted to whip a human who'd been raped," I begin.

I proceed to tell Temper the rest of the story, from the moment Des first exited the throne room to the moment he carried me out of it.

By the time I finish, Temper's mended my broken wings completely. They itch where the new skin and bone growth has occurred, but itchiness aside, they might as well be brand-new.

I exhale a shaky breath. "I owe you one," I say softly, trailing a hand over one of my wings. She's healed me before but never to this extent. I feel shaken but so unbelievably grateful.

"Well, I think I owed you one after you used your glamour to get me that deal on my car, so you know, we're even now," she says, her expression soft. It hardens a moment later as a thought comes to her. "Now that you're all better, where is the *fucking* monster who did this to you?" she demands, referring to Mara. "I will kill her."

Her words have Des smiling nefariously, and oh my God, the only thing worse than these two being enemies is them being friends.

A knock on the now doorless doorframe interrupts Temper's rant.

Outside, a human servant waits, his head bowed. In his hands is a bouquet of wildflowers.

"Yes," Des says, moving to the doorway.

"I have a gift for the Night King's mate," he says, lifting the flowers a little as he speaks.

I push myself off the bed. "Callie," I say, crossing the room. I take the bouquet from him. "And thank you for the flowers."

His head hesitantly lifts, and I stare into his cool-green eyes. "Thank *you* for what you did," he says softly. "None of us will forget."

He doesn't need to clarify who *us* is.

He dips his head again, and then he leaves, heading down the steps.

"Wait!" I call out, stepping onto the walkway beyond the suite.

He swivels back to me.

"You don't have to live like this," I say. "None of you have to. There's a place for all of you on earth."

He smiles. "We appreciate you and your strange ways. Perhaps one day we will leave. Until then..." He tips his head then resumes walking once more.

I feel my shoulders deflate. Rome wasn't built in a day and all, but still, it's a hard pill to swallow, knowing these humans will continue to live here, where they have precious few rights.

"So," Temper says when I reenter my rooms, "I propose we blow some shit up then leave."

Des doesn't look completely opposed.

My despair and my pain fill me up, choking the life out of me. Suddenly, I can't take it.

Lightning heats my veins. Maybe, if I boil away all my suffering, all my petty insecurities, all my frustration and toil, I'll hit an indestructible core. Something that cannot be broken by greed or lust or violence. Something that isn't quite magic but is still power.

"No," I say, facing Temper. "I'm *not* running from this place."

The beginnings of a smile tug at my mate's lips when I meet his eyes.

I say, with steel in my voice, "It's time the Otherworld understands just how strong a human can be."

CHAPTER 40

That evening, I stare at the beautiful gown waiting for me.
It's a deep plum color, so dark that it's nearly black. The
shoes that go with it are nothing more than leather and
ribbons—shoes for dancing.

I take a deep breath.

Time to don my battle armor and see those fairies again.
I still feel the echo of those lashes against my wings.

Des walks up to the armoire the gown hangs from and
closes the doors.

I glance at him in confusion.

"Tonight, we're not attending," he says.

"But—"

He cups my cheeks and cuts me off with a kiss. His
lips move against mine until I've forgotten what exactly I'm
objecting to. My hands drop to his forearms, sliding over his
exposed skin. Goose bumps rise along his flesh at my touch.

To have such an effect on the King of the Night.
Sometimes I forget he's just as moved by me as I am by him.

His lips break away from mine before dipping just below my ear. "My mate hasn't been satisfied *nearly* enough since we arrived here."

My core heats at his words. What, exactly, does the Bargainer have planned?

Des's breath ghosts against my skin, right at the juncture where my neck meets my jaw. He presses a kiss there. "What a poor soul mate I am, to deny her this."

Des backs me up, up, up until my wings brush against the wall, effectively trapping me.

One of his hands moves from my arms to the low-cut top of the wispy fae dress I wear. It elaborately laces up the front, tying together at the scooped collar.

The Bargainer slides a finger along that collar before grabbing the end of a ribbon. His eyes meet mine as he pulls on it, undoing the bow. The blouse loosens, the binding unraveling inch by inch.

Des pushes the material down my torso and exposes my breasts. He presses a kiss to the valley between them.

"Gods, you are exquisite," he says, his voice hushed.

The same can easily be said about him.

I remove the leather band that holds his shoulder-length hair back and run my hands through it.

He helps me take off his shirt before tossing the piece of clothing to the ground.

I smooth my hands over his large pecs.

"Do something magical," I whisper.

Des's lips twitch, like he finds my request both funny and endearing. "Name your price, cherub."

Now it's my turn to suppress a smile. There's always a price with him, but these days, it's not always an unpleasant one.

Rather than name my price, I let my dress do the talking, sliding it the rest of the way down my body.

The Bargainer sucks in a breath as he takes me in. All I have left on is a scant pair of panties, and judging by the way my mate is eyeing them, they're not going to be on for long.

I feel the brush of Des's magic as it leaves his body.

A moment later the vases of flowers perched around the room all upend themselves at once, and the water and flowers inside each slide out. But rather than fall to the floor, they begin to float in midair as though they were experiencing zero gravity. The effect is dazzling.

"Magical enough for you?" Des asks, his eyes on me.

"Just barely."

He smiles. "You tart thing." He kisses me again, and as he does so, my panties slide off my hips, another bit of Des's magic at play.

He pulls away long enough to run his hand down my torso. "My brave mate, my fierce mate. No fairy has ever been prouder of his woman."

His words move me. Being here, in the Kingdom of Flora, has made it abundantly clear that humans aren't seen as equals. But if there's one thing Des has always made sure of, it's making me feel like I'm his match in all ways.

He smooths his hand over my skin until the tips of his fingers brush my core. In response, my skin lights up. We stare at each other, something about this intimate act made all the more vulnerable because we won't look away.

I move my hips against his touch, forcing his fingers to slide in, then out, in then out. I was already wet when he undressed me, but now my inner thighs are slick.

The rest of his clothes peel away from him.

Did I mention I freaking love magic?

His cock presses between us, so hard that it's straining.

I move against him, and he groans at the friction.

"Can't resist you..." He lifts me then before easing me slowly back down. The head of his cock pushes against my entrance, and then it's sliding in, filling me inch by inch.

He drinks in my expression as my back arches, my lips parting as he seats himself all the way to the hilt.

He takes my hands in his and presses them into the wall on either side of my head. The only thing holding me up is his body.

"Nothing has ever felt so good," he says, "I'm sure of it."

He slides out, the sound thick and wet, then slams in again. I gasp at the sensation, arching into him, my legs tightening around his waist.

"Faster," I breathe against him.

But, stubborn fairy, he doesn't move faster. He goes slow and deep, driving me frantic. His wings spread around me, enveloping us in a cocoon of his own making.

"What if I wanted you to be my queen?" he asks as he thrusts in and out of me, his eyes glinting in the near darkness he's created beneath his wings.

"Mmm." I close my eyes against him, enjoying the sensation.

He continues to slow, the pace becoming increasingly agonizing.

I shift against him, my eyes fluttering open. "*Des*," I complain.

He stares at me, his eyes serious. "What would you say to that?"

To what?

He presses his lips to my ear. "Give me the answer I want, and I'll give you what you want."

What had he asked me? Something about being his queen...

I should know better than to give in to Des's bargains; they're always weighted to his benefit. But pinned to the wall, with his cock buried deep inside me, I'm not exactly a strategic expert.

And Des's thrusts have pretty much come to a halt.

"Yes," I breathe, eager to resume where we left off. "Sounds great."

Anything to get him to move again.

He smiles, looking like the cat that ate the canary. "*Good*," he says.

His thrusts pick up, and *sweet baby angels*, this is everything.

Des releases my hands to scoop me against him. He pulls us away from the wall and moves us across the room. Flowers and droplets of water that still float in the air now brush across my skin as we pass them by. The room looks as though time itself has stopped.

"My future queen," Des says as he gazes up at me.

I wrap my arms around his neck, holding him close. "Faster," I whisper.

"Ever demanding," he says.

Laying me down on the bed, the King of the Night rocks against me, each stroke stronger than the last. He drives himself deeper and deeper, his wings flaring out once more.

"About to come," I say.

"*Wait.*"

Wait? I'm not sure I can. My climax is climbing up and up, and it demands to be released.

His hands tighten on me. "*Now.*"

That's all the encouragement I need.

I shatter apart, my orgasm lashing through me. The

sensation is made more intense when I hear Des groan, his cock thickening inside me as he pounds out his own release.

It feels like it lasts a lifetime as wave after wave of pleasure washes through me.

It's not until several minutes later, once Des has slid out of me and the two of us lie in a tangle of limbs, that I remember his words.

What if I wanted you to be my queen?

Give me the answer I want, and I'll give you what you want.

What had I just agreed to?

CHAPTER 41

I doze in Des's arms, feeling his hands stroke my wings. I never used to be a fan of post-sex cuddling, but that was before the Bargainer became mine. Now I'm finding I have quite an appreciation for it.

The flowers and water are back in their vases, but now hovering above us is a thick sheet of parchment and five separate paintbrushes, which are all painting at once. Where Des found the brushes, or the parchment, or the five little ceramic pots of paint that rest on a side table next to the bed, I have no idea.

Just like when he first started making his art for me, I'm completely enchanted.

The painting is quickly coming along, though it takes me minutes to figure out what, exactly, the image is of. Eventually, however, I realize I'm staring at feathers, lots and lots of iridescent feathers.

"You're painting my wings," I whisper.

"Mmm," he says in response, running his hand over them again.

One of the paintbrushes wanders away from the parchment, floating down to the side table next to me. It dips its bristles into one of the pots of paint, and then, once it's coated with black paint, it floats up and over my body.

Before it makes it back to the parchment, a glob of the paint hits my shoulder.

"Des!"

He laughs, totally aware of what just happened.

"You did that on purpose!"

"Maybe," he says evasively, a grin in his voice. He brings his hand up to my shoulder and, using his thumb, rubs the paint into my skin.

I breathe in the smell of him, his scent mixed with mine. "I think we should skip more events," I whisper.

He turns his face to me, his lips brushing my forehead. "Now *that*," he says, "is an absolutely brilliant idea."

I smile a little as I run my fingers over his chest, where his sweat still slickens it. I draw swirls into his skin before continuing on, my touch tracing over the tattoos that wrap down his arms. One day I'll know the designs by heart.

He finishes the painting in silence, the two of us watching it reach completion. Once it's finished, it and the paintbrushes all lower themselves to the side table.

"I have a secret to share," Des murmurs, his mouth pressed close to my hair.

I still.

He's shared secrets in the past but often only after prodding. For him to offer one up... When he did it earlier in the day, while I was getting healed, I thought it was a one-off event meant to distract me from the situation. But now, it's possible he's simply opening up to me more, *trusting* me more.

I angle my head to look up at him.

Where minutes ago he was carefree and content, now he looks somber.

"When I close my eyes, all I see is the shape of your face and the brightness of your smile. You are the stars in my dark sky, cherub."

That isn't at all what I expected to come out of his mouth. My heart, I'm finding, is simply not big enough to hold everything I feel for this man.

Des swallows gently. "You and I share many tragedies. Mothers who died too soon. Terrible fathers..."

He said something similar days ago.

He takes a deep breath. "My father was killing off all his heirs when my mother discovered she was pregnant," Des begins, repeating what he already told me. "She fled the palace before anyone else could discover this fact.

"The kingdom simply thought she'd deserted her king—a grave enough offense. And the slight didn't go unnoticed. From everything I've learned, my mother had been my father's favorite concubine. It must've bruised his ego.

"He spent years searching for her, but she'd had a career as a spy; she knew how to hide.

"She raised me in Arestys, shielding the truth of our identities and the extent of our power from the world. She did a good job hiding us, but...I exposed us." He says this with such guilt.

"As soon as he discovered our existence, my father came for us, and—he killed her."

I feel horror closing my throat.

Des's eyes are far away, as though he's seeing the memory unfold all over again. He runs a hand over his face. "I was fifteen when I watched my mother die."

I can't even fathom…

"Des, I'm so sorry."

Has a *sorry* ever, in the history of the world, made a situation like this better? And yet I can't *not* say it.

He blinks several times, pulling himself out of the past. "I killed my father."

My eyes snap to his. For several seconds, I don't breathe.

Des…killed his father?

So many emotions bubble up. Surprise, horror, fear… *kinship*.

You and I share many tragedies.

Now I understand. His father and mine both died by our hands. It makes me wonder anew what he saw that first day he met me. I always assumed my depravity had shocked him a bit. I hadn't imagined this.

"Was it an accident?" I ask.

He laughs. "No," he says, his voice bitter, "it was quite deliberate."

My skin prickles. "Why are you telling me this?"

His hand slides around my waist, locking me to his side. "Sometimes I see you, and the past is alive. It overlays who you are and what you do." He squeezes me closer, almost to the point of pain. "I'm reminded of my old wounds, and I feel…I feel my vengeance rising.

"I cannot change my past, and I cannot change yours. I cannot even stop you from getting hurt…but I can make others atone for your pain." He says this last part so silently, so malevolently that a shiver escapes me.

That's foreboding.

"What are you thinking of, Des?" I ask him. Because it's clear to me that he's scheming.

He glances down at me, his white hair and silver eyes looking more Otherworldly than ever.

"Nothing, cherub. Nothing at all."

CHAPTER 42

"Did you hear the news?" Temper asks the next morning. The two of us eat breakfast in the same large atrium I ate at on my first morning here.

This morning, when I woke up alone in my bed, I headed over to Temper's room and asked her to join me.

I was determined to show those here at Solstice that they hadn't seen the last of me yesterday.

"What news?" I ask now before ripping off a piece strudel and shoving it into my mouth.

Dozens of other guests in the atrium keep glancing at me and my repaired wings, their voices low as they whisper into their friends' ears.

I want to throttle every last one of them—even those who weren't closed up in Mara's throne room with me. How can anybody be okay with what's happening to humans here?

Meanwhile, the waiters keep finding reasons to come by my table, some to whisper a quiet thanks, others to discreetly drop off an extra pastry here and another warm drink there.

"You're missing out on all the juiciest gossip," Temper says, pulling me back into the conversation.

"Not if you tell me." I kick my heels up on the table, the action earning me more whispers.

Temper leans forward. "The fairy who raped the human woman yesterday?"

The food in my mouth turns tasteless. I force myself to swallow. "What about him?"

"He disappeared sometime during the night. Apparently, the only thing left of him was a finger, though some people say it wasn't a finger at all—that it was his junk."

I grimace. "Ugh, Temper, couldn't you have waited for me to finish breakfast?"

Last thing I want to think about is a sexual predator's severed bits.

"That's not all."

I raise my eyebrows, picking up my cup of tea and taking a swallow.

"The queen's harem went missing—supposedly, they were taken right out of the queen's bed, though no one saw it at all."

I nearly choke on the tea.

A rapist and the queen's entire harem all go missing on the same night?

There's only one person with both the motive and power to do such a thing, and he wasn't in my bed this morning when I woke.

Temper steals a slice of bacon from my plate. "People are saying Des did it."

Just as they blamed him for the soldiers' disappearances. Only now...now I'm not sure where to begin and end defending him.

"Where is he anyway?" Temper asks.

I shake my head. "I don't know."

She sits back in her seat, a smug little grin on her face. "That cheeky bastard did it, didn't he?" she says. "I think I like him."

I feel Des's magic lasso me, tugging me and my seat backward.

Speaking of the cheeky bastard...

"Shit," I curse under my breath, grabbing the edges of the table as my crossed ankles slide off it. The chair I'm sitting in begins to slide away from the table in jerky fits and starts.

Temper pauses. "What is it?"

My blood quickens. "Des is back."

CHAPTER 43

It's not just that Des is back, it's that he wants me to train yet again, hence the magical leash all but dragging me out to one of the queen's gardens. It's only once I arrive that the Bargainer's magic dissipates.

I catch sight of the man himself leaning against a tree. In front of him, he holds the pommel of a sword like one would a cane, his outfit today 100 percent human, from his Kiss T-shirt to his leather pants and black steel-toed boots.

"Morning, cherub," he says, stepping into the sunlight, looking far too chipper for his own good. He tosses me the sword.

"Morning," I say back cautiously, catching the weapon with ease. I'm wearing a flimsy fae dress and thin leather-and-lace sandals. From my attire alone, I can tell this training session will be tougher than the others.

I watch Des as he heads to the side of the gardens and procures another sword for himself.

"What?" he says, his back to me.

I've long since stopped wondering how he can figure out my expressions when he's not even looking at me.

There's no sense beating around the bush. "Are the rumors true?" I ask.

"What rumors?" He swings the sword in his hand as he approaches me, loosening his wrist.

Only once he's mere feet away does the weapon drop to his side so he can pull me in for a quick kiss.

I close my eyes at the rush he sends through me. He tastes like secrets and deception, my wily king.

I pull away, my eyelids lifting slowly. "That you're responsible for the disappearance of the queen's harem?"

He stares at me for a long moment, those silver eyes ever enigmatic.

"That question will cost you," he says softly.

My breath leaves my lungs all at once.

He did it. God damn it, he did it.

"Sword arm up, love," he says, pulling away from me. "Fall into your battle stance."

I do as he asks, even though my heart's pounding from his evasion.

"Why?" I ask as he takes his position. He and I both know I'm not referring to his instructions.

The two of us circle each other.

"I think you know why," he says, all but confirming the rumors are true.

He rushes me then, his sword lifted high.

I spin away, my skirt trailing behind me.

"Is that all you're going to do, Callie? Run from me?" he asks as I move between the rose-lined pathways. He's right on my toes. If he wanted to, he could appear right in front of me, but for now, he's content to chase me like this.

All at once, I swivel to face him, bringing my sword up to meet his.

"Are they dead?" I ask.

The corner of his mouth quirks. "Define *dead*."

Jesus.

Our swords spark as I drag mine down and away from him. I spin under his shoulder before coming up for an attack from behind. The Night King turns just in time, deflecting my blow.

"Why?" I ask again.

"*No one* whips my mate." The vehemence with which he says that takes my breath away, so much so that he almost lands his next blow. Instead, I hear a rip as his blade slices through layers of flimsy fabric.

"Defend yourself, Callie," he growls.

I shuffle backward. "But...how?" I ask, referring to his previous answer. "You agreed to peace with the queen."

He comes at me like a force of nature.

"And I will have it. There are many handsome men she can fill her bed with."

But none would be replicas of men she once had relationships with. Des hadn't harmed her mate, but he'd taken away the men she distracted herself with.

"How will you maintain peace? Won't she know it was you?"

"Cherub, have you ever considered the possibility that it *wasn't* me?" he says, bringing his weapon down like an anvil.

I sidestep the blow before swiping my sword at him. "Are you taking the soldiers?"

He parries my attack. "What if I am?" he asks. "Will you love me less? Hate me more?"

The answer is eerily like the one he gave Mara when she asked him a similar question.

I push away from him, backing up. "Damn it, Des," I whisper hiss, "I am not some fae queen to trick with your words. Just be honest with me."

The world seems to go silent, the chirping birds and rustling trees quieting.

He comes at me, swinging his sword menacingly left and right, the blade crisscrossing his body.

As soon as he reaches me, it's all I can do to block and evade his barrage of attacks.

Our blades lock again.

"Do you trust me?" he asks.

All I hear is the rustle of my dress in the wind and our soft exhalations.

Do I trust Des, the man who saved me from my father, who loved me from afar for years? The man who rescued me from myself and sets me aflame over and over?

"*Yes*," I breathe.

His eyes soften. "The answer to your question is no," he says, his wolfish eyes boring into me. "Mate of my soul, I did not have anything to do with those soldiers' disappearances."

I feel the truth of his words, like a hit to the center of my chest. Des's confessions all have a weight to them, like he's handing over a little of himself in the process, but this one feels particularly heavy.

"Do you believe me?" he asks, our swords still locked together.

I nod, sucking in my cheeks. "I do."

His body relaxes, and I sense my opening. I drop my sword, sidestepping Des, then spin, bringing my sword around with me.

The tip of it grazes his forearm, a line of blood sprouting in its wake.

The moment I register that I injured him, I drop my sword, staring at the wound in horror.

Did he let me get him on purpose?

Just as quickly, I answer my own question.

No. This was unplanned.

Des stops fighting to stare at the cut in shock.

"You *struck* me. You landed a blow." He tosses his sword aside, the battle utterly forgotten. A beat passes, and then he begins to laugh. "You did it. You finally did it."

He's gone mad!

Des sweeps me up in his arms, spinning the two of us around. "Do you know what this means?" he asks, staring up at me.

I don't.

"You are finally ready."

CHAPTER 44

This evening's Solstice ball doesn't exactly go as planned.

As Des and I descend to the ballroom, I feel the comforting weight of my two daggers, which are currently strapped to a set of inner thigh holsters and hidden under my dark, iridescent dress. Is Solstice a peaceful festival? Yes, in theory. Do I plan to use these weapons? Not unless provoked. But after yesterday's events and Des's encouragement, I've decided to come to this party armed.

And I'm not going to lie, I feel like a bad bitch tonight, which I totally dig.

Des and I have barely entered the subterranean ballroom when Mara falls on us, and just from one glance alone, it's clear the Queen of Flora is out for blood.

She grabs the Bargainer's lapels. "Where are they?" Mara growls. She shakes him like a madwoman, the floral scent of her power filling the air "Desmond Flynn, where *are* they?"

"What are you talking about?" he says, his voice low.

"You know damn well what I'm talking about. I swear

to the Undying Gods, I will do everything in my power to break our vow of peace if you don't tell me where my harem is."

The Bargainer pries her hands off his clothing. "Pull yourself together, Mara, your subjects are watching."

They are in fact watching us, drawn in by the latest drama between rulers.

Many of them, I notice, have their wings on display. Apparently, the Night King and his human mate have had some effect on Otherworld fashion, despite—or perhaps because of—our taboo relationship.

I turn back to Des, watching him with fascination. I'm half convinced by his performance that he really has no idea where the queen's consorts are. But, of course, he's already all but admitted to me that he's not innocent.

"You have been nothing but trouble since you entered my kingdom," Mara growls, "from attacking Janus to your *human* wife questioning my authority in front of my own people."

At this, the room begins to darken, no doubt because Des is vividly recalling just what happened when I questioned her authority.

"Not to mention," she continues, "that the Fauna fae want you dead, and several people think you're behind the missing soldiers. And now my men are gone—"

The Green Man joins us then, lovingly brushing the Flora Queen's hair off her shoulder as he does so. She shudders at the touch, not so subtly shrugging his hand off. Her gaze flicks to him, and she gives the Green Man a tight smile.

Okay, that whole interaction was *not* normal. Mates aren't repulsed by each other's touch, and they don't just bear each other's company.

The Green Man smiles at Mara then us, completely oblivious to his queen's reaction. "Why don't we take this somewhere quieter?" he says.

"*Fine*," Mara whispers, spinning on her heels.

"I'm not going anywhere with either of you," I say. Not after yesterday's events.

Mara gives me an incredulous look. "Excuse me?"

"I didn't stutter," I say.

The groups around us fall quiet, shocked by my words.

"You may be their queen," I say, motioning to the room, "but you are not mine."

I hear some quick inhalations of breath.

God, it feels good to tell this woman off.

"Desmond," the Flora Queen says, "tell your ma—"

I step in front of Des. "*No*," I say. "The King of the Night is no message boy, and I can understand your words quite clearly, so if you have something to say to me, say it to my *face*."

The ballroom is serene for all of five seconds. Then Mara's power builds until it's shaking the very walls of her palace. The plants in the room come alive, twisting and snapping.

"You idiotic waste of—"

Desmond steps to my side. "Careful, Queen. Any offense given to my mate is an offense given to me. And I do not tolerate slights."

That's the closest Des will come to admitting he's behind the disappearances of Mara's men. The Flora Queen reads between the lines. Her eyes blaze as she takes in the Bargainer.

"You son of—"

The Green Man lays his hands on Des and Mara's shoulders. "*Privacy*," he emphasizes.

The room continues to darken. I can feel Des's magic

336

coiling around me, steeping me in shadow. Around us, the guests have gone utterly silent.

"Say it," Des goads her, a smile drawing the edges of his lips up. "Finish the statement."

A chill slides over my skin.

"Say it," he says, quieter.

The plants are whipping about, and Mara's sharp green eyes are flinty. "You son of a whore. You'll never be more than a bastard king, and your mate, a slave. You and your ilk disgrace my halls."

Des smiles, and the world goes dark.

CHAPTER 45

Solstice expectations: everyone shall set aside their quarrels for this week, hold hands, and sing in harmony.

Solstice reality: everyone shall come within an inch of death at least once.

Fairies everywhere in the room begin to panic as darkness cloaks our surroundings.

I feel the breath of a hundred different types of magic trying to illuminate the room only to be snuffed out by Des's power. Along the walls, I hear plants rustling. It takes several seconds for me to realize they're withering, *dying*.

"Before there were plants, before there were animals, before there was even light, there was darkness," Des says, his voice silky smooth. "From that darkness, all our deepest desires and most secret fears were born. And I know all of yours. Perhaps I should share them..."

I swear I hear Mara suck in a breath.

"Or perhaps I should simply hurt you where you stand."

"The truce..." she says.

"Yes," Des replies, "that damnable truce, the same one you managed to find your way around when it came to my mate. You think that will save anyone now? Surely you realize I can outmaneuver that promise just as well as you can."

The plants are still withering around us; I hear their unearthly death rattles.

She doesn't say anything, but the smell of rotting flowers is thick in the air.

"Or maybe I'll do it all. Spill your secrets then break your pretty throne. Shall I start with how you hate your mate's touch?"

Air hisses through Mara's teeth, but she doesn't deny the accusation.

"I know you desire my touch—and my mate's."

That last little bit of Des's confession is met with whispers in the dark. I guess wanting a human woman to fondle you is *extra* scandalous.

"There are other things I've learned. Should I keep going?"

She won't say no. I know it, Des knows it, and she must know it as well. There's both her pride and appearances to keep up. She can't just bend to a visiting fae's will. But I also know Des is unearthing truths she'd rather leave buried.

As it turns out, she doesn't have to worry about answering the Bargainer.

From the darkness comes light. It's dim at first, but with each passing second, it gets brighter and brighter, shaping itself into a man—into Janus.

His whole body radiates light, casting the room into a dim golden glow. He makes his way to our group, his guards flanking him—Aetherial one of them. He gestures for his soldiers to fall back before coming to our side.

"My friends," he says, grasping both Des and Mara on the shoulders, "why don't we find a quiet place to rip each other's throats out?"

Half of me thinks that Janus's presence is only going to agitate Des more, but my mate looks around the room, seeming to awaken from whatever state he's in. Ever so slowly, the darkness recedes, and Des rubs his mouth, reluctantly nodding.

The fairies in the ballroom blink as light returns, their gazes quickly finding us. And then the whispers begin. They stare at Des with more than a little fear.

Now it's not just the Fauna fae who distrust him; it's everyone here.

The Bargainer's silver eyes find mine. "Enjoy yourself, love. I'll be gone only a minute."

He signals to some of his soldiers, who come to flank my sides, and then, with a parting kiss, he slips away with the other royals.

I watch the four of them retreat, their stifling power leaving with them.

After they leave, Aetherial steps up to me, putting all my guards on edge. I wave them down.

"Your mate's really going through the bender with the whole bonding process," she says, looking at the door they exited through.

I glance over at her. Is that what's going on? He mentioned his instincts getting the better of him, but the Desmond I know always was the epitome of control.

"I hear Night rulers get it particularly bad," she continues. "Something about their ancestral blood apparently makes them hyperaggressive."

Des had mentioned he'd descended either from dragons

or demons. I suppose either creature could cause the mood shifts.

Her gaze slides to me. "I've also heard rumor that a white-haired man has been snatching soldiers from Solstice festivities."

I groan. "Not you too."

"So you don't believe it?"

"That my soul mate is taking soldiers?" I say. "No, I don't."

And I mean it. Wicked though Des is, he's no monster, not like the Thief of Souls is.

I step closer to Aetherial. "The truth is that since I laid eyes on your king, I've assumed he's the one involved with the disappearances."

Aetherial's head snaps to me. "Seriously? Why?"

I frown. "When I was delivered to Karnon, I saw the man who captured me—it was *your* king."

"Impossible," she says.

"Why do you think Des attacked your king the night you all arrived?"

Aetherial searches my face. "You're telling the truth," she murmurs. She shakes her head. "But it's impossible. I've seen my king's truth too. He's had nothing to do with these disappearances."

I lift a shoulder, my attention moving to where we last saw the fae rulers.

We are all turning on each other—this person points the finger at that person, that person points the finger at yet another individual. The truth of the matter is that we are all being played by the Thief of Souls, whoever they are.

The Thief of Souls...

I rotate to Aetherial. "You wouldn't happen to know the

last known location of the Day soldiers who've gone missing during Solstice, would you?"

She shakes her head. "They disappeared all over the palace grounds—mostly just outside the royal gardens."

Mostly just outside the royal gardens.

The reports I've been given corroborate this; they mentioned the men vanishing on the outskirts of the palace grounds.

The only thing beyond the gardens is the queen's sacred oak forest, which rings the entirety of the property. I've been in that oak forest a time or two, but more than that, I've dreamed of the place, over and over.

What had the Bargainer told me weeks and weeks ago?

In the Otherworld, dreams are never just dreams. They're another sort of reality.

My skin buzzes as if with electricity. It's the sensation I got as a PI whenever I felt particularly close to solving a case.

"I have to go," I say.

Aetherial gives me a quizzical look. "Didn't you just get here?"

I wave the question off. "I'll be right back."

The Thief of Souls has been hunting during Solstice, and now I know just where to find him.

CHAPTER 46

I walk through the Flora Queen's sacred oak forest, frowning at the soldiers shadowing me.

"It's not safe for any of you to be here."

Had I taken a moment when I left the ballroom to consider the fact a handful of Night soldiers would be guarding me, I'd have tried to slip past them. At the very least, I'd have requested all women, considering the Thief of Souls isn't trying to capture them these days. Of the six soldiers surrounding me, only one is a woman.

"King's ordered that we guard you," one of them says.

It's the same answer they've given me the last several times I've tried to shake them off.

I turn back to the forest ahead of me. Other than a few warm droplets of blood on my skin, I haven't found anything suspicious or unsettling about this place.

Fairy lights hover between the boughs of the trees, casting the woods in an ethereal glow.

"You could always return to the dance," another soldier suggests.

Ugh. Back to those schmoozing, scheming fairies? Back to Mara, with her cloaked insults and brittle smiles, or the Green Man and his leers?

"Give me a few more minutes."

Just thinking about the Flora rulers has me rubbing my skin. There's something off about those two.

"*Callypso...*"

I pause. "Did you hear that?" I ask the soldiers.

Two of them nod, their faces grim. One of them grabs my upper arm. "Time to get back to the ball, my lady."

Of course they're right, but I still hesitate. Finally, something slightly spooky happens out here, and now I'm about to be whisked away to safety.

I let them steer me back toward the gardens anyway, which I can just barely make out in the distance.

"*Enchantress...*"

My spine goes stiff. I glance back, toward the origin of the voice. For a split second, I catch sight of a shock of white-blond hair in the darkness.

"Des?" I whisper, before I can help it.

As soon as I breathe his name, my guards hesitate, looking back to the woods for their king. But where he once was is now dark as ever.

One of my guards yelps.

I whip around. "What happened?"

They glance at each other, each one as perplexed as the last. It takes a few seconds for all of us to put together what exactly is off about the situation.

A second ago there were six soldiers at my side.

Now there are only five.

"Move, move, move!" one of them shouts.

The soldiers don't stop to search for their comrade. They grab me and begin hustling toward the gardens.

They're not fast enough.

We've barely taken ten steps when a slew of vines drops from the treetops, reaching for one of the soldiers.

It happens in less than a second.

They wrap around his arms and shoulders and jerk him up into the canopy overhead.

"Oh, *shit*," I curse.

I've never seen *that* before.

The soldier's feet kick at empty air as the treetops swallow him up.

My wings open on reflex.

Not going to lose another soldier.

Before any of the others can stop me, I leap into the air. My wings beat furiously, lifting me toward the guard. He's still tangled in vines, and they pin his body to the trunk of the tree.

Using my claws, I slash through the plants. But as quickly as I cut through them, more form, winding around the soldier.

What in the world?

I manage to free one of his hands, and with it, he pulls out his own sword and hacks away at the vines.

One of the ropy branches darts out, wrapping around his wrist and squeezing, *squeezing*. I hear the crack of his bones breaking. The soldier cries out, his weapon falling uselessly to the forest floor beneath us.

I rip through the plants, freeing his mangled wrist. As I do so, vines snake around my own body, twisting around my torso.

Shit.

I'm pried away from the guard, and my body is flung to the ground. I land on my hands and knees, and for several seconds, I just rest there, breathing heavily.

The four remaining soldiers close in around me, helping me to my feet. Already several of them have their wings out. No doubt they were about to join me up in the canopy.

I glance above me. As I watch, the vines completely ensnare the soldier, cleaving him to the tree.

And then—horror of horrors—with a wet rip, the trunk of the tree parts around the fairy and begins to suck him in.

"Holy *fuck*."

Once more, my wings flare out, but the remaining soldiers hold me fast.

"We need to leave," one of them says.

But I can't look away.

It only takes seconds for the trunk of the tree to fully wrap around the fairy and then another several seconds for it to reseal, starting at the soldier's feet and working its way up, leaving a thin line of blood in its wake.

And then it's over.

A tree just swallowed a soldier before my eyes.

I did this. I led these guards into this sinister-ass forest, and now two men are gone.

I spend several seconds glaring at the treetops and berating myself as they lead me away before I remember.

I am the Night King's mate. I'm no victim, I'm a survivor, a fighter.

I'm someone's nightmare.

"Let me go," I say calmly.

The soldiers ignore me.

"I said, *let me go*." This time when I speak, it comes out as a command.

"My lady—" one of them protests.

I begin to glow. "This is not how you treat your king's mate. You *will* listen to me, and you *will* follow my orders."

Now they do listen. Their hands fall to their sides.

I turn around before stalking back to the tree, my skirts swishing around my ankles. "Men," I call over my shoulder, "leave this place and go find your king. It's not safe for you here."

This time, they don't follow my order. Seconds after I give it, all four remaining soldiers flank me. "We're not leaving you," one of them says.

I want to growl at them. Surely, they know how dangerous this is for them.

But I push my worry and frustration aside. I can only focus on one thing at a time.

Several feet away lies the captured soldier's sword. I grab it then face off with the tree that ate one of Des's men.

This was a bad day to piss me off.

I pull the sword back like a baseball bat, well aware that this is not how you hold the weapon.

One of the soldiers at my back says, "It's against the law to cut down—"

I swing the blade, embedding it into the tree trunk. With a swift yank, I jar the sword out.

"I'm not cutting the tree down," I say over my shoulder. *WHACK.*

I strike the trunk again.

"I'm saving one of my guards."

Again, I yank the blade from the bark, wood splintering away as I do so.

"There's a difference."

There's not really a difference. Sure, my goal isn't to cut the tree down, but I probably will chop the fucker down to save this soldier.

The tree moans, and I hear the neighboring ones hissing at me, some of their branches bending down and swiping at the group of us.

I'm pretty sure I just made enemies of the oaks.

I look over my shoulder at the guards at my back. "Well, are you all going to just stand there, or are you going to help me get your comrade out?"

That's all the encouragement they need.

My remaining guards and I take turns sawing into the tree trunk, bits of bark splintering off with every hit. The tree begins shrieking, the ungodly sound carrying through the woods.

We do this until we see a swath of skin.

The night soldier is still cocooned in vines, his body curled inside the core of the tree.

That is not a sight you see every day.

I drop my sword, and together with my guards, I pull out the coughing soldier from the heart of the tree.

He pants, pulling off fine, spindly roots that seem to have wedged their way *under* his skin and into his veins.

"Thank you," he wheezes to his comrades, clasping one of them on the shoulder. His eyes move over the group until they find me.

The rescued guard gets up, dusting dirt and bark off himself. He kneels before me, taking my hand and pressing it to his forehead. "I owe you more than just my allegiance, my queen. I vow that as long as I live, my shield and my sword will protect you. My life is yours."

CHAPTER 47

The oak we hacked into is making strange wheezing noises, and its neighbors have quieted for the moment. The vines that once entrapped the soldier now roll up into the tree's core, withering away.

The soldiers, meanwhile, are tending to their comrade, leaving me to assess what exactly just happened.

A voice called to me, I saw Des's likeness, and then two soldiers disappeared: one we recovered and the other still missing. The sequence of events is hauntingly similar to the tales that have been coming in.

I turn to the other trees that surround us. Never have I been so sick of the color green in my life.

But green isn't the only color in this forest. Dark blood drips down many of the branches around me, turning the sacred wood into something macabre, something I'd be more likely to see on Memnos, the Land of Nightmares.

An ungodly thought hits me.

The men who are missing...

I stride over to where I dropped the soldier's sword. Picking it up again, I head to a particularly bloody tree several feet away. Once more, I lift the weapon.

"My lady," the female soldier calls after me, "cutting one tree to save a soldier is bad enough. To cut down another will be seen as an act of war."

Too bad for Mara, she already swore an oath of peace with Des's kingdom.

"I don't give a fuck what the Flora Queen sees this as."

I roll my neck and then pull the sword back and take a swing. The blade embeds itself into the thick trunk, something warm and wet spraying from the wound.

The tree screams—the sound like a pig squealing—as I cut into it.

I yank the blade out of the bark. From the gash, blood oozes.

Bleeding trees. What a grisly, grisly sight.

No one else dares to join me, though they all avidly watch.

I swing again and again, ignoring the strain in my arms. Each successive blow cracks a bit more of the bark, spraying shards of wood and bits of blood. The tree continues to shriek, its canopy rustling.

I'm covered in gore. It speckles my hair and paints my face, reminding me of that fateful night years and years ago when I stood up to my stepfather...and watched him die.

Slowly but surely, the hardened bark of the oak gives way to its soft core. I begin using my claws to rip it away, studiously ignoring the fact my hands are now coated with blood. With one final rip, I unearth exactly what I feared.

In the heart of the tree, covered in gore and a web of roots, is a sleeping man.

Like this whole outing, it's downright spooky. I'm staring into the face of a man who's been missing for who knows how long, his arms crossed over his chest as though someone laid him out.

Unlike the Night soldier we just retrieved, this man looks like he's been here a particularly long time. The vines wrapped around him have now fused together, and his long hair is matted to his skin.

Whatever color his uniform originally was, it's now crimson, steeped in blood. But I don't need to make out the color of his uniform to figure out which kingdom he belongs to. The curving ibex horns indicate he's a Fauna solider.

"There's a tree-cutting party, and I wasn't invited?" a familiar voice says at my back.

I turn around.

Des leans against a neighboring oak, watching me with those eyes that see everything, his white hair stirring in the breeze.

His arms are folded over his chest, his biceps looking massive and his tattoos seeming particularly menacing. I have to remind myself that the three bronze bands on his other arm are for valor because right now, even clad in fae attire, he simply looks like the Bargainer, the man who strikes deals for gain and breaks bones for slights against me.

"If my mate is going to break the law, she should at *least* invite me along," he says, pushing away from the tree.

His face changes seconds later when he takes in the scene.

"What happened?" Des asks, all humor gone from his voice.

I wipe my bloodied hands off on my dress. "I think I found the missing soldiers."

CHAPTER 48

Des disappears before materializing at my side a moment later. He scrutinizes the man sleeping in the tree.

"*Mara*," he whispers.

Mara, the vain Queen of Flora, has been hiding men in her sacred oak forest, one of the places where it's forbidden to strike down a tree.

No wonder no one had found the soldiers—they'd been hidden inside the one place that could not be disturbed. Only an outsider like me would be ignorant and ballsy enough to desecrate this grove.

I feel the breath of Des's magic a second before it hits the vines. The tree shrieks as it blackens and decays, the vines that hold the man fast now curling away.

Motioning with his hand, the Bargainer uses magic to pry the sleeping soldier out of the tree. Vines groan and snap as the man is released.

His body is covered in gore like a new baby's might be

when Des's magic settles him onto the grass. And in some ways, this is a dark rebirth.

"The bleeding trees," I say to Des. Each one must house a missing soldier, his body cocooned inside it.

The Bargainer nods. "I know, cherub." His eyes meet mine.

The plants aren't rotting from a disease at all—they're coffins.

Des leans over the sleeping soldier, his eyes scouring the man. "He's just like the women." A muscle in his cheek ticks.

The trees rustle and shake as a wind kicks up. It lifts my hair and lashes it about.

"Mara's coming," Des says, his voice ominous.

My skin chills. This whole time, the Queen of Flora was behind the men's disappearances.

The wind picks up speed, beginning to tear leaves from their branches.

I feel rather than hear her approach, her magic thickening the air with scents of pine and honeysuckle.

When I finally see her, her dress is whipping behind her, her bright red hair billowing around her like a fiery corona. At her back, a regiment of guards follow, their faces solemn.

"Who has struck down one of my trees?"

Struck down—like it was a man, not a plant. Perhaps to her it was. Perhaps these trees are far more beloved than the men lying dormant inside them.

I straighten as she closes in on our group.

Mara's eyes move to the tree I just demolished, and her low moan carries on the wind, rising higher and higher until it becomes a shriek.

"My sacred oak!"

For a moment, we're forgotten. She rushes to the tree and falls to her knees at the foot of it, her hands going to its bloody trunk.

Now's probably not the time to tell her we actually took out two oaks, not one.

She doesn't spare the sleeping soldier laid out near her a passing glance.

"I never thought it would be you," Des says quietly, menace riding his voice.

His wings snap out, the bone-white talons gleaming in the darkness. The shadows are gathering around him.

Mara's head is still bowed. "You entered the Fauna King's palace and defiled it. I invited you to my kingdom, and you dared to do the same. First with my harem, and now with my holy forest."

Around us, roots and vines begin to snap and stir.

"You thought promising peace between our kingdoms would earn you immunity." Her hair begins to whip about her as her power rises, the floral scent now mingling with the cloying smell of rot. "You—thought—*wrong*."

Mara screams, and a hundred different roots and vines shoot toward us. Des steps in front of me, and shadows blast out from him, snuffing out the fairy lights and blocking out the heavens above. The roots wither and die away before they can do more than caress my skin.

Everything is inky darkness. I can't tell up from down, left from right. There is no ground, no forest, no soldiers, no sky. Nothing but primordial night.

From the darkness, I hear Des chuckle. "Oh, Mara."

The air fills with power, and the fae queen shrieks.

BOOM!

The earth shakes as Mara unleashes another wave of her magic.

"Is that the best you have?" Des taunts a moment later.

I can't tell what's happening; I can only assume the two rulers are fighting.

The magic in the air crests again—and again and again.

"*Callypso…*"

The hairs on the nape of my neck stand on end. Des's voice calls to me from an entirely different direction than where I assumed he stood.

"*Enchantress…*"

I spin at the sound of his voice.

From the nothingness around me, a figure appears in the distance. Des watches me from afar, not coming any closer.

And yet, I swear I can sense him still engaging with the Flora Queen somewhere else in the darkness.

Des beckons me toward him. When I don't budge, he turns around and heads deeper into the inky blackness.

What is going on? Is this an illusion? Is this real? What happens if I follow him?

What happens if I don't?

On reflex, I begin to move, throwing a glance over my shoulder. I don't know why I bother. Aside from Des, there's nothing here but unending darkness. I understand now why one of Des's titles is the King of Chaos. This world of perpetual night could drive a person crazy.

Slowly, however, the shadows give way to forest once more. It's not until I see the fairy lights overhead that I look behind me. A swell of darkness still swathes the forest. From it, I hear faint shrieks and grunts.

When I swivel back around, my mate waits for me in the distance, surrounded by those bloody oaks.

"Des?" I say, confused.

How can he be in two places at once?

"How very beautiful you are," he says.

Again, my gooseflesh rises. Something about his voice is...off. But what?

"Callypso Lillis, the enchantress," Des says, strolling forward.

"Des, what's going...?" My words die away as he nears.

That hair, those eyes—it's a spitting image of Des. But the shape of his face is a little squarer, and the curve of his mouth a little crueler.

Not Des!

I take a step back.

"I've wanted to meet you for some time."

My heart's thundering, my gaze moving from the fairy's pointed ears to his white hair and sculpted frame.

Not Des, but similar.

This man's body is a shade more compact than my mate, his frame a bit wirier.

Despite the incongruences, I recognize him from my dreams.

Dreams are never just dreams...

"Who are you?"

He disappears, only to manifest behind me.

"*A ghost.*"

I whip around, expecting to see him at my back, but there's no one there. I spin in a full circle, but the man who could be Des's doppelgänger is gone.

"So the Bastard of Arestys found himself a human mate." The man's voice comes from above me. "Here I was, ready to pity him."

The Bastard of Arestys...I've heard that from somewhere...

"But you are nothing quite so ordinary," he continues. "A human with wings and scales. A siren who can ensnare mortals with her voice alone. Even I might've made an exception for a mortal like you."

I stare at the canopy above me, trying to track his voice.

"How did you lead me here?" I ask. *How did no one sense you?* Des rules the darkness and everything in it.

The fairy laughs. "By the time your mate was learning tricks in the darkness, I had already mastered them."

I glance around me, trying to pinpoint the man's voice. Damn him, he keeps moving about.

"The foolhardy ruler of Night is everything he is because of me—but not for long."

The fairy reappears in front of me, brandishing a dagger.

"Shit." I jerk back just as he slashes it across my chest. Silk rips as his blade cuts through my dress, and a line of blood blooms in its wake, seeping into the frayed material.

The sting of pain and the thick rush of adrenaline are enough to call out my siren. My skin illuminates, and *yessss*, I feel my own viciousness rising.

The man backs away, his eyes drinking me in. "A shame to kill you when I could keep you as a pet."

His words are the very thing I need to push me over the edge.

I come at him, feeling the wild, chaotic power I was born with. *Men like him die by my hand.*

I swing at him, left, right, my own instincts now bolstered by my training.

He dodges the hits, his eyes brightening like Des's so often do when he gets excited.

The fairy vanishes.

I spin just as he appears at my back, lunging at me with his knife.

Oh God, he doesn't just look like Des, he fights like him too, disappearing and manifesting at will.

I bring up my arm, blocking the swing, and then I grab his wrist, twisting with all my strength.

He winks out of existence, but not before he releases his weapon.

I swipe it off the ground as he forms at my back. I just barely miss his fist, but I'm unable to avoid the booted kick to my back.

I grunt, sprawling across the grass. Dagger still in hand, I scramble to get back on my feet, unable to roll away because of my unwieldy wings.

Before I can, my attacker's hand threads into my hair. He yanks my head back. With a shriek, I turn into the motion, twisting and swiping out with my stolen blade. The knife cuts through the air before slicing into my attacker's side.

Hissing in air, he releases my hair and steps back.

I rotate to face him, my lungs heaving.

Almost in a daze, he touches his side. He stares at his bloody fingers, shocked.

Bloodlust surges in me. I rise to my feet, my wings billowing out in a show of power.

The fairy's face morphs, turning sinister. "You cut me."

I smile at his anger and his words.

I'll take and take and take until this fairy is nothing but pulp and bones.

My surroundings darken.

"Cherub," Des says, appearing at my side and dragging the darkness along with him, "what are you doing out…"

His words die away when he catches sight of my attacker.

"*You.*"

Across from us, the fairy's cruel mouth curves.

"Hello, my son."

CHAPTER 49

Son?

But Des's father was supposed to be...

"You died on my sword, Galleghar," Des says. He stares at the fairy like one would a ghost. By all rights, he *is* a ghost.

His father—*Galleghar*—tilts his head. "Did I?"

My eyes dart between the two men. The similarities between them are uncanny. No wonder there were so many rumors of Des being the last person seen with the missing soldiers. His father has been haunting these woods.

"*Desmond!*" Mara shrieks from somewhere in the distance. "*Coward! Come back and finish the fight.*" She sounds like a broken woman.

Galleghar uses the momentary distraction to disappear. A second later the air behind me stirs. That's all the warning I get.

The fairy's arms wrap around me. Then I'm jerked off my feet and into the sky. He propels the two of us high into the night air.

"What do you think your mate desires more—love or life?" he whispers into my ear as my mate charges after us.

I struggle against him. Higher and higher, the two of us shoot into the sky.

"Why don't we find out?" Des's father says.

His arms open, and abruptly, I slip from them.

I hear Des shout as I pinwheel in the sky.

At the moment my wings might as well be useless. I can't get my bearings, and the oak grove is growing bigger and bigger beneath me.

All at once I'm scooped out of the air and into Des's arms.

"I've got you," he says.

No sooner does he speak than Galleghar appears at the Bargainer's back, his hands braced against Des's wings. He jerks sharply on them, and I hear the snapping of bones.

He broke my mate's wings!

Des roars in agony and anger, those massive wings folding at an unnatural angle. And his father, his damnable father, laughs before disappearing just as quickly as he appeared.

The Bargainer tucks his broken wings around me as the two of us tumble, trying to shield me from harm despite him being the injured one.

Several seconds later, we slam into the treetops, and Des grunts as he takes the brunt of the force. The two of us tumble from branch to branch until we finally hit the earth below.

I moan as I stare up at Des. His eyes are unfocused with pain, but he rises to his feet without hesitation, pulling me with him.

"Going so soon?" Galleghar appears on a branch before us.

Even battered and broken, Des is furious. My normally contained mate is losing his long-practiced control.

The shadows gather and spill over the forest.

The man above us may have sired my mate, he may even know a few tricks Des doesn't, but right now the darkness is bending to the Bargainer's will, not his father's.

Des's entire body hums with pent-up rage. I *feel* that unnatural wrath churning beneath his skin.

"How did you escape death?" Des demands.

Galleghar gives his son an indulgent look. "As the Lord of Secrets, you should know better than to ask." He hops off the branch, and I get my first good look at the wings spread out behind him.

They could be carbon copies of Des's own wings except Galleghar's talons look a little bigger, his wingspan might be a little narrower, and the skin of his wings is soot black, not silver. They fold behind him as his feet hit the ground, and he strides toward us.

"How I have longed for this reunion," he says. "How I will savor killing you." His eyes land on me. "Maybe I'll be merciful and keep your mate for my new harem—I'll save her for only my most unspeakable acts. Kings have their needs."

Okay, this fucker needs to go *down.*

Des releases me slowly, stepping forward. Darkness pours off him in waves.

Galleghar disappears in the next instant before reappearing right in front of Des, his arm cocked.

The Bargainer dodges the hit, and then, grabbing the collar of Galleghar's shirt, he thrusts his own fist into Galleghar's face. Before he lands the blow, both men disappear. They materialize in the sky above me, grappling as they fall. And then they vanish once more, winking into and out of existence over and over.

My trembling heart lodges itself in my throat. My mate

is mighty, but he's fighting the one man who might be his match. And unlike his father, Des's wings are broken.

I hear the two leviathans roaring as they fight, the world shaking with claps of their power as their magic meets.

Never have I felt so useless as now, staring up into the sky. "He'll be fine."

I jolt as the Green Man steps out from the dark woods, his green skin glowing softly in the moonlight.

"What are you doing here?" I ask, edging back a little.

I came into the forest looking for answers. So far, I've only been met with questions.

He comes right up to me, reaching out to stroke my dimming skin.

"You are utterly singular," he says, his finger moving over the scales that dust my arms. His eyes flick to mine. "I find I've become quite...*enthralled* by you."

I step away from him, grimacing a little. "Where's Mara?" I ask, looking over his shoulder.

Something about this situation is off, but what?

"Mourning her beloved trees," he says, not taking his amber eyes off me. "I admit, I was utterly titillated when you struck down those oaks." He shakes his head. "That brute human logic of yours does indeed stir things up around here."

The Green Man reaches for me again. I slap his hand away. That earns me a nefarious smile. "The one wife I couldn't have, the one soul I couldn't claim," he says.

My skin goes cold. "What are you talking about?"

"Did you miss me while I was away?" He begins to circle me. "I've looked forward to chatting with you since our last little encounter in the Fauna Kingdom."

CHAPTER 50

I walked Des and myself into a trap. One I can't figure out.

Des's father is back from the dead, and the Green Man claims to have memories he shouldn't.

The Green Man smooths down his shirtfront, looking at his body. "This bloody sot died *long* ago."

I swallow, beginning to back up.

"Deep in the forest, the Green Man met a stranger who wanted to harvest the most *peculiar* fruit." The Green Man—or whoever this guy really is—laughs. "The weakling sought to strike me down." He flashes me a sly smile. "But I am a hard thing to kill.

"He died, I lived, and I indeed harvested the most magnificent fruit." He lifts his hands, gesturing to the bloody trees around us.

He was responsible for the disappearances?

I'm itching to reach beneath the hem of my dress and grab my daggers. Slowly, my hand moves to my skirts. I hike the material up slowly.

Keep him distracted.

"How did you hide this from Mara?" I ask.

No wonder the Flora Queen was utterly uninterested in her mate. Whoever this man is, it doesn't sound like he's the true Green Man. Which means she's been living with an impostor for who knows how long.

He laughs. "You mean her bleeding trees? She thought they were dying of rot—which they are—and she sought to hide it from her kingdom. Little known fact: sacred trees die when Flora rulers are too weak to sustain their kingdom. She feared she was losing her hold on her reign."

I continue to gather the fabric of my skirt in my hand.

"And Karnon?" I ask. "How did you infiltrate his kingdom?"

The Green Man's eyes light. "Ah, Karnon. That mad, clever king was my greatest conquest yet. To slip into a skin not yet dead... It was effortful, to say the least."

My flesh crawls. How could I not have noticed before the lingering *wrongness* of this man?

"But, as you saw, living bodies have their drawbacks. I fought with his mind for dominance, and I didn't always win."

Karnon's split personality! The mad king had still been in there when this body snatcher took it over.

But...*how?*

The Green Man continues talking, unaware of my thoughts. "That animal made you in his likeness to escape me. He sought an end to his life by provoking the King of the Night, and what better way to do so than to harm the Night King's mate?"

I've hiked up almost my entire skirt. So close to my daggers.

"What *are* you?" I ask.

For one second, his body morphs. Inky-black hair and eyes replace the Green Man's more vibrant ones. His skin pales, his features turning sinister.

Those upturned eyes, that pouty mouth and plaited hair. I've seen that face before! It's the dark-haired man from my most recent nightmare.

"What is a body really?" he says. "Something that constrains you, something that perishes."

The image dissipates, and he's the Green Man once more.

"I have a thousand eyes and even more souls. I am what happens when even darkness dies. Look at me and see the truth."

I do look at him. I can't bear to take my eyes off him. This is the man who has hidden thousands of soldiers and raped thousands more.

The Thief of Souls.

CHAPTER 51

I desperately grasp one of my daggers. The metal zings as I pull it out of my thigh holster.

He smiles at the sight. "Come now, Callypso. Have I not just warned you that killing me is pointless?"

"Stay away from me," I hiss at him, lifting the weapon.

"Alas, I cannot. You, my sweet, have presented me with a unique problem." He rubs his lower jaw as he talks. "A prophecy demands you must die in order for me to get what I want, but if you do, you are beyond my reach."

Above us, the sky quakes as my mate battles with his father.

"What is it you want?"

He grins again, the sight unsettling. "Wouldn't you like to know. Ask yourself this: Why would a thief such as me steal as many soldiers as I have?"

That's one of the many things I could never figure out about this mystery.

"Think on it, enchantress."

"Don't call me that."

"Would you prefer *slave*?" he asks. "Personally, I think you seem ill-suited to the title, but if that's what you desire..."

I begin to back up. "I don't understand—what does Galleghar have to do with any of this?" I ask. Even now, the sky thunders with the sounds of father and son.

The Thief of Souls smiles. "There's an old prophetess who can answer that question—for a price. One way or another, you'll figure it out."

I fight the next question on my lips. I know it's no use asking; no answer will be good enough. But I ask anyway. "Why are you doing this?"

His eyes seem to dance. "Perhaps it is time for you to learn more about me, as I have you." He reaches out to me again, cupping my cheek.

All my confusion, all my fear and rage, pulls the siren from her depths.

As my skin illuminates, I swipe out at the Green Man with my dagger, relishing the moment the blade meets flesh.

A normal fairy would've flinched from the pain, but he doesn't react. Doesn't even bother moving his hand. He just continues to talk. "I do have one problem, enchantress. As exquisite as I find you, you are beyond my control. There is, however, a remedy for that."

Moving so fast that I can barely follow, he grabs my dagger-wielding arm and twists.

I let out a cry, half in pain, half in rage. Bringing my heel up, I slam my foot into his chest, knocking him away.

He chuckles, the sound like nails on a chalkboard. He holds up my dagger. "Missing something?"

Shit.

Hastily, I reach for my remaining dagger. My gown is

368

already bloody and shredded. I look like a wraith, like a ghost come to haunt these cursed woods.

My hand closes on the weapon's labradorite handle, and I draw it out.

Des and his father continue to duel overhead, the air thick with their magic.

I shift my weight, tossing my dagger from hand to hand. Somewhere along the way, I became comfortable with the weapon.

The Thief smiles, and then he charges.

Unlike Des's father, the Thief of Souls cannot appear and disappear at will. He can, however, harness the Green Man's power.

The oaks begin to hiss and shake, their large bodies bending to swipe at me.

I duck and dodge the attacks as I square off with my opponent, my body thrumming with energy.

When I get within arm's reach, I swipe out at the Thief, the dagger slashing him across the chest. I follow with my claws, slashing his cheek.

His blood looks striking against his pale green skin.

More. I want more.

I thirst to see him bleed. To see him die.

The sight of all that dark liquid sends me into a frenzy. I move with fluid grace, parrying the Thief's blows with my blade, slashing and kicking with the rest of my body.

It takes minutes to cover the fairy in his own gore.

This is power.

Foolish of him to fight me.

"You're going to have to fight a little harder if you really want to hurt me," I goad the Thief.

He smiles. "That can be arranged."

Moments later, Mara walks into our clearing, looking a little worse for the wear. The flowers in her hair are wilted, she has dirt smeared across her cheek, and her clothes are nearly as stained and ripped as mine.

It takes her all of two seconds to take in the scene. The Green Man—her mate—covered in blood, dueling the human woman who cut her beloved trees.

"*You*," she practically hisses at me.

Vines come at me from all sides, and it's all I can do to shred through them with my claws and dagger. And still more come at me.

No longer am I fighting the Thief of Souls so much as I'm defending myself from Mara's attacks. Right in the middle of the melee, he strides toward me.

The Thief runs his blade down my cheek then my arm. "So bloodthirsty. I had *no* idea."

I swipe out at him, which he easily dodges.

"Mate," Mara calls out to the Thief, "what are you doing?"

"Exacting our revenge," he says over his shoulder.

That seems to appease her. The plants continue to pin me in place, squeezing me slowly.

The Thief of Souls drags my blade down my other cheek, slicing open the flesh. I feel a brief sting and then the warm sensation of blood slipping down my jaw. "The only problem is, the moment I truly hurt you, your mate will be on me." He taps the blunt part of his blade against my nose. "But I think I've figured out a solution."

I'm a fly caught in his web. The vines have completely overpowered me. My arms are pinned to my sides. I still hold my remaining blade, but I cannot move enough to saw my way out of my bindings.

He leans in close. "Why don't I explain exactly what I plan for you?

"Right now, my magic is incompatible with yours, and that ruins all my fun. But it doesn't have to be that way—not if you drink a certain something.

"Have you heard that lilac wine, the rarest of fairy elixirs, can not only bestow longevity to mortals, it can heal the wounded?"

I thin my gaze.

"It's a cure-all of sorts, and if you drink it, well, then you *would* be able to fall victim to my power, and your soul… your soul could be mine for the taking."

This sicko.

"I could just give the wine to you here and now, but"—he seems far too giddy—"I have an even better idea."

He lifts my blade to his eyes, inspecting it. His gaze flicks to mine.

"This might hurt."

With one swift movement, he buries the knife in my gut.

CHAPTER 52

I choke, my skin flaring even brighter.

So much pain!

From behind us, Mara gasps, her vines loosening. "What are you doing?" she asks, aghast.

Rather than answering, the Thief yanks up on the hilt. My body jerks as he cuts through vines, flesh, and organs. I let out a scream, my glamour making the cry sound lyrical.

In the distance, Des roars, the sound eclipsing all others. In an instant he's in that forest with us, bloody and broken and angry.

He drags the Thief of Souls away from me before throwing him to the ground with an enraged cry.

Mara's vines release me, and I fall to my knees.

My surroundings are darkening, and I can't tell if it's the Bargainer's doing or if I'm just that close to blacking out.

Cannot black out.

Dimly, I'm aware Mara is watching the scene unfold and that Galleghar, wherever he is, has not joined the group of us. But more than anything, I'm aware of my mate and the Thief of Souls.

The Bargainer stomps on the Thief's calf, snapping the bone.

"I could scalp you alive or remove your entrails and make you eat them," Des says as he breaks the Thief's other calf. "Or perhaps I should start with your teeth and nails?"

Mara screams. "Please, Des, no more!"

"He harmed my mate," Des snarls. "By law, I'm entitled to retribution—and I shall have it!" His battered wings flare.

The Bargainer looks like some dark god; never has he seemed quite so Otherworldly. And I can barely see him through my dimming vision.

I clutch the gash on my stomach, blood pouring from it. I feel myself weakening with each breath I take.

Mortally wounded. I might have minutes left.

And the agony! I squeeze my eyes shut and swallow down my bile.

Des circles the fairy, staring down at the Thief. He lifts his hand, the land darkening.

I know what happens now. It's the same thing that happened when Karnon faced down my mate.

Utter annihilation.

"*Stop!*" Mara cries.

She knows it too. She's a far cry from the haughty queen I met a week ago, her clothes ruined, her face confused, her pride in tatters.

I pick myself up, holding my stomach. Each step is pure agony, but I force myself onward. I wrap my hand around the hilt of the dagger buried inside me.

Don't think about it.

Des's eyes widen when he sees what I'm about to do. "*Callypso, no—*"

I yank the blade out, gagging on the pain, the nausea, and the screams that should be rising out of me. A torrent of blood gushes out of the wound, making me sway on my feet.

Some of the shadows—*Des's* shadows—are receding, but a different sort of darkness tugs on the edges of my vision.

Death.

My mate is at my side in an instant, relinquishing his vengeance for love. He presses a hand to my stomach. Within seconds, his fingers are coated with my blood.

"Cherub, what are you doing?" he asks, his voice torn up.

I meet his crushed gaze. He's a man watching everything he's lived for slip through his grasp.

Even he fears I'm going to die.

I can see him desperately grasping at his anger because if he lets it go…it's a long way to fall, and the abyss that would swallow him up—it would be world ruining.

"Let go of me, Des." There's steel in my words.

Wordlessly, *reluctantly*, he releases me.

I stagger forward, right up to where the Thief lies sprawled on the ground. He's managed to flip himself over, onto his back. His eyes move to my wound.

I kneel next to him. "You robbed thousands of soldiers of their lives. You robbed them and their families and their friends." All those soldiers who became victims just like me, their bodies buried in the hearts of trees or laid to rest inside glass coffins.

He swallows, a bit of blood leaking out the corner of his lips. "You're not going to—"

In one swift motion, I draw my arm back and plunge my dagger deep into the Thief of Soul's heart.

Mara shrieks somewhere behind me, sounding as though with that one blow, I stabbed her as well.

The Thief of Souls laughs, even as blood seeps out of his wound. "You can't kill me," he says.

His face changes from that of the Green Man, earning another shriek from Mara. The queen didn't even know the man she slept next to wasn't her husband. Raven-dark hair and inky-black eyes replace the Green Man's evergreen hair and amber irises.

"Want to know a secret?" he whispers. "Janus had a twin, a twin who died. The first time you met him, you were really meeting me."

I reel back. Whether it's from pain or blood loss, I can't seem to put his words together.

He says, "Ask yourself this: Do the dead ever really die?"

I stare down at the monster who's already ruined so many lives, feeling my own life force seep out of me.

He reaches for a lock of my hair. "Utterly singular…" he breathes. He smiles at me. "This is our little game—and trust me, enchantress, it's far from over."

A gust of wind sweeps through the forest, a dust devil rising around him.

"I'm still coming for you," he promises me. "Your life is mine."

CHAPTER 53

The Thief's eyes close, his body going still.

It's only once his life has fled him that his features revert to those of the Green Man.

Now that the Thief no longer animates the Green Man's body, the fallen ruler looks benevolent, kind.

Mara pushes past me, falling to the side of her dead mate. She cries over the Green Man, clutching her chest like the loss physically hurts.

I rise on shaky legs, one of my hands still pressed to my stomach.

I feel my own life ebbing away from me. That horrible darkness creeps in from the edges of my vision.

I stagger then fall. Des catches me before I hit the ground.

"That was the Thief—"

"Ssshhh," he says, laying me out on the ground before shucking off his shirt. Efficiently, he rips it into strips, making a tourniquet of sorts for my wound.

It's too late for that. I know the Thief shredded vital

things when he stabbed me. The soldier in Des knows it too.

I touch his battle-weary face, gazing into his fathomless eyes. They're like a beacon, calling me to life. But the shadows are closing in on me…

"I love you, Des."

"You are *not* leaving me, Callie," he says fiercely.

My cold hand slips from his face, and I start to descend into that final, eternal darkness.

CHAPTER 54
DESMOND FLYNN

She's not going to die.

She can't.

She may.

Just like my mother.

This is what happens to brave women. Strong women. If you're worthy enough, they'll bleed for you.

They'll die for you.

I feel my throat working.

Please, not again. Never again.

And not *her*. My mate.

Life was bleak enough without my mother. But with Callie, with Callie, everything changed. Life was a thousand times sweeter than I could've imagined.

If she dies…there will be no surviving this.

I stroke her cool, clammy cheek, desperate to coax life back into her. She stares up at me, and there's such brutal truth in her expression.

She knows what's happening to her.

My heart is crushing. I almost can't breathe through the pain of losing her. So much worse than my injuries.

This is not how I thought it would all end. But everything Callie is, everything that makes up her essence, is fading.

I run my hand over her bracelet.

Her bracelet! While she lives, she's still bound by her vows.

I'm not above exploiting them.

"You will *not* die," I command.

My magic flows out of me, and one bead begins to fade...then another and another. She draws in a shuddering gasp.

"Des, what are you doing?" she asks, breathless.

"Saving you."

And by the gods, it's *working*.

Row after row of beads disappears.

Take them all, just bring her back to me.

The beads start to vanish slower and slower until, finally, they stop disappearing altogether.

Only a little over a row remains.

Her breathing is still as shallow as ever, and her wound hasn't stopped bleeding.

I'm no healer, but if the magic took, then something should've improved.

But it doesn't.

And then, with a *whoosh*, the whole thing reverses.

The magic slams back into my body, sending me backward, and the beads begin to reform one by one.

Nooooo!

Can't complete the spell.

Beyond my control.

Callie's eyes widen, like she felt the balances tip as well.

I gather her body closer to me, rocking her in my arms, my head bowed over hers.

I've never fallen apart in front of Callie. Not even when she was at the mercy of Karnon. But now I do.

Because this is the real thing.

"Till darkness dies, love," she says, her voice faint.

"No." I'm shaking my head. "Even then, *no*." The night could end, and she'd still be mine.

Always mine.

Her eyes slip shut.

"*No*," I say more emphatically.

Where is Temper?

I glance up, frantically looking around. The sorceress could heal her. But finding her and flying her back here would take minutes at best.

Minutes I do not have.

I look back down at Callie. My mate is fading so fast. Too fast.

This is the moment I've dreaded since I met Callie. The moment I lose her.

I'd rather do something unforgivable to keep her alive than let her slip quietly into death.

Something unforgivable...

"Mara, where is the wine? The—the lilac wine."

The Flora queen looks up from her own dead mate, her eyes dull. "The royal cellar," she mumbles, as if in a trance. And then her attention returns to the Green Man.

The royal cellar. I've been there several times over the centuries. The wine wouldn't take minutes to locate and bring back—it could be done in mere seconds. But the cost of such a solution—it's a steep one.

Fuck the ramifications.

It takes an instant to leave Callie's side and materialize there, then several precious moments to locate the telltale purple glass bottles.

Grabbing one, I disappear before returning to my mate's side.

With a swift jerk, I snap the narrow neck of the bottle clean off. Already I catch faint whiffs of the wine.

I promised my mate that I'd protect her from this side of myself, the selfish, immoral side.

I lied.

The thing is, I'm both a fairy and the son of a tyrant king; I've descended, undoubtedly, from demons. Wickedness is in my blood.

For once I will give in to the depraved thoughts that revolve around my mate.

Callie's face is ashen, her skin already cold. Her pulse is a weak, fluttery thing.

I'll take my mate's mortality from her just as I have always imagined.

Bringing the bottle to her lips, I tip the lilac wine into her unresponsive mouth. Using a little of my magic, I force her throat to swallow it.

I pour it all down, every last drop, my hand never once wavering.

And then I wait.

I comb her hair back then stroke her iridescent wings.

Never should have brought her here. Never should have rekindled what we had. Never should've entered her life in the *first* place.

It's a peculiar kind of agony, knowing the love of your life would be alive if not for you. Loving her enough to want that life for her even if it means erasing all that you had together. Because then, at least, she'd still be alive.

Movement draws my attention to her wrist. Where a minute ago, my black beads had reappeared, row after row of them now vanishes once more.

Only death or repayment can fulfill a bargain. Death or repayment.

Death.

Fear—true, heart-crushing, sweat-inducing fear—flows through me.

She really is leaving me.

A chasm inside me opens, and it's filled with all my pain, all my dread, all the suffering I've borne throughout these long centuries.

I let out a choked cry and run my hand down the side of Callie's face, her skin damp from where the lilac wine spilled.

My skin begins to tingle, itching right over my chest. My magic gathers there, the pressure from it building to such intensity that it's almost painful.

Out of nowhere, it blasts out of me. I groan, my back bowing at the sensation.

And then…and then I feel my power *fuse*. Fuse with another's.

I lean over Callie's body, drawing in several ragged breaths.

I search her features. I've been around archaic magic long enough to know when it's at work—as it is now.

Seconds later Callie's chest rises then falls, rises then falls.

It worked.

Gods' hands, *it worked*.

Callie's *alive*.

Her body arches, her lungs heaving in breath after breath. Before my very eyes, her wound stitches itself up.

I look to the heavens above me and laugh once, a wild, manic sound. The night, in all its infinite chaos, moves around me and through me.

She's alive, and she's *mine*. Really, truly, entirely mine.

I rub my chest, right where my heart cradles our *completed* connection.

My broken wings fan wide with my triumph, and I don't even register the pain through my elation.

She's not mortal, not any longer, but *everlasting*.

Her magic and mine sing together through our bond.

Nothing—*nothing*—has ever felt this good.

I made her one of us. True, she'll never be a fairy in the most honest sense of the term—her rounded ears are still proof of that—but she's immortal like us, strong like us, and her magic is now compatible with mine.

I glance at Callie's bare wrist, her beads all used up.

Only death or repayment can fulfill a bargain. Death *or* repayment. My demand that Callie live, the lilac wine I poured into her mouth—it fulfilled her end of the bargain.

"You gave her the wine," Mara murmurs from where she crouches.

I nod, not bothering to glance away from my mate.

"Any regrets?" she asks.

"I would do it again a thousand times over."

Wrongs can be forgiven. It's death that one cannot return from.

Mara's final words linger in the air between us: "Let's hope she feels the same way."

CHAPTER 55

My eyes peel open, and I blink at my surroundings. I lie in the same suite Des and I have been staying in throughout Solstice.

I'm...*alive*.

Strange. I thought—I thought I died.

But I don't feel dead. I don't even feel like death warmed over, which is usually the case after I get my ass handed to me over and over.

My hand moves to my stomach. The Thief of Souls, the dagger to the gut—had I just dreamed it all up?

Hastily, I push away the clothes covering me. There, low on my abdomen, is a thin white scar.

Not a dream after all.

I sit up in the bed.

How could I possibly recover from such a wound? I don't feel terribly different, all things considered. That is, except...

My hand goes to my heart. I gasp when I feel a tug that has nothing to do with the beat of it.

Being a soul mate means being connected by a very real magical cord. I've known this, and yet it's only now that I truly understand. I *feel* the bond beneath my rib cage, reaching out across the world and connecting me with Des.

Before I can dwell too long on that, I realize the third oddity of the day—

I've been sleeping on my back.

I reach around to touch my wings, but they're gone.

What in the world? Where did they go?

I glance at my forearms and nails. Both are wholly and completely human.

Frantic, I will my scales to appear. To my surprise, I feel a tug on my connection. A moment later, the skin of my forearm flushes a golden hue as hundreds of shimmering scales take shape.

That shouldn't have happened.

I will them away, and with another tug on the bond I share with Des, they vanish, my skin returning to normal.

This is Des's magic. It thrums through me.

Somehow, he saved me, and in the process, our magic unified—our *bond* unified. At least, that's the best theory I have at the moment.

To test it out, I lift my arm and try to use my borrowed magic to levitate the vase of flowers next to the bed. Other than vibrating a little, it does nothing.

Okay, maybe I'm wrong.

"Not even out of bed and my wily little cherub is already exploiting her side of the bond."

The man himself appears at the threshold of our room, leaning against the door. He's wearing a Def Leppard shirt, leather pants, and his shit-kicking boots, his white-blond hair tied back in a little ponytail.

My favorite outfit.

At the sight of him, my body blooms with excitement. "Des—we're *bonded*."

His entire face breaks into a smile. "We are."

I touch my abdomen. "And you healed me." Everything about me thrums with life. I feel new and powerful in the most exquisite way. "How did you do it?"

Temper? Had she healed me and fixed our bond in the process? I didn't suspect she could do such a thing.

"I have my ways."

Des pushes off the wall, coming over to my side. I touch the side of his face, and he leans his cheek into my hand, closing his eyes to savor it.

"What happened?"

"While I fought my father, you battled the Green Man."

"The Thief of Souls..." I murmur. Even now, the thought of him sends a shiver through me.

He's still out there.

And Des's father... "But I thought your father—"

"Was dead?" he finishes for me. His expression darkens. "So did I." Des's eyes grow distant.

"Where is he?" I ask.

"Licking his considerable wounds, I imagine," the Bargainer says.

Whatever happened between father and son, it's plain enough to see that Des won this round. It's also plain to see his victory gives him no joy.

He works his jaw. "Wherever he is, one thing's clear: he's in league with the Thief of Souls."

Just hearing the Thief's name turns my attention back to my immediate situation.

The knife wound to my gut. All that flesh the Thief

ripped into when he dragged his blade up my stomach. The chill that set in as my blood exited my body...

I remember Des demanding I live. I still feel the phantom fingers of his magic trying to bar me from death.

But it didn't work. I remember that. I felt it when his magic released me.

And yet here I am—*alive*.

My gaze cuts to my bracelet. All that stares back at me is my bare forearm.

For eight years, I wore it, and now it's gone.

I run my hand over my wrist. "Where is it?"

"You fulfilled the rest of your repayment last night." By living, he means.

"But it didn't work."

"I found another...alternative." He says this almost defiantly.

I rub my arm, trepidation crawling up my back. "What alternative?"

His silver gaze searches my own.

Have you heard that lilac wine, the rarest of fairy elixirs, can not only bestow longevity to mortals, it can heal the wounded? The Thief of Souls's words echo in my mind.

"There was only one way," Des says.

I'm already shaking my head, a wave of dread washing over me. "*No*," I whisper.

It's a cure-all of sorts, and if you drink it...your soul could be mine for the taking.

"I gave you lilac wine." The normally remorseless Bargainer is beseeching me with his eyes to understand. "I couldn't let you die."

Do the dead ever really die?

It was a trap. One the Thief of Souls set, and Des, the master of trickery, walked right into.

I drank the wine and escaped death—for a price.

This is our little game—and trust me, enchantress, it's far from over.

All that dark magic the Thief wields can now be used against me. I'm more vulnerable as an immortal than I ever was as a regular human.

And the Thief of Souls knows it.

I'm still coming for you. Your life is mine.

EPILOGUE

Deep in the queen's sacred oak forest, the royal trees bleed, rotting from the inside out. The sound of chopping and the unearthly howls of the oaks fill the air. Tree after tree is cut down, and the bodies of sleeping men are pried from them.

The Flora Queen keeps herself locked away in one of her towers, weeping over her fallen mate, her missing harem, her dying oaks.

One by one, each great fae kingdom leaves the Flora palace grounds, heading home from Solstice and carting their sleeping comrades with them.

All are somber, all are solemn.

Dark days lie ahead.

Across the Otherworld, strange, deadly children lie in wait, their glassy eyes staring at some distant point.

An ocean of glass coffins rest in four separate lands. The women inside them lie unmoving, their bodies sheathed in their uniforms, their weapons laid across their chests. Months and years may have passed, but their skin is just as supple as the day they closed their eyes.

They sleep away the sands of time, waiting, waiting…

It's coming.

Something is coming.

Fingers flutter. Muscles twitch.

Not dead, but also not alive—not *yet*.

The sacred oaks groan, their branches swaying as a network of vines retreats from their inner membranes.

A crack forms along one of the glass coffins, spider-webbing across the transparent surface. Wood splinters down the center of an oak. A devilish child smiles.

And then, as one, several thousand eyes snap open.

The time has come.

Dear readers,

Thank you so much for reading A Strange Hymn*! Reviews and word-of-mouth recommendations are really helpful to authors, so if you loved Des and Callie, please consider leaving a review on your favorite book website or telling your friends and family about it.*

Hugs and happy reading!

Laura

Keep a lookout for the next book in
Laura Thalassa's The Bargainer series:

The Emperor of Evening Stars

CHAPTER 1
MISBEGOTTEN

257 years ago

Bastard.

Bastard. Bastard. Bastard.

It's an ugly word, one I've come to hate a great deal, mostly because I can't escape it.

I hear it whispered beneath people's breath as I pass. I see it in their eyes when they look at me. I smell it in the sour breath of the town kids who like to push me around for it. My knuckles are scabbed over from the number of times I've had to fight for my honor.

But the worst is when people use it idly.

"That Flynn boy came at my son again."

"Who?"

"You know, the scrawny bastard."

"Oh, him. Yes."

The word is only a step or two up from *slave*. And I have to wear the title like a badge of shame.

I head into the Caverns of Arestys, twisting my way through the tunnels, the flickering candle in my hand my only source of light. Not that it matters. I can see quite well in darkness, light or no.

My mood blackens as I pass through the shoddy door to our house. A bastard son living in the worst area of the poorest floating island in all the kingdom.

My mother still isn't home from her work as town scribe, so I move about our house, replacing the nubs of candles with the fresh candlesticks I procured.

All the while, I seethe.

Every *plink* of water dripping from the cavern ceiling, every draft of chilly air that slides through the myriad of tunnels—it all mocks me.

Bastard, bastard, bastard.

I grab the beets that are laid out on the table and drop them into the cauldron in our kitchen. It's only once I pour water into the mix and then light a fire beneath the hanging pot that I actually relax enough to rub my split knuckles. Flecks of dried blood coat the skin, and I'm not sure whether it's mine or someone else's.

Bastard.

I can still hear the name, spoken like a taunt, on my way home from town.

Beneath the fresh cuts are old ones. I've had to defend my shitty title for a long time. Of course, it's not necessarily *bastard* that set me off. Sometimes it's all the insults that spawn from it.

You'll never be anything more than your whore mother. The street kid had said that to me today. His voice still rings in my ears.

It was the wrong thing to say.

The next time you say that, I warned, *you'll have a few less teeth to work with.*

He hadn't believed me then.

I slip a hand into the pocket of my trousers and touch the tiny, bloody incisors resting there.

He does now.

Behind me, the front door opens, and my mother comes in. I know without getting close to her that she smells of old parchment and her fingers are stained black with ink.

A scribe cries words and bleeds ink, she used to tell me when I was little and didn't know better. I thought it was true, that this was part of her magic. That was before I truly understood what magic was—and what it wasn't.

"Desmond," she says, flashing me an exhausted smile, "I missed you."

I nod tersely, not trusting myself to speak.

"Did you do your reading?" she asks.

We might be the poorest fairies to exist in this godsless world, but Larissa Flynn has always spent what little hard-earned money she makes on books. Books about kingdoms I'll never see and people I'll never meet. Books about languages I'll never speak and customs I'll never endure. Books about lives I want but will never live.

And under her roof I'm to learn everything within their pages.

"What's the point?" I ask, refusing to admit that I did in fact do the reading because I can't help but return to those damned books day after day, determined to change my life. Our lives.

My mother's eyes move to the candles.

"*Desmond.*" Her voice drops low as she gently chastises

me. "Who did you swindle this time?" She gives me her no-nonsense look, but her eyes twinkle mischievously.

As much as she pretends to disapprove of the deals I strike, she subtly encourages them. And on any other day, I might say something to butter her up even more. Because most days I enjoy helping her.

"Does it matter?" I say, pausing over the small cauldron I'm stirring. I smell like beets and my clothes are stained a reddish-purple where the juice has splattered onto me. I gave up a decent meal to trade for those candles. Hence, beets for dinner.

I should be thankful. It could always be worse. There are nights I go to bed with a full mind but an empty belly. And in the morning, I wake up with sand in my eyes and between my toes, like I'm the Sandman's favorite damned person, and the whole nightmare starts over again.

I hate poverty. I hate feeling like we're only entitled to the worst this realm has to offer simply *because*. But more than anything, I hate having to make hard choices. Books or food? To learn or to eat?

"This wouldn't even be an issue if you would just let me use a bit of magic," I say.

I can feel my power burning under my skin and beneath my fingertips, waiting for me to call it forth.

"No magic."

"Mom, everyone thinks we're weak." The strongest fairies wield the most magic—the weakest, the least. Everyone who's met me believes I'm one of those poor, rare souls born without it entirely.

A fatherless, *powerless* fairy. Aside from slaves, this might be the worst fate for a person living within these realms.

The rub of it all is that I have plenty of magic, and now,

so close to puberty, I can feel it like a storm beneath my veins. It's taking increasing effort just to *leash* it.

"No magic," she repeats, setting her satchel next to our rickety table before taking over the stirring from me.

"So I'm to have powers but never use them?" I say heatedly. This is an old, scarred battle of ours. "And I'm to read but never speak of my knowledge?"

She reaches for my hand and runs her thumb over my knuckles. "And you are to have strength without abusing it," she adds. "Yes, my son. Be humble. Speak, but listen more. Rein in your magic and your mind."

Which only leaves me my muscle. Even that she'd have me hide away from the world.

"They call me a bastard," I blurt out. "Did you know that?"

Her eyes widen almost imperceptibly.

"They call me a bastard and you a whore. That's why my knuckles are always bloody. I'm fighting for your honor." My anger is beginning to get the better of me, which is problematic. And under my mother's roof, I had to live by two hard and fast rules: one, I must never use my magic, and two, I must control my temper. I'm decent at the former and shit at the latter.

She turns to our sad pot of beets. "You are not a bastard," she says, so softly I barely hear it over the bubbling cauldron.

But I do hear it.

My heart nearly stops.

Not…a bastard? Not a misbegotten? The entire axis of my universe shifts in an instant.

"I'm not a bastard?"

Slowly, her eyes move from the pot back to me. I swear I see a flash of regret. She hadn't meant to tell me.

"No," she finally says, her expression turning resolute.

My heartbeat begins to pick up speed at an alarming rate, and I have the oddest urge not to believe her. This is the kind of talk you sit your son down for; you don't just casually slip it into the conversation.

I stare at her, waiting for more.

She says nothing.

"Truly?" I press.

She takes a shaky breath. "Yes, Desmond."

Something that feels an awful lot like hope surges through me. Bastards live tragedies. Sons live sagas. All my mother's books are very clear on that point.

I am some man's son. His *son.* Masculine pride rushes through me, though it's quickly doused by reality. I am still the boy raised by a single mother, and I have lived a fatherless existence. Perhaps I'm no bastard, but the world still sees me as one, and knowing my mom's love of secrets, the world will continue to see me as one even after today.

"Did he die?"

How? How did our lives come to this?

She shakes her head, refusing to look at me.

"Then he abandoned us."

"No, my son."

What other answer is left?

The only one that comes to me has me scrutinizing my mother, my hardworking mother who keeps many, many secrets and who has taught me to do the same.

"You left him," I state. Of course. It's the only logical answer left.

She grimaces, still refusing to look at me, and there is my answer.

"You left him and took me with you."

It feels like someone's stacked stones in my stomach. This sense of loss is almost unbearable, mostly because I didn't know I had anything *to* lose in the first place.

"Who was my father?"

My mother shakes her head.

This is the kind of revelation that I shouldn't have to pull teeth to get.

"Tell me. You owe me that." I can feel my magic hammering beneath my skin, begging for release. A name is all I need.

Again, she shakes her head, her brows furrowed.

"If you have *any* love for me, then you'll tell me who he is." Then I could find him, and he could claim me as his son, and all those kids that called me a bastard would realize I had a father...

My magic builds and builds. I can feel it crawling up and down my back, pressing against the skin there.

"It's *because* I love you that I won't tell you," she says, her voice rising in agitation.

This is where I'm supposed to drop the subject. But this is my *father* we're talking about, one whole half of my identity that's been missing all my life. She's treating this conversation like it doesn't matter.

"What kind of answer is that?" I say hotly, my annoyance turning into anger. My power becomes frenzied at the taste of my heated emotions. Harder it presses against my back, becoming an itch.

"Desmond," she says sharply, "if you knew the truth, it could kill you."

My heart beats faster. Sharp, sharp pressure at my back. *Who* is my father? I need to know!

"You're the one who's always droning on about educating

myself," I throw at her. "That 'knowledge is the sharpest blade,'" I say, quoting her. "And yet you still won't tell me my father's identity." My words lash out, and with them I feel the skin of my back give.

I groan as the flesh parts, and my magic shoves its way out of me. I have to bend over from the force of it, leaning my hand on the nearby counter.

My wings are sprouting, I think, distantly. My back throbs, tingling with my magic, and it's not quite pain but it isn't exactly pleasant either. My power consumes me, darkening my vision and making my body shake.

Didn't know it would be like this.

I sense rather than see my mother turning away from the cauldron to give me her full attention. This is about the time I get a verbal lashing. And then her form stiffens as she takes me in.

I breathe heavily between waves of magic.

Why, now of all times, did my wings have to sprout?

They tug at my back, and they should feel heavy, but my magic is making them buoyant, about the weight they'd be if I were submerged in water.

I blink, trying to bring the room into focus. My sight sharpens for a moment, and I see my mother clearly.

Her eyes are wide as they gaze at my wings. She takes a shaky step back, nearly knocking into the heated cauldron.

"You have his wings," she says, sounding utterly terrified.

Her form slips out of focus, and my attention unwillingly turns inward. I fight against it, determined to finish the conversation.

"*Whose* wings?" I say, my voice sounding very far away to my own ears. I feel like I'm in another room. My magic pulses *tha-thump, tha-thump, tha-thump* inside me.

I don't hear her answer, and I'm not entirely sure whether that's because she never spoke, or I simply didn't hear it over the *whoosh* of power deafening my ears.

"Tell me and I'll swear to the Undying Gods never to tell."

My power begins to ebb, the darkness clearing from my vision. I make out my mother, and she gives me the same sort of pitying look all the townspeople give me.

"My son, that is not a vow you can keep," she says softly, her voice breaking. Her terror and her pity are giving way to a more hopeless expression, something that looks a lot like desolation.

She's not going to tell me—not today and from her expression, probably not anytime soon. She'd have me endure the taunts and insults for years more. All so that she can shelter me. As though I'm a defenseless babe!

My anger rises swiftly within me, dragging my power along with it.

…You are a man now…

I am. My wings are proof enough of that. My wings and my magic, the latter of which is building on itself, darkening my vision once more. My wings flare out, so large I can't fully extend them in our cramped quarters.

Too much magic.

I sway on my feet. My anger amplifies my power, and my power, in turn, amplifies my anger, building to some elusive crescendo.

Can't control it.

I know a split second before I lose control that my magic is too big for my body and too strong for my will.

And then the storm trapped beneath my veins is trapped no more.

"*Tell me.*" My voice booms, my power rippling across the room. Our dining table slides across the floor, the chairs tumbling. The kitchen utensils hanging over our cauldron now fly across the room, and our crude stoneware plates shatter against the far wall.

It's a testament to my mother's strength that my power only manages to make her stumble back a few feet. My dark power coils around her. I can actually *see* it, like tendrils of inky smoke.

As soon as I release my magic out into the room, it loosens its hold on me. Again I can think clearly.

Horror replaces anger. Never have I spoken to my mother this way. Never has my power slipped its leash—though never has my power felt so *vast*.

I can still see my magic in front of me. It circles my mother's throat and seeps into her skin.

I feel sick as I watch her throat work.

What have I done?

...*Don't you know...*

...*Can't you feel it...*

...*You've compelled her to answer...*

Gods' bones. Now I can feel it, like a phantom limb. My magic is clawing its way through my mother's system, prying the secret from her.

Something flickers in her eyes, something alarming, something that looks an awful lot like fear.

Fear of *me*.

She fights the words, but eventually she loses.

"Your father is Galleghar Nyx."

Glossary

Arestys: a barren, rocky landmass belonging to the Kingdom of Night; known for its caves; smallest and poorest of the six floating islands located within the Kingdom of Night.

Barbos: also known as the City of Thieves; the second largest of the floating islands located within the Kingdom of Night; has garnered a reputation for its gambling halls, gangs, smuggler coves, and taverns.

Borderlands: area where day meets night; the border between the Kingdom of Day and the Kingdom of Night; boarders between fae kingdoms.

changeling: a child swapped at birth; can alternatively refer to a fae child raised on earth or a human child raised in the Otherworld.

dark fairy: a fairy that has forsaken the law.

Desmond Flynn: ruler of the Kingdom of Night; also known as the King of Night, Emperor of the Evening Stars, Lord of Secrets, Master of Shadows, and King of Chaos.

fae: a term denoting all creatures native to the Otherworld.

fairy: the most common fae in the Otherworld; can be identified by their pointed ears and, in most instances, wings; known for their trickery, secretive nature, and turbulent tempers.

glamour: magical hypnosis; renders the victim susceptible to verbal influence; considered a form of mind control; wielded by sirens; effective on all earthly beings; ineffective on creatures of other worlds; outlawed by the House of Keys because of its ability to strip an individual of their consent.

Green Man: king-consort of Mara Verdana, Queen of Flora.

House of Keys: the global governing body of the supernatural world; headquarters located in Castletown, Isle of Man.

Isle of Man: an island in the British Isles located between Ireland to the west, and Wales, England, and Scotland to the east; the epicenter of the supernatural world.

Janus Soleil: ruler of the Kingdom of Day; also known as the King of Day, Lord of Passages, King of Order, Truth Teller, and Bringer of Light.

Karnon Kaliphus: dead ruler of the Kingdom of Fauna; also known as the King of Fauna, Master of Animals, Lord of the Wild Heart, and King of Claws and Talons.

Kingdom of Day: Otherworld kingdom that presides over all things pertaining to day; transitory kingdom; travels around the Otherworld, dragging the day with it; located opposite the Kingdom of Night; the eleven floating islands within it are the only landmasses that can claim permanent residence within the Kingdom of Day.

Kingdom of Death and Deep Earth: Otherworld kingdom that presides over all things that have died; stationary kingdom located underground.

Kingdom of Fauna: Otherworld kingdom that presides over all animals; stationary kingdom.

Kingdom of Flora: Otherworld kingdom that presides over all plant life; stationary kingdom.

Kingdom of Mar: Otherworld kingdom that presides over all things that reside within bodies of water; stationary kingdom.

Kingdom of Night: Otherworld kingdom that presides over all things pertaining to night; transitory kingdom; travels around the Otherworld, dragging the night with it; located opposite of the Kingdom of Day; the six floating islands within it are the only landmasses that can claim permanent residence within the Kingdom of Night.

Lephys: also known as the City of Lovers; one of the six floating islands within the Kingdom of Day; believed to be one of the most romantic cities in the Otherworld.

ley line: magical roads within and between worlds that can be manipulated by certain supernatural creatures.

Mara Verdana: ruler of the Kingdom of Flora; also known as the Queen of Flora, Lady of Life, Mistress of the Harvest, and Queen of All that Grows.

mate challenge: a duel between two rivals for the hand of a mate; usually ritualistic as mate bonds cannot be transferred.

Otherworld: land of the fae; accessible from earth via ley lines; known for its vicious creatures and turbulent kingdoms.

Peel Academy: supernatural boarding school located on the Isle of Man.

Phyllia and Memnos: sister islands connected by bridge; located within the Kingdom of Night; also known as the Land of Dreams and Nightmares.

pixie: winged fae are roughly the size of a human hand; like most fae, pixies are known for being nosy, secretive, and mischievous.

Politia: the supernatural police force; global jurisdiction.

portal: doorways or access points to ley lines; can overlap multiple worlds.

Sacred Seven: also known as the forbidden days; the seven days surrounding the full moon when shifters remove themselves from society; custom established due to shifters' inability to control their transformation from human to animal during the days closest to the full moon.

seer: a supernatural who can foresee the future.

shifter: a general term for all creatures that can change form.

siren: supernatural creature of extraordinary beauty; exclusively female; can glamour all earthly beings to do her bidding; prone to bad decision-making.

Somnia: capitol of the Kingdom of Night; also known as the Land of Sleep and Small Death; biggest island in the kingdom.

supernatural community: a group that consists of every magical creature living on earth.

Thief of Souls: the individual responsible for the disappearances of fae warriors.

werewolf: also known as a lycanthrope or shifter; a human who transforms into a wolf; ruled by the phases of the moon.

About the Author

Found in the forest when she was young, Laura Thalassa was raised by fairies, kidnapped by werewolves, and given over to vampires as repayment for a hundred-year debt. She's been brought back to life twice, and with a single kiss, she woke her true love from eternal sleep. She now lives happily ever after with her undead prince in a castle in the woods.

...or something like that anyway.

When not writing, Laura can be found scarfing down guacamole, hoarding chocolate for the apocalypse, or curled up on the couch with a good book.

You can find more news and updates on Laura Thalassa's books at laurathalassa.com.